LET'S GO PLAY AT THE ADAMS'

Mendal W. Johnson

GOLDEN APPLE PUBLISHERS

To my wife,
Ellen Argo Johnson

This low-priced Golden Apple Book
has been completely reset in a type face
designed for easy reading, and was printed
from new plates. It contains the complete
text of the original hard-cover edition.
NOT ONE WORD HAS BEEN OMITTED.

LET'S GO PLAY AT THE ADAMS'
A Golden Apple Publication / published by arrangement with
Thomas Y. Crowell Company

Golden Apple edition / December 1984

ISBN 0-553-19829-7

PRINTED IN CANADA

COVER PRINTED IN U.S.A.

0 9 8 7 6 5 4 3 2 1

Prologue

On the keyboard of a piano—in this case, it is an up-right—are two neatly positioned pairs of hands. To the right is the pair (at C above middle C) which may be fairly said to be the hands of a girl. They are terribly slender—only girls, only the young have hands like that—and they are firm and strong and tanned. There is a decorative ring on the right hand but nothing on the left: the girl is not yet engaged or married. The hands are spread into a C-major chord and waiting. They begin.

What they are playing—and well enough—is "The Happy Farmer." It's a rather insistent small tune that goes, "Dum *dum*—boom, boom—dum *dum*—boom, boom—dum dum dum *dum*," etc. It goes to a similar conclusion. It is an inevitable tune; people have been toying with it for centuries.

The hands disappear.

"OK, now you try it."

Now it is the turn of the other pair of hands, the ones to the left, the pudgy, sunburned (but well-scrubbed) little hands. They strain awkwardly. They achieve the necessary chord and begin: "Dum *dum*—boom, boom (mistake)." They reposition themselves and begin again.

"Come on now. You can do that after church."

"Just let me. Just once more—now?"

"OK, but you come when I honk the horn. I don't want to be late." The longer, more slender hands pull

1

on a pair of short white gloves that stop exactly at the wrist. "Now, where's Bobby? Bob-*eee!*"

"I'm coming. But it's early. We never leave until—"

"Let me see *your* hands."

These hands are also more or less clean, but they are definitely boy's hands. Against the white gloves that hold them, they look knuckle-barked, calloused and innately grubby in spite of their recent washing. Nonetheless they pass inspection.

"OK, let's go, Cindy."

"*Com*-ing, Miss Barbara." There is some truculence here.

"You don't have to use Miss with me."

"Mommy said to."

"All right, if she said so."

The parents are in Europe, so that the children are driven to church by the baby-sitter. They make a pleasant sight.

Cindy Adams, the smaller piano player, is an impish little girl of ten. She is pretty enough, and she has brown hair cut rather short for summer, because with swimming and moist heat, it wants to spring into curls and spirals and tangles and become unmanageable. She is the sort of child that grown-ups instinctively want to pat.

Bobby Adams, her brother, is oddly enough the beauty. He is about thirteen, thin and fair, with high coloring to his cheeks and fine, blond hair that requires water and sticky stuff to keep it from floating around his head in an unruly halo. He rarely smiles, and he often stands in thought with his hands thrust straight down, as deep as they will go in his pockets. This position, rare in a youngster, is an unconscious copy of the position his surgeon father often takes in conversation.

The white-gloved hands that swing the family station wagon into the churchyard, belong to the baby-sitter—pianist, Barbara. When she gets out of the car to let the children out, it is with an athletic little leap. She is

2

probably twenty—not much more. She wears a white dress of extremely diplomatic appeal. It is short enough to show off her legs and pass with her generation and yet long enough to show her deference to the older generation and the social order of things.

Barbara is also not pretty in the sense that movie professionals are pretty. She is better than that: she is young and downy—or so you would say from looking at her face—and she likes everyone. You can see it in the way she shepherds the children off to Sunday School and in the way she is rather instantly accepted by the older, generally cautious group in the churchyard, all of whom are strangers to her.

The morning passes easily enough. Downstairs in Sunday School—Cindy squirming, Bobby sitting with that thoughtful look of his—they hear about how Our Lord cured people. Upstairs they hear—Barbara sitting with white gloves folded neatly in her lap—that in times of change and uncertainty the words of Jesus have even more relevance than before.

Afterward they all sing. It is a pretty and simple sound: "Jesus, our God and Father," and so on and so forth.

When services are over, everyone stands in the shaded yard—it will be paved next year; now it is all dust—and discusses the county news. Call it gossip.

The Adams are well known here, for all the fact that they are not natives. Dr. Adams has contributed to the paint, the piano, and the plantings. Mrs. Adams has participated in the cake bakes and fund-raising affairs.

There is a little cynicism in this, and there is a certain amount of friendliness. For cynicism, everyone knows that the Adams are not godly people, at least not in the sense of this county of the Eastern Shore of Maryland. It's all for show. Quite on the other hand, everyone understands that by so participating in the church doings, the Adams are doing their dead level best to be friends with their adopted community. Dr. Adams' hand is extended and taken, and—in his absence—the hand of the community is extended into the

3

slender one of the baby-sitter, Barbara, who stands daisy-white and bright outside beneath the mimosas.

Tomorrow, or on some tomorrow, she will be a part of some community with children of her own and plans and—well, sometimes we *must*—cake bakes. It is a soothing future, one which she has considered all her life, or perhaps a picture instilled into her long ago. Nonetheless, it is nice, and here she enjoys the vision.

Her thought—this is as close as it comes to words—is, Who will he be who gives me all this? Ted? She frowns to herself.

So, everyone mills around until Sunday School lets out—late today—and the children come out to claim parents. Because there are a lot of fond old-timers here today, there is also a lot of ohing and ahing by the grandparents' groups, and this the children endure with as much good grace as possible. After all, the Lord said to be kind. Then Bobby and Cindy and Barbara get into the station wagon to go home and go swimming in the river on whose banks the Adams house is built.

There is a last item. As they get into the rather flossy wagon—it is air-conditioned and has tinted glass and pretty much the whole option sheet—they find their way out momentarily blocked by pickers. This is a group of migrant workers walking along the country road on foot.

Nearby—it is woodsy hereabouts—there are commercial orchards, and at this late time of summer, the pickers arrive and harvest the fruit. It is hard work, back-bending work, and very poorly paid. Nonetheless their arrival signals the end of the summer, and when they have gone again like a flock of dark Latin birds, fall will begin.

"Who are they?" Barbara, with 425 cubic inches of piston displacement under her small foot in the family wagon, is impatient.

"I dunno."

"Pickers," Bobby says. "Nobody."

4

Then the road is cleared, and the car spins gravel. They pass the pickers without looking back.

"How long to get into the river?" Barbara says.

"Fifteen minutes."

"Twelve." Cindy goes her brother three better.

"Then let's *go-o-o!*" In white-dress and white-glove exuberance—though she drives well, she rarely gets the chance to drive a powerful car like this—Barbara floors the gas pedal for home. Clearly she feels a little naughty about the surge of speed—there is that touch in her—and clearly she enjoys the squeal of tires when they take pavement and accelerate.

It is afterward that it begins.

1

In the first moments, her mind floated up still webbed in memory of the most recent hours. After seeing the children through baths into bed, she had made herself a small highball with Dr. Adams' Scotch and sat out on the steps nearest the river—it was reward at the end of the fourth day. Later she had showered and gone to bed.

Then, somewhere in the middle, there had been a commotion, something brief and frightening—perhaps a bad dream—that seemed in the now clearing mind to have nearly made her sick. Her thought in that fright had been *the children*, but instead of going to them, she had fallen dreamlessly back into this sleep that released her so slowly.

Yes, the children. Get up.

She made all the drowsy efforts of rising but did not actually move at all. The mind reaching consciousness understood few things at once, but these came first.

Daylight.

She was uncomfortable, stretched out in an odd position for sleep—flat on her back with her arms and legs flung out. She was stiff and in some pain at her wrists and ankles. She could not move. Her mouth was filled with wet cloth—like terry cloth—and the lower part of her face was covered with something stiff that hurt and pulled at her skin.

More struggle—quicker, more anxious now, more

6

coming awake—but nothing gave or changed. She was helpless, a condition caused by—a nervous craning and twisting of her eyes showed her the reasons—rope, a gag, adhesive tape. She was tied up. Beneath the sheet someone had thrown over her, she could see that she was bound to the four posts of the bed and thus made entirely, tightly, a prisoner.

This, of course, was not acceptable fact: it simply couldn't be, particularly under the circumstances. She was still in her bedroom at the Adams'; she hadn't been kidnapped or moved. Beyond the tightness of rope, some stiffness, and a mild headache, she seemed well: she hadn't been harmed or raped (or so she felt). Moreover young Bobby Adams was asleep in a chair beside the bed.

In the early light, his young face was all innocent composure—blond hair, high pink on the cheeks, full lips—a fine-looking boy at his dreams. Under the conditions—her helplessness: his freedom—sober, reliable Bobby seemed perhaps a too young sentry sleeping off-duty at the front.

All totally impossible.

Here was a familiar, late-summer morning, and the only thing out of its appropriate role and place was Barbara, the incredible, incredulous prisoner. At once, her shock and surprise turned to fully awakened indignation. It was as if she were victim of some cosmic practical joke aimed at her alone, and she resented, rapidly hated it.

Getting Bobby to untie her was obvious, but with that inherent, adult feeling of superiority over children, she struggled for herself first. Although the ropes were tight and her position unfavorable, she arched and wrenched, jumped and pulled at her bonds. Athletic and young, even she was impressed by her strength and the violence and coordination of her movements. The bed itself complained at assault.

Some lessons teach quickly, however.

Though it worked and cracked, the bed did not yield. Though the rope slacked in her favor, the slack came out of the turns on her ankles and wrists, and these turns tightened like wire. Though she tugged and twisted, she could breathe only through her nose and soon became winded and weak. A minute, a minute and a half, and she fell back. The hunter, the captor, whoever he was, had won for the moment. Still indignant, more indignant for being more convinced, she nonetheless stopped spending her strength and lay still. Now she would take help.

The noise, of course, had waked Bobby. Careful, constant Bobby—he stood up by her side in detailed, somewhat sleepy confusion and alarm.

"Um I ee," she said through her gag, or tried to. "Ere. Um I ee." Demandingly.

Bobby reacted quickly. His hands flew to hers but only to tighten the knots that held her. He flung back the sheet—she was still in her shortie, she saw—and he checked the ropes on her ankles.

This done, his face relaxed, changed. She saw it.

He suddenly realized *what day this was!*

"Cindy!" No longer his sober self but shouting as if it was Christmas, he ran from the room toward his sister's.

Helpless, still breathing hard but now exquisitely attentive to what the children would say, Barbara heard Cindy's usual morning complaints. "What is it? Hunhh ... ? *Stop* it, now!" Then after an interval, there was faster, lower conversation. "Don't you *remember?* Listen ... !"

Then they came bounding back into the bedroom. Bright and now energetically awake Cindy—she was tousled joy—jumped right up on the bed and peered down at Barbara's helplessness. Convinced it was so, Cindy kissed her on the nose and hugged her as if Barbara were the greatest present in the world.

"We got her," she yelled. Jumping down from the bed, she did a round circle dance with her brother.

"We got her, we got her ... we *got* the baby-sitter!" She and Bobby hugged each other in rare, delirious agreement. "And *they* won't be back for a *week!*"

8

The girl on the bed was not stupid: the visible and physical fact was fact. In some way, for some reason, she was the prisoner of children.

Beyond the reach of such logic, however, beyond reason's control, her habits of inner being continued. Spirit, will, vitality, told the mind that it was wrong, and at their command, the body continued its motion. She raised and turned her head and carefully explored her ropes. She tested them again and again, finding first hope and then disappointment in a constant, steady rotation. Straining, her fingers reached for unreachable knots and curled back again. At length, unconvinced but impotent, her inner self desisted. From discovery, shock, indignity, and astonishment, her mood by induction grew angry.

Lying there, she rethought the classic thoughts of the vengeful, disobeyed adult: *Wait'll I get my hands on them,*" and *"Wait'll I tell the Adams."*

However satisfying this might be, however, the now coming thought of how distant a day that would be, made her pause. The Adams were leaving England today if she had the itinerary right: later they would be in Paris. They were still in the "going-away" phase of the trip: the bleakness of time and distance this thought summoned up, made her consider further.

During the four days she had been here—one with Dr. and Mrs. Adams and three alone with Bobby and Cindy—she had met few other adults. The Tillmans, who ran the general store, one or two of the Adams' church friends, the mother of one of the kids the young Adams played with, and that was the lot. Sooner or later perhaps, one or another of them might stop by, but in three days, it hadn't happened yet. The web of reliance on others, wisely or falsely taken for granted, was abruptly torn. She had momentarily slipped through the mesh entirely.

Finally there were no neighbors closer than half a mile across a field, some woods, and then a stream that joined the river. This was gentleman farmer country—the houses were placed like islands so that the privilege

9

of privacy and view was maintained—and privacy was severely respected. Even if she were to work her gag off, she could scream from this quiet, air-conditioned room for a month, and no one would hear her, except, of course, the children. Everything came back to the children.

As she lay there, she could hear them in the kitchen two rooms and a hallway distant. After their dance of glee, they had fled as if in need to talk secrets and all sorts of delicious mischief. Now they were heating frozen Pop-Ups in the toaster—she knew the sound—and slamming the refrigerator door and giggling. The mood was exuberant, naughty and a lot of fun, and it didn't promise to subside.

"Umnn!" It was Barbara's first sound of complaint, discomfort, exasperation. This all might go on for some time.

Shifting her body to find relief that barely existed, she sighed. Then she closed her eyes. *All right, don't think about the time. Think about the children. Think about making them let you go.*

Think, Barbara Miller, age twenty, baby-sitter, money-needer, college junior, education major, history minor, B-averager, free-style swimmer, prom chairman, sorority sister, dutiful daughter, runner of errands, dreamer of lovely futures, think.

She tried.

Even given that thought was difficult in this all new, never-before-experienced situation, however, the fact of the matter was that Barbara was just not the true thinking type. She was intelligent and sensitive enough—perhaps a little too sensitive—but her instinctive manner was to intuit life, to sense it, to feel where it was flowing and then run there. It gave her a grace and liveliness, but it did not well fit her for the role of analyst and planner.

When faced by such a need, she always automatically said, "Mother, what do you think? Daddy, what do you think?" or "Ted, what do you think about it?" "Terry, what's the best thing to do?" The situation was

10

so recurrent with Terry—even unavoidable—that the resultant joke never lost its flavor. When she was so interrupted, Terry had taken up the habit of turning back and mimicking, *"Ter-ree . . . ?"* Barbara was never insulted; actually, she could barely stifle a giggle when she saw Terry's irritation. "Well, what is it?"

Barbara and Terry had been KKGs and roommates at college for two years, and in that time, Terry had advised, adjudicated, and planned things in almost every part of Barbara's life. It was that way: Barbara kept things light and busy, and Terry kept them tracking. "Terry, what'm I going to do?"

Barbara turned her cheek down on the pillow and closed her eyes; and of course, *that* very question came to her mind. "Terry, what . . . ?"

It wasn't hard to imagine what she'd say.

"But Barb, for godsakes, *how?*" Terry was head-shaking amused. "You're bigger than they are, you're stronger, you're smarter. How could you let them do a thing like this to *you?*"

"It was after I went to sleep"—Barbara felt guilty at once—"Maybe I snored, and that's how they knew I was sleeping, or something. Anyhow, the children or Bobby alone—I guess it had to be Bobby—came into the room with something, drugs or something, in a rag. I had a bad dream. That must've been when he was making me breathe it. Afterwards, they tied me up."

"But *why?*" Imagined Terry was unconcerned with sympathy. Her inaudible voice was disbelieving, of course, but now equally amused. Possibly she smiled.

"I don't know."

"Then find out," Terry said simply. "They can't keep you gagged forever. You've got to eat and drink—even *they* know that. Anyhow pretty soon they'll get curious, they'll want to know what you think about their grand joke. And when they *do* ungag you, don't yell or scream or lose your temper. You're three fourths of a teacher by now, you've read your learning psych, you know how their minds work. Use some of it. Talk to them; be interested in all this. There're only two of them, they know you, they like you. Sooner or later they'll get bored silly and let you go."

Terry, as always, was hard to refute. Hers was a practical, a reasoning, an analytical mind devoid of whims and enthusiasms. Moreover, at this moment, hers was a welcome—if imagined—argument.

"That's right. . . ." Encouraged, Barbara pursued the thought. "And they can't keep me tied up forever. I've got to go to the bathroom and get some exercise and blood circulation. That could be my excuse for getting up, and when I do. . . ." In time, however, she became aware that she was thinking toward an absent audience. Terry vanished—bored or called away on more important matters—and was gone. The room was empty once more. On the other hand, it was perceptibly more bearable.

Reminded now, Barbara considered all the realities, the unpleasant and impossible chores the children would face by themselves. Cooking, once the sweets were gone, restarting the well-pump when it was air-locked (Dr. Adams had showed her how), shopping, replacing fuses, fending off possible visitors, answering telephone calls, making excuses for her own absence, even amusing themselves. They could never do it all. It was an adults' world, and alone in it, two youngsters their age would soon discover their weaknesses. Well then, wait it out, she told herself.

Periodically one or another of the pair came in to inspect her and make sure that she was not freeing herself, then leave again. They were up and down the hall, in and out of their rooms, back and forth outside and inside with the doors banging heedlessly behind. The liquor of freedom was in them, and until it burned down, she could only lie quietly and wait.

Finally, after about two agonizing hours, Bobby—now fully dressed—came into the room, and after checking her security again, picked up the phone by her bed, and dialed. There was a *br-r-rttt* at the other end of the line, and then conversation.

His face, which had been thoughtful, quickly assumed a Sunday-scrubbed smile (like yesterday). "Good morning . . . Mrs. Randall? This is Bobby Adams. Is John there? . . . May I talk to him, please? . . . What, ma'am?" Bobby paused and then said with enthusiasm, "Real great! And Barbara's taking us swimming in the river this afternoon, again. You should see her swim; she's on the college team . . . yeah. Yes, ma'am, we *will* . . . OK, thank you." There was silence.

Bobby put his hand over the receiver and yelled, "Cindy! Pick up the phone in the kitchen, but keep your hand over the mouthpiece. OK?"

From far away, Cindy yelled, "OK."

After a moment more, Bobby removed his hand. "John," he said cautiously. "Yeah, is your mother right there? . . . OK." Again his face changed, this time to very serious, almost possessed. His voice became imitation adult, clipped. "Red Fox One to Freedom Leader, do you read me? Over."

Silence for a second or two.

"OK, Freedom Leader," he continued. "Mission going OK so far . . . Yeah, no kidding! Yeah, I told you. We have her . . . Yeah, Code Urgent from now on. No, I'm looking right at her right now just like we planned. Right, Red Fox Two?" He yelled this last at Cindy (in the kitchen). "Yeah, *see?* OK, Cindy, get off the phone, now. Now listen, John, can you do what you said about this morning? Yeah, you call the other kids and meet us here as soon as you can get over, right? . . . Cool, man . . . OK. Roger. This is Red Fox patrol out." And he hung up.

For a few seconds, Bobby stared off into space above Barbara's head. Eventually, he dropped his glance to her, and Barbara understood that there was a lot more to this than she had imagined.

About midmorning, they heard the sound of someone whistling through his teeth—shrill, powerful,

13

outdoors, some distance away. Cindy, who was desultorily working on a dress for her doll, looked up.

"It's John."

"It's *them!*" Bobby had been moving restlessly around the living room. Now he hurried through the kitchen to the river door and out onto the steps. Being thirteen and being Bobby, he did not accomplish this without a certain clumping, banging, and thumping, and he arrived on the second step down with a thud. Then, putting his fingers between his own teeth, he whistled back.

From down in the woods at the northeast end of the Adams property—maybe beyond the woods from Oak Creek—there came a shout. The sound rose and fell. There were words in it which couldn't be understood at the distance, but Bobby knew them by heart.

"Freedom-m-m Five!" His first shout drunk up by the vastness of sky that hung above the river and land, Bobby gathered his biggest lungful of air and yelled again. "Freedom-m-m Five!" He panted. "This is Red Fox One!"

There was quick reply—whistles, shouts—slowly coming closer.

Bobby jumped down the steps and started along beside the vegetable garden with Cindy down the steps one clump behind him. Then he stopped. From the outside it would have been possible to see, perhaps, a look of caution, of newfound responsibility, on his face. He was discernibly proud of what he had done, possessive, nervous: it wouldn't do if at this last minute his captive escaped and descended on Freedom Five like an avenging goddess of some kind.

"Aren't you going to meet them?"

"You go on. I'll stay here." But he put his fingers between his teeth and whistled once more for reassurance.

Torn between the desire to run and tell everything first, and a new feeling of duty to her brother, Cindy hesitated. Then she turned back. "OK, I'll wait, too."

Bobby was a little startled. Being a girl, being little,

being the darling, Cindy could get to Bobby politically about as often as she wished, and she wished often. She cried and accused him, she tattled, she tempted and set female snares, she rushed out and told all the good news first, and so on and so forth. Bobby was used to this and used to the discipline that followed if he so much as tried to defend himself against her. Though they had not invented the fabled law of fang and claw, brother and sister lived by it inflexibly.

"Why?" Like any man, Bobby was dumbfounded by this offer of peace.

"I dunno"—she shrugged it away quite lightly—"I just will, that's all."

Touched (unknowingly), Bobby smiled, and so they went back and settled down, Cindy on the bottom step—nearest the coming action—and Bobby sort of hanging on the railing, one foot swinging impatiently over it beneath him. "Do what you want," he said. There was something almost managerial about Bobby: he took his truces where he found them and enjoyed them while they lasted, and he trusted his sister about the way he would a cottonmouth.

At last, the other three kids appeared from the shadows of the woods. They were walking slowly because the mowed stubble between the ending of the tree line and the vegetable garden was August-hot, splintery, and dusty. John Randall, the biggest—he was seventeen—led the way. Behind him (protectively in the middle) came Paul McVeigh, thirteen, and following, his daintily stepping (excessively thin) sister, Dianne.

Something about their steady, collective approach seemed to relieve Bobby. When they reached the edge of the garden, he deserted his place on the steps and ran to meet them, half tackling, half throwing himself at John.

There was something like a ritual dance (again).

"Did'ja really do it?"

"Yeah! Really!" Then they were all bobbing around, slapping backs, and laughing, except for Dianne who at seventeen plus stood an even one step aside. "Barbara's in there right now. Wait'll you see it!"

"Was it hard?" Paul said.

"It was real cool," Bobby said. "Just like TV. I swear it must've taken me an hour just to get in from the door to her bed." They all came along now, Bobby waving his hands and talking, Cindy jumping ahead like something on springs. "She kept turning over and waking up and yawning and stuff like that. I was scared she was going to turn on the light or get out of bed and step on me or something like that. . . ."

"Did you keep the cholroform in the bag like I told you?" Dianne said.

"Yeah, but you could smell it all over the place. At least, I could. And I kept thinking, boy, if this doesn't work, we're really going to get it."

"Did it?"

"Well, when I finally got there, see, I stood up and took the cloth out of the bag, and I sort of just held it up in the air near her nose. And I had to hold my own breath, I *mean*." They had reached the kitchen steps now and stopped to hear Bobby finish. "And she sort of reached up and pushed my hand away."

"Really?" Paul's eyes spread wide with imagined participation.

"Yeah, and when she touched me, I jammed it down over her mouth—" Bobby paused, amazed in retrospect at his own courage.

"What'd she do then?" John said.

"Well, I guess she made a noise and really grabbed my hand, and I sort of jumped on her. She kept pushing the rag away, and I kept getting it back, and then she just sort of gave up and quit shoving at me."

"You were on top of her?" John said.

"Sort of like halfway, like wrestling," Bobby said. "Boy, she's strong for a girl, even when she's asleep."

"So what then?"

"Well, anyhow, I held it over her face a little bit longer, and then put it back in the bag again. I was scared she might wake up, and I was scared I might give her too much. Then after that, I got the rope from my room and tied her hands and feet, and then the rest was easy."

"Weren't you scared?" Paul was still deeply excited.

"Yeah, man. If she'd sneezed when I was creeping up on her, I'd have run right across the river."

"But you haven't seen her yet," Cindy said. "Come on!" She ran up the steps and opened the kitchen door. "Come *on!*"

Bobby, host in his own house, captor of the baby-sitter, hero of Freedom Five for the moment, followed proudly. There was a barely perceptible hesitation in the other three. It was as if they dare not see what they were going to see, but then John gruffly nodded his head and led the way behind Bobby.

When they emerged from the woods, John, Paul and Dianne had been carrying bathing suits rolled up in towels. Now, in the coolness of the Adams kitchen, they dropped these on the counter and muddled their way into the living room, their feet impelling them forward, their caution holding them back. Cindy, however, was already down the hall—had, in fact, been in and out of Barbara's room in her impatience.

"Well, come *on,*" she said. "Are you scared or something? Bobby and me aren't."

She, of course, led the way. Bobby followed, succeeded by John, Paul, and Dianne. In that order, they entered the bedroom and came to the foot of the bed. Silence followed.

Given that Bobby and Cindy had three to four hours' advantage, the fact was that until today none of them had ever seen an adult human made helpless—chained, pinioned, bound, gagged, brought down beneath adult level. The sight itself was a fundamental experience that, while it affected each differently, carried some common meaning for them all.

Each person expects to grow up. Ascension to power is a given part of existence. Usually, however, it lies distantly ahead—we shall have power when we have the years, the means and experience, for power—and meanwhile, we shall coast along being simply what we are and no more. Now, of course, all of this was capsized. They had done the unbelievable thing, they had captured a grown-up.

The baby-sitter was theirs, the Adams property was theirs, the next seven days—give them luck!—were theirs, life for these hours they held it was theirs. It was like a dream, a wish, an indolent fantasy, come all too suddenly true, for beyond the boldness, beyond the impetuosity, the success, lay inevitable tomorrow. Now they had done it, now it was fun, now the adventure had begun, now they were really in for it. What now?

After some moments the trance was broken; the not-believable sight was believed. They moved a foot, an arm—Paul scratched his nose—and they stirred from their frozen positions. They looked; they moved around the bed; they breathed again.

"Y'see?" Bobby said.

"Her hands are all blue and purple," Paul said.

"That's the ropes. Maybe they're too tight," Cindy said.

Bobby sighed. "Aw-w-w, if they were looser, she could get away."

"She has pretty feet," Paul said.

"You always say that." Cindy giggled.

"Cindy, get *away* from her," Bobby said. "If she grabs you, you'll know it."

John Randall, who alone had not moved from the foot of the bed, said, "I guess we better have a meeting about this."

"A meeting, a meeting!" Cindy sang.

"No. You stay and watch her," Bobby said.

"I don't *want* to. She isn't doing anything."

"OK, I'll watch, and *you* go to the meeting."

Now, Cindy was surprised. Under fang-and-claw rule, Bobby was in command here and entitled to step on her, and he hadn't. She didn't even remember having been nice to him: she only knew that this was nice.

18

"Whatever you want," she said. Bobby looked at her, and they made an uncertain pact.

John Randall looked from one to the other. "It's OK," he said. "We can all come to the meeting. We'll have it in the house, and then we can hear if she starts getting away."

Victorious through diplomacy (a rare act), Cindy smiled and skipped out first. Paul and the rest followed.

Although the Adams living room had furniture, none of it seemed to suit the children. John, who most needed big chairs, slumped instead on the coffee table, legs apart, elbows on knees.

"OK, let's get going," he said. "We've got a lot to talk about."

Paul sat down before him, cross-legged on the rug; Bobby lounged against the edge of the old captain's desk; and only Dianne sat in a chair, an overstuffed chair with rather regal lines. Cindy flung herself full-length along the back of the couch as if she were riding it bareback; then she slowly let herself slide down the front side onto the cushions where she rolled over once and lay staring up at the ceiling.

"Cindy, stop that," Bobby said. "You know you're not allowed to play on the furniture."

"We can do anything we want now," she said defiantly. "There's no one to stop us, and you're not my *father*."

"No, we can't," John said. "That's why we're having a meeting. We've got to make a lot of new rules about this thing."

"Like what?" Cindy was obviously against rules of any kind. Nonetheless, she sat up.

"Like, for one thing, we have to stand watch over her. Take turns," John said. "If she ever gets loose. . . ."

"She can't get loose," Bobby said quickly. "I put the knots where she couldn't get them."

"What if she found something sharp and cut the rope or reached over and knocked the telephone over?" Cindy said.

"Aw, that's only like you see on television. Where could she get hold of anything sharp enough to cut rope?"

"Just the same, we ought to watch her," John said stubbornly. "Take turns, one at a time."

"We ought to write this down like the other rules we used to have," Paul said. "Hey, Dianne, get some paper. . . ."

"That's a good idea," John said.

"Where's something to write with?" Dianne, who at seventeen was slightly the oldest, got up and went searching. There was an opening and slamming of drawers before she found a telephone pad and a ball-point pen. "OK," she said, "Number One: watch her."

"Right. Now, since Red Fox Patrol will have to watch her all night, Blue Fox Patrol and me'll watch her while we're here. OK?"

"Blue Fox, Roger," Paul said.

"OK?" John looked at Dianne.

Dianne did not say Roger. In no way did she condescend to say it. "Certainly," she said coolly.

"OK, and another thing," Bobby said. "We can't keep her tied in one place all the time. How're we going to move her around?"

"Why move her?" Cindy said.

"She has to get some circulation sometime, and she has to go to the bathroom like everybody else."

There was general giggling.

"Yeah, but she's strong," Bobby said. "You should have seen her this morning. Man, I thought she was going to tear the bed apart."

"Really?"

"We'd better all be here when we do have to move her," John said thoughtfully. The idea didn't appear to cheer him. "There're five of us—we ought to be able to do it."

"I got some things figured out—" Bobby began.

"Write that down," John ignored him.

"Then what about feeding her?" Cindy said.

"Yeah, that's something, too."

20

"I think we ought to put her on bread and water once a day," Paul said quite seriously. "You know, like a diet."

"Why?" Cindy said. "She's not fat."

"To make her weaker. Bobby says she's strong, so make her weak. Our mother diets. She doesn't eat anything at all during the day, except for carrots and celery and skimmed milk and junk like that, and she's always weak and tired out. Besides," he said, "we can do anything we want with a prisoner."

"Does your mother really eat that stuff?"

"All grown-ups do. They're afraid of getting fat and dying."

"Aw, you only get that from smoking and cancer," Cindy said. "Don't you watch TV?"

"Shut up, Cindy," John said, but kindly enough. "OK, how're we going to feed her? What happens if we take off the gag and she starts doing a lot of yelling?"

"We've still got the chloroform from Bobby's father," Paul said. "We can tell her if she screams, we'll put her to sleep and not feed her at all."

"There's enough stuff in the rag still." Bobby thought and had to agree. "I put it back in a tight jar."

"No one could hear her way down here anyway," Dianne said coolly.

"I know! We'll turn up the TV like they do on TV," Cindy's redundance was unconscious. "That way, anybody'll think it's that."

"Well, at least we all ought to be here whenever we take off her gag," John said. "Five are better than two. Write that down, Dianne."

"Another thing," Dianne spoke while she wrote. "Bobby and Cindy are supposed to have a baby-sitter to do all the housework and keep them clean," she looked up at Cindy. "If the house isn't neat, and the yard's a mess and the trash piles up, anybody stopping by'll want to come in and find out what's wrong."

"I'm *not* dirty," Cindy said.

"You ought to wash your face and brush your hair."

21

"Aw, I thought we were going to be free after *her*—"

"We are free, stupid," Bobby said, "but that doesn't mean you can do everything you want."

"It specially doesn't mean you can do what you want," John said. "We've got to be extra careful from here on. We have to do the things they usually do." *They* meant adults, clearly the other team (and the children all understood this).

"Right. First of all, we have to stay neat. Don't make a mess. Second, we all have to chip in and help clean things up," Dianne said. "Well, we *have* to," she added to the silence with which she was heard.

"I liked it better the other way—when *she* did all the work," Cindy said. "At least, she was our friend and played with us."

"Friend," John scoffed. "She was plain bossy. If I was your age, I wouldn't want her to sit for me."

"Besides, grow up," Bobby said. "We're too old to play all the time. Even you."

"What'd'ya mean?" Cindy sat up with the beginning of a tantrum in her voice. Whatever brother-sister love they had shown earlier was erased just now.

"Leave her alone," John said. "Now what else?"

"Phone calls," Dianne said.

"Yeah, we got to be careful about them—"

"And food," she said. "You've both got to eat for a week. We have to shop. . . ."

"*That's* easy," Bobby said. "We have a charge account at Tillman's. That's closest, and he delivers. Somebody can phone in an order, and he'll bring it up on the porch and leave it. He does all the time—"

"And he has Pop-Ups!" Cindy said.

Dianne looked at her with a frown. "And you have to cook. . . ."

"We'll barbecue things on the grill like Daddy does!" Cindy was slowly rekindling some enthusiasm.

"And vegetables, too."

"You're not my mother."

"Do what she says," Bobby said. "Eating has to

be just the same as always. Just as if nothing was wrong."

"Then why're we doing all of this?" Cindy's smile sort of stopped.

"You want to go swimming anytime you want to?" Bobby said. "You want to stay up late and watch the movies on TV you're not allowed to see? You want to try some of Dad's Scotch?"

"Well. . . ."

"It's just that there have to be rules."

"Yeah, but that takes the fun out of it."

"No, it won't," Paul said with a tic. "C'mon. Just wait."

Cindy sighed and flounced up and went to the kitchen. She went as if she felt she carried some immense veto power over the older kids. She let them wait. Then from the kitchen—slam of the refrigerator door—she grudgingly acquiesced. "OK."

John snorted, but not without mild amusement. "Well, OK. What're the rules so far?"

Dianne handed him the pad. On it, she had written in a neat, tiny hand:

1. *Watch her.*
2. *All be here—move her.*
3. *All—gag out.*
4. *Be neat, clean up.*
5. *Watch telephone calls.*
6. *Eat—shop.*
7. *Cindy's hair.*

"Yeah, what about the telephone?" John passed the pad to Paul. Bobby leaned down over his shoulder and read with him.

"Tell everyone she's taking a bath," Dianne said.

"Or she's down at the beach with the rest of us," Paul said.

"Or she took Cindy up to Bryce," Bobby said.

"OK." John was convinced. "Anything else?"

"Read your own rules," Dianne said. "First, let's

23

clean up what needs it, and then we can find out if *she* needs anything."

"I'll do the kitchen," Cindy said from the doorway.

"You wash your face and hands and put on a clean dress and brush your hair," Dianne said.

"It hurts."

"All right, I'll brush it for you."

"Still hurts—"

"Not if I do it."

"Cindy!" Bobby looked at her. He was the stronger.

"Aw-w-w—"

"Anyhow I'll do the kitchen with somebody. I know where everything's kept," Bobby said. "Afterward we can get Barbara up."

"Cool," Paul said. "That's neat."

Barbara had guessed in advance who the rest of Freedom Five would be. She had taken the same five children swimming the afternoon before—Sunday—helping the boys with their flailing Australian crawls, herding Cindy back from the part of the river where the current was strongest, and getting in some workout herself. (Dianne had only waded around a little and then withdrawn to sit on the bank and watch.)

Freedom Five was simply a community of kids—well, call them children, Barbara thought—stuck down in the country with no one else to play with except one with the other. And, just as Barbara had characterized Bobby as manly and reliable and Cindy as spoiled and funny, so had she formed rapid, friendly opinions of the others.

John was quite big and strong for his age, which she took to be about sixteen. He was a good-looking boy; his voice had settled down toward what would be its steady, mature tone: he was mannerly and thoughtful toward the others even though—except for Dianne—they were younger, possibly irritatingly younger. Still, there was an air about him which had to be called vague, lost. Even in the short hours they had all been together at the small river beach north of the Adams house, he had seemed now and then to drift away, to be thinking about something else or, more accurately perhaps, to be *trying* to think of something beyond his experience or present ability. Not to make too much of too little—particularly in the young—Barbara assumed that since he was no longer one of the children and yet not an adult (as she firmly felt herself to be), he was merely in the fashionable process of making himself, of finding himself. It made him rather nice, and made her rather more kindly toward him. Toward John, she had the Christian sort of superiority that made her want to help, made her want to see him succeed.

Paul—poor little thing—was absolutely a mess. This instant assessment rested not so much on his small skinny frame, thin lips, brown hair, gnomelike steel-rimmed glasses, as upon his manner. Paul was *squirmy*. In girlish reaction, Barbara was a little revolted: in motherly reaction, she was full of pity.

Paul twitched; he moved from foot to foot as if the ground was burning; he twisted his head and craned his neck when he talked. It was as if he were straining to put into words and actions some pouring torrent of ideas that could be neither checked nor investigated. His voice cracked and warbled; his eyes darted about. He was obviously a creature in torment caused—again—by trying to translate back and forth between the world he found himself to live in externally and the one within that was visible only to him. He would eventually grow up to be something quick, bright, complicated, and comically deformed—a full professional inventor of the useless, a doctor to computers, a teacher of the theoretical and distant. In short, he too would become civilized, "normal," and useful, but that would be long after the itch in him was tamed. For now, he remained squirmy.

Dianne, of course, was a stick. It wasn't unlikely that she was so considered by classmates at school. Oldest of the five by possibly half a year, she approached her eighteenth birthday unblossomed, unfavored and, at this late date, unpromising. Even Dianne, hopeful as she might allow herself to be in moments of absolute privacy, must now begin to sense the cold cast of the future. Where other girls had by this time begun to spread their child-bearing hips and lift out their breasts, she remained a tall, thin girl with long, white feet, bony legs in which the knees were prominent, absent hips, flat chest, prominent collarbone and sharp-edged elbows and wrists. Dianne rose to some height, and then dangled down again. Probably to combat this, she was agonizingly neat, quiet, withdrawn, undemonstrative, and chilly. Her hair was severely pulled back—strand by strand, each exactly parallel; she was spotlessly clean and smelled (nicely) of soap. She always stood a fastidious step apart, and only by her occasional use of authority over the other children—an authority they seemed to grant her willingly for some reason—did she reveal that there might be a person within the stick.

Because she felt superior—again—Barbara had felt her heart envelop the girl. She was extra kind to her and wanted to be more so. She wanted to tell her things, coax her: after all, no one need be *that* unattractive. But how to approach the wall Dianne had around her? Well, that would come in time.

So it had been, so they had seemed, so they had all behaved on the bright Sunday—yesterday—after church and a picnic on the beach and a swim. And among them, Barbara had moved and directed with assumed, cheerful responsibility, already the pretty new teacher with her first class of pupils. How different now.

By bright yesterday afternoon, Barbara realized now, her capture had all been fixed as a plan, her indignity assured except for chance and error. Bobby would have had his father's chloroform hidden away in a plastic sandwich bag in a jar, perhaps: there would have been rope in his own closet in the dark. Even

26

Cindy would have been primed to silence in spite of her voluble, willful nature.

Seen in that light, how unreal their innocent splashings, their carefully taken instructions, their casual obedience seemed. What a bad job new Teacher had done in her analyses, how easily Teacher was made the fool. Beneath the glib little caricatures she had drawn of the children, they were people—learn that! They were organized; they could plan; they could keep their own counsel; they could execute; and now it appeared that they could keep their composure once commitment had been made.

How quickly the tables were reversed. The children were children no more, and Teacher was Teacher no more. With a neat, short plot, they had erased her advantages and made her just a girl again, one who was now no better than they.

Less better!

Having heard the meeting which they took no trouble to keep secret, Barbara, of course, knew her captivity was not intended to be short. The moment of release, triumph, retribution, that she had felt to lie only a short while ahead, was not here or even near. Only another hour lay beyond this hour, perhaps only another day beyond this day.

With that conclusion, of course, she began to hurt. Her flesh and her muscles and tendons and body began to hurt very much. Something like her first panic almost returned.

No, Barbara said (remembering Terry's advice). I'll be calm. I won't hurt myself. I won't scare them again. I'll be careful.

Help me, Barbara said.

For anyone inclined to see humor, Freedom Five's second visit to their captive offered subtle possibilities. They entered the room together—very closely together—and moved to the bed in silence. It could be guessed from their manner and the sound of rapid shallow breathing that the wardens were more nervous than the prisoner.

The law had been broken, of course, and they had broken it. Since Barbara's capture had been accomplished before, however—last night, offstage, remote from them—all except Bobby might conveniently regard the crime as not theirs. The resulting situation—Barbara's helplessness, their ascent to power—might then be merely an abstract, a set of conditions discovered on their awakening this morning. But with their meeting, their decision to go on, their confrontation of the girl right now, things must obviously change. Now they began to break the law hour by hour, deliberately, forewarned of all the possible and unpleasant consequences. They became entirely responsible and answerable for their own actions. The door to innocence, real or pretended, had closed behind: from now on, there was no way to think of themselves except as bad and wrong and to be punished. So clearly did this appear to impress them, that they looked down at their prisoner but took care to avoid her eyes.

Barbara, of course, felt their tenseness and had the momentary, crazy impulse to laugh—if she could have laughed—at the whole improbable scene. She saw it as one both sees one's self and *is* one's self in dreams, the not-quite-Lilliputian captors and their possibly dangerous captive, each afraid of the other and yet each locked in with the other. Because it was true, of course, there was an hysterical edge to her thought.

Finding after several moments that Barbara indeed remained helpless, however, Freedom Five gradually relaxed. All right, here they were, out in the open, breaking the law between children and adults, and nothing was happening. They ignored the taboo, and no lightning fell.

"Well, what're we going to do?" John's voice was a little tight and dry, as if he were having difficulty in speaking.

"We don't have to do anything if—"

"I thought we were going to ask her if she wanted

28

to go to the *bath*room!" Cindy giggled at the idea. To her the capsizing of roles seemed endlessly funny.

"If she wants to go," Dianne said. Then she said directly to Barbara, "Do you?"

"Umnn?"

"Do you want to go to the bathroom?" Dianne said with painful clarity. "We can take you."

Barbara looked back up at her and then closed her eyes. The situation was, in actuality, more desperately impossible than she had foreseen. Going to the bathroom with five youngsters in tow! First, she thought that she'd never go to the toilet again rather than this. On the other hand—caution slowed her— the matter would have to be faced sometime if they held to their plans, and anything was better than simply being forced to lie here forever.

The *other* selfish thought skipped through her mind, of course. She hardly dared think it lest the kids somehow intuit it. This might be a chance to break free.

"She wants to go," Paul said. Squirming from foot to foot, he now seemed to be enjoying himself.

"OK, now. Like we talked about it," John said. "Are you ready?"

"Yeah"—Bobby had some more rope in his hand—"but, remember, she's strong for a girl if you let her get even a little bit loose."

"I won't." John rather squared himself. "Let's do it."

"Well, OK, I'll tie her hand first."

With one piece of the new rope he had brought, Bobby tied her right wrist just above the point where it was already tied. Then he took the free end of this new rope and squatted down beside the bed. "Now, we'll run it through here—"

Her momentary objectivity gone, Barbara watched them a little apprehensively. She could not see all they were doing, and she was afraid it might hurt.

Bobby straightened up. "OK, now, when I untie

29

her hand up here, you all hold her arm and move it down there and Paul pull on your end."

"All right," Dianne sighed. "Just *do* it, will you?"

There was a moment's silence with Barbara looking up at them, and John and Dianne looking down at her arm as if it had more-than-human strength in it. Barbara despaired.

"OK, that's it." Bobby jumped up from the head of the bed. "Move her—hurry up." He went around to help Paul.

The plan at last became clear to Barbara and everyone. At no time was she to be free. When Bobby released her wrist from the headboard of the bed, it was already tied by a longer rope to the lower part of the frame; all they had to do was to move her one defenseless arm down more or less by her side while Paul took up the slack. She was helpless at each instant of the operation.

"There, see? It did work."

"Yeah . . ."

They all straightened up.

Barbara now lay, legs still apart, one arm tied down by her side and the other up to the headboard. It didn't really hurt, at least no more than before, but it was frustrating and disappointing. At no time could she have done so much as free that one hand even for a minute.

"She looks like she's doing semaphore," Paul gave her one of his squirmy little smiles and looked around for approval.

"Or dancing," Cindy said critically. "Like Mrs. Gulliver." She giggled.

"*Miss* Gulliver," Dianne said.

"OK, never mind that. Let's do the rest of it."

With the same engineering care, they brought her other hand down by her other side and tied it, too. Her shoulders, stiff and sore from the hours of unnatural position, throbbed. Here, at least, was circulation and movement.

"Now, she has to sit up."

"What if she won't?" Cindy said. "How're you going to make her do it?"

"She's the one who wants to go to the bathroom. If she doesn't, we can always put her back the other way." It sounded reassuring when John said it, but, in fact, Barbara had more freedom now than at any time since she had awakened. She could do nothing with it, but she was more free.

"Yeah," Bobby said. "Sit up. You can if you want to." It was the first thing like a command that they had given her, and he did so with hesitation in his voice.

For the same reason, Barbara just slightly held back. The lessons in this relationship were painfully few, and yet she seemed to have so much trouble learning them. Were the youngsters, on the one hand, demanding that she sit up and, on the other hand, threatening to retie her if she did not? Indeed they were, indeed they would. Barbara must realize that no matter how far beneath her station she felt the kids to stand, they were absolutely in command. There was no alternative with dignity. She would obey, or she would be returned to a less pleasant position, and this would be repeated until she submitted. Barbara sighed and then, being a swimmer in good condition, managed to do the sit-up demanded.

They all looked at Bobby expectantly.

"OK, here—" He passed the rope around her body. "Now we tie her arms to her sides."

This was done. After that, her left wrist was released and tied up behind her back with a rope that went up over her right shoulder, crossed her body between her breasts, hooked under her elbow and returned to her wrist. For the left side alone, it was the same position she would have been in had someone been "twisting her arm" except that it *was* twisted and held there.

They were so cautious, everything took so much time and was so elaborately done that Barbara began to grow irritated. All right, she was doing what they wanted; she couldn't get away—she knew it, they knew

31

it—why so much fuss? When they got ready to move her legs together, she impatiently did it for them, or nearly did it before she fell over backward.

Cindy laughed, but Bobby, remembering his struggle this morning, quickly hobbled her ankles before she took the notion to kick out at someone. He seemed almost fearful when he released the last of the rope that held her to the bed.

"What about her other hand?"

"She needs one free, stupid. Besides, she can't do much with the elbow tied like that."

"Can she get up now?"

"Yeah, I guess so." Actually they had to swing her feet over the side of the bed and help her sit up again.

"How're you going to make her go just where you want her to?"

"Well—" Bobby hadn't thought of that.

"I know. Put a rope around her neck," Paul said. As he did when speaking most of the time, he sort of ducked his head and came up sideways like a myna bird struggling to say a difficult word.

"Yeah! That way, if she doesn't follow, we can choke her or at least pull her down."

"No, I've got a better idea," Bobby said. "Sit up," he told Barbara. He didn't hesitate this time, nor did she. She actually leaned towards him.

"Here—" Bobby looped his last long length of rope around her neck with ends trailing in front and in back. "One of us goes in front and one of us behind, and if she doesn't behave, each one *pulls*."

This was a little frightening. Barbara looked from one child to the other. She felt as if her upper body were embalmed in clothesline. The shoulder of her shortie was no longer on her shoulder, and she was a trifle bare-feeling.

"Choke her?" Cindy said.

"Don't worry. Not unless we have to."

"I'll lead," Paul said quickly.

"No, you won't," Dianne said. "Let Bobby and

John do it, and you follow and just don't get in the way unless we tell you to."

More foolishness. All right, she would go. More than anything else now, Barbara wanted to get this thing over with quickly. She looked at Freedom Five and made her only sound: "Umnn?"

"OK, stand up."

She tried and found that she couldn't do it without the fear of falling forward. "Ull mmnn," she said.

They looked at her blankly. All her sounds sounded the same.

"Ull mmnn!"

"Help me," Dianne translated.

Obediently, John and Dianne took her bare arms and helped her to stand. Briefly, she recorded the fact that they were much stronger than she would have guessed. Then Bobby gave a timid tug on the rope around her neck—it worked as he had said—and she turned and followed him, the rest coming behind.

The trip down the hall was a mile and a half long. Barbara was hobbled just above the ankles, and Bobby had tied his loops too tightly. When she stood up and put her weight on her legs, they swelled and the ropes cut in. Moreover, he had hobbled her too closely so that she advanced only by short little slides no more than nine or ten inches a move. Finally, her feet finished each step nearly in line so that it was like walking a tightrope. She was afraid of falling and kept her right hand out to steady herself against the wall as they went.

When the slow procession reached the bathroom at last, Dianne told the rest, "You can't see," and let Barbara slide in ahead. The whole time afterward, Dianne stood inside against the wall near the door, her gaze primly averted.

"Well, we'll have to feed her *some*time." John was sitting, elbows on table, heels hooked over the rung of a kitchen chair. He chewed while he talked, and in front of him lay part of a sandwich Dianne had made.

"How'll we get the gag back in her mouth if she doesn't want us to?" Cindy said. "She might bite."

"First of all, what if she starts yelling, you mean?"

"That's easy." Paul gave a twisted shrug. "Let John have a pillow, and if she does, he wraps it over her face."

"She'd smother," Bobby said.

"Just for a little while, while we open the chloroform, and then we put her to sleep."

"*How about the gag* though?" Cindy persisted.

"Same thing, stupid."

"I'm not stupid. You stop calling me that!"

"Why don't you leave her alone, Bobby?" John sighed.

"Somebody better stand guard and watch the road in case anyone drives in when she isn't gagged."

"You want to do that, Cindy?"

"No, I want to watch." She lazily ate the icing off a piece of cake she had wheedled out of Dianne.

"I'll stay out here," Bobby said.

"No, we might need you."

"I'm only out *here,* for godsakes. Besides, it's Paul's turn to do something. If he wants to chloroform her, let him try it for a change."

"Finish your sandwich, Paul. Hurry up"—Dianne was already straightening up—"It's getting late."

"Yeah, and I want to go swimming after my hour," Cindy licked her fingers slowly.

The kids approached Barbara more familiarly now. She was back in her room but sitting in a chair to which they had tied her—amid endless debate and engineering discussion—over an hour ago. It would be obvious to an outsider that half the rope would have done the job, but that was not the point. The more they used, the safer they felt.

This was apparent in the way they lounged around while Dianne explained about the pillow over the face and the chloroform and the lookout to watch the road. "Now, will you be quiet if we take your gag out?"

Barbara nodded solemnly. Her jaws ached from being spread.

Since the boys never offered to touch Barbara unless they had work to do, Dianne removed the adhesive tape. As usual, Bobby had used enough to set a broken bone, and it took a long time to come off strip by strip, each one protested by Barbara. When they were finally gone, balled up and discarded with the paper trash to be burned, Dianne reached in the older girl's mouth and pulled out the damp terry-cloth wad. Barbara swallowed immediately and painfully, and extended her tongue to touch her dry lips.

"Can I have a glass of water?"

At the sound of her voice, John and Paul stiffened slightly. This, clearly, was the beginning of danger.

"I won't scream," Barbara said carefully.

Don't lose your head when they ungag you, Terry had said in her phantom conversation this morning. *Talk to them. Be calm.*

"I'll get some," Cindy buzzed out.

"Turn on the TV—*loud*," John yelled behind her. He was still quite nervous.

"I won't scream," Barbara repeated in a low, steady voice. When no one said anything, she added, "You can put the pillow and bottle down. I *know*. I won't make any trouble."

Dianne, also tense, seemed to relax. "All right, then. I'll get you something."

"What?"

Dianne turned and left the room. "Cereal," she said over her shoulder.

"I want more than *that!*"

"That's all you're going to get." Paul instantly picked up the bottle again; the cloth was visible inside it, and his fingers were on the lid. "You're on a prisoner's diet."

"You—" Barbara stopped herself and sighed. "That's not going to make me any weaker, Paul. It's just going to make me hungrier."

"Well, you're still on it." He shut his lips tightly.

35

There was silence.

"The more you do to me, the more you'll get punished, you know?" Barbara finally said. She could not bring herself to say more, to grant them additional powers. A certain stubborn insistence on her adult superiority forbade it, particularly now that she had her voice back. "What do you suppose they'll do to you for this?"

The boys acknowledged her shot. Paul became embarrassed and looked down at the rug. Behind Barbara, John remained silent.

"Why don't you have another meeting and talk about it? You *know* what's going to happen: just decide for yourselves what's best. If you keep on going and somebody finds out before you let me go, you'll be in even worse trouble. If you let me go now, I'll"—Barbara was still ticked off—"I'll think about it. We'll all take a swim and talk about it."

The boys' silence became concrete and cold.

"Isn't that better than what you're going to get this way?"

Nothing.

After a bit, Dianne came back with the cereal on a tray and, being Dianne, a napkin. "What were you talking about?" She set the things on the vanity.

Paul's relief at seeing his sister was pathetic. He writhed in gratitude. "She wants us to let her go. She says she might not tell on us."

Dianne snorted in a ladylike way. "Can we move her over here?"

"But what's going to happen to all of you after this?" Barbara said.

"We don't want to talk. Come on." Getting over on the opposite side of the chair from John, Dianne helped him slide Barbara up to the small vanity.

Barbara sighed again and shook her head.

"Here's the water."

Dianne took it from Cindy and held it to Barbara's lips.

"Aren't you going to untie at least one *hand?*" The

36

caution, the insistence on detail, the silence, the refusal to be sensible or communicate with her, brought Barbara close to losing her patience. "I can't run away on one hand."

"It's too much trouble."

"But I want to feed my*self*."

"I know, but it's too much trouble. It takes too much time, and everyone wants to go swimming," Dianne said. "Do you want this or not?"

Barbara looked at her—Barbara felt crushed—and nodded. For all the fact that it was metallic well water, however, it was cool and healing and smooth. The sheer comfort to her throat erased part of her irritation, and when Dianne asked if she wanted the cereal, she simply nodded again and submitted to being fed like a baby.

Afterward Barbara felt the tension in the room begin to rise again. The boys positively radiated it. Paul picked up the bottle again.

"Wait a minute!"

They waited.

"You don't have to gag me again this afternoon. Nobody's coming, and I won't make any noise if they do—" She looked mostly at Dianne.

Instead of diminishing the tenseness, however, she only seemed to increase it. Even Dianne looked warily across at John, who reached over and fingered the pillow.

"But it hurts." Barbara looked from one to the other now. "I can't move my tongue or swallow. Can't you think of something else without that rag? I've had it in my mouth all day. Even last night." They appeared unyielding and yet reluctant to force her quiet yet. "Can't you tie something around my mouth or just use adhesive tape if you have to?"

"Aw, that's stuff like you see in old movies." Paul twitched. "You can talk through a gag like that, and you can lick tape off."

"You use saliva," Dianne said.

"How do you know?"

"He's right," John said from behind her.

Barbara hung her head and breathed deeply. They were probably right at that. "All right, but you're not ready to go swimming yet. Can't you at least leave me alone for a few minutes?" She raised her head and tried to look over her shoulder. "Come on, John."

He sighed—the put-upon male. "OK. For a few minutes."

Barbara had no one to talk to, however. They all left the room to change into their swimsuits, and when they came back, they meant pure business.

"Thank you," she said bitterly and opened her mouth for them.

After that—nothing—just tape and numbness and immobility and silence.

With a whoop of relief, Freedom Five banged out of the house and down the path toward the river, leaving Dianne to watch the prisoner first. Barbara tried to make sounds and get her attention several times, but it was no use: being ignored by her only made Barbara's ears and cheeks burn pink with anger and humiliation. And she *was* ignored.

Dianne unconcernedly curled up on the bed behind Barbara and began to read. Barbara had heard of the book not long ago—it seemed pretty grown-up for Dianne—a book club selection about mythology and ancient times (which were often sexy and sometimes gruesome, if the reviews were half right). In spite of this, Dianne read with absorption: Barbara could see her by looking in the vanity mirror and thence backward over her own shoulder.

The girl's face was pale and stern and distant. If Barbara had been able to speak to her, she would not have been sure of getting an answer at all.

2

It was evening but still light. Having helped with the dishes and separated the trash—"hard" things for fill, paper for burning, vegetables for compost—John Randall descended his veranda steps and stood looking toward a spot indeterminately between sky and earth.

The Randall house was next upriver from the Adams', the dividing line being Oak Creek. Like the Adams house, it faced the water but after that, the situation was quite different. An older, much added-to frame building with porches and gingerbread, oddly placed chimneys and roof angles, it sat on a knoll facing almost due west across the confluence of creek and river. From it, a mowed lawn—John's work—rounded down to a marsh on the river side. Where the cropped grass ended, water pooled, and a meadow of drowned reeds began. On the creek side, the same lawn ran right to tide's edge, and there hung a single-plank, weather-grayed dock.

The appeal to the senses offered by these sights was pleasant enough. The wind was still, the river reflecting twilight was deceptively blue and clean, and its surface was rippled only by feeding fish here and there. By contrast, Oak Creek was sunk in shadow to the left: in another twenty minutes it would merge with the dark stand of pine on the Adams property. Lightning bugs were out, frogs disputed, a faint smell of dust came from the cooling ground, all pleasant enough, indeed. Nonetheless, the view had not been pleasant to John

39

for a long time now. In many ways, it even appeared as the confines of a prison, not so much one of place (though it was) as one of process, a system from which he could not escape or even imagine escape. He was growing up, and they were waiting for him. Plans were laid.

If he got good grades—and they were fair enough—two years from now on an equal evening of late August, he would be all but departed for college. Four years more with working in the summer plus these immediate two, made it six years in all. Afterward he would go into the family business in Bryce or get a job and— What?

John's lack of clarity and motivation at this point was not blamable on poor training. Cause and effect, work and reward, had been hammered into his head and reinforced from the beginning. It was simply that being familiar with both, he found them commonplace, worth neither waiting nor striving for.

The fact was that John—quite predictably—wanted freedom now. By nature (if he disclosed it), by size, weight, strength, intelligence and desire, he was ready to become an apprentice adult, to be where wars were fought, rockets were fired, ships were steered and ice caps crossed. He was ready for girls and love. His spirit not only bent under the weight of years that separated him from these things practically, but cracked at the realization that such visions would never come true without enduring the same heavy and future years.

Before colonels commanded or astronauts flew, they were nearly forty! They told you all these things you could be, but the truth of it was that when you wanted it you couldn't have it, and when you got it, you were old and boring like everybody else. It quenched ambition—growing up simply took too long— and he made no plans and few starts. John was allowed his judgment: most people are. And in his judgment, nothing that grown-ups offered him—given the prerequisite qualifications—was worth a good goddamn. What the world was out to do was kill him, or at least the part of himself he considered best. Well, the hell with them all. He put himself on answering service—yes, sir; no, ma'am—and drifted on the *now*. Such was the John Randall of the background, the one revealed by himself to himself in long, not infrequently self-pitying moods.

To see John Randall at the moment, however, would be to miss this entire personality. Indeed to the unfamiliar eye he would seem—standing at the foot of the veranda steps—alert, wholly engaged, mentally charged, and even impatient. If he had been vague for several days, it was only because he was suddenly dazzled. Without expecting or intending to, he had stumbled into *life;* though he dare tell no one, he all at once felt himself to be living.

Flinging away from the house and the noise of the endless TV, John descended the lawn to the dock and slipped into his rowboat. There, not twenty yards across the creek, the Adams property began. Go up the clay bank, back through the woods by the path, across the field to the vegetable garden and you'd be at the house. It wouldn't take forty-five minutes—fifteen minutes going, fifteen there, and fifteen back again—and he would have seen Barbara again. Unfortunately, of course, they had all agreed to do nothing unusual to attract attention, and normally he never went over there at night. Dropping down on the center thwart of the boat, he sat knees together, shoulders sloping, chin in hand, inducing and savoring a new feeling of miserable bliss.

Actually, when it comes to sheer exposure of flesh, John Randall had seen much more of Barbara the times that everyone had gone swimming together than he ever had today. Her bikini bathing suit worn unconsciously in their presence, left exactly three and a half small things to the imagination, and while John admired her more than he hoped was noticeable, still it was somewhat abstract admiration.

Barbara was fun and friendly and a helluva good swimmer; she was almost like one of them, but it frosted him that like other adults, she just seemed to take it for granted that all kids were dumb and innocent and friendly and everything else, and that all they thought of was staying in line and having fun. Her obvious assumption that down deep they were just what she wanted them to be—good and well-behaved—was a real put-down. Her stupidity, her cheerful bossiness, that coercion he could forgive in someone really older—and so, really stupid—could not be forgiven in someone who looked like, who pretended to be a girl not much older than John himself. It rankled. It aggravated. Who would ever go for someone like that? Well, that was what he had thought, all right.

How different today!

He sighed, shifted position slightly, and—thus reminded that there was water in the boat—began idly, mechanically to bail. From time to time he stopped and stared, preoccupied, at the surface of the creek.

John had been scared and embarrassed this morning. Barbara was tied and gagged pretty well, but it had seemed like they only had *her*. It was as if the weight of law and order she represented must have allies everywhere, as if something terrific was going to happen to them any second. Even now, he wasn't sure it wouldn't occur sooner or later.

Nonetheless, the afternoon had been great, the greatest experience John Randall had ever had. He didn't know exactly what it was: it was just something about the way she acted (as if, indeed, she could have acted any other way—John didn't think about that).

When it was his turn to watch her and Dianne had left to keep an eye on the kids at the beach, he went into the bedroom, and Barbara was looking at him as if something different was going to happen. When he simply sat down a little to one side, pulled his towel around his neck and propped his feet on the bed, however, she had turned away, and after a while her head had slowly dropped forward. It was then that something about the smooth back of her neck, the curve of her shoulders, the way she sat there barelegged and sort of innocent and kid-looking, entirely charmed him.

John Randall was largely truthful with himself in regarding this as a surprise. The day had been filled with emotions—nervousness, embarrassment, daring, excitement, foreboding, and perhaps some covetousness—but yet he had entered the room feeling more a sense of danger and disbelief than anything else. It was impossible not to think of the trouble of keeping this whole game going, the chances of being caught, the things that would happen when it was all over—quite truly, he had a number of sober thoughts in his mind—and it was only after some time that he really studied the girl before him.

Silent, subdued of body if not of spirit, sweetly patient (or so he thought) enduring just enough picturesque pain and discomfort to keep her alert, Barbara became minute by minute a kind of girl he had never seen or suspected to exist. In fact, as he became attentive, even hypnotized by the sight, it became clear to him that he had never seen a real girl, a woman, before in his whole life.

Girls—in John Randall's estimation—were a pain in the ass. They came at you and were friendly enough, but if you responded, they turned and ran again and stood giggling in clutches of their own kind. They might touch you now and then, but if you touched back, they pushed you away as if you had broken something—or something. They came around in fantasies and kept you awake at nights, and yet—such was John's conclusion—girls really didn't need boys now or ever in their lives. Despite the fairly steady sight of marriages and enduring romances in the community and even in school, he was convinced of this. You needed girls—sleepless nights attested to it—and they didn't need you. That was the pain in the ass. But Barbara was different.

She was *now*.

Though it was imposed and enforced, of course, she had during the afternoon, exuded a feminine quality of submission that literally drenched the room. Moreover, the tension between John Randall and Barbara perceptibly changed as his guard hour wore along, changed between the girl and *him*. Before, it had been Barbara tied up by the kids—for so he still thought of himself—and now suddenly, as delicately as a bubble appearing, there came before him a girl brought to her proper, humble place by (in part, at least) her master. She was given to play her role, and he was—divinely—given his. It was all a stunning conception. He had the feeling of being in the presence of profound reality, the kind that smashed away laws, manners, and all the crap they handed you. He exhaled and only then realized that he had been holding his breath in order to hold the spell. The most mysterious and wonderful thing in the world was simply what was going on right there beneath his nose. He was engulfed in living as he had always wished.

What sort of spoiled it every now and then was that she would try and shift around. The way her hands twisted and searched behind her back, the way she suddenly breathed more heavily, the way she looked accusingly at him, brought back the truer shape of things. She was only Barbara after all: released, she would become her busy, cheerful, uninteresting self soon enough again. And he was only John who was going to get it good when all of this was over and finished. The magic was broken.

Only to rise again.

With the sigh of someone who throws himself before a wonderful fate, John Randall flipped the rowboat's painter off the dock piling and let himself float slowly toward the river. It was dark now, and he felt more sheltered and private. With exacting mental care, he picked the needle of memory up—it was all like replaying a good record—and set it back again to the precise groove when everything seemed to change between him and her. Then he sat back and let himself and the boat drift, and he lived it all over again.

Things were harder for Paul.

Everything was harder for Paul.

He knew, for example, that he laughed too loud and too soon—brayed in fact—when nobody else saw anything funny. He knew he let himself become sad or frightened and cry too easily He knew that—being his size—he dare not fistfight, and yet he couldn't hold his temper one bit. He always realized afterward that he missed stupid questions at school because when they were asked, he stopped to think of all the possibilities and ramifications, and then the questions weren't simple anymore. Things were all more complicated than anyone seemed to understand. The world constantly reported itself to him as louder, harsher, funnier, sadder, more menacing and intricate, than it did to others.

All of this had been observable from the beginning.

"See the dog, Paul"; Paul understood at once. "Say *dog*," "Spell *dog*"; Paul did it first. So far, so good. Paul McVeigh was as superior as his forebears would have expected (and they were very WASP forebears). How bright-eyed, how interested, how quick. Yet Paul also saw terrible terrors in the most familiar shadows. And he felt things that were not entirely warranted—more grief than a dead bird demanded, more beauty and grandeur than a winter night's sky possessed. His sensitivity, in short, went beyond the useful to the useless and to the harmful itself.

Growing up, Paul had assumed that everyone else felt exactly as he did, saw the exact same things he did. The difference was that—somehow—everyone else seemed to control themselves better. The question of why puzzled him very much. Why shouldn't they twitch and cry out, too?

Later, of course—now he was thirteen—Paul decided this wasn't true. They didn't understand and never would. He was a stranger in the world. See simple, act simple, home free—that was the way of the world after all. To Paul alone fell the struggle of controlling an uncontrollable self.

Dianne, for example, could come home from a day like today at the Adams' house and help around the kitchen obediently and unconcernedly. To look at her, an outsider would conclude that it had been merely another day among many.

Paul, on the other hand, appeared at the dinner table still flushed and trembling with inexpressible—and they had better *be* inexpressible—thoughts of the hours just past. The transgression of the children against adulthood, the possibilities of the Barbara game yet to come, the inescapable punishment, before which he writhed in anticipation, were burned more than vividly upon his mind. He dropped his fork in his plate—a splash; he knocked over his iced tea; he sniffed and twitched and stared into space; he heard no words when he was spoken to. At length, sent from the table by parents embarrassed by his bad manners (for themselves), he stomped to his room and sat in furious confusion, half over the events of the day and half over his rage at the world. When Dianne looked in to say, "Be careful now, don't give anything away," he jumped up and shouted nearly in tears, "Get out of here! Leave me alone!" And even this wasn't the end of it.

He was dreaming (oddly enough, he knew this but could not break the hold of the dream). One of the grown-ups said that he had seen big fish, and Paul went to the river by the Adams' to look, except that the river was huge—at least a mile wide—and its color was crystal and clear and green as morning air. Watching from the beach, which fell like a cliff into the well-lit depths, Paul saw unimaginable shapes moving in the deep shadows at the bottom. Then, gradually, these rose to the middle depths, and he recognized whales and sharks and barracuda among the undulating currents. Terrified, disbelieving, yet drawn helplessly to look, he knelt down on his knees in wet sand to see better. Then—again it was instant—he was out in the water itself, yards from shore, and beneath him were the horrible fish coming up from the black at the bottom of the clear. Now there was no shore anymore, and he looked around and

46

floundered helplessly as he sank toward the dark fish. He screamed, even underwater.

"It's all right, Mother." Dianne was the first down the hall. "Paul's just having another nightmare. I'll take care of it. Don't get up." Entering his room and switching on the light, she saw his thin, bone-rigid face.

"The fish," he said confusedly, "the fish—"

Dianne actually smiled, but from relief, amusement, or contempt it would have been impossible to say. She looked down on her younger brother like a thin, white Mona Lisa.

Throwing back the sheet, she saw that Paul's pajamas were soaked, his hair limp with sweat and his eyes abnormally wide. "The fish again," she said. "Well, you *look* like you've been swimming." She shook him. "Wake up now. Sit up a minute." Going down the hall to the bathroom, she busied herself and then returned with a little white, plasticlike capsule, some water, and a towel to dry him with. "Here—"

Some time afterward, when he had quieted down a little, she turned out the light and stroked him. She began to tell him all about the scary book that she was reading and he lay listening, rapt.

At the Adams house the sun took an uncommonly long time to set and the evening forever to pass. After the older kids left, Cindy tried out her newfound freedom by walking back down to the river. There, alone, she kicked up pebbles with her big toe and tried skipping them on the water the way she had seen John and Bobby do, but even her rare successes were uninteresting. Shadows were stretching out; the river was quite still; and there wasn't anyone around. At length she stood by herself, absolutely free and solitary, a small person beside the water, and it all bored her to death. In fact, freedom—the way the older kids described it—was not all that great. She missed the presence of adults.

In grown-ups' comforting company, there was noise and purposefulness and direction all the time.

Meals must be gotten, potatoes dug, trips to Bryce made, shopping completed. Telephones rang; meetings were arranged; plans were made for taking the tractor to the shop. Moreover someone was always asking what *she* wanted, what *she* was going to do, and someone was always watching, correcting, encouraging, and applauding all *her* deeds. Freedom was no one there: freedom was no one caring (and Cindy didn't like to perform without her audience).

Just now, for example, she could drift up from the beach, skirt along the lines of pines to the north of the house, fall in with the private road into the Adams property, play in the abandoned tenant house—Freedom Five's meeting place—and return when and as she pleased, even after dark if she pleased, and yet none of this was tempting. The woods, the road, the scary old tenant house, the yard, all were empty. Nowhere was there anyone waiting expressly for Cindy.

Oddly, she didn't miss Mommy and Daddy. She had prepared a little hollow place in her mind to allow for their trip, and—given surety that they would be back on the *dot*—she endured their absence cheerfully enough. Who she really missed, however, was Barbara, not of course the *person* of Barbara which she could see at any time she chose, but the fun and excitement of Barbara.

Cindy remembered the flurry of Barbara's arrival with special pleasure. They all drove up to Bryce and had ice cream while they waited for the bus. Then it was there, hot and clattering with the door opening, and then there was Barbara on the steps all neat and clean and trim and pretty in a pale-blue summer dress just like a big sister delivered in answer to a prayer. She was nicer and quicker, more dashing than Mommy, and yet she was younger and closer and more understandable to Cindy.

Once home, Barbara swept into the guest room and opened her bags. There were dresses and brushes, underthings and bathing suits, books and perfume, all the fascinating things Cindy would have someday for herself. Barbara swished and ordered, kissed and patted—she brought real life into the house. She could even drive the station wagon. And now Barbara was gone—at least for practical purposes—and Cindy missed her most.

Of the wonderful surprise, the pretty big sister, there was little recognizable in the person tied to the guest-room bed, led by a rope, and fed like a pet. Except that Cindy was one of the kids and had her part to do in Freedom Five's adventure, she would gladly untie Barbara and set things running again. Lonely enough, angry enough—just let them call her stupid one more time—she just might do it to *show* them. But not yet. Cindy sighed: she would just have to make do with old Bobby.

That evening they had frozen TV dinners. Bobby carefully and methodically heated them in the oven, and he and Cindy ate them from the foil trays while they watched a twilight serial on the tube. After they cleaned up, Bobby went to his room and tried to take a nap while Cindy sat up to be the guard. Now the whole house, the television set and living room were hers as well, and she had the same unpleasant feeling of being bored.

Having fed Barbara a sandwich and a Coke, the kids had gagged her again, engineered her to bed, spread-eagled and tied her there. Afterwards—from her point of view—she was very nearly forgotten, discarded as simply and with as little thought as a toy. She was embarrassed and angry—indeed, she had been mostly so all day—but at the same time, she was strangely relieved. After the morning's shocks of discovery, the hours of discomfort sitting in that chair, the ordeal of being watched and guarded all the time, she was almost pleased to be lying down again, quiet and—for the instant—alone. The same position that had seemed intolerable before now seemed bearable.

That's not true, Barbara said. People who are tied up don't just lie around in comfort. Soon enough the muscles around her underarms and in her hips would begin to ache, and the blood would slow down and her hands and feet grow numb. It would hurt. Above all, however, was the burden of time to be passed. If the same pattern were followed tomorrow as had been set today, it could be sixteen *hours*—twilight, evening, night, morning, and midmorning—before she would be allowed the barest movement, and that would only be to the end of the hallway and back again. Fear-leading-to-panic can begin in soft, quiet ways, and it began now liked a velvety moth circling around in her mind.

Sixteen hours, Barbara was appalled. Yes, that's the very soonest too. Maybe more. I can't stand it, Barbara said. But it's going to happen anyway.

The anticipation alone was enough to throw her into unreasonable hysteria, make her exert every ounce of her energy in one more desperate struggle to be free. Young Bobby was improving as a jailer, however; he had used his longest length of rope this time, and her wrists were tied with hitches in the middle and the ends out of sight somewhere behind the headboard. There was nothing to tempt her or raise hopes. And she could not even sleep.

Out in the kitchen Bobby and Cindy clattered and bickered over their simple dinner. Barbara's nose, sharpened by a day's unsatisfied hunger now, could smell it nearly the moment they peeled off the foil— fried chicken. When Cindy came to check the prisoner, her fingers and mouth were greasy with it, and she seemed to reek of food. Barbara had the disgusting thought that if she were free just then, she'd take a bite out of the child as if Cindy were a plump little chicken herself. And the TV blared.

During dinner the children had silently watched the old TV reruns. Later, after they cleaned up and Bobby went to his room to nap, Cindy sat vacuously through the whole long evenings of shows, one after the other, favoring those on which there were child or animal characters and after that, the most exciting and violent. Often—perhaps simply to exercise her exclusive control over all the knobs of the set—she switched from channel to channel seemingly able to follow all the simple stories at once. At one point, she dawdled away a long commercial break by also trying to play "The Happy Farmer" on the piano. It gave Barbara a headache. The child's mind was obviously spinning loosely, shallowly, from this to that to this to that without any anchor of attention to hold it, and *she* was the jailer and Barbara the captive. It was insane.

Finally, during the late-late show, things steadied down, and there was no further movement from the living room. Planes dove and strafed; Japanese died with endless screams; the surviving Marines formed up and marched out presumably to new battles; the Orioles beat the A's 9–5 to keep their hold on first place; the dollar was again under attack in Europe; and then there was "The Star-Spangled Banner" and, at last, only a gritty, staticky, blue-white buzz. Cindy, Barbara supposed, had long since gone to sleep, likely as not on the rug. Bobby was still absent—probably asleep in his room—and Barbara was truly alone.

Now was the time for the heroics and daring of fiction. A subtle flick of her fingers and a hidden razor blade would suddenly appear; snick, slash, and she would be free. Unfortunately, of course, it was only on the tube that such things happened. Now, here, in life, victims remained pretty much what they had been before—victims.

The callousness with which the children were able to leave her thus—save making it worse by guarding, of course—was astonishing to Barbara. They seemed to have no ability or desire to project themselves into her situation or imagine how much she hurt. They had no gods—or, if they did, they weren't charitable and loving gods—and they had no heroes unless the name Freedom Five implied that guerrilla fighters had some hold on imagination. They just went along. Like Cindy, they all just sort of went along buoyed up by their automatic, thermostatically controlled, smoothly running house machines and credit cards and charge accounts. Adults weren't really needed or heeded at all.

Oh, stop that, Barbara said, frightened. *You're going off the wall. It isn't that way at all. Oh, yes, it is. Why not? O god.* She strained not to strain at her ropes; that would only hurt more. *Lie still.*

I'm trying. I'm trying.

If she could momentarily will her body to quietude, however, Barbara could not silence her mind. As an Ed major, her young head was full of everything from Group Needs and Interaction down to Gestalt Psychology (a lot of it, undigested). Her head—in enforced solitariness, *would* spin on—would keep her awake. *If I could only make something out of all of this,* Barbara said. Instead a tune came to mind; it emerged out of "The Happy Farmer."

> School-days, school-days,
> Dear old golden rule days,
> Reading and writing and 'rithmetic,
> Taught to the tune of a hick'ry stick. . . .

Stop it, Barbara said again. I want to *think*. And she did, but the silly music went on and transposed itself into:

> The automatic children and the prophylactic pup
> Were playing in the garden when the bunny gamboled up . . .

No, I do want to think!

It was no use, thinking had gone. Barbara hurt and ached now: at her best, possibly, she could not have pursued the matter. It wasn't her sort of thing, not like it was Terry's.

Terry could settle down, not mannishly of course, but settle down with a relaxed attitude that at least indicated the absence of body concerns from mind. Chin on left palm, right hand scribbling notes in swift, efficient shorthand, she exuded concentration, isolation. A wall existed around her. At the other end of the room by contrast, Barbara sat twisted and twined around her chair like a vine. Her legs were crossed and recrossed, foot hooked behind ankle. Her hands willfully played with things on her desk. She brushed her hair out of her eyes three times a minute, it seemed like. She looked at words and understood them and then forgot them the moment she passed to the next paragraph. She could not structure and comprehend wholes. Movement, pleasure, warm and direct human contact and joy were her world, not this one of contemplation. At times of absolutely forced study—exams, term paper deadlines—she even had the notion to speak out, yell, dance, sing, throw something to break the holy quiet. "What's the use, Terry? I mean, really like what's the use? How can you just sit there and grind like that? What's the difference between us?"

Snagged, touched by a memory, Barbara drifted, recalled clearly, saw their room in the dormitory with Terry studying that way, Terry dressing, Terry doing her small wash. Terry moving in and out with her self-possessed assurance. It was so momentarily vivid that there even seemed to be a faint superimposition of this room at the Adams' upon the old one at the university, Barbara lying in the one bed here, then a curious light/time effect, and finally Terry moving about on the other side of *her* bed in *their* room not ten feet away. What if it was really like that and not simply imagined? The daydream begun and interrupted this morning, began again.

"Terry?"

"Terr-ee-e-e . . . ?" Terry said.

"They didn't let me go," Barbara said unnecessarily.

Terry said nothing.

"I don't think they're going to let me go until they have to."

"Maybe not." Terry was beginning to get ready for bed herself. She was a plain, not to say an awkward-looking girl, but she had beautiful copper-colored hair and enviable green eyes. Now, on her side of the room, she turned to Barbara, tipped her head, swung her hair away, and undid her earring. "What're you going to do?"

"What can I do?" Barbara was miserable. "What would you do?"

"I don't know." Unhelpfully, Terry swung her head the other way and unscrewed her other earring. Turning to her dresser, she opened the top drawer and dropped the jewelry in her hand into a small, laquered box. "In the first place, I wouldn't get into such a fix."

"That's right."

In ordinary conversation with all guards up, Barbara would have objected, but in this privileged, short-hand conversation of the imagination, she automatically yielded ground. "That's right," she said more thoughtfully, "but why? What makes you so smart?"

"Nothing." Terry shut the drawer. "It's not me, it's you. You're a square, Barbara." She went into the bathroom and stood, taking off her makeup.

"You wouldn't have taken the job here."

"Um hmnn." Terry pulled out a tissue, wrapped it around her forefinger and began to wipe away her lipstick. "If I needed the money, I'd have gone out and gotten a real job in the real world. That's number one." She twisted her jaw unglamorously and wiped lipstick from the other corner of her mouth. "You're a dreamer, a dropout. You try and slither through by taking a job way down here in the country—friends of the family—for nickles and dimes because it doesn't make you change your mind about anything. You're going around wrapped up in white cotton. You're playing little, rich, middle-class mother. It's like a vacation with pay, and if you can just keep it going like that, Ted or somebody else is going to come along and really *make* you one, and you never will have had to face up."

Barbara agreed. It wasn't as if Terry hadn't said very much the same thing before; it was just that Terry really said it more diplomatically than Terry imagined.

"And if I did take that kind of job"—Terry leaned toward the mirror, eye-to-eye with herself as she dabbed—"what would the difference be?"

"The children would be afraid of you. They wouldn't do this."

Terry threw the tissue in the toilet and pulled out another. "That's right"—she wrapped it expertly around her finger—"and why?"

Well, Barbara didn't know. But she did.

"That's what I mean when I say you're a square." Terry pulled back from the mirror and finished off with a few deft swipes. "You go around with everything hanging out, Barb, and what hangs out looks like sweet, simple affection. You make yourself be nice, and you think that if you keep on being that way and don't do anything to the world, it won't do anything to you."

"What's wrong with that? If I like people, why shouldn't I show it?"

"Because you *don't* like them." Terry dropped the tissue in the toilet again and turned on the taps in the sink. Standing in her slip, flat-footed, un-made-up, she pulled down her washrag from the bar and spread it out beneath the running water. "You turn everybody into little Disney puppy dogs and pussy cats. You like them for what you make them and not for what they are with warts on. You make everybody want to act out for you, and it isn't comfortable."

"I like to see . . . I like to try and see what's good in people," Barbara said stubbornly. "Everybody else goes around seeing the warts as you call it, so why isn't it nice to see the good for a change?"

"Right-schmight. If somebody's ticked off, they want to be taken the way they are—ticked off. They don't want to have to play-pretend for *you*." Terry pulled out her complexion soap—the hopeful soap she called it—and began lathering her face according to the rules prescribed in all the womens' magazines. "For example"—she worked at her forehead with rather short, strong fingers—"you think of me as your smart roommate who knows everything in the world to get you out of jams. Right? I mean, that's *all* I am. And the fact I just might be lonely or in need of cheering up or worried about finding a man just doesn't get into your idea, right? You miniaturize me and take the sweet part. Where 'serious' begins, you leave off."

"That's not true—"

"And if the boys smile at you, you like to think they're being friendly, and when they want to put their hands on you it's not because they really want to take you to bed." Terry plunged her face into handsful of water. "Barb, you're square."

Barbara said nothing.

Terry pulled down her towel and began to pat her face dry. "I mean, when did we ever *talk?* The minute I say something that bothers *me,* I can just begin to see it coming—some kind of blip goes off in your head. Your mind begins to wander. You change subjects and go back to something stupid and safe. You just sort of slide away." Terry tossed the towel back on the bar. Tomorrow, she would be sorry she hadn't spread it out to dry evenly, but just now, she forgot it. Whatever good qualities she had were at least somewhat offset by the fact that she was also sloppy.

"I can't help it," Barbara said more slowly and sleepily. "When people start to get too close to me, it makes me feel—crawly." She paused, considering this fact.

The ache in her body that she had foreseen had set in now. Muscles must be extended and tried—as a swimmer she had absorbed a lot of coaching—and then they must slack and relax again. Her muscles could not. She was extended tightly, permanently, and immovably, and now the muscles protested.

"That's silly." Barbara drowsed. "This shouldn't really hurt anyone in condition. But it does—it hurts like hell. Anyhow we were really talking about the children and I didn't really like them, right?"

"Terry . . . ?"

"I'm here." Terry turned off the bathroom light

56

and came out to finish undressing. Barbara was relieved that she was still there.

"So?"

"Well, you didn't like them, and you didn't land on them either. You just horsed around, and you lost respect. They weren't afraid of you." Terry pulled her slip over her head and dropped it negligently on the chair. "You were just a kind of super playmate, and so you got pulled down into their games. You're just a Barbie Doll—you walk, you talk, you wet, you say real words. If they want to tie you up and play monster, why not?" A certain, ritual modesty made Terry turn her back when she took off her bra and slipped on her nightgown. Only then did she pull off her panties and toss them with everything else on the chair. "You're more naive than they are and a lot less tough. You're just bigger, that's all."

Barbara was silent. Imagination's game, imagination's conversation, required more effort of mind than she now had left to give.

Terry pulled down the covers and slipped into a largely unmade bed (she had only pulled the bedspread up over it to hide the disorder on whatever morning it had been before). "Anyhow you were in charge here last night, and now the kids are. Why?"

"They're a bunch of little animals." Barbara seemed to have to rise from a long way down to even reply to this. Everything else was ache and oncoming exhaustion.

"You're going to make a lousy teacher."

"Monsters then. Let me alone. I want to sleep. God, I want to sleep."

Terry said nothing. Released, blurred out somehow, she was silent at last. Barbara imagined, however, that she was still over *there*, asleep in her own bed, and the comforting fantasy made everything better.

"Good night. . . ."

"Wait a minute. You can't go anywhere looking like that," Barbara's mother said.

She was right.

Barbara had been going into town just to get away for a few hours—near/far away, she could see where she wanted to go—but Mother was right. She was still in her nightgown, and it was too small. It hurt. She'd have to change into something else as soon as the car coming down the road had passed. Its headlights were too bright to do it here.

Then Barbara opened her eyes.

Young Bobby Adams, sleepy, sober, subdued-looking, was standing beside the bed in the light of the night lamp he had just turned on. He inspected her bonds carefully, hand and foot, and then thoughtfully pulled the sheet up over her. Afterward he went out to the kitchen. She could hear him rummaging around for a snack.

Oh, god, at least turn the light back off, she said.

3

The kids arrived earlier the next morning. Awake and squirming for hours, Barbara heard them yelling their way through the woods, heard the morning's exchange of news on the back steps and heard them come clumping into the kitchen. Anxiously, she watched them fan into her room. She was frantic to be allowed some movement, and it was at the top of her mind that she would not be allowed so much as a twitch if she frightened them. She lay very still and very docile.

At once it was apparent that whatever else had happened in the twenty-four hours or so that she had been captive, her jailers at least had lost their nervousness. To the extent that this downgraded her in relation to the children, it was discouraging. To the extent that it speeded things up, it was a godsend.

"Shall we do it the way we did yesterday?" John said.

"Yeah." Bobby was a little sleepy and out of tune, but he remained conscientious. "Only this time, I'm going to put two turns of rope around her neck when she walks."

"Why?"

"Oh"—there was no malice in his tone—"it'd hurt more."

(Barbara agreed.)

"Let me pull her today." Paul's eyes darted with morning energy from Bobby to John.

"You don't *pull*. You just walk in front of her," Dianne said. "You only pull if she doesn't follow."

"He wants to choke her." Cindy gave, for her, a very sly and knowing smile.

"I do not!"

"Do so."

"It's OK." Though he spoke to the bickerers, John turned his eyes squarely to the girl on the bed. "Let him lead. He can. Bobby can follow; I don't care. Get the rope."

Far more quickly than yesterday, they had Barbara on her feet, elbows tied to her sides, one hand tied up behind and almost between her shoulder blades, her ankles hobbled. They were rougher, quicker, surer— they seemed to have no further fear that she might somehow escape or overpower them—and Barbara made no resistance except that when she finally sat up and before she stood up, she bent forward and eased her hurting back a moment. This, they allowed her, and like any prisoner, she supposed, she did not prolong her pleasure. She stood up stiffly; she moved as they wished; and she cooperated fully. What had been humiliating and infuriating yesterday was simply more expedient, less painful today. Moreover it avoided the futile defeat a one-handed struggle would bring against five determined youngsters.

Barbara began to realize how people could be broken. It would be just the way you read about it in books. Everything would be brought down to the tiniest little pleasures measured out by the cc. from the tiniest little eyedropper. Drop, pleasure; no drop, misery. Someone else's hand would be on the little bulb, and you'd do anything to please them. Even as the recognition occurred to her, moreover, she was padding out of the room behind her captors.

They shuffled her to the bathroom where Dianne once more stood guard. Then they put her in her chair with yards of cordage around her, and gave her the same breakfast of cereal and juice except that they let her feed herself. Awkwardly. One hand was free from the elbow down, and she was gagged, of course. She had to bend and strain and more or less slurp. Quite naturally she dribbled, and Dianne was there to wipe her gown as you might wipe a baby's. She slid her hand inside the shortie top and held the cloth away so that she could dab it with a dampened napkin. Barbara would have given up, bent over, and wept for her own helplessness in all of this had it not been that she was now terribly hungry and that this little meal was one of the pleasures she had been thinking about.

Afterward—and she pleaded for this—the children even allowed her to remain ungagged, though her free hand was once again bound up with the other behind her back and the rag and chloroform were left in plain sight to remind her of the children's power. It was another little pleasure. Speech.

"Why are you doing it, Dianne?"

"Hmnn?" Dianne had finished her share of the morning's chores and settled down on Barbara's bed (which she had neatly made) with her rather lewd book on ancient practices—or so Barbara thought of it. When Barbara spoke, she looked up coolly.

"Me. Why are you keeping me tied up? Why did you do it in the first place?" Barbara was sitting faced away from Dianne, but she could see her in the vanity mirror.

"I don't know. It's only a game—" Dianne spoke offhandedly.

It stabbed Barbara. They did not know how much they were hurting her; even she did not entirely know. It was only just beginning to pile up. Last night had been—appropriately—a nightmare.

"It's only a game," Dianne said, "and besides, we aren't hurting you."

"You are, too," Barbara said, definitely.

"I haven't heard any crying and moaning and groaning."

"How *could* I?"

"It isn't hard."

"How do you know?"

"The same way." Dianne continued to cradle her book though she had given up any pretense of reading. "They've tied me up. Worse than you. We've all taken turns."

"You? The five of you? All of you?"

"Um." Dianne was nonchalant. "It's a game we used to play. One time I let them tie my hands to a tree limb, and they left me there most all the afternoon. In the woods. That really hurts."

"And that's a game?"

"Um." Dianne shrugged again.

"Where did you ever get the idea to do something silly like that?" Barbara almost said "like this."

"I don't know. You see it on TV or in the comics." She looked down at her book. "Do you know what people used to do when they were binding up the last sheaf of wheat in the fall and somebody came by the threshing floor while they were doing it? You know what they did to a king of England with a red-hot poker? Do you read very much in college?"

"Yes," Barbara yearned upward toward the ceiling and tried to stretch her shoulder muscles. They had tied her overtight again. It hurt. Still, she was careful; at least, she didn't have a gag in her mouth. "Not *that*, though."

"Oh." Dianne seemed disappointed. It was as if college wasn't going to be for her. "Anyhow, playing Prisoner's not all that great an idea. You used to do stuff like that when you were young yourself."

"No, I didn't." Barbara wasn't used to being included in some older generation. It startled her.

"Hmnn." Dianne barely made the sound at all, but she looked at the captive closely.

Barbara felt the scrutiny. Looking up into the mirror, she met Dianne's eyes. Perhaps Dianne didn't believe her, or perhaps she did and thought it odd. Whatever the cause, there was a degree of contempt in her look, and Barbara lowered her head and broke off the match.

In fact, Dianne's question had started up a memory. Barbara had been raised in an apartment building until nearly her senior year of high school. What she remembered now was an entire and uncomfortable relationship with the other kids in the immediate—and crowded—neighborhood. Specifically she remembered the whispering and sniggering of kids at one end of the apartment parking lot at twilight after dinner in the summer, a low, confidential murmur that dropped and turned to hostility if she approached. "Been helping your mother with the dishes?" "Hey, Barb, what d'ya do for *fun*?" "I know what I'd like to do with her—" Guffaws in the grand old manner.

If she had been walking toward them, inwardly anxious to be folded into the warmth of the group that laughed and talked so intimately, this immediately repelled her. She might try to face it out by asking one of the girls her age a question, or she might veer off and pretend to be going somewhere else on an errand, but either way she would hear over her shoulder the resumption of confidences and giggles.

They *wanted* her. She felt that boys and girls alike wanted her to do something or that they wanted to do something to her, and afterward, form had it, she would be one of them. Barbara didn't know what this suspected ritual act of initiation was—in her imagination, it was variously any number of wild things—but she felt it would take place somewhere far from help, that it would be in a crowd with a lot of snuggling up and hands on her body and the same knowing sniggers the next day, and she knew that even if she forced herself to begin, she would cry or get frightened in the middle of it and so wind up farther away from the group than now. Thus the wall of privacy and selfness that the others wanted to break down in her was thickened. She moved as closely to the other kids as she dared, but in the end she went her own sweet and deliberately shining way. Barbara would not be dirtied. It wasn't anything that had been taught her; it was just her own way.

"I don't know what the other kids did," she said to Dianne. "I never played that way."

Something of what Barbara had been thinking in her moment of silence—perhaps it was conveyed simply by the set of her face—seemed to reach Dianne. Her mirror image smiled a faintly contemptuous smile, and Barbara thought how like one of the parking-lot gigglers Dianne was at that.

At lunch they had been talking about her, though all they said, Barbara could not hear. Afterward, when John came to take his turn at guard, he brought with him a certain tension that quickly filled the space between them. It was so real that although she was still ungagged, Barbara said nothing at first.

John came over and needlessly checked her ropes. Then he moved to the room's other chair, which was out of her comfortable line of vision and beyond the mirror's angle. Barbara heard him sit down, and then it was quiet again, except that the room still held that tension.

After a while, Barbara turned her head back to the left and saw from the corner of her eye that John was knotting one of the unused pieces of rope (it amazed her that there were any). "What're you doing?"

"Nothing."

"Are you sure?"

"Sure." He looked up, mildly surprised. "What did you think I was doing?"

Barbara frowned and faced forward again, definitely a little nervous now. There was something in the air that just wouldn't go away. When John said or did nothing, however, she said, "John, why're you doing this to me?"

"I don't know." He was quiet a long moment. "We thought it'd be fun, I guess."

"Is it fun, hurting people?"

There was no answer, but the tension in the room tightened still more.

Barbara sighed. Yesterday the kids had not noticed or cared that she hurt. Now she was *telling* them. It seemed to make no difference one way or the other. What she could not understand was why—all right, so they were going to go on with it—but why she couldn't raise even a hint of guilt or sympathy or fear of punishment from any of them. Dianne was barely polite.

I just can't get through, Barbara thought. They don't care. In fact, I'm getting farther from them all the time. But it isn't my fault, is it? Barbara thought about it for some minutes.

When you got right down to it, what did fault have to do with anything, anyhow? What she wanted was results, relief. Maybe she had been embarrassing them. Taking a deep breath, she contritely said, "I'm sorry, John. I won't ask you that anymore."

John seemed somewhat relieved. The tension in the room seemed to drop a degree. "Aw, that's OK," he said, "there's nothing to be sorry about." When Barbara remained silent, he said, "Is it too tight?"

There!

Sympathy!

Barbara was astonished. She almost held her breath so that she wouldn't frighten the discovery away. Something had happened. Something *was* happening; she could feel the tension definitely lowering now. By accident, she had touched some control, and now the situation was better/possible. But what was happening?

Think, Barbara said (as usual). It was there, it was just out there. No, I won't, she said. I don't like it. Nonetheless her mind like a piece of photographic paper received a pale impression, and she suddenly saw a pattern in all of this. It seemed incredible for these sub-teen and teen-aged children and yet the truth of the matter was that the kiddies had fallen in love with Teacher and determined to play an erotic game with her. I don't believe it, she said. But she did.

Children, pupils, students falling in love with their teachers—it was all in something she'd read for some course or other, nothing more than a footnote but there. *Here.* The feeling she was getting from John, the

65

one she had not been able to understand when he came in, was in fact the same feeling she got from older men who thought they just might have the chance to make her. It was the thing of the party traps, the automobile traps, the arm around the shoulder traps—how well she knew them, how carefully she avoided them (usually)—and here it was again. Absolutely. No mistaking it at all.

Dear god, Barbara thought a little wildly, what now? If she continued to be complaining, accusatory, aloof, it would spoil their game, she supposed, but would it make them turn her loose? From somewhere inside her came a nice, neat answer: no. Where did *that* come from? Old "Group Needs and Interaction?" From experience? Never mind. People and animals in packs were socially merciless. What was more likely was if she continued the way she was going, they'd turn angry and vengeful. Like the gang of children snow-balling the odd-child-out on the playground, they'd punish her: as the parking-lot sniggerers had never been able to do, these kids would make her play the game. But they couldn't, Barbara Miller said to herself. Oh yes they could, said another voice within her, one that sounded very much like Terry.

On the other hand, Barbara said, on the other hand. . . .

No. This was a direction in which her mind moved only with reluctance. The path of thought was dark and impeded by a lifetime of avoidance.

On the other hand, Barbara still said, if I changed myself somehow, if I was a little bit more like what they want me to be, what would happen then? She rapidly imagined herself through the day or days ahead and thought that perhaps she saw a time when one of the youngsters in a fondness then returned, would become sorry for her and let her go. After all, Barbara said, what have I got to lose?

Still a nicety held her back.

Deep inside of her in a place she delicately and indistinctly located below her navel and above her knees (associations like that are Freudian, Terry always said) was another, separate and very neatly independent Barbara who had always been there. Not unusual. Not unusual at all if what Barbara read in her psych courses was even nearly right. Over the years, Barbara had located, recognized and isolated this shadow self that she called Sexy Barbara.

To the extent that Sexy Barbara had individual existence at all, she appeared as a slightly slipped image of the self that necessarily followed but did not always exactly obey her mistress. Where real Barbara conventionally waited for love to find her, Sexy Barbara was almost anxious to try sex and adventure for themselves. Where real Barbara went her own way believing that her essential worth and merit would eventually be discovered, Sexy Barbara bleached real Barbara's short hair, darkened her eyebrows and lashes, chose padded bras, shortened her skirts, walked in a certain way at certain times and for certain other people. She invited closer investigation.

The way it came out, Sexy Barbara—everything mock-adult, mock-dangerous, mock-heavy—was a plain hazard to have around, and the relationship between the two Ms. Millers had to be clear all the time. Real Barbara controlled, and Sexy Barbara was forcibly submerged, a willful creature who day- and night-dreamed and occasionally slipped out to be a trouble. Now, however, Sexy Barbara might be just what was needed.

If Freedom Five liked Barbara the way she was now, if John had a thing on about her, what in the world would they think of Sexy Barbara? What would the chemistry be? Well, anyhow, her mind was made up about it. The only problem was that after a lifetime of suppression, Sexy Barbara wasn't the easiest thing in the world to just turn on. Besides, she didn't respond to everyone anymore than did Barbara herself. Oh, well.

These rather complicated considerations did not, of course, come to Barbara as any neat, little mental essay. The component ideas were there, they had been there forever, and they simply flashed into a vague plan. She went from insight to surprise to possibility to conclusion in a very few seconds. Her only question to herself was, Can I?

"Is it too tight?" John said it again as if somehow he was now the one who had offended her.

Barbara made several experimental, anguished, twisting movements in her chair and permitted herself the smallest sound of someone in pain. She felt rather amateurish about it, but it was a beginning. "Yes," she said, and said it very meekly.

John dropped the rope he had been fiddling with and sat up indecisively. Perhaps he was even timid.

"Come feel for yourself. Please, John."

He got up and came over behind her. "What is it? Your hands?"

She was able to use the vanity mirror to both bend down away from him physically—as if in fear? pain?—and yet look up at him through her eyelashes (unfortunately not made-up). "Mostly," she said. "Couldn't you loosen up just a little bit or untie one hand and let me move it around and get some circulation? You're going to really hurt me badly if you keep this up."

John could see that this was true. Only her one wrist had been free that morning and now it was tacked up behind her again. Besides, keeping her sitting up had been his own idea.

"Hmnn—" He considered and savored a bit.

"*Think* of something, please? I couldn't get away if I wanted."

"OK," he said with magnanimity. Going to where he had been sitting, he brought back the spare piece of rope and bound her upper body more securely to the chair back. Then, however, he released her wrists, both of them, one by one.

"Oh! Oh-h-h—" The sound she made was sincere enough. There had been rope on her wrists almost without relief for over thirty-six hours. As she disbelievingly allowed her hands to fall by her sides, it was like when she was a child and her hands were cold from playing in the snow and burned when she came in the house. Blood seemed to rocket straight out to the ends of her fingers and pulse there. She flexed gently and brought her hands up to her lap where she could see them (rope around her body prevented her from doing more). They were red splotched with little white freckles in the palms and blue veins on top, and there were deep indents in the wrists where the cord had been.

If her complaint was real, however, the accompanying gestures were not. She closed her eyes and bit her lower lip and furrowed her forehead. Unfortunately she was not an actress and could not cry on demand. It was outchy enough (a term they used on the swim team), but it wasn't going to kill her nor could she pretend that it would.

"Umnn—" She tried to stroke her sore hands, but one would not quite reach the other.

"What is it?"

"The blood's starting to run back. It burns." She moved her fingers like someone rubbing sand or powder between them.

"Is it better, though?"

"Yes." She bit her lip again. Bravely this time.

Impulsively, even daringly, John reached down and took one of her free hands in his and began massaging the inside of her wrist.

"Ow!"

"Does it hurt?"

"No." In fact, it did. What her hands really needed was just to be let alone, but she did not say it. "That's nice, but be gentler. Please?" She looked up at him briefly and then lowered her eyes again. She made an effort to relax. That was going to be the nicest, softest, most maidenly hand that any boy ever stroked, even if it killed her. It worked, and after a while, he took her other hand and chafed some color back into it. Such a game could not go on forever, however.

At length he stood back. "What about your legs?"

Sexy Barbara looked up at him demurely, and he colored a bit.

"Oh, I see. Only my ankles. The corner of the chair legs—" In the morning, Bobby had tied her upper legs together above the knees and then tied each foot out to its own chair leg, and the chair legs were uncompromisingly square and sharp (to her). This, John proceeded to change, eyes discreetly upon his work which nonetheless seemed to go slowly. He untied each ankle and then retied them—loosely—together in front of her but not to the chair. She could swing her legs up and down like a child in a swing if she wanted to, but she did not. Afterward he slightly eased the rope about her bare knees.

During all of this, Barbara—both Barbaras—had the opportunity to examine her captor more closely. He was, as she had noticed straight along, a manly boy but more manly than she had taken the time to see before. He had strong, suntanned shoulders and arms, smooth and babylike perhaps, but definitely developed. And he was a clean boy with none of the acrid smells she associated with men on the make. He was like a big, strong pup.

No, stop that, Barbara said. The whole mental sequence, her entire imagined conversation with Terry came back to her. You don't turn people into bunny rabbits. They are people; John is nearly a man. He's bigger than I am, stronger than I am, and he can do a lot of things to me that I can't stop—now. And why stop it, Sexy Barbara said.

Sexy Barbara, indeed, allowed herself to be handled with grace and opportunism (such as was allowed her). She flexed her toes and rubbed her feet—sole on top of top—together when she was free, and docilely pressed her heels together when he retied them. She moved her legs together as if there was pleasure when he eased the line above her knees—actually, she could barely feel the difference—and sighed with gratefulness when he was done. There was truthfulness in this, and there was manliness in John.

70

Moreover John Randall seemed to have a streak of kindness in him. After the preceding day and a half, he was the only one who had now gone out of his way to help her. Both Barbaras found this his most endearing trait. While she was not any more free—she could not have gotten free in a month of uninterrupted labor—she was suddenly in a state approaching endurability, and she was making progress.

"Thank you, John." Sexy Barbara flashed him another calculatedly shy look from beneath eyelashes and held up her right hand a bit.

For a moment he seemed about to shake it, but at the last instant, he clumsily squeezed her fingers as he had seen polite adults do. There was about it a touch of the minuet. "You can stay that way while I'm here," he said.

"That'll be nice," Barbara said. "Wait a minute—don't go away."

"I'm not going anywhere."

"I mean, don't go over there in the corner where I can't see you. Stay here and talk to me."

"Well . . . what about?"

"Anything," Sexy Barbara said. "Just don't leave me alone."

John wavered. Then he sat down on the dresser, one leg along the top, one leg extended down to support himself.

"Well . . . where do you go to school?"

"Here. Bryce High."

"Junior?"

"Next year. I mean, next month."

"Do you go out for sports?"

"Yeah, football."

"Do you get to play?"

"I played JV last year. I'm supposed to go up to varsity now."

"Do you like it?"

"I dunno." He shrugged. "It gives you something else to think about."

"You ought to be good at it. You're big enough."

"I'm not very fast." Nonetheless John accepted the compliment with a faint coloring.

"Do you go steady?"

"No."

"Do you have a girl you like?"

"Well . . . yeah, I guess so."

"What's her name?"

"Sue," he said. 'Susan."

"What's she like?"

"It's hard to just say. Usual, I guess. Brown hair."

"Does she know you like her?"

"I suppose so. I've taken her to a couple of the school dances. We go to the movies sometimes. It's pretty dull being stuck down here all the time. There's not much to do."

"Oh." Barbara paused, somewhat defeated. During the silence, she twisted back and forth several times in a way that emphasized her (unfortunately) not-large breasts.

"Is it still too tight?"

"Oh . . . I guess I'm all right." Tiredly.

"When you're at college, do you go steady?" John became a little more sympathetic.

"No, not really."

"Why?"

"I don't know. I guess I don't want to." Since this was not quite correct, she amended it. "I mean, nobody's asked me to that I like enough. Anyhow it's more fun to go with a lot of different people."

"Yeah," he was unconvinced. "What do you do on dates?"

"Well . . . unless there's something big going on somewhere over the weekend, I guess we do about the same things you do. Get off campus, go downtown for dinner. Have a few drinks at a place where everybody likes to hang out. Go to dances. You know."

"Does everybody have a car?"

"A lot of them do."

"I wish I did." And then as if the thought instantly

72

gave rise to another, he said, "Do they try to kiss you afterward?"

Barbara looked up quickly and caught him faintly blushing again at what he must consider boldness. Found out, however, John did not give in to his shyness. He continued to wait for his answer with interest, and it was Barbara who dropped her eyes first.

Looking down at her useless hands lying beside her bare legs, she actually felt her femaleness in relation to John no longer a matter of amusement or disbelief. It had taken Sexy Barbara only a few minutes to prove suspicion right. The youngsters—this one, at any rate—most definitely did regard her as having a sex, and from old habit, she stiffened slightly. Enough of the come-on.

"Some of them do," she said with what of a shrug she could manage.

"Do you let them?"

"No."

"Really? Never? Not even when you were in high school? We do."

"Well . . . ," Barbara was forced to nod. "Every once in awhile if it's someone I really like."

"I thought you didn't like any one person very much."

"Oh, you know," she said shortly, "what I mean is nice boys. Some of them are so—" She made a wry face. "It's like wrestling a bear or something."

"Wrestling?" John was curious and interested.

"Not wrestling. Just . . . grabbing and pawing. Girls don't like that," she said. "I hate it."

"Can *I* kiss you?"

"No, John, I don't want to."

"Why?"

"It's silly. It doesn't mean anything that way."

"Yes, it does."

"How can it?"

"Well—I like *you*—"

"Ah." There were a great many directions in which Barbara suddenly did not want to see this little

73

conversation develop, and in self-defense and puzzlement she fell silent.

"Are you mad or something?"

"No," Barbara said quickly. "No. Really. It's . . . nice. I'm glad you like me but. . . ."

"You still don't want to."

"Well, it's not very romantic for *me*"—she was a little short—"like this."

"You couldn't stop me."

"That makes it worse."

John slid to his feet and stood beside her and very much over her.

Barbara turned and looked the other way but said nothing. It was suddenly very quiet—to her, at any rate. She expected any second for him to put the moves on her, grab her hair, pull at her gown—it could be anything—and she decided not to make a fuss. He was right; she couldn't stop him anyhow.

Instead, however, she felt him take her wrist and pull it around behind the back of the chair again. "Give me your other hand."

"Oh, John, no. Please."

"Give it to me."

"I don't want to. Please! It's early yet."

"All right, then, *don't* give it to me."

"Ouch! Ow! I will, I will. But don't make it so tight. You're doing it worse than it was."

"No, I'm not."

"But my hands are sore now. . . ."

"I can't help it."

"Please stop. You can kiss me if you want to. I don't mind."

He had begun tightening the rope around her body and the chair. When he spoke, he hesitated only a second and then went on with his work. Afterward and silently, he retied her ankles to the cornered legs of the chair, cinching up on them vengefully.

Ouch, Barbara said. Damn. I pushed him away and made him mad. He's just like a man, or men are just like children. They try and grab you and kiss you

74

and run their hand up under your dress with that terribly randy look in their eyes, and you might even let them if it weren't for green teeth braces or pimples or if a kiss would get rid of them. The trouble is, Barbara said, a kiss never ends anything but an old movie. Quite the contrary, she had found out: it was a place to begin with the other hand coming around under your breast and fumbling with buttons and all the rest. And if you stopped them, they went back to the frat house or wherever and called you frigid or did something mean when they got the chance. Men had just one use for women, and women—Barbara, most certainly—wanted so much more.

She watched John stand up, obviously satisfied with his work. He hurt me, he is hurting me, that'll *teach* me, she thought. Moreover, he wouldn't kiss me now if I begged him. I'm dirt. Instead he's going to let me learn my lesson well, hours of it. Barbara would have liked to do any number of womanish things—slam doors, yell, throw something at him, slap him—but none, of course, were possible. Instead she bowed her head, chastised, and weakly said, "I'm sorry, John." The tone of her voice was very soft and nice, but it didn't regain anything.

Instead he was the silent one now. He stood looking her over—Barbara did not raise her head but she could feel it—on an almost inch-by-inch basis. After a long while, he said, "I'll be back later." Quickly, Barbara heard him out in the living room, rummaging around in Dr. Adams' liquor cabinet. Although he had not done anything like it so far, he was obviously going to take a drink and get himself into a teen-aged mood. So much for Sexy Barbara's activities.

I could never be a sexy person, anyhow, Barbara said. I just don't like what happens when everybody gets going like that.

An hour later, when Cindy came in so that he could take a swim, John's conversation with Barbara no longer seemed as disappointing to him as it had.

Unaccustomedly expansive after several ounces of Scotch, he even considered the talk something of a success. Pulling on the chopped-off jeans he used for swimming, he reviewed the afternoon with even a degree of satisfaction.

It was as good as yesterday. Again he had felt the new, the still heady mixture of the girl's submissiveness and his own mastery, but today he had *used* that mastery. He had discovered that he could tie and untie her, himself. It changed a lot.

John did not think these thoughts out in sequential manner, but he understood what he had learned well enough. For favors which he was able to give, she more or less had to consent to being handled. For things he wanted which she could give, he could withhold his favors. That the favor to be traded was the giving or taking away of pain—he had no doubt that she was right: it hurt—was a very interesting bonus. The most clear kind of power. As with yesterday, he felt that he had lived through, been shown something terribly fundamental and important, not simply about himself and Barbara, but about life itself.

Swinging out the kitchen door and jogging down the steps, he paused a moment at the bottom loosely swinging his towel in one hand. It was another burning afternoon, summer-humid and hazy, the kind of day that usually produced thunderstorms in the evening but had not done so now for over a month. At his feet, brown, hard-shelled insects jumped and buzzed through the weeds, busy at trying to survive their baked existence. There wasn't a breeze nor the hope of one. Everything seemed hanging and waiting, but he hardly noticed it.

Tomorrow he might leave Barbara gagged, or he might not. She was a dumb person to talk to anyhow: he preferred her muffled sounds and eye movements to her words by far. In any event tomorrow he would bargain far more shrewdly. If she wished more freedom, she would really have to beg for it: if she wished to be ungagged, she would also have to be kissed. And other

76

things. As the interesting details of these adventures to come eased through his mind, John Randall understood that he was making progress. Progress toward what, however?

John's sex education had been sufficiently liberal and vivid that he knew—in theory at least—exactly what the act of sexual intercourse involved. When in imagination, he approached the matter flat-footed, straight out—call it fucking (a word that actually, somewhat embarrassed him)—his mind imposed a near mythic taboo. He was not exactly afraid, but the act was something that lay ahead in a not-now time. Moreover he expected that once it had been done the first time, some cataclysmic change would come over the world and that nothing would ever be the same again.

To ease the slight pall this thought brought over the otherwise successful afternoon, he broke into a trot across the field, leaped down the sandy bank, crossed the river beach in two strides and threw himself out across the water in a shallow surface dive. The brown, tepid water closed over him and burst back again, cooling but not entirely erasing his mild foreboding.

Afterward, pleasantly winded from a short but furious swim, he waded up the beach and stood toweling off near Paul and Bobby. "Aren't you going in?"

"We've been."

"Where's Dianne?"

"She's putting the laundry in the dryer. We have to go pretty soon. . . ."

"Yeah. We'll have to move *her* again."

"That's easy." Bobby stretched out on his back and looked up at the sky. "She can't get away anymore, anyhow."

"Yeah." Paul twitched unconsciously.

John sat down and was quiet.

After a while, Bobby sighed. "This is boring."

"What?"

"This. Her. All of it," he sat up impatiently.

"I think it's. neat." Paul twitched again. "How

many kids you know have ever done something like it?"

"What's the point, though? Move her here, move her there, feed her, and do the same thing over again the next day."

"I think it's fun."

"*What's* fun? *You* don't have to sit up half the night every night."

"Well, OK. Not that part maybe." Paul leaned over and began to draw idly in the sand with his finger. "But what'd be tough would be if we could do all the things you do to real prisoners."

"Like what?" John said.

"Aw-w-w, like we used to pretend. You know. Only really. Take off all her clothes . . . and whip her and stuff like that." He let his voice trail off nervously.

"We can't do that," Bobby said.

"I don't know why not. Really."

"Yes, you do. We're in enough trouble as it is."

"What do *you* want to do with her? Turn her loose? Then you'd really find out what trouble was."

"Anyhow, how would you do it?" John said carefully.

"Easy."

"How?"

"Scissors." For all its pinched and twisted features, Paul's small face took on a look of angelic radiance. He was imagining things.

"What?" Bobby said.

"Scissors. Dianne has it all figured out." Paul began one of his rapid-paced, squirming explanations. The angelic expression faded to one of intensity. "When we come in the morning, she's all spread out and tied up, right? And before we untie her, Dianne just cuts the things over her shoulder and along the side and . . . and . . . opens her up." His pupils seemed to grow tiny and bright.

"Aw, she wears underpants, too. I've seen 'em."

"It's the same thing. Two sides."

"Yeah. Maybe." John admired.

"Then what? What'd Dianne say?"

"Nothing. But we could think of the rest."

Bobby, looking at John, became suddenly unhappy. He assumed his father's thoughtful frown again, more so because John seemed to be entertaining the idea. John seemed silly and far off.

"But after that," Paul was encouraged by the silence, "we could do all other kinds of cool stuff to her . . ." He stopped. They had all played together for several years. They knew what he meant.

"No, you couldn't," Bobby said. "It'd make everything twice as bad as it already is."

"Why not?" All the world of his odd imagination seemed open to Paul at the minute. He saw things the other two could not.

"Shut up," Bobby said.

"Dianne said that—"

"Shut *up!*"

"John?" Paul appealed for help.

John avoided his glance and scowled across the river for a moment. Since they had all first become a gang together, he had been the leader. He was the biggest, strongest, and he had lived in the neighborhood the longest.

Among the things John had gradually learned to accept, however, was that he seldom led, that is, invented the things to do. The whole thing was really like following from ahead. You sort of knew what everybody wanted, what was going to happen anyhow, so for better or worse, you gave it a reason for occurring, helped it to become. Further, John had learned—and in this, he self-confessed a certain lack of imagination—that if no suggestion or solution appeared, you simply pulled your chin and looked gravely down at the ground. Someone else came up with the proper idea.

In this case, it was Paul—how often it seemed to be Paul—who, for being younger and possibly less embarrassed by what he was saying, had put into words exactly what John vaguely wanted but dared not face alone. Moreover the suggestion came complete with a plan—Dianne would do it, John and Paul would help if necessary, Cindy would stay out of the way—and that left only Bobby. There was a peculiar air of fate about the whole thing, as if from the first day they saw Barbara, they knew they were going to capture her, as if from that moment on, they had been moving toward this further heightening of the adventure. At this, the faintest worry clouded John's thoughts, and yet what he must say and do was somehow foregone. Choice, if it ever existed, had simply slipped away.

"We'll have to make some new rules," he said finally.

"When?"

"About what?" Bobby was negative.

"After Dianne takes off her clothes."

"What kind of rules?" Paul went into a trembling spasm.

"Wait a minute. . . ."

"Well, we still have to watch her—stand guard."

"Sure. . . ."

"But we ought to be able to say what we want, and everybody should help. You know, like if you want her gagged when it's your turn, OK. If you don't, OK. If you want her in the chair, OK, and if you want her in bed or anything else, OK. What the person guarding wants, we all agree to. And we help. If you want the door closed, OK."

"The door?"

"Hers—Barbara's."

"Why close the door?"

"Just if you want to," John shrugged.

"*No!*" Bobby jumped to his feet.

"No, what?"

"You're not going to get Cindy'n me in any more trouble."

"It's the same for everybody."

"No, it isn't. It's *my* house and *my* parents and *my*—" He waved his hands in exasperation. "It's *our* sitter. If it wasn't for me, we wouldn't be doing this at all and you're not going to take off anybody's clothes."

80

"Dianne is."

"No, she isn't either!"

"Who's going to stop it, then?" When he got to his own feet, John's size and weight advantage over Bobby were unarguable. For a second, they stood face to face.

"Let me alone!" Before a blow was struck, Bobby quailed. Tears of anger and frustration made him blink and brush his eyes. "Let me alone now!"

"I haven't touched you."

"Then get away from me. This is my *beach,* too!"

"Well, are you going to help us then?"

"No!" Ducking to the side, Bobby suddenly ran across the sand toward the bank.

"Get him!" Paul did a little dance of excitement.

John caught Bobby as he tried to scramble upward and dragged him back down on the beach, kicking and screaming. After a short wrestle, he got Bobby's arm twisted around behind his back and gave it a hard tweak. He got Bobby's face down in the sand and held it there. It made him less noisy.

Bobby began blubbering harder. "Ouch! Damn it, stop it, John. You don't have to do it that hard. Ow-w-w-w! *Please.*"

"Down then. Shut up."

Bobby lowered his face right on the sand and quieted, hurting badly.

"Now, are you going to help us or not?"

"No—*yes-s-s!*—no. I can't, John. Don't make me." He was sobbing now.

For the second time that afternoon, John felt a sense of cosmic power. The only difference was that this time, it frightened him a little, and he slowly eased up on Bobby. There had been the barest moment when if Bobby had stood between him and Barbara, he might actually have hurt him. At length John even released him.

Bobby rolled over slowly and sat, sobbing and cradling his arm in his lap and trying to get the sand out of his eyes at the same time. John and Paul sat on

81

their heels and watched him cry himself out. It took a while.

"What are you going to do? Give all this up?" Paul said.

"Nope," John said, "we'll just have to make him a prisoner, too."

Bobby looked up now. Both their faces were slightly wolfish, and it was apparent that they were ready to pounce. Somewhat like Barbara, Bobby was no fool for his age. The notion that they could take virtually everybody captive and do everything was out of the question. "Everybody" was a terribly vague thing: however, to *him*, they could do it, even to Cindy, and a lot of bad things could happen before it got better. Memory of Paul's cruel streak alone made him more afraid of Freedom Five than of any adult power ever to come.

"Make up your mind. Hurry up."

Bobby sighed, still sniffling a little.

"OK, get the rope, Paul. I'll watch him."

"No, wait a minute . . ."

"What?"

"OK, OK, I'll do it. I'll *help* you."

Paul dropped back on his heels, a little disappointed.

"No telling lies and then letting her go by yourself some night?"

"No."

"Because if you do, when everything's blown over, we're *really* going to get you."

"Yeah. OK," Bobby said dispiritedly. Something of the sort had been going through his mind. "But I'm still scared."

Paul gave a yell of triumph and leaped to his feet. "Man, this is really *neat!*"

"Yeah, all right," John sighed and rose, too. "We can talk to Dianne about it on the way home."

Bobby—humiliated, still sitting, still cradling his arm (it still hurt like hell), still occasionally brushing tears and sand from his eyes—encountered the dilemma so known to adults and so unknown and even unsuspected by him—conflicting loyalties. On the one hand, he had promised to do what he knew he must do to survive—be loyal to the kids, to Freedom Five—while on the other, the same pledge had committed him to see and accept the stripping and humiliation of someone from the adult world (Barbara was certainly that) to which he owed equal loyalty.

Well, there was that other thing.

Bobby liked Barbara, and she wasn't entirely just "adult." He liked her for reasons unknown to himself, but then he did and that was that. In submitting to loyalty to Feedom Five to escape pain and punishment directed from them toward himself, he had equally submitted her to their whims.

Bobby Adams did not know what manly meant nor did he remotely know what unmanly meant. In not letting John break his arm, in agreeing to everything, in abandoning Barbara, in not sharing her fate, Bobby Adams had done something that made him extremely ashamed and sad. He did not know why. It was sensible not to let yourself be hurt, and it was senseless to let Barbara get hurt, and the two arguments collided. Hegel had a thought on the matter, but Bobby Adams had never heard it and would little understand it if he had.

What Barbara thought of as her second night in captivity—actually it was the third, but she had been unconscious Sunday night—began about four-thirty in the afternoon when the McVeigh children and John Randall were ready to go home for supper. Then, with their endless caution—each of her limbs was always tied to something or other—they fed her, got her to bed spread-eagled, and bound her tightly again. Afterward began the impossible hours between daylight and her distant release into troubled sleep, hours when she could only look up at the ceiling and mark the slow fading of August twilight.

During the forty some hours that she had been a

83

prisoner, Barbara had passed far beyond shock or injured dignity. Her mind, if not her active body, accepted the idea that there would be no early escape or release now. She was the it of a children's game that had not run its course yet and might well become worse. The matter was simply how to endure.

Of the two main problems, the first was mental, of course. In her survey psych course at school, she had heard the classic example of the prisoner in the round gray room with nothing to do, nothing to hear, nothing to see, nothing to attract his attention—the ancient case of the man who went insane from boredom. Her own situation, she considered neatly parallel. Her room at the Adams' was neither round nor unfurnished, but with the ever-humming air conditioner and the pale curtains covering the window, it was dimly and evenly lit at the brightest time of day. Moreover, the walls were a light blue which could easily be considered gray if you wished it. To further the similarity, while the textbook prisoner could at least move—amuse himself with the flow of sinew and muscle—she was forbidden even this distraction. The challenge to the normal, intelligent person not to go mad was strikingly real.

With—for her—unaccustomed objectivity, she realized that she spent most of her time in fantasy. From the beginning she had been able to imagine the voice and, at times, the person of her roommate, Terry. Last night Terry had been quite real, but there had been a wall between them even then—Barbara here, Terry there. Now the wall thinned: it was easier tonight than last night to call Terry forth, and when she came, she was no longer in their room at school but almost *here*, almost real.

Pretty soon, she'll start coming here without my asking, and I'll really be out of it, Barbara thought.

The longer she remained a captive, however, the more fantasies crowded in with Terry and the more real they were. Barbara was doing laps in the pool, and it was so vivid that she could feel the curdly water resisting as she kicked, could smell the chlorine and hear the echoes around the pool building. She was in her room at home, and it was last week again; her mother had put flowers on the dresser, and they were pretty. She was at the Refugee Bar, and Ted was buying her a beer and talking long and seriously about trying to get a job abroad. In detail, in color, feel, smell, and taste, the pictures of her normal life crowded in and, being more interesting than her present immobility, claimed equal reality with the actual world. Moreover, they cascaded, toppled, spilled across her mind out of sequence, out of context, even simultaneously until her head hurt with the many attentions required of it. The mind, deprived of normal stimulus, was beginning to create its own out of itself.

If they keep me here long enough, they'll have a real tripper on their hands, she thought. Wild imaginings of a female Rip Van Winkle emerging back into the world, out of time, out of place, invaded her imagination. Aloud—within the mind—she said, No, stop that! And like startled birds, her fantasies scattered into air only to perch again nearby, in the safe, dim periphery of active thought.

Mingled with this totally mental struggle, was a second—the physical.

The mind, of course, received messages from the body—Teacher had studied *that* well enough. In the case of being prisoner, however, she found these messages to be of a new and unknown kind. Held fast, unmoving, suddenly stopped after twenty years of waking and even sleeping action—willful, selfish, unhindered movement—the body became capable of panic of its own. Yesterday, last night, she had been seized with spasms of irrational, physical, non-thought terror in which her arms and legs wrenched at ropes that her mind knew would not give. It produced needless pain, tightened loops which would remain tight until they were untied hours later, and yet as well as she recognized this, she still could not stop her body's fearing movements.

This afternoon, this evening, she seemed to have

85

gained some control over these struggles. Occasionally, she was still overwhelmed by the desire to break ropes, push down walls, demolish houses, sweep away all physical restraints with the irresistible swing of gloriously free arms, free legs. With effort and attention, however, she was able to restrain herself. Biting down on the rag between her teeth, she willed herself to lie quietly. In this enforced motionlessness, however, came another sensation.

Emanating from the body, inarticulate, thoughtless and blind, it nonetheless arose within her. Mankind's grip on life, on nature, is secured only by unceasing alertness, thought and action. Stopped, held fast, we watch helplessly as the weeds and jungle creep back in over the land, as the home untended falls to rot, as the garden unwatered withers to straw. Made prisoner, isolated, held immobile, we lose our claim on, our place in life and begin to sink.

Barbara, of course, thought little enough about mankind, gardens and all that. Nonetheless she understood it all. In willing herself to stillness, she felt the bed beneath her back grow cold, as if she were lying on a black, tidal flat whose slowly rising tides would climb until they drowned her and took her back into nothingness again.

This thought, more frightening than the loss of mental control, brought her close to tears she could not cry with a gag in her mouth. I can't, she said, not caring which of the terrors she defied. I just can't let go.

Against this and from another side of her mind came the interrupting thought, I'm free when I'm asleep. And she prayed for sleep which was many hours away in exhaustion.

As the evening grew darker, it became more sullen. The trees drooped; an early dew developed; and it became still enough to hear the wing whir of swifts and bats hunting in the deepening dusk. At full dark, nervous spasms of heat lightning flared back and forth above the trees, the silent river, and the fields beyond.

Briefly illuminated by these glows, heavy black clouds stood down the distant bay toward the ocean to the east. The giants were walking again.

Sitting alone on the back steps, barefoot, ragamuffin, knees and elbows together, chin on palms, Cindy watched the growing fullness of night with ancient unease. Now that she was ten, Cindy was no longer afraid of lightning and thunder as such, yet they still reminded her of the time when she was little and when, in the second's flash of lightning, she always thought she saw the dim forms of nameless, terrible gods stalking across the sky. In the next moment their eyes might fall on her, their great strides crush her into the earth. She had cried and demanded much comforting.

Now, these things better understood, she endured squalls and storms as well as anyone—outwardly. Giants in the sky, there were none. But on those nights, there was *something* abroad in the world, something always there but rarely seen by eye. In the approach of thunder, wind, and rain, she remembered it coming and she remembered crying.

Tonight she felt the giants might not come. The amber, faraway play of lightning was dim and remote. Nonetheless, she was lonely. The older kids had been gone for hours; she and Bobby had eaten; and he was trying to sleep until his watch. Television was more boring than ever, and she was left by herself to watch the night in blackness. The responsibility and solitariness were unendurable. She lifted her head and put her palms down on the step restlessly. How to escape freedom?

The answer was the same now as on the more gentle night before: *Barbara.*

Though she was not as spoiled as people thought—indeed she was as spoiled or as obedient as she thought the traffic would bear—still Cindy knew with a child's certainty that while one foot was planted in her life and doings, the other was firmly anchored in the adults' distant world. She depended upon it and wished it so, particularly when she felt like this. And when the problem was solvable—as now—it was frustrating not to be allowed to do anything. John and Dianne and Bobby and Paul might move Barbara as they would, but Cindy could only watch. Her own existence within the group, in fact, was based on the understanding that all she could do was watch. Thus Barbara, dearer to her than to any of them, was just as removed as if *she* were the one in Europe. This, too, was unendurable, and with her mind half on the grumbling evening and half on her own needs, Cindy imagined what she might do.

No more than Bobby did she dare turn Barbara loose. No more than John or Dianne would she move her alone. Still—if Barbara agreed—she might remove the gag and at least *talk* to her, and that's all she really wanted just this minute. It was a dangerous thing; it was daring; and yet without it, how could Cindy live until it was time for Bobby to take over? With resolution, even with a smile, Cindy rose and entered the kitchen with a screen-banging crash.

Barbara was awake.

At the quiet click of the overhead light, she blinked her eyes and turned them toward Cindy, who in turn assured herself that all was safe, that the prisoner was still imprisoned. This silent, if mutual acknowledgment completed, Cindy walked to the side of the bed and then, with sudden courage, sat down on its edge, her hands in her lap.

There was a brief moment in which child and girl, captor and captive, met with eyes and attention. Then Cindy said, "Are you awake?"

Nod—yes.

"Do you want to talk?"

Barbara did nothing for a moment. She could not shrug, but after a bit she tossed her head in an imitation of I don't care.

The gesture seemed weary, and Cindy suddenly felt sorry for her. Nonetheless, Cindy's problem came first. "Will you make a lot of noise if I take off your gag?"

Tired nod—no.

Cindy reached up to the back of her own head and, taking a curl of her own short hair, twined it around her finger sensuously. She smiled, "Will you let me put it back when we're through?"

Yes—yes. A nod, a nod.

Cindy hesitated just another moment, feeling both frightened and daring, righteous and naughty. Then she leaned down over Barbara. "OK, turn your head a little. . . ." Putting her small fingers on Barbara's cheek, she managed to get her nails under the adhesive tape and pull. It was something she had seen the older kids do, but until this minute, she had never realized how sticky the tape was and how Barbara's skin pulled up with it. Nonetheless she persisted, and slowly, slowly, the adhesive strap came away until it parted from the other side of Barbara's face.

"Umnn—" Barbara opened her mouth and at least partially disgorged the scrap of folded terry cloth she was forced to accept each time they gagged her.

It looked disgusting to Cindy—it was like some obscene, unknown-to-children bodily function—and yet she daintily reached down and pulled it out and laid it aside on the night table. Barbara licked her lips.

"Are you OK?"

"No. I'm stiff. I hurt all over," Barbara tried to shift the smallest bit and obviously could not. "Just untie me."

"I'm sorry—" and Cindy truly was.

They looked at each other a minute.

"Well, I'm hungry." Since the children had never cared about this, Barbara said it in a bored voice. "Thirsty."

"We've eaten everything that's good—Dianne's going to shop for us tomorrow—but I can make you a peanut-butter sandwich and a Coke."

Barbara sighed.

"OK?"

"OK."

Cindy rose and went to the door. There she

turned primly and said, "Would you like jelly with the peanut butter?"

"Fine. Anything."

In the kitchen, Cindy self-importantly fulfilled her promise, and neatly. The realization that adults would not be in to clean up after her was gradually imbuing her with a sense of proprietorship. Cindy was for the moment mistress of the house and keeper of the prisoner. It was a demanding role. When she had made the sandwich, she put the bread, jelly, peanut butter, and knife away and wiped up the crumbs. She put the Coke in a glass with a bendable straw and everything together on a little tray her mother used if someone was ill and had to eat in bed. Returning to Barbara's room, she was even somewhat proud of herself.

There was a great deal of clearing things and making room for the tray and adjusting of the light. Finally she said, "What do you want first, the sandwich or the Coke?"

Barbara drank greedily and then ate a little more slowly, Cindy administering to her as if she were a child. After a few sips and bites, they had everything worked out tidily—no crumbs, no spills. When they were done, Cindy carried the tray back to the kitchen, but there she abandoned her neatness. She just banged the tray on the counter and ran back to Barbara's room. This was fun! Or, at least, it was something. It would've been more fun if they could just have sort of sat cross-legged on the bed and talked like real friends or sisters or something instead of *this*.

"Does it really hurt that much, being tied up *all* the time?" Cindy sat down gently on the edge of the bed.

"Yes."

"I thought so." Cindy frowned as if confirmed in some private suspicion of her own that had been nagging her. "It does me, too," she said, "or it did."

"You?"

"When we used to play that way. I didn't do it much, but once in a while they let me go with them."

"Where?"

"In the woods, down in the tenant house, wherever they wanted to play Prisoner."

"They did it to you, too? You must have been too little."

"Yeah," Cindy agreed. "But everybody took turns—it was part of the game." Cindy was flattered that Barbara suddenly looked more interested.

"What was the game, really?"

"I don't remember all that much about it." Cindy tried, however. "John was king, and Dianne was queen, of course. And Bobby was the general—we all had things to do. We had maps of the country and everything."

"And that's when you captured prisoners?" Barbara said.

"Yeah," Cindy twirled a ringlet of hair in her finger again. She would have put it in her mouth if it had been long enough to reach: instead she just tugged it down the side of her face and stared off into space a little wistfully. "After a while it got boring."

"Then that's not what you're playing now?" Barbara was coaxing.

"Um mnnn!" Cindy was emphatic. She shook her head and continued to look off somewhere above and behind Barbara's bed. "I guess this is Freedom Five. Paul invented it; it's more fun. We're a bunch of guerrilla fighters living in the woods and shooting people and blowing up trains and stuff."

"Oh. . . ."

Cindy smiled down. It did seem to her that Barbara more or less understood what was a rather complicated history. "And we kidnap hostages and take prisoners and torture them and stuff. It's kind of fun."

"Fun!"

"Well"—Cindy was a little apologetic—"when it isn't your turn to be caught. Even then, it isn't too bad most of the time. Paul's the really mean one though. When he's jailer, watch out."

"How?"

"Oh . . . he's always thinking up new things to do. Once he tied me up so tight he even tied my toes together. Then he tickled me."

"But where were the rest of them?"

"There. It was just my turn."

"Didn't they do anything?"

"Yeah. After a while I started yelling and crying—I was littler then—and they had to let me go. They were afraid I'd tell."

"Oh."

For a moment neither of them spoke. Pursuing her own thoughts, Cindy didn't notice at first. When she did, she resumed where—to her—they had left off. "Paul likes girls' feet," she giggled. "He's the best at torturing."

"Real or pretend?" Barbara said levelly.

She really *did* understand, Cindy decided. That was just the way Freedom Five talked about it. "Both," she said brightly.

"Well, they better not torture *me!*"

"No," Cindy conceded. "I guess not. Mommy and Daddy are coming home, and you have to go back to college. It's too bad, though. . . ."

"*What's* too bad?" Barbara seemed like she was beginning to get mad slowly the way grown-ups do.

Cindy sought to placate her. "I dunno. It's just kind of fun having you here to play with us, too."

"I'm—not—playing."

"Well, you are, *sort of.*"

"I'm not at all. What I want to know is when you're going to let me go again. This *hurts.*"

"Well, they won't do it until after tomorrow anyhow. I guess."

"Why tomorrow?" Barbara seemed to have calmed down again. At any rate she was sweeter.

"They're going to take off your nightie."

"What?" Barbara suddenly lifted her head from the pillow and stared straight at the little girl. You could almost hear the individual letters coming out of her mouth: *W-h-a-t.* "*What?*"

"It's just like the 'nitiation," Cindy jumped back a little.

Cindy could enunciate as well as anyone else and even be prim and clipped about it if she was angry. When she was just noodling along, however, she slurred childishly (and sometimes to be cute). "Guerrilla" came out at "gorilla"; "initiation" came out as " 'nitiation."

"We've all done it," she said. "It isn't all that bad anyhow. Well—it's bad when it's you and everybody's laughing and all, but when it's somebody else, it's funny. Boys look—"

"Where did you hear this?" Barbara didn't raise her voice, but she suddenly had that adult sound of now-you're-going-to-get-it.

Cindy got up off the bed and backed away to safety. "Bobby said so at dinner. He'd been crying. They beat him up and made him promise to help."

"Well, that's the *end!*" Barbara looked up at her wrists in turn and jerked on her ropes angrily. "You get Bobby in here right now, and I mean *now,* or I'll start screaming."

"But you're not supposed to be ungagged," Cindy quailed, her heart suddenly thumping. She was thinking *trouble . . . trouble . . . trouble.*

"I said *now!*"

Cindy sighed unhappily. This was unexpected, uncontrollable. The other kids would get her for it.

"Bobby! Bob-bee-e-e!" Barbara shouted. "Bobby, get up!" Then she screamed. It was not a completely abandoned shriek—she had little practice at screaming—but it was loud enough for openers.

Badly scared now, Cindy ran out of the room for Bobby, followed by another scream this time a little higher. In the hall she all but knocked him down.

White, rumpled, wide-eyed and only half seeing and understanding, he more or less danced back and forth from one foot to the other, trying to get by her. "What is it?"

"Hurry-*yup!*" Cindy said.

"Is she loose?" Bobby pulled back sharply, ready to run.

"No. No! She wants to talk to you. Come on!" Cindy finally got him moving, and together they stumbled into Barbara's room.

She was still wrenching at her cords and shaking the whole bed. "Bobby, let me go right now. I mean it. Untie me."

Caught by the terrible unanswerable tone of adult anger and command and yet unable to obey—quite—Bobby froze.

"I said *untie* me!"

"The bottle, the bottle!" Cindy was quick thinking in her terror. "Give her the bottle of *stuff*."

Instead Bobby turned on her—for once, he had lost composure—and began yelling, too. "You ungagged her. *You* did it. Now we're going to get it. We all are."

Then Barbara screamed again. This time it was right on; it was abandoned and shrill and animal and prolonged. It galvanized Bobby.

He ran over, pulled the pillow out from beneath Barbara's head, and threw it down across her face and held it there. "The bottle's on the dresser. The *dresser*, not the vanity!"

Cindy turned around twice before she saw it. Behind her was a frightening chaos she preferred not to see. The bed was tossing like something in a high wind. On it Bobby rode a pillow life raft, his face lip-bitten and determined.

"Bring it here," he yelled.

From beneath the pillow came muffled sounds of desperation.

"Now hold the pillow. You can't be afraid now! *Hold* it."

Cindy did, but badly and weakly. Barbara was able to turn her head underneath it and shout—it was now muffled—in a kind of terror of her own.

"Stop it. *Stop* it! You're going to smother me. I can't—stop it!" It was all ugly to Cindy.

With shaking hands her brother finally got the

bottle open and pulled out the reeking rag. "Keep holding her. I don't care what she says." He bent over and pushed the rag under the pillow where the noise was coming from and threw himself down beside Cindy to hold it there. After a while, the nightmare subsided and Barbara went limp. Afterward, still shaking badly, Bobby threw the pillow off and let her get some air. She was still breathing; in a little while, the breathing became more or less regular. Even so, he sat by the bed and waited a long time more before replacing the gag doubly secure.

By the door, ready to run if things got worse, Cindy said, "Is she all right?"

"You still there?" Bobby seemed to have forgotten her. "Yeah." He turned around still pale. The high pink spots on his cheeks were scarlet. "She's out."

Cindy came back cautiously. "Look, she hurt herself."

In fact, she was right. Barbara's wrenching at her ropes had slid them down to her wrists, leaving bare, scraped, red places on her arms and flaked, roughened skin. Bobby pulled down the wrinkled sheet and saw that she had actually scraped down to blood on one ankle, but nothing looked serious. He sighed.

"She's OK enough"; and he went outside on the back steps and sat down.

After a little interval of not knowing what to do, Cindy—still frightened and now remorseful—went out and sat down beside him wordlessly. She watched the giants walking around in the sky—now they were more distant—and waited for the police or the sheriff or the FBI to come and get them for all that screaming. When they did not, she surrendered to the need to sleep and went off to hide under the covers.

4

Barbara awoke with sudden fear. The gag and tape were like the hand and rag on her mouth. She couldn't breathe. She felt she was being suffocated again; the pillow was back over her head. Jerking her eyes open wide in fear, she raised her head and strained as if struggling to reach the top of the water after a deep dive, and then, of course, remembered. There was the room; there was the ceiling; there was—she turned her head—Bobby sleeping exhaustedly. There was the whole world again. This was only another day, the third day like this. Everything else had been last night.

Lowering her head and closing her eyes again, she took in long slow breaths of air the way she tried to do before a swimming event. She had a headache—oxygen was the answer—because Bobby had forced her to breathe too much chloroform last night. Moreover her wrists and ankles hurt where she had scraped them raw in her struggles with him. Her hands and feet were icy cold and numb; she was stiff and muscle-sore all over, and later on, they were going to take off her nightie somehow. It all leapt back to mind.

Each day instead of beginning newly, as it did when you were normally free, seemed—to her in helplessness—to begin with the weight of the previous days upon it, almost as if she hadn't slept at all. Unconsciousness was merely unconsciousness; it didn't restore. When she awoke, she was that many more steps down a road, down a process, down a ladder whose bottom she could not see.

As the weight of this realization, this particular hour, resumed its place on her shoulders, she was overcome by a peculiar sorrow and loneliness, something almost akin to the feeling of being lost. Outside it was going to be another calm summer day. The lightning, the threatened night squalls, had passed once more, and there was a soft light in the sky—she could tell by its presence in the room—and the birds were singing around the house as they did only at the very early morning. The river would be sparkly, and it would be so pretty from the kitchen.

If I could just. . . .

Barbara formed a thought of freedom so wide that no words could even suggest it. She saw herself sitting up on the side of the bed, somehow miraculously released, rubbing her wrists in disbelief. Then she was getting up, walking free, almost running to everywhere her mind would imagine her to go. So simple a thing was freedom. The little scene, so enchanting and unattainable, was also so sweet that she repeated it to herself several times. Then, of course, it faded.

If someone would only just find me, Barbara said. Help me. *Please help me*.

This was given a little in the tone of her childhood prayers. "God, please let me find my new wristwatch that Daddy gave me." "God, please let me get [whatever] for Christmas." "God, please. . . ."

In fact, and naturally enough, Barbara had had poor service from God. Though her nature required Him, she had long ago made the young's private conclusion that He was no short-order solver of small problems. One might conclude (to save the respect) that He was too busy or too remote *there,* at some higher level of management.

"God helps those who help themselves," her mother had said, and Barbara had always tried to help herself. Cheerful Barbara, busy Barbara: she had found, indeed, that God did help them who helped themselves. *Good things happen*. It was square, and it was also an article of faith with her.

No one was going to find her, no one was going to help her unless she helped the event to occur herself. At this moment—if she were awake—Mother was probably thinking how nice it was for Barbara to be down in the country for two weeks. The Adams were thinking how lucky they were to have such a competent young baby-sitter. God was thinking his thoughts, and Barbara must think hers.

Squirming around for the elusive comfort that was never there, Barbara said, OK, I'm part of a game. It probably began a long time ago with dolls and toy soldiers and stories the kids made up themselves out of what they saw and heard. Then when they got older and toys faded a little, they moved outside to more freedom, but the game went on. That is, they moved into the dolls' roles; they *became* the dolls—playing is practice living: this was rote for teachers—and made themselves a bigger kingdom to rule over. And it was unsupervised—another teacherly word—and completely outside the adult world. Barbara could understand this. Who has not had a private kingdom at one time or another? She almost saw the way they would jealously keep its secret integrity against the grown-ups' environment, the one in which they were powerless.

But age and knowledge corrode. There had come the time when they no longer believed in kings and queens, when new models were needed, and the game moved on.

It moved on, Barbara said. It moved on idly, whimsically, almost as if it were an accident (which she thought it was not). Still, from the kids' point of view, it would be that one day they were playing this game, the next day they were bored and irritable, and the third day they were playing something new (which was not new at all). They withdrew into the hills and woods and became their ex-kingdom's harried guerrilla fighters, its Resistance Movement. And then that got boring—hadn't Cindy said they hadn't played much until now?—and then Barbara came along.

And then I came along, Barbara said. Something in the sentence attracted her. And then I came along. It was all so bitterly clear. I am the fourth level of the game.

The parents were gone; they were to be gone for quite a while by children's standards. Now the children could, now they could—what? Who knows? And the only thing to prevent it was silly Barbara, dumb Teacher, who had come flouncing onto the scene in a blue summer dress and not much else. How easily the children's impatient imaginings and the opportunity of Barbara/target would come together with a bang. Now they could *really* play the game.

If they could. If they dared.

And they dared.

But *what* was the fourth level of the game?

Something chilly and dark passed just behind Barbara's immediate attention and then waited somewhere in the out-of-reach part of her mind. An intimation.

She thought.

OK, I am their new toy. Like Terry said. I walk, I talk when they let me. They can move my arms and legs. They can even dress and undress me if they want. But how do they *play* with dolls?

One could imagine and find no harm in the imagined scene of a child like Cindy—in tantrum—hurling her doll across the room in fury. Tears would pass: if the doll was broken, someone would fix it or buy her a new one. Cindy would thereby learn not to break things anymore. But what if one were suddenly the doll itself? At the thought Cindy's face grew huge in Doll Barbara's imagination; Cindy's clear, curious, simple eyes became as threatening as a cat's in their uncaringness.

Again one could see and find little harm in Paul's marching his toy soldiers to the dungeon and tieing them to twig stakes with string and shooting them on command. Paul was working out his boy aggressions. Anyhow tomorrow morning, metal-smart and cast-to-attention, they would be ready to fight and lose and be executed again. Real soldiers, real people, of course, are only executed once. Once. In Barbara's mind, Paul suddenly became even more a horrible little boy.

And in the woods, in the disused tenant-house gathering place of Freedom Five, hadn't Cindy said they took prisoners and hostages and tortured them for secrets? Even here, little enough harm. Erotic play, discovery, a sorting out of values. The next day, the next raid, the prisoners would be back intact, surly and unwilling to tell, and hence ready for torture again. But if the prisoners, if the prison*er* were real?

At this point the logical step was obvious. At the fourth level of the game five kids just-before-teen or crossing through their teens, were going to torture Barbara to a slow death. Barbara dismissed this out of hand. She wasn't a toy; they were *not* free to do as they wished, and the world of spankings, punishment, and authority remained. It only troubled her that they might *think* about it.

She was also troubled as to why they should think about it.

In play, children acted out life as they believed or wanted it to be—that had been back in freshman year that she had learned that—but if what Teacher Barbara had been taught was true, why did these children want to believe life to be *this* way? The rope, the adhesive tape, and all the hurt went into the thought.

Children's materials are all the materials they can see and imagine and imitate. Their whole world. Nobody says there isn't too much war and crime and trash for them to pick up, Barbara said. Lord, they've even criticized fairy tales for being too violent. But there are other things, too, the total environment of love and warmth and fun and helping. These children have certainly had that, and money as well (I wish I had as much, Barbara said). So why, given the everything of life, would these kids choose the darkest parts for their most interesting games? Were they *naturally* bad? And if they were, who then wasn't a little naturally bad? What would Terry say?

Terry said (without bothering to materialize completely), Maybe they don't like what they see of what
100

we think is the "pretty" world. Maybe it's too complicated or too dull or too hard or too something. Maybe they feel they have to hold themselves in too much in order to be a part of it. Maybe what we think of as rewards are only penances of different kinds to them. Maybe they don't want to grow up at all. Maybe the world is closed off now, and there's no place left to live.

Barbara said nothing.

Do *you* want to grow up, Barb?

Again Barbara said nothing.

You think these kids are oddball and different and dirty, but how do you know they're all *that* different from the rest? What did you think of them when you came here? You thought they were pretty and fun. What did you think of them when you took them over to Sunday school? You wished they were yours by some handsome, well-known man like your Dr. Adams. What did you think of the way they obeyed and had fun when you took them swimming? You were all over yourself with love, love, love, Terry said.

You make me sick, Terry said. A person's a package deal. Prime ministers probably go to bed at night and play with themselves. What these kids are doing to you is the rest of their playtime; it all goes together. What they're doing is natural enough.

Barbara shook her head silently. Again the logical airy step invited, and again she refused to take it. I don't believe you, she said. All kids aren't this way. We weren't.

Weren't we?

Barbara stopped. Something in imagined Terry's tone summoned to her mind the remembered image of the parking-lot sniggerers of her own early teens. She saw them clearly again, heard them clearly again. Their faces moved back and forth interchangeably with those of John and Dianne and Paul, Cindy and Bobby.

No! They didn't do anything like this though.

No chutzpah, Terry shrugged.

Well, maybe, Barbara granted. What would they *really* have done? What would any person do given entire power over another person? What—in particular—would inexperienced children do? Who knows what people think when they're children and we haven't broken them yet?

It was high, shimmering, full day.

Barbara no longer doubted that the children would strip her naked. It wasn't that difficult; the kids were getting more confident, and in final count, it would hardly be fatal.

I've been naked before, Barbara said, but as she waited, she continued uneasy—squeamish.

On the swimming team, in dormitory life, with doctors and—by accident, of course—with the family, she had certainly been seen without clothes on. These transactional occasions, however, had been brief, businesslike and not particularly pleasant. In a generation that at least vocally favored frankness, skin, and more natural sex, she remained private and self-possessed, avoiding exposure and usually averting her eyes from the exposure of others. Naturally she worried that she was a prude—it was a death sentence in her age group—that in the imminent upswarming flight of love and mating she would somehow be kept out of the action by being timid and hesitant. None of this, however, seemed to internally alter the rather maidenly shyness, the almost wordless taboo that inhibited her.

Rationalizing, she told herself that it was only a matter of time, place, and values. She could see—if no one else told her, Sexy Barbara did—that in a moment of faith, trust, and love, it could be joyous to free the body and live. There was an element of confession, submission, of oneness about it. Indeed she had had a good many girlish dreams on the subject. It was just that the occurrence hadn't come along quite yet, and that, as a result, she was getting nearer a time when she could look back and find that she had "saved herself for her husband" or at least a serious affair—surely an old-fashioned approach—but one that was rather nice in a way, or so she felt as she got older.

Today's indecency, however, had nothing to do with necessity, love, confession, or the unfolding of sweet offerings. What disgusted her, made her feel crawly, was that there was dirt and malice in it, sneakiness, a shades-drawn, sex in a rented-room furtiveness about it. She was being hauled back into a primitive stupid world of grayness and feeling around and smirking and giggling. The object was torment, and she was afraid she would show how well it was succeeding.

Actually, the event itself was at least quick and sparing of the lewd pawings she had imagined. The kids arrived a bit earlier than their usual midmorning, and after some whispered conversations in the kitchen, sauntered into her room with affected casualness. They knew that she knew that Cindy had told her, and so it was all straightforward between all of them. Dianne had brought a small pair of sewing scissors in her lunch bag, and while the others stood back, she used them carefully.

Folding back the cotton lace of the shoulder straps of Barbara's summer nightgown, she cut almost on the seams concealed there, right and left. Barbara could not see what Dianne was doing, but she felt the metal go carefully along, dull edge of the scissors against her skin, and she sensed that it was a proper job. Among her other talents, Dianne apparently sewed as well. Having then bared Barbara's shoulders (Barbara felt a loss even here), she went on with it.

Beginning at the hip, Dianne cut up the side seam to the armhole on the right side. It was all very much like opening a pretty Christmas package and trying not to spoil the wrappings.

When she felt the gown being lifted off her body, Barbara closed her eyes and felt the tears she had so much wanted not to show them. In another minute, the side seams of her bikini pants had been cut, and she was as awkwardly, gracelessly, naked and helpless as it was possible to be. Of course there were giggles—she could hear each one separately—and she thought, It finally *did* happen. After all. Every woman has thought the same under some circumstance. Now they would begin to *do things* to her.

When nothing further happened, however, she

opened her eyes, still teary wet, and raised her head. The children were caught as in a frieze—Cindy half bent in mirth, two small hands covering her mouth to stifle laughter, bright eyes half-peeking through her fingers; Bobby solemn; Paul in spasm; Dianne still holding the scissors; John unable to raise his head for some reason—and seeing them, Barbara was partially calmed.

Outside of the shock of seeing and feeling herself naked, there was yet no real harm in all of this. Hers was hardly the kind of beauty that would drive beholders to madness anyhow. Then John raised his head at last, and she saw *his* eyes.

Instead of being teased and tormented as she had expected, Barbara was handled as if the morning was no different from yesterday or the day before it. The children untied and retied her, marched her to the bathroom and back, bound her to her chair, and fed her the skimpy breakfast of cereal and toast, and then scattered to work on their list of daily chores. The only difference was that Barbara was naked.

In place of the rather voluptuous feeling the flow of air over her bare body usually had—as before a bath, for example—she was, of course, acutely demoralized and self-conscious. Without her looking down, it was possible to feel every part of herself sticking out here, rounding in there, and so forth. It really was; it was amazing. Moreover it did no good to think that clothes were the barest fraction of an inch thick, that their presence or absence made no difference, that we are all born naked to begin with. The real fact was that clothing was privacy, protection, and (in the variety to be chosen from) personality. Naked, Barbara was somehow less Barbara than before, and the children—without benefit of such extended thought—somehow knew it. Nakedness heightened the captor-captive relationship, and it was probably meant to. Barbara sighed.

Outside it was hot, probably the hottest day since she had been here. In spite of the continuous hum of the air conditioner, a still, dead atmosphere steadily filled the room and made her skin moist and uncomfortable. A fly buzzed. Her hair tickled her damp forehead, and she shook it around as best she could. Helplessness: torment.

Right now Terry was on the beach at Cape Cod, spreading out her blanket and settling down with a book or maybe someone to talk to. Barbara's mother was probably on her way to the Seven Corners' Shopping Center feeling late, impatient with traffic, and wondering what it was she had forgotten to write down on the shopping list. The world went on so freely and carelessly without Barbara. I know what it's like to be dead, Barbara thought. Everything's just like it was before.

She could hear Dianne—just barely from where she had to sit—telephoning in a grocery order on the kitchen phone. Dianna was half disguising her own voice, half imitating Barbara's, and she wasn't doing badly at all. Barbara could picture easy Mr. Tillman at the local crossroads store, where the city-people bought in-between things they hadn't bought in Bryce on Thursdays—he would have no doubt that he was listening to the Adams' young baby-sitter at all. Not on your life. He would very nearly testify to it on the stand.

Oh dammit, Barbara thought. Everything's so smooth; everything's going so well without me. I'll never be found. I have a headache. Even Dianne would be comfort of a sort.

When Dianne finally did look in on her, Barbara asked for aspirin. When Dianne brought them, Barbara was forced to lean forward and mouth them from the palm of Dianne's hand like a horse getting sugar cubes. Afterward Dianne carefully gave her a drink of water.

"Thank you."

"It's OK." Dianne put the glass down. "Hope it helps."

"Thanks for cutting up my nightie, too."

"Oh, I'll fix that. This afternoon. You'll never know it. I could do it at home—we have our own sewing machine—but Mrs. Adams has a much better one

105

right here. It does buttonholes and zigzag, everything. . . ."

"Why did you do it, Dianne?" Barbara said it impatiently, perhaps, but confidentially. After all, Dianne was a girl; she must know the fear of nakedness. "I mean, was it just because you wanted to get at me for some reason, embarrass me with them?" Them was clearly the boys.

"Not really." As her part of the shared duties, Dianne dusted Barbara's room and made the bed each morning and turned it down each evening. She did it with a mother's half-annoyance and a perfectionist's dislike of mess. Now as she did this, she moved out of Barbara's vision. Barbara turned and tried to follow with her eyes.

"Do they do everything you tell them to?"

"Me? No." Dianne might have been speaking with a toss of the head but Barbara couldn't see. "We vote. We voted."

"I mean in the game, Freedom Five."

"Oh." Dianne audibly laughed. It was the first time she had done so, and it did not have a funny sound. "That's all over."

"Then, what is *this?*"

"I don't know," Dianne said honestly enough, plumping the pillows back into place. "This is just this, I guess. We used to play the other when we were younger, but not anymore."

Barbara sighed, but in exasperation. "Well, if you're not keeping me tied up because it's part of a game, and you're not doing it because you're mad at me, and you all vote, then what *is* it? Why did you ever start it? It's stupid. . . ."

"Well. . . ." There was the sound of that last thumping a well-made bed gets. Dianne was obviously not in a mood to confess inner thoughts—it was almost unimaginable that such a time would ever come—but again she wasn't being coy or obscure either. The conclusion might be that she had not thought it out herself, or that she had and simply wasn't saying.

106

"I don't know," Dianne said. "We just got to talking about it, and then we just did it, that's all."

"Like on a dare?"

"Yes. Kind of. I guess so."

"Then why keep it up? I mean, you did it after all—you won."

"Why not?" Dianne was dusting. Barbara could hear things being moved and replaced behind her.

Barbara bit her lip. It was all a wheel and a circle inside of an oval with these kids. It wasn't real; it wasn't a game, and yet it *was*. The illogic of the position didn't seem to bother them at all. "Then, how are you going to get out of it," she said, "when the Adams come back and all?"

"I don't know," Dianne said. "What could they do anyhow? What's the harm?" Dianne came back in front of Barbara and dusted the vanity top, moving bottles and things deftly and quickly. "Have you been hurt? Really? Has anybody done anything to you?" She turned and looked down at Barbara. "Well . . . ?"

Barbara looked up into those clear, gray, flawless, and conscienceless eyes and was frightened somehow. She had never been naked, helpless, stared at—it was more like inspection or inventorying—by another woman before. Moreover there was no guessing what went on behind those cool eyes.

Dianne and the others had no gods and heroes to exemplify the good and proper life for them, nor did they seem to have any pursuing demons either. Within their smoothly-managed, automatic world, they were serene, secretive, knowing, adept and without fear or respect. They paid no tax to their Maker, their parents, nor to anyone else—not really, not within their hearts, Barbara *felt* that—and they operated free of standards other than their own. In the power of Freedom Five, Barbara was more alone than she might have been in some classic, solitary confinement. How could you guess what children like that might do, might dream of? She swallowed.

"What now?"

"I'm going to dust," Dianne said with practicality.

"I mean with me," Barbara said.

Barbara was really too squeamish. Her actual thought—there was horror in it—was that you just don't leave a naked, helpless girl sitting around for young boys to fool with. And though she was the object/victim, she was too *nice* to protest. She said, "What are they going to do with me next?"

If Dianne caught Barbara's mood, she ignored it. "I don't know," she said. "I mean, after all, what *can* they do? Really?"

When it was Paul's turn to watch, he didn't think he was going to be able to walk into Barbara's room. It was as if he were carbonated on the inside, a bottle of fizz that someone had shaken too hard; everything tingled. He felt that he had some kind of haze over his eyes; there was a knot in his throat. He was afraid.

"Wait a minute," he said when Bobby told him his guard time had come. "Don't go yet—I want her gagged again."

"Why's that?" John was sitting half-a-saddle against the kitchen sink, eating a sandwich.

"I just do. That's the new rules. You have to help me do what I want with her," Paul had been eating too, but now his appetite disappeared. "Isn't that right, Dianne?"

She shrugged. "OK."

"Don't go out of your tree, man. I was just asking why. That's all." John swung down to his feet. "Come on if you want to. Let's get it over with."

"Really?"

"Let's!" Cindy said.

When they all got into the room together, Barbara looked up. When Dianne got the gag and tape from the dresser, she looked alarmed.

"What's that for, Dianne? Please—"

Paul thought that she had a nice pleading tone to her voice. "You're going to get gagged." With the others around him, he was assured again. "Do it, Dianne."

"But why? I didn't make any noise . . ."

"I know," Dianne said. "It's just the new rules. Paul wants it, so that's what we have to do."

"What new rules?"

"Whoever's on guard, gets what he wants. We all help."

"When did this start?"

"This morning," Dianne folded the terry cloth square. "Don't worry, I'll take it out when it comes my turn later on."

"But why do you want me gagged? What're you going to do?" Barbara averted her head a moment and looked at Paul.

Paul squirmed and grew red. This was exactly the kind of confrontation he didn't want.

"He just does," John said, short of patience with them both. "Now are you going to do it or not?" He looked around for the bottle of chloroform.

"You'd better *not* do anything," Barbara said to Paul, but she opened her mouth and allowed Dianne to put the cloth in. She complained, but she didn't fight when Dianne fixed it there with three wide strips of adhesive tape over her lips.

Then they were gone. After pretending disinterest for a few minutes, Paul went over and softly closed the door to the hall. Then he came back and walked around Barbara. It had all come true. His heart was very loud: he could hear it from within his own head.

When they had first talked about taking Barbara's clothes off, he had pictured her like the girl in the book Dianne was reading—she was tall, slender, terrified, bound to the stake in the middle of the stone platform with the magic signs drawn on her body in blood and the priest with his dagger ready to rip her heart out from beneath her breast. Reality, of course, had been quite different.

For one thing, Barbara had hair down between her legs, and this not only surprised him, but disappointed him. He imagined a woman's genitalia from air-brushed pictures he had managed to see—something small, rounded, utterly smooth, and somehow, magically attractive (else why could they not *show* it?).

In this sense, she had let him down. For another thing, Paul had seen enough of the mass media to know that Barbara wasn't exactly shaped like a film star. His idea of anatomy was not so vague that he didn't realize that he'd seen better and more rounded figures—clothed, remote, of course—many times.

Nonetheless Barbara was here and helpless, and that made up for a lot. He was discovering the particularness of a separate person. He walked around in front of the chair to which she was tied and reached in his pocket.

Paul had a knife. It was the ordinary kind to be bought in Tillman's store for a dollar seventy-five, but today it was hot as a poker and weighed a ton in his thirteen-year-old hand. He took it out and opened the big blade. Only when he had done so did he allow himself to look up and meet Barbara's eyes. She wasn't looking at him as he had expected, but looking at the blade, following the movements of his small hands with attention.

Paul turned the knife this way and that, made as if to feel the edge, which was dull enough. He moved the knife from side to side and again watched her eyes follow; it was like holding a switch over a dog and not beating him yet, but it was far, far better. An extreme, a delightful sense of going-to-be-bad filled him. His fear had begun to fade. He whipped the blade past her at arm's length—it was perhaps as close to him as to her—but she stiffened nonetheless.

Only that?

Paul paused.

Probably Barbara wasn't at all afraid that he would kill her (this, he wished her to fear): she probably wasn't even afraid that he would hurt her much. Paul was obviously in command in one way, but as an adult, she was obviously and still in command in quite another way. He better not or else. It hurt Paul. Cross him, belittle him in any of his crazy whims, and you had a very angry boy on your hands.

Well, she'd better believe me, Paul said. Leaning forward, he put the flat part of the knife blade on her throat and pressed the dull side into her gently and safely. She wouldn't know that of course; she couldn't see under her own chin. She shook her head no-no angrily, and in so doing, cut herself. There was, after all, a sharp side, too. It was no more than a prick, but she felt it, and it slowed her down perceptibly. Afraid that he'd really hurt her for a moment, Paul almost withdrew, but when he saw that she was merely scratched, he left the knife on her neck and continued to press— less gently. There were the tiniest, whitest little blonde hairs on her skin—you wouldn't even see them unless you bent close and tested her neck with a blade—and Paul was fascinated. The point of the knife made a little shadowy indent that was white at the tip and flushed all around and then all of those pale little touches of light on her skin and she stopped moving at all. Now she knows, now she knows, he thought. Then he began to trace the long tendon of her throat up and down, a little harder each time until she had to withdraw. This continued until she had her head practically flat on her far shoulder.

Delighted, Paul held her there with the point of steel just under her ear. They had invented a new game: he could make her move her head anywhere he wanted, and she resisted. It was exciting and dangerous. If she became angry or tired and thrashed her head around again, and he did not get the knife back in time, she really would be hurt. He might kill her that way. And if he held the knife in one place too long, he might just do it—accidentally. But still he held the blade there another second and another and pressed harder. Then finally he relented, only to walk around the chair and begin the game over from the other side again.

During all this, of course, Paul was painfully aware of her naked breasts just below his arm, sometimes nearly touching it. He thought that somehow there was something sacred about a woman's breasts— it was one of the very reasons he had wanted her nightgown off—but he wasn't going to touch either of them, certainly not yet anyhow. Instead, when he had tired of

111

his present game, he let the point of his knife trickle down between them to her navel and her pale white belly where he pressed in just hard enough to make her wince and squirm. Then a new game began. Stick her here and make her twist that way; stick her there and make her twist back again. This way, that way. Harder.

When he finally straightened up, it seemed that he had been holding his breath for a hundred years. He let it out slowly and listened. The life of the house went on as usual. He could hear the other kids' voices somewhere, but they didn't seem to be caring. It was better than he'd dare think, and his turn at guarding wasn't half over. He looked at Barbara—the complicity of victim and tormentor—and he smiled.

Much more slowly now, with much less fear, he began to test her whole body with his knife. He found that by keeping the blade flat and pressing in on the point, he could leave a faint white line on her skin wherever he drew. He could make designs even if they lasted but a moment. They were chanting in the cave now: by the flickering light of greasy, animal oil torches stuck in the rocks, Paul prepared the victim for the final act. Even he trembled when he thought of it.

When Paul straightened up a second time, he found he had been lost in his dreams for nearly an hour. Barbara's body was crossed and marked with a number of now-pink lines that were slowly becoming more vivid. After that, they would fade; at least, he guessed that they would. He found, however, that he really didn't care. There would be no beating for this tonight, and the remoteness of punishment plus the number of possibilities formed something like an inescapable corridor down which he must go, each step leading to the next. He had to do what he was doing.

Barbara, too, was thinking. Paul was glad he didn't know what. She still didn't seem very much afraid—though she understood it well enough when he hurt her—and she was still angry. But there was something else. She kept looking at him as if she just couldn't understand any of this, as if she were trying to look inside of him and figure it all out. He bore this

112

uncomfortably while he regained his normal breathing: she was spoiling things. Then he had an inspiration.

Going to the chest, he opened the drawers one after another until he found the one with her own things in it. As he had hoped, there were several summer scarves neatly folded and stacked to the side. Taking one and laying it on the bed, he refolded it from corner to corner and then again and again until it was no wider than a belt. He had a blindfold.

Barbara saw him coming and would have no part of it. She shook her head no-no and twisted away from him violently. Nonetheless, by putting the blindfold under her chin and trapping the back of her head against his skinny chest, he was able to work the cloth up over her eyes and tie it in place. It took several tries and some struggle, and when he had finished, they were both breathing hard again. The change in things, however, was remarkable.

Instead of Barbara's put-down looks, there was nothing. It was as if *she* had left the room. The prisoner was anonymous—like the ones they used to do things to down in the woods: nonexistent—and the taboo over her was gone.

Taking his knife again, Paul McVeigh reopened his game, this time pressing in here and there as if daring himself to break the skin and draw blood. Now. *That* ought to hurt for a change. He even touched her breast. When lightning did not strike him dead—like John, he rather saw lightning as the all-avenging blast that evened justice out—he put the point of his knife on her breast and ran it luxuriously down to the nipple. Hers were bigger than his, bigger even than Dianne's, and they had little bumps in the pink part and he had a long time to go yet, and so he toyed with his knife point.

John, too, was half-afraid when it came his turn to guard Barbara. Though he felt himself to be the leader in most things, he was all the more shy about saying what he wanted done with her. It would be like a pane of glass—everyone would know then—and he almost

113

let the whole thing pass. Then he called himself coward, and faced the whole matter down.

"I want her back in bed. Like she always is."

"OK," Paul twitched. He had just joined them on the kitchen steps. He seemed pale and a little breathless.

"It's too early," Dianne said logically. "We'd only have to go to the trouble of getting her up again to eat. And then put her down again."

"Yeah. Anyhow, that's no fun," Bobby said.

"It's my turn to say."

"OK. All right," Dianne sighed and got up. The rest of them followed her.

This time Barbara resisted. When they released her from the chair and got her to her feet, she refused to move, and when they pushed her, she knelt down on her knees and doubled up and let them choke her with their halter. When they grabbed her upper arms and tried to lift her, she squirmed free, rolled over and shot out her hobbled ankles, hitting John and nearly knocking him down. Blindfolded, she continued to kick out in all directions until they finally caught her bare legs and pinned her down. In the end, it took all five of them to drag her up onto the bed and tie her wrists and ankles to its four corners again. Bobby and Paul got knocked back several times; Dianne got scratched; and John nearly lost his hold on her once or twice. When it was over and the other kids had left, he sat down to catch his breath and think a moment. The fact was that he was still afraid of what he had dared himself to do.

There were so many Barbaras in his mind. The first one, the one he had met when she first came to sit for the Adams kids, was busy, athletic, and bright. She ticked him off the way she whipped the Adams kids around in the station wagon as if she owned it. She wasn't anywhere near a grown-up, and yet she acted more like a mother than Mrs. Adams did. She ticked him off the way she let the old ladies at the church make over her and take her in. Barbara could swim better, run as fast, manage twice as well, talk better—she knew everything—and all the time that she was

114

being so smart-ass and bossy, she knew that she was pretty and that all the guys were watching her out of the corner of their eyes. Even the old men. She had that look-and-eat-your-heart-out manner. It made it easy to want to take her down a couple of notches—as, indeed, they had—but remembering that girl did not make it any more easy to approach her.

Then there was Barbara the first day after they captured her, not stuck-up and busy anymore, but finally silent, gagged, helpless, and bewildered. She was still recognizable, but it was an improvement.

Yesterday there had been a friendlier Barbara. He now realized that she had been putting him on with all that talk about his school and his girl and all—what did she care anyway? That was all kid stuff to her—but, in fact, he had enjoyed it. He wished now that he had kissed her when she gave up: he wished now that he dared ungag her and talk to her some more, but her kicking around said enough for her mood.

So that he got down to Barbara today, naked for him to do anything with that he wished, and he was still scared, actually scared. John Randall was also disgusted with himself. When Dianne had cut off Barbara's nightgown this morning—John, of course, consenting—he had thought he would go blind. She was so pretty. A kind of blankness came over his mind; he hardly seemed able to look. His legs were all sort of weak on the insides: he thought he was going to do it again, right then and there. Did just looking at a girl do that to you? Nobody had ever told him about that before, and he felt a little betrayed. It was unfair that women had *that* advantage over you. It had dismanned him the rest of the day, right up until now.

Now.

He swallowed with some noise.

Just now, as a matter of fact, he would have liked to get up and go out of the room, but he couldn't. He was trapped. On the one hand were the rest of the kids who would laugh at him: on the other there was the reason for it all—Barbara. OK, he managed to look at her long and steadily from where he sat, and while he still felt a little bit of that heady, half-blindedness, he found that he had *some* self-control. He even found, at length, that he could stand—a better view—and that he could walk as if in a dream, half stuck to the floor, half gliding. He found that he was able to move to the side of the bed and sit down on it beside her and endure that, too.

At such close range, he felt he was in the path of some kind of death ray. Something was happening inside him. He was irresolute: it was difficult to breathe. Very hesitatingly, he touched the inside of her calf and moved his fingers up her leg—John Randall enormously avoided what he considered Barbara's "private parts" (despite the fact that on the team, the word "cunt" was used standardly)—across her flat stomach and down again.

Of course, the stroke was lustful. To the extent that he felt or understood lust *per se,* he wanted the girl. But there was much more in his hand: his fingers traveled with a truly admiring caress and one of understandable wonderment. Barbara *was* so different from him and from his experience. The obvious but suddenly made discovery filled him with awe. By revelation, he came to understand something about love. I mean, John said, if it wasn't this way and we were really friendly and she didn't mind me touching her this way, then it would really be great. In fact, given that possibility, he would have freed her on the instant and knelt before her upright body. His mind could barely hold the many possibilities that followed. But it wasn't like that.

Instead she was in there, inside her own skin, inside of her own mind, inside of the gag, the rope, the adhesive tape and all, and he was out here inside of himself as well. The mutual isolation was complete, and to John, it was quite honestly sad. I don't want to do this to you, John said, but how could I any other way?

No way.

What was left was at least bittersweet. If he couldn't be her grown-up, voluptuously welcomed lover, it was sad and nice at least to touch what he

116

loved, and—like Paul—he, too, lost some of his fearfulness. Increasingly his hand moved over all of the parts of a woman's body that he had only daydreamed about, and moved gently, almost protectively. There was nowhere he could look and not be dumbfounded by a sixteen-year-old joy.

The sharpness of ankle running over the thinness of shin to the strength of knee; the fullness of inner thigh merging into the complex of hips, belly, navel; the body, the breasts, the nipples (as if in defiance, they were cold, tiny, and shrunken); the slenderness of throat, the chin line, Barbara's hair. John loved. For the moment, he rather desperately loved.

Throughout all of this, Barbara lay absolutely rigid. It wasn't simply that she was bound but that there was an inner rigidity that was somehow her hopeless defense against him. Her nearly covered face—taped and blindfolded—was turned away from him. No matter what he did, he received no response at all. He was not there. Thus he arrived at the second part of last night's plan rather defeated and elated all at the same time.

How easy it had seemed then. How he had tossed and turned with impatience. Now, as it turned out, his hands were shaking as he stood up, unbuttoned his cutoffs, kicked off his moccasins, and fearfully lay down beside her. Don't be mad, John Randall said, don't be mad; and he turned against her.

Barbara's flung-out position made the whole episode difficult. Nevertheless there was an instant touching of his whole body—even the parts he rarely had occasion to touch himself—with hers, the conjugal experience never before felt or imagined. It wasn't her nakedness that so impressed him but his own, and yet not so much his own but theirs. Although it was wrong, that is, although the moment was gained by theft in a borrowed hour at the Adams' house with an older girl who was helpless to reject him, although the sureness of punishment came steadily closer, still the feeling changed his life forever. As he knew it would. He loved her, and he felt himself rising in proof. Getting up on all

117

fours—elbows and knees—he crossed to between her legs. At last she acknowledged him, shaking her head violently from side to side, No, No, No. That was when he did it to her.

Dianne had the last guard duty of the day. When she looked at her tiny silvery watch and got up and left the beach, it meant that Cindy and the rest of them (except for John, who was on watch) had to come out of the water, dry off, and follow her up to the house. Afterward there was always the elaborate and possibly dangerous business of moving Barbara and feeding her, the dull thing of getting out of wet bathing suits and hanging them to dry, and then the unhappy part of having to watch everybody go home. The sun was still high up and all, but it was the end of the day, and Cindy hated it.

Not only was the boredom of spending nights alone with nobody to talk to, becoming harder to endure, but each finished day was one closer. Reckoning time was coming.

For Cindy, of course, time did not race by with adult speed. Preoccupations, duties, schedules, arrangements, meetings were no part of her life. Instead she drifted, sometimes pleasantly, sometimes petulantly, in a vague continuum of night-day-night needing only amusement, approval and a little petting to be happy. Nonetheless she marked treats and punishments accurately enough. Mommy and Daddy would be home *this* Monday, and today was the end of Wednesday. Five more days.

Presumably by then, the kids would have let Barbara go, and she would have turned around and let them have it good. The *first* time. Afterward she would tell Mommy and Daddy. What would happen then, Cindy couldn't even guess—she had never been so bad—and it worried her.

Immersed in this mood with a child's singular intensity, she banged into the house and down the hall unaware of low serious conversation ahead of her. Not until she reached Barbara's room did she realize that

118

anything different was happening. Then she stopped at the door, dirty, dragging beach towel coming to a stop on the floor behind her. John and Dianne were talking.

"What did you do to her?" Dianne was angry.

John glanced down at Cindy and back again. "Everything," he said.

There was an extra second's hesitation in which Cindy thought that they looked at each other with a kind of secretiveness; certainly, they weren't including her, at all. Then she looked at the bed and saw a small amount of blood on the sheet between Barbara's legs, right *there*.

For a child of her age, Cindy was singularly unshocked. She had seen it before. Sometimes there was blood on the sheet where Mommy slept. Mommy had explained it to her—needlessly; Cindy didn't care much one way or the other—that it was something which happened regularly and normally to a woman once a month, but Cindy knew better. She herself was a woman, that is, female, and it didn't happen to her nor could she believe that it ever would. Cindy would be careful; she wouldn't *let* it happen. It would be easy.

Straight out, the blood on the bed had something to do with what men and women did alone in the dark of night, had something to do with the whisperings and smiles of the older kids—the "mystery." Had she been possessed with adult vocabulary, Cindy would have said something like, "Oh, the hell with it." So John had done it to Barbara. Cindy's only reaction was mild surprise; she didn't think either one of them was that *old*. After all, they weren't married, and that had something to do with it. She looked at John and Dianne.

"How did you move her legs?"

John looked odd for a moment. "I didn't."

"Then you couldn't have done it," Dianne said.

"But I did."

Dianne looked at Barbara and bit her lip. "Well, you did something anyway."

"Are you going to let her get up?"

"We ought to feed her."

119

"She's going to be mad again. . . ."

"Oh." Dianne seemed to think for a moment. Then she shrugged, still upset. Going over to the bed, she removed Barbara's blindfold. Cindy watched her and saw that Barbara's eyes were wet, not with sorrow, not with happiness, nor with any other emotion she had ever seen before. Maybe what men and women did, hurt.

"Umnn—*umnnn!*" Barbara couldn't talk, but she did. She looked at Dianne, raised her head, looked down at herself, over at the door, and back up again. She wanted to go to the bathroom. Even Cindy could understand that, and so could Dianne.

"We'd better let her get up."

John, who had watched this a little embarrassed, seemed somewhat relieved. Barbara wasn't mad at him, Cindy thought, or at least anger wasn't the thing she felt *most*.

"Go get the others," John said, and Cindy went, taking time only to toss her towel across the doorknob.

Using the normal, drawn-out manner, Freedom Five shifted Barbara to her feet and led her, rope around the throat, to the bathroom. She didn't fight now, but when they got her inside, she began to make sounds again. She bent low and rubbed her taped mouth on the wash basin. She wanted to be ungagged.

"Do you want to go to the toilet or not?" Dianne said.

More hopeless sounds.

Dianne just shrugged.

Barbara gave her a look of anguish that even Cindy could feel. Then Barbara sat down on the toilet and all except Dianne went out into the hall. Afterward they could hear a great deal of water splashing and bathing inside. Eventually Barbara came out again— shuffling, hobbled—and they led her back to her room and tied her to the chair by the vanity.

Dianne fixed her a sandwich, a good one for a change. It was chicken, white bread, and mayonnaise, and it smelled good to Cindy, who was getting hungry again as she did hourly. When Barbara was ungagged

120

however, she didn't use her free hand to eat it. Instead she said, "Dianne, you've got to untie me now. You've *got* to."

Dianne said nothing. She was standing to Barbara's right, near but not leaning on the vanity.

"That boy raped me," Barbara said. "You know about that; you're a woman. I've got to wash myself out or something."

"Don't you use the pill?" Dianne said with curiosity.

"No, of course I don't. Do you? Does anybody?" Barbara wrenched at her ropes angrily. "Dianne, unless you're married or you're set on going to bed with every boy you meet, there's no *need* to."

"I thought all girls who went to college did." Dianne seemed to consider this a most odd piece of information. She regarded it with scholarly surprise.

"Dianne, it doesn't make any difference one way or the other. What makes a difference is that I may be pregnant by that boy. *Already* pregnant. It only takes *one* sperm cell to fertilize. You've got to let me go *now*. You've got to let me *try*."

Dianne remained silent, but Cindy thought that she looked aware, concerned about Barbara in some way.

"Dianne?"

"How could he do it?" Dianne remained quite puzzled about it.

"He *did*."

"Did he?" Then Dianne looked down at Cindy and said with a rather quaint prudery, everything considered, "Well, never mind. We can't let you go. You know that."

"Why?" Barbara was on the edge of crying. "Dianne, he could make me have a baby. The baby would live to be someone like you or me or any of us. You know, can I make it any clearer? You've got to let me get out of here and douche or something."

"I can't." For the first time, Dianne didn't use the word "we" when speaking of Freedom Five's joint action. She took the decision to herself, and Cindy

121

thought—also for the first time—that Dianne was a very strange girl.

Barbara accepted the ruling in silence.

"Do you want your sandwich or not?" Dianne said.

"I'd throw it up," Barbara said. Her head dropped forward, and Cindy thought she might really begin to cry, but she didn't—quite. "Just go away and leave me alone."

A few minutes later, with a display of temper on both sides, Freedom Five gagged their prisoner again, forced her to bed, and tied her down. Very tightly. The sandwich sat uneaten and drying in the air; eventually Bobby and Cindy split it between themselves and washed the plate clean.

5

As on the night before, it was hot, still, and humid. The marsh mosquitoes—obviously infuriated—whined about his head. And again, as on the night before, the end-of-day squall had gathered, threatened and then dissipated without giving rain. Remnant clouds sat high in the distant darkness, a castle of corridors and halls through which dim lightning and dull thunder wandered without giving any true action. Unlike Cindy, John Randall had never had any superstitions about storms. Instead, he cast a sailorly eye aloft and concluded that the rain, if any, would fall on the lower Eastern Shore or even drop wastefully into the ocean beyond. He dismissed the intruding consideration and returned to his first—it could be said his utterly consuming—passion. Barbara and/or the thoughts provoked by her.

Considering that he had helped capture a girl and hold her prisoner, that he had raped her, that the punishment for this was going to be so severe that he had literally destroyed himself, he was singularly elated. He had broken out of the prison of childhood; he was no longer someone just to be ordered around, he had solved what he too considered the "mystery." He could *do it* from here on as well as any grown-up—he could fuck: what all the others talked about—and he had done it. With a defiant, self-immolatory glee, he was absolutely delighted with himself. He had executed a real, fundamental, human act: he had entered life in

123

spite of them all. (*Them* he defined as adults—those tedious, living pains-in-the-ass who held you down so long and took such pleasure in doing it.) And he had sampled something of love as well, not simply the physical side, but the spiritual and revelatory side, too. He saw now—at last—the possibility of falling in love himself someday. To that extent, his thoughts were both characteristic of the male and quite uncharitable.

When he had lain beside and then atop Barbara, he had loved and admired her—quite more than that, he had been nearly rabid with passion—but the insertion accomplished, the deed done, everything had faded rapidly. Old Barbara's body was pretty much OK; what you could expect, he guessed; but in retrospect, he had to remember that under the tape and blindfold was only the girl herself, the goody one with something to say about everything. Her undeniable appeal and submissiveness were enforced, almost created by the kids—Freedom Five—and, of course, only temporary. In her place, John Randall would far rather have—at the same, harsh terms—any number of girls at school and around here, girls at home with their parents right now, girls not knowing that his thought like a closely defined spotlight was picking them out one by one. John swatted at a mosquito, shifted position on the back steps, and sighed. Life was going to be endless and suddenly wonderful.

John Randall, his punishment for present sins served out, was going to plough through the world screwing everything he could get his hands on. Never mind love or babies or God or any of that crap. His mind focused on the moment-of-first-clutch. Just exactly there. That much, Barbara had taught him. And, if in the end, he did marry, it was going to be a mild, sweet, meek girl he could do anything with that he wanted. That much more, Barbara had also taught him—no smart-asses. Meanwhile he had better things to think about (in truth, the same thing but in more particular terms).

"Tomorrow and tomorrow and tomorrow," Macbeth had said—it was one of the few things John's memory had salvaged from endless, boring English classes—and it entirely suited John's present mood. Tomorrow, indeed. Tomorrow he was going to rape a girl captive. Again. Few men alive could say as much: few people knew as little about technique required as the impatient re-rapist.

Dianne had said—another bossy girl—that the woman's knees should be raised and parted to open the vagina. At least, if you were electing *that* position. She had read it in a marriage manual her progressive, not to say permissive, parents had thrust on her shortly after she began to menstruate. This John now took in with great and attentive care. It could explain a number of things.

When he had tried to get himself inside of the girl—dumb Barbara shaking her head No, No, No—he had had the worst time finding out *where*. With humorless concentration, not to say intensity, he had taken the failure hard: it defeated manly dignity. Nonetheless he knew approximately where to look and so got his finger in: thereafter, he attempted to put his penis into the same opening (were there *two?*). His reactions were discouraging. First, it hurt; second, he was so excited that he came almost at once. If there was further remnant memory, it was that Barbara made an angry-animal sound not at all like the sighs of love and passion satisfied the world had led John to expect. Thereafter, considering the unsatisfactory nature of the coupling, there was drowsing, desirable bliss. It was something one could grow to like *if* done properly. There, exactly, was tomorrow's problem.

He was going to do it again, of course, but better if possible—for himself anyhow. No other thought—no consideration of Barbara's actions and reactions, thoughts or feelings—so much as shadowed his mind. Had he been asked about her, he would have said—male fashion—that he didn't give a shit.

125

Paul, obviously unaware of John's thoughts, had—equally and obviously—the same principal subject on his own mind as the somewhat thwarted night settled down. Unlike John, he was not free to roam the creek in a rowboat or even ramble around the rather considerable piece of McVeigh property. Instead he sat encapsulated in his room, a beating heart in the unresponsive body of the house. But tomorrow—such was the relieved contract between parents and child—he would not only be released again, but pitched out, free to run and play and torture a grown girl. This whole adventure was for Paul like a string of erotic Christmas Days all in a row.

Like John—again—the thrust of Paul's thought was entirely sexual. Compared to other thirteen-year-olds, Paul was very nearly jaded. At five he had peeked at his naked older sister; at eight, he had found his father's magazines; at ten, his imagination had already taken him far beyond what the world could ever offer. At twelve, he understood that he was closed in and that his best dreams would never come true because of "people."

Like John—still again—Paul loathed adults.

Yes, they held you down; yes, they dominated; yes, they kept you away from the fun; but Paul had a deeper complaint. Yes, they were more stupid—by far. His contempt was the entire heap of contempt of the "mind people" against the "no-neck people." He despised no-necks, and on this point at least, he felt himself on sound footing.

Adults *were* unseeing, insensitive, slow, dull-witted and catastrophic in their makeup. They smashed and blundered about. How could they be human at all? Paul was not related. He held like the blade of his knife an absolute division between himself and them, and the division would never be mended. He could *see* where they could not; he was cheered when they wept; he was clear where they were unclear. The only hitch to this was that *they* dominated. They ran the world.

Paul's feeling was less one of hatred than pure

separation. *They* were not people. He did not grant their existence anymore than after waking he granted the existence of his strange dreams. He did not grant the existence of his parents (though he had to grant their power, surely enough). He did not grant the existence of schoolmates; he did not grant the existence of so imperfect a world. Paul was—given other times and circumstances—capable of an Auschwitz, an Inquisition, a Rape of the Sabine Women. He would kill cheerfully, simply because the victims offended the patterns of perfection he would then create. A world of Pauls would be—to his mind—a perfect world.

To that extent, when he thought of Barbara, he thought only of her skin and of his knife blade passing in and passing out, passing in and passing out, accompanied by the instant appearance of blood. *There!* He would *show* them. In his night imagination he heard a scream, but it was *them* screaming, not anyone in particular at all. It was great.

Only Dianne escaped his fervor: first, because she understood him and told him things; second, because she was bigger and older; third, because she was fairly ugly and uninteresting; and last, because she was his sister. Within this unsentimental roster of priorities, her chief value to him remained that of storyteller, exciter.

Dianne was widely—though not well—read. She devoured her mother's book-club novels as fast as they fell through the mail. She poked and pried around the house and read everything in it from *Organic Gardening* to *High-Speed Emulsions* (photography). She was off to the library every time the family car went into Bryce. She was a fund of scattered, not too well-considered, knowledge. Those things she shared with Paul, however, had a certain direction.

For him she reserved her tales of the Nazi atrocities, the Salem witch trials, the fate of the early Christian martyrs, or the human sacrifices of primitive peoples, and when she did so, her cool gray eyes became abnormally large and intense. Paul ate it up. He saw, he saw it all as she talked. He saw the small iron cage

127

hoisted by rattling chains, up, out, over, and then down into the waiting bonfire built in the medieval town square. He heard the shrieks, saw the dimly lit figure in the cage flinging itself around in captive agony, heard the flesh crackle like bacon in a skillet (his simile), saw the iron grow red until its content was entirely consumed. Paul nearly fainted at the force of his—tutored—imaginings. This wasn't a make-believe story, this wasn't the comics or TV—they were all tame and boring—this was what had happened to real people, *done* by real people.

It was too much for a small boy, and yet from the time he could think, Dianne had treated him to such fare. (In fairness to her, it must be said that he had never put his fingers in his ears. He listened.) Their natures coincided at this point, and the Freedom Five "game" insofar as they were able to influence it, was their game. (In fairness again, it must be admitted that though the others might change the plot here and there, they *played*. They liked it.)

Thus, when Paul considered tomorrow and the prisoner they called Barbara, he considered it from a most special point of view. He lay in the darkness of his room turning over all the possibilities. Actually you ought to have more than just a knife to do any good.

Bobby, awakened on the same night, hardly knew what to think. Cindy, sleepy and untalkative, shook him to consciousness and then went stomping off to bed, fell in, and was almost instantly asleep, knotted hair, dirty dress, dirty pants, dirty socks, and all. In the smoothly purring automated house, Bobby was alone again. Though he did not think of the house in just those terms, it seemed a ship. The flavor of the hour was easily assimilated. It was a ship on which he was at once both master and passenger—the black night sailed by outside. He had his duties and his burdens.

After he had yawned and scratched himself to life, Bobby made a cursory inspection of the prisoner, though it was hardly necessary on this fourth night.

128

He had observed—excepting when Cindy ungagged the captive—nothing more from Barbara than the occasional movement of a hand, the turn of the head, an occasional opening and closing of the eyes, or a twisting of this foot or that. She simply could not escape, and each tieing up made it less likely. The children steadily inproved as wardens, and Bobby was the best of all.

The difference tonight—her nakedness—did not much affect Bobby. Barbara appeared to be sweet, defenseless, and all that, but to him, she was also a trifle repugnant. The raw thrust of genitals and hair was a little too much for him at his age; everything was over-scale compared to his own slight build. Her nudeness was simply another grotesque item in Bobby's troubled week.

Nonetheless, walking into her room and finding all of this so—still so—Bobby felt a true sympathy for Barbara. They *were* hurting her. She had not put on makeup in days, so that her eyes were as naked as her body; nothing was left to imagination, and in her eyes he saw the change the Freedom Five had caused. There were dark smudges under those eyes. He knew Barbara had slept, but she seemed not to have slept in a long time. Her eyes—possibly from sleeplessness—were red with irritation, and wide open and dry, and the pupils were abnormally dark (or so it seemed to Bobby). Her wrists and ankles were chafed and scraped from the rope; her hands which he did not dare touch and her feet (he touched one foot knowing what he would find) were dark colored and cold. Circulation. Her stomach was flat, not to say hollow. The torture was beginning to show.

Bobby knew what he would do if it were up to him, what he *could* do even now—the sooner the better. Son of a surgeon, he had sat around enough dinner tables listening to his father talk about patients. Bobby would untie her, get some circulation going, feed her, cover her up, and let her sleep in absolute secure peace until she wanted to get up and become some part of Barbara

129

again. He remembered asking his father some question about his work and hearing Dr. Adams tell him, "We stop a person from getting sicker and make him comfortable, but patients get *well* by themselves. All you can do is to try and help."

And Bobby did want to help her, but it wasn't one of tonight's possibilities. Boy fears were at war.

Free Barbara, and in all probability she would beat him half to death. If she did not, Freedom Five (only then it would be three) would do it for her later, Leave her prisoner and let the others toy with her another two or three days, and his parents would accomplish the same end. There was no way out and no way to take action just now.

Personally he felt bad about Barbara. He—they—had proved the point. They had taken and successfully held her captive. Now the responsibility weighed on him. For a boy who should have been living on parental guidance, kindness, and protection, he had turned out to be extraordinarily self-disciplined. How else could he have made the initial capture, stood the morning watches, avoided catastrophe last night, and so on? Like his surgeon father he had the inborn willingness to subject himself to the test again and again. Someday—again like his father—he might hold life and death in his hands, and they would be good hands. But for the moment he was tired of it all and quite frightened over what would happen next. (Cindy had told him what John had done.)

At one o'clock in the morning, however, he just couldn't seem to think about it clearly. Like any adult faced with similar imponderables, he simply postponed thinking about the matter. Barbara, momentarily released in imagination, was—with some misgivings—returned to captivity. Bobby left her room and went into the kitchen to make himself a milkshake.

Ordinarily a treat, this ritual repeated alone three nights in a row (no one to give permission, admire, or share) had become like so many other things he found himself doing now that Barbara was captive, his par-

130

ents were gone, and he was in charge. It was simply another duty; having fun was practically a duty. Like Cindy he felt ennui. He wondered why in the world adults bothered to grow up. You had to get physically bigger of course, but why *grow up* if it was like this? He shook his head.

Well, anyhow.

He carefully plopped in the ice cream—chocolate—added chocolate syrup for true taste, just enough milk to liquefy, and pushed the bowl of ingredients up under the blade of the Adams' milkshake-maker (as separate from Mother's mixer and Dad's blender, each in its own place, too). He set the automatic timer for forty seconds, pulled down the lever, and pushed the button to On. Having at thirteen years old executed this maneuver without even thinking about it, Bobby turned and idly surveyed the kitchen. It was in the instant of turning that he saw—perhaps a trick of reflection—what appeared to be a light down in the marshy woods by Oak Creek where nothing else could be.

Bobby wasn't alarmed. Parallax and prism effects, particularly in a house with duothermal panes, air conditioning, and random condensation, were not only known to him but actually the objects of games he played alone. (Move the head this way and make the light disappear, etc.) Instead of being startled, he summoned up his interest and tried to figure out what light source could cause so funny a bounce back. The color varied; it was white and then quite yellow. It danced. Bobby moved his head. No luck; the light stayed pretty much where it was no matter what he did. Behind him the mixer whirred on: fifteen seconds to go.

The conclusion he reached in the next five seconds was that the light was not his old friend reflection but truly a light in the marsh, not a flashlight, not coming closer, but simply an unknown light in the marsh. This meant *somebody* was in the marsh.

Bobby's first thought was John Randall. John had talked big about coming over and helping watch at night, but Bobby knew the problems of sneaking out of

131

that house and returning too many times. Also the light was not near the path by which John would come. Therefore it was not John. Behind Bobby, the mixer purred to a stop, leaving only the little orange-colored On sign blinking at him.

As if wishing the whole matter to go away, he turned, opened the kitchen cupboard, got out a tall glass, and with a steady, exact hand, poured his milkshake into it. Then he detached the mixer blade, rinsed it, and put it in the drainer to dry. When he had done this and turned back, however, he saw the light again. Once in a while, it disappeared only to reappear again. In his imagination, it was a small campfire, and someone was passing back and forth between it and his eye. Gathering wood, perhaps.

Bobby got his milkshake, turned off the kitchen light, and stood holding the cold glass and sipping from it, his heart beginning to step up tempo in the darkness of the room. As soon as his eyes became accustomed to the night, he understood once and for all that there *was* a light in the marsh, that it was man-made, and that there was a person there feeding the fire.

There followed two very quick trains of thought:

1. Adult. Power of adults. Kids holding a captive girl in the bedroom. Discovery. Alarm. Punishment.
2. Pickers.

Although the Adams did not own enough ground to farm seriously, they were surrounded by commercial spreads farmed by traveling machinery and—when the fruit was ripe—Pickers. And in the fall—it was almost time, now—the Pickers came to help. They were dark Latin people with oily shiny skin, dark luminous eyes, "heavy faces" and volatile natures. Their futures were also hopeless. If Bobby had had the ability to phrase his opinion, he would have called them slaves—to his parents, to his group.

For two or three weeks Pickers filled the countryside, spent their meager pay at Tillman's or the local bars, and then disappeared again. They spoke an incomprehensible language Bobby's parents called pachuco, and no one Bobby knew, knew any of them.

During the period of their stay, Pickers might appear anywhere at any time doing anything. By turns the local community depended upon, tolerated, persecuted and then drove them out. And then they returned the next year unchanged. To Bobby, however, the idea of a Picker camping in his marsh under the present circumstances, was menacing. The man might come to the door; Barbara might make a noise; and then the whole plot might be exploded. In the darkness he became much as his father was—careful.

He put down his milkshake half drunk, turned, and went down the hall, down the stairs into the rec room where the guns were kept. There he put two shells into a .410 shotgun, several more in his pocket, and went back upstairs, his heart now beating very irregularly. From Freedom Five, Bobby had gained rather advanced notions of tactics. The way to defend a castle was not to sit on the walls but to leave it there like a tantalizing target. What you really did was go out into the woods, lie flat, let the enemy pass through you, and then shoot them from the rear.

This, in his thirteen-year-old manner, he did, opening the kitchen door (away from the fire), sneaking out and down into the vegetable garden where he was concealed. Wild little thoughts flitted. Wake Cindy? No, she was no use; she might get hurt. Let Barbara go? Again no use. Go for help? It was too far away, too risky, too unavailable. Instead he crept down between the lines of tomatoes (to the right) and beans (to the left) and knelt in the dust. Except for distant thunder he could hear nothing, and he kept his cool.

As on the night his dog had been put to sleep by his father's merciful hand, as on the day he was too sick to graduate from grammar school and had to miss the party, as on the day . . . as on the day . . . he found here was nothing to do but accept life. It ran you, and

133

you did not run it. The problem was to do the best you could with what you had—that was another of his father's sayings.

So he lay down in the vegetable garden alone, aware both of the unknown person or persons down beside the marsh and of Barbara and Cindy inside of the house. They were all in his hands, and they didn't know it. He felt quite brave. And scared.

The fire in the marsh burned on, but no one came. The night wore out in wet dew, and green became the color of the sky. Any adult walking past would have been hit by a shotgun blast, but luckily (Bobby thought) it wasn't required. Eventually—nodding, fighting it—he went to sleep, pink cheeks on crossed hands, the gun at his side.

The physically painful side of Barbara's captivity continued to worsen. Because of her several struggles with Freedom Five, her wrists and ankles were so raw that she bloodied the ropes that held her, and of course she could not hope to heal under the circumstances. From containment and inactivity, her body steadily became more stiff and cranky; she was slowly acquiring a form of bed sickness, so that when the children came and made her get up, she felt dizzy for a moment. Her mouth was perpetually dry—the wad of cloth in her mouth kept it so—and her throat from trying to swallow when there was nothing to swallow was swollen and tender. Her lips, from being taped and untaped, were dry and sore, and hunger pains came and went like menstrual cramps. The kids had never fed her much, and refusing that chicken sandwich tonight had been stupid.

None of this was fatal, of course. She knew that. None of it would leave so much as one scar, and yet—considered as one—her small complaints added up to torture.

To Barbara's thoughts tonight were added new problems. Paul had indeed scratched and pricked her with his knife. John had indeed taken her virginity, clumsily, but taken it: she had been opened for the first time, and she had bled a little (a very little, she noted when she had been allowed to get up). All that was left now was a distant, burning sensation between her legs.

Also, of course, there was the mental affront—humiliation, but more than that—a feeling of "going down." With every day, her status as an adult, her hold on Freedom Five steadily declined. Where she had begun as their keeper, she was now down to being their equal—less than equal for being the it of the game. Where this morning they had barely dared strip her naked, she had become by afternoon the object of rape. Tomorrow she would be little better than the Barbie Doll that Terry had foreseen her becoming.

Tomorrow, Barbara said. I've got to think. Oh, why am I always saying that, when I *can't?*

One thing she had learned. If her body was a prisoner of Freedom Five, her mind was a prisoner of her body. The steady complaint of nerve ends to the brain—stop everything until you take care of *this,* and this and this and this—created an interrupting static that made her jump from subject to subject. However she tried to imagine tomorrow, the most that she could come up with was that it would be worse than today.

Tomorrow Paul would invent new ways to tease and hurt her (and here, she felt true fear). This afternoon, when he had begun to drag his knife over her just short of breaking the skin, he had just been Paul. As time passed, however, his face had assumed a smooth cast of pleasure, even righteousness, as if what he was doing was for him the most correct thing—for him—in the world. Here was the revengeful soldier putting the torch to Joan of Arc's pyre; here was the good gray friar listening to confessions of heresy from the rack. Barbara had thought, this little boy is very nearly insane. The string that held him together—fear of parental punishment—might have snapped this afternoon, might well snap tomorrow when he no longer felt novelty in the situation. If it did, he would really stab her or worse, and if he did it

135

once, he would do it again and again in a frenzy. Barbara could see it; she could see that tomorrow she might die sitting up, bound to a chair in the guest room at the Adams'. Whatever other thoughts came across her mind, that picture remained—the little boy stabbing her again and again—and she was afraid.

Tomorrow—again her mind took a sideways jump—John would probably attempt to rape her again, and he would probably succeed. Here her thoughts shattered and ran off in several directions at once (again). There was fear of pregnancy ... sorrow ... John ... Midge. ...

In college, during Barbara's first year, there had been a girl called Midge, who, as the nickname implied, was short, petite, brunette, vivacious, and pretty much everyone's choice as the Most Fun To Be With. The night after the Indiana game, she and a boy were goofing off, horsing around the freeways in their car when they hit an overpass bridge abutment and were killed.

Such things, of course, produce shock on campus, even on so large a one as that. For several days following, the conversation rather typically ran to "I knew her ... ," or "A friend of mine knew her ... ," or "She was in my American Lit class last year ... ," etc. The main point of it all was that one of us is dead, already dead, actually *dead*. There was awe. Afterward there were sophomoric, if better considered, discussions of life, love, God, philosophy, and so forth.

In the dorm where Barbara was living, the second clear point to be derived was, If you knew you were going to die tomorrow, wouldn't you be sorry you hadn't jumped in bed with every boy who ever asked you? It was hardly an original question, and it elicited what was hardly an original answer. Yes, I would, I most certainly would. The girls had shaken their heads. Since they were not going to die, of course (it was true: that was the only student death incident that year), they had not altered their various standards. They had simply thought about it.

Midge's death had had no further meaning for Barbara until tonight when it was reflected as this: if you had known you were going to be taken prisoner by a bunch of kids and raped by a sixteen-year-old, wouldn't you have given in to Ted when he wanted you to? Yes, I certainly would have, Barbara said. Absolutely. It would have had something nice about it then.

Ted swam, too.

He wasn't Olympic caliber—on the team there was a standing joke that when you were twenty you were over the hill in swimming—but he was good as most young men went. They had met at the pool and gone stroking off like a pair of sleek young otters, and afterward, Barbara was considered to have a boyfriend.

Ted had a number of other qualities, too. He could be serious; he hit the books with fair results and even thought about them afterward; he was kind and considerate for a young man; he smelled good, and though he was strong as a bull, he was remarkably gentle and restrained with Barbara. One night after a different game (it was the next year—last year) they, too, had been goofing off and coasting around in *his* car when he turned into a vast, empty parking lot, parked and put the moves on her. He was the first one whose attack did not cause revulsion. She was surprised.

His hand circled under her arm and covered her breast, his other hand moved under her skirt and stroked her thigh (well, I guess there just isn't all that much different you can *do,* she had thought), and she had consented. She had liked it. There wasn't that wild, randy look that some of them had. If she had had to put it into words, she might have said that she was being worshipped—it had seemed so, anyhow—and that was certainly permissible. I just might, Barbara had thought, I just might, and if I do it and like it, I just might keep on doing it. But she hadn't. There was her innate "niceness."

Barbara's mother and father hadn't reared her to do it in a parking lot. Or in a rented motel room (at least, she didn't think so). Or in the woods (not most

137

woods, anyhow). Just exactly where she would consent to Ted's loving, Barbara hadn't decided (at that time). She supposed she would know it when it happened. Anyway cars kept coming and going with their headlights; it was cold and cramped and just out of the question. At best, she wordlessly promised to go to bed with Ted at some unspecified time and place and to submit—she used it in the grand sense of girlish surrender—to his whims (which appeared safe and pleasant). Yet even that hadn't happened.

Mostly because of money, because of time, because of the lack of a place to be safely alone, because of her own aversions, they simply hadn't connected. Instead summer had come, and they had split until this coming fall. Therefore young John Randall, many and many a mile away and unknown then, had ultimately taken for his own what was honestly promised to Ted.

Again, it wasn't fatal, she supposed.

I'll live, Barbara said. After all, I'll live. Some girls lose it to a bicycle seat.

Nonetheless she felt sorrowful, deprived unfairly, and changed against her will for the rest of life. John had altered her. He might also have made her pregnant. She thought about it—it was too late to do anything else now.

On the one hand, marriage and children were what Barbara considered herself best suited for. She just wasn't an activist; she had no desire to compete; politics were like real-life comic strips, and teaching—her field—was only meant to fill in the time until some young man came along to organize her and get her tracking in the right direction. Sometimes this seemed grim (particularly at school where there was so much talk of careers, and so on), but most of the time it seemed nicely possible. Moreover, at her age, this might happen at any time: it could happen this fall, or it could be three or four years from now. The way she regarded it, she had "four years left at best." At that time, if not before, her focus would properly shift to love, impregnation, gestation, birth, and rearing of
138

young. If sometimes she seemed to swing along in cropped hair, suntan, cotton frocks, and carelessness, it was all something of a put-on; the older she got, the more she thought distant thoughts.

Being pregnant, that is, being trapped by a baby out of wedlock, however, was another thing entirely. In no way was she a Libber. Getting knocked up, *there* was the commonly shared nightmare that walked the halls of the girls' dorms, visiting the poor ones (automobile back-seat girls) in their small suites and the richer ones (motel doubles, ski-weekend girls) in their sorority bedrooms, causing each young transgressor to frown into the darkness and wonder, "Am I, am I?" That was the situation where, having broken the deep taboo, you suddenly felt cosmic, impersonal consequences coming out of the night to expose you: life was over, finished, and how much too soon, too.

How could I have been so stupid? Well I got carried away, etc., away, away, far away.

Such was the rehearsed, the long-avoided fear that came with Barbara's troubled thoughts tonight. She would have to have an abortion; surely in these circumstances, they would let her. At the necessary idea, however, she shrank back a little.

Barbara knew a girl who had had an abortion, a legally arranged, expensive, fancy one, and the girl had told her about it. She had described checking into the large university hospital (in another city) accompanied by her parents (everyone shifting embarrassed in their plastic chairs), had described signing in, being shown her two-bed room, getting undressed, having the tests, getting pubic hair shaved off, having Daddy come up later with candy, magazines, and flowers and that absolutely betrayed that noble look in his eyes. What remained highest in Barbara's mind, however, were *the forms*. In the evening, a brisk, young lady doctor had brought the girl several papers to read and sign for herself, and the lady doctor had sat there, coolly efficient, ready to answer any and all questions while the girl read.

The patient understood that she had requested and was to have an operation for the removal of certain tissue matter from her body; the patient understood that the hospital would be held blameless from the results, mental and physical. The patient understood that the operation might be witnessed by qualified medical students; the tissue removed from her body might be laboratory studied or disposed of by suitable means. The patient understood, the patient understood. . . . The girl had nodded dumbly, signed, and gone back to looking at a magazine she couldn't seem to read. Afterward, the parents—Mommy and Daddy—also had to read and countersign. They understood that as parents of the above minor, etc.

What the patient, what Mommy and Daddy understood quite clearly, was that they had mutually agreed to kill a baby-to-be, one presumably in healthy condition and fully capable of becoming *one of them*. (That was the part that really horrified Barbara.) So be it.

The operation was performed as announced, at seven o'clock in the morning—neatly, quickly and with professional speed. Forty-eight hours later, the patient was home again, sick with nausea (womb returning to normal size), nausea of the spirit and nausea of living. Which would it have been? What would it have been like? Who would it have resembled? What have I done?

Nothing save death is fatal, of course. Some few months later, Barbara observed the girl—hardly penitent, hardly broken-hearted—swinging out with that little bottle of pills her mother's GN had prescribed. The abortion, she referred to simply as Mommy and Daddy's little d and c: "It really shook them up." Thus lightly the matter was concluded.

Barbara, however, could not view it so. To her, the entire experience lay ahead like an insurmountable barrier to further life. She would rather die first (and knew, of course, that she would not). The invasions of the body so far endured might soon enough come to be trifling compared to the curette and the removal of a possible baby from her womb. The time had come for *her* to look at the dim ceiling and wonder, "Am I, am I?" Then somehow she was over it, and thinking about John.

Barbara, too, had varying opinions of her coupling partner. There was John the young boy, John the captor, John the damned rapist, John the just-possible-father-of-her-baby, and John the First One. Without surrendering an iota of her shock, sorrow, and bitterness, she was still forced to remember the event with at least a degree of after-the-fact clarity.

By afterthought Barbara supposed that if it were her destiny to be raped at all (a large if, but there was some measure of fatalism in her nature), then she was fortunate that it had been a boy she knew and not some man animal up an alley or in the woods or wherever. With John, lust was at least somewhat tempered by fondness. His touch—unwanted, repugnant, unsure—had been gentle, even so. He had tried to arouse her, tried to coax her, and if at the last moment he had gone ahead and satisfied himself at her expense, give him marks for effort.

Had she enjoyed it? Indeed not. She had been spread and torn (in a minor way, she suspected; after all, she couldn't *see*); she had been pumped, and there had been friction, enough so that going to the bathroom afterward had made her burn.

So *that's* it, Barbara said, and considered.

Teacher Barbara was well enough sex-educated—technically—but there is always the little trick of actually *doing* a thing to really understand. Shouldn't I have felt anything at *all* that was good? She couldn't remember; rape was more of a dorm subject than classroom topic of discussion.

Here she was interrupted. Bobby ran down the hall outside her room. She raised her head and watched him run back by the other way, shotgun in his hand. The vision was a momentary one but sufficient to impress on her the set, frightened look in his face, the

141

measure of desperation in his movement, the utter need for haste.

After the first two days, when she had given up hope of release, Barbara had begun paying as little attention to Bobby and Cindy as they did to her. They interrupted her difficult sleep, came to gaze with large, innocent, and yet impersonal eyes on her misery, and then went away. She neither feared them nor held them out as a medium of hope. At night when she was dozing and dreaming of Terry or Ted or other things, the children came and went more as pictures, things of imagination equal only to other things of imagination. Now this changed.

Impossibly, Barbara knew at once what the trouble was. Bobby's manner, his quick strength, the gun in his hands told her. She heard the kitchen lights turned off, heard the opening and closing of the river door, and understood. There was a prowler somewhere. This, more than anything else that had happened, really frightened her.

Enduring the small tortures of children, even child-rapists, was one thing, but helplessness before the unknown was another. Whatever noise had startled Bobby was made by a human not an animal, a male not a female, someone powerful and not weak. It could be no other way.

Moreover Bobby, gun and all, would be no match for the man-in-the-dark of Barbara's sudden imagination. He would be taken care of if necessary, and then the kitchen door would open again. What would happen to her when the intruder finally learned what was going on here was unimaginable, better *not* imagined. She held her breath to hear the sound of scuffling, the sound of a gun—the sound of *something*—and heard nothing for an hour and then a second hour. She looked at her wrists seeming miles away, neatly bound with Scout knots—clove hitches if the correct terms were used—and felt that tomorrow, if there was one, she must absolutely get away.

Gingerly, very gingerly, she exhumed the outlines

of a plan she had invented earlier and been too "nice" to effect.

In the garden Bobby was late-awakened by the sudden heat of a risen, huge August sun; he was cold, damp, dirty, and stiff with the barrel of the .410 glinting wetly where he had laid it against the beanpoles (the gun was still dangerously cocked). He awoke with a start, a physical jump, all of the past night's fears and suspense, all of the guilt at having had to abandon guarding Barbara, immediately on his shoulders. A moment's consideration, however, told him that everything was all right: he could *feel* it. The sky was pale green with very tropical, moist clouds just warming their eastern faces to the light. The birds were making their usual morning racket, and the river—when he cautiously stood and surveyed the place—was flat-moving and peaceful. Most important, there was no concealment for anyone now, no shadows, no darkness, no confusion. Was the Picker gone, too? (In Bobby's mind, it was definite now: there had been someone, and the person was a Picker.) Or was the Picker still sleeping on the pine needles, a ragged shirt pulled up over him for dryness and protection against mosquitoes?

He was gone. Bobby could feel that, too. The new day was clear of menace. Taking up the shotgun, Bobby carefully lowered the hammer back into place, broke the piece, removed the shells, and walked neatly down the rows of vegetables, up the river steps, and back into the kitchen, his mind sleepily remembering.

What if the Picker had really come and found him asleep in the garden, gun all ready and free for the taking and using? Or what if he had come and passed unseeing by as Bobby had planned? Would Bobby have shot him or shot in the air and bluffed him away? Would Bobby have done anything at all? Really? It was yes-no, no-yes. He didn't know that nor know what he would do when it was night again. And what if the Picker came around today asking for work and somehow discovered—it wouldn't take a genius—that

143

there was no one in this house but a bunch of kids keeping a girl tied up in bed? I don't know, Bobby said, I just don't know.

In the living room, he carefully propped the gun up against the side of the fireplace, took the shells out of his pocket and put them on the mantel before sinking down, exhausted. He was still there—sleeping—when Cindy, all tangled and sleep-eyed, came through on her way to the kitchen and her morning treat of Pop-Ups.

"There was somebody here last night," he said when he had waked up a second time.

"Oh?" Cindy's mouth was full, her voice uninterested at first. Then, as all the slow, complicated thoughts that Bobby had had hours ago began to occur to her, she stopped eating, and very, very carefully put her pastry down.

"Who was it?" She was subdued.

And he told her.

6

Freedom Five—all assembled in meeting—heard about the Picker with gravity but no panic. John laid out a first plan: Cindy and Dianne would watch Barbara and the grounds around the house and sound the car horn if they wanted help; Bobby and Paul would come with him and investigate.

They went armed. John carried Dr. Adams' pump-action 20-gauge shotgun; Bobby his .410; and Paul a scope-.22 loaded with shorts. Guns were familiar objects to them. Even twitchy Paul went ducking with his father in the winter. All three kids had fired, and all three had killed small game and a few birds. They were, in fact, a rather formidable little group if their trigger-nervousness be taken into account.

They went down the private Adams road, past the vegetable garden, past the way to John's house, and around the first turn to just beyond the marsh. Generally they were paralleling the bends and turns of Oak Creek until they got to the area they called "the pines." Here the untended woods and wetland ran together in an almost impenetrable thicket of trees and underbrush, each tangled with the other, each fighting for survival, sunshine, and air. Failed trees stood dead, leaning against their neighbors, unable to fall because of the crush, and vines twined up their trunks and spanned their limbs and made green caves to hide in.

At John's wave they fanned out reconnoiter style, but the deception was useless. Dried leaves and brush broke under them and broadcast their movements. Squirrels chattered and ran, sending showers of dried bark clattering down through the dimness. Jays scolded, and little invisible things ran invisibly off to the left and forded marsh pools with small splashes. The boys paused—each alone—peering into the green shadows and seeing anything their minds suggested, but in the end each grayness turned out to be tree and each movement, light on the foliage. At length John yelled from on the right.

"Found it!"

"What?" (Two separated voices)

"Over here . . . !"

What there was to find was a charred campfire. It had been built in a hole, hand-scooped out for the purpose, and provided with an underdraft which could be closed with a rock, and it had been neatly covered over afterward; in the straw-dry woods, someone accustomed to living outside had pretty much gone by the book. There was also—Bobby had been right—a rather thick bed of the greener pine needles and branches. Beyond that, there were a few blurred footprints— wide—where the ground had been cleared for the fire, there were a few cigarette butts (not filters), an empty stew can, and a couple of empty beer cans. Nothing more. Freedom Five—except that it was now three— stood in silence and absorbed this.

John bent over and laid his hand on the uncovered ashes. "Can't tell."

Bobby and Paul nodded; together they had all built and extinguished many Freedom Five campfires.

"Well, this is where I saw it, OK," Bobby said.

"Yeah." John straightened up, broke his gun, and unloaded. The others unloaded with him and felt a trifle more naked in the woods, even though they were quite certain they were alone.

"Who do you think it is?"

"Like Bobby said, some Picker."

"But why's he *here?*"

"Drunk, hiding out, fired from the job—how should I know?"

"He was hungry," Bobby said.

"How do you know?"

"The stuff he bought, stew, spaghetti, beer. It fills you up." He kicked over a can. "Nothing left in it, like he used his fingers to get it all." (As an old icing-bowl cleaner, Bobby knew his fellows.)

"If he's hungry, he's looking around." Paul twitched.

Both John and Bobby looked at him somewhat in surprise. Paul was growing snarter. He might be right.

"And if he keeps looking around, he might find us."

"Yeah."

"Well, there's nothing more here," John said. "Don't mess anything up."

"Why not?" Paul said. "Then he'll know someone has found out about him."

"No. Then he'll move somewhere else," Bobby said fast.

"Sure, he'll go away!" Paul writhed.

"Or he'll come up to the house."

"Let's talk about it with Dianne," John said, and they turned back.

Dianne, when she heard about it, narrowed her gray eyes down and said nothing for a minute. In the last five days—counting the Sunday when they had planned Barbara's capture—she had lost a lot of her diffidence and become more assertive in making the plans for all of them and seeing that they were carried out. Her province had expanded until the Adams' now seemed *her* house (Cindy was miffed). All of them, even John, asked her even by just a lift of the eyebrow for approval before making a serious move, and so they waited now.

"What're we going to do if he comes up and asks for food like Bobby said, and then he finds out that there aren't any grown-ups here?"

147

"He *hasn't*, has he?"

"He hasn't been around long. . . ."

"No, but what if he does?"

"Then let me talk to him, and the rest of you hang around. We'll say that Mother's in town, Daddy's at work, and besides we have somebody to do the field-work. Keep one gun up here on this floor, and somebody like John or Bobby to shoot it, and we'll just see." Dianne reached her decision with decision. "Don't worry about it."

"And what if we have to shoot him?" Cindy said brightly.

"Then we'll shoot him," Dianne said.

Freedom Five considered. What she was talking about was killing an adult, not a very important one perhaps (adults varied) but still *doing* it. The idea was not in any way unacceptable except that other grown-ups would find out about it and punish them for it.

"Won't that blow everything?" Bobby said quietly.

"Not if we do it my way."

They nodded. Nonetheless the day had begun on a somber note.

The next problem of the day—it became a crisis—arose with Barbara. Because of the Picker, the children were late in shifting her from bed to walking and taking her to the bathroom: nonetheless she went docilely enough and performed her usual ceremony (ever more brief as she ate less) with such grace as was possible. Only she and Dianne knew exactly what happened next.

While Barbara was washing one-handed, she dropped her washcloth on the floor and being tied, couldn't seem to bend over properly and pick it up again. Dianne went in, bent to get it, and Barbara grabbed her. Strong, elastic swimmer's fingers dug into Dianne's neat hair and seized a handful at the roots. Though only Barbara's right hand was free and then only from the elbow down, all her strength was concentrated there, and it was clear to her and to Dianne that

148

she was never going to let go. The hair strained at the roots with the force of the grip. Moreover, Barbara threw her hip and cracked Dianne's head against the side of the sink for emphasis. Then it was all confused.

Dianne yelled, of course. The sound was one of surprise, sudden pain, and anger but—it was still cool Dianne—not quite panic. Her own hands shot above her head and engaged Barbara. Then she was hipped against the sink again, and her eyes momentarily lost clear focus.

The rest of Freedom Five came banging into the bathroom, wide-eyed and thoughtless, and there was instant battle. Barbara seemed determined to never, never let go, and even hobbled, resisted their tries at getting her fingers loose. Dianne hurt, and she continually made just exactly that noise as she tried to get up from her knees where Barbara had her forced. In the tumble of bodies, naked and clothed, nothing was clear except the central issue of Barbara-must-let-go-or-Dianne-will-be-hurt, versus Barbara-must-hold-on-and-hurt-Dianne. They swayed and twisted; Paul was pushed across the edge of the empty bathtub and fell in it; Cindy fled; Bobby got his hands tangled up with Dianne's and Barbara's. Only John could solve it and only his way.

He doubled his fist and, in contradiction to all his upbringing, hit Barbara on the face. His blow aimed at the chin went high and struck her just in front of the ear, but it was delivered with such sincerity that she, in turn, lost focus, and her hand in response released Dianne and tried to reach up to the hurt, and then John hit her again. There was no one to catch her. Hobbled, she could not step back and so fell against the wall and slid down sideward, spinning the roll of toilet paper out in a stream as she did so. Then everything was changed again.

In the succeeding tableau—it was a half second later—Dianne was sitting, crying, on the tile floor, her head in her hands, face out of sight. Barbara, bound as ever, lay twisted and half out of sight behind the toilet, and John, now the frantic one, was grotesquely trying

149

to get at her and rip the tape from her mouth. She mustn't cry or she might suffocate behind her gag. Finally everything subsided.

Dianne, crying, got slowly up and stumbled blindly from the bathroom, down the hall, into the living room, and threw herself onto the couch, still cradling her face in her hands. For some time she remained there, her tears gradually slowing, her control returning. In the bathroom itself, Barbara lay in a fettered S on the floor, her face white, her cheek against the cold tiles. Paul followed Dianne and stood over her in helpless spasm; Cindy stood timidly behind him while John and Bobby watched over the prisoner. More minutes passed.

When Barbara's eyes showed clear and intelligent again, John and Bobby dragged her feet first, breasts down against the floor, to a space where they could get at her. Rolling her over, they took the free hand and tied it back to the other behind her. She said things like "Don't—" and "Please— " and "It hurts—" and all they got out of it was that she was OK now. Afterward, they regagged her and doubled the tape over her mouth. The rebellion was over for the time.

Barbara's brief night view of Bobby with his outsized shotgun (or so it seemed to her), his boy's face frightened and determined all at once, the silence that followed when he abandoned his post in the house and slipped outside, all produced in her a new degree of desperation. She would *not* be passed on by captors to a new captor, winners to new winner. A possible escape plan she had formed much earlier came back to mind.

Because the children were not getting more careless with her but only more expert, she could expect only less and less possible freedom as time went by. Already an opportunity to put her idea to work had slipped by her because things had not been serious enough, because she was too squeamish. Because, because, because. But I have to now, Barbara said.

It had begun as a simple if desperate proposition. During a moment when she had even partial movement of one hand, she would grab one of the children and hold on until the rest of them let *her* go. Since with the chloroform and by weight of number they could easily thwart this, she shifted to a variation. With the momentarily free hand she would *hurt* one of the children. This would eventually cause adult investigation, and investigation would lead to her rescue hence release.

She could easily have conned Cindy the night before last, but she had not wanted to hurt *that* child—who would? Barbara's sense of nicety would not permit it. Moreover there was no sense in trying to catch Bobby; he not only went by the book; he had written it. He stayed carefully out of reach. That left the outsiders—John, Dianne, and Paul. She would send her message to the outside via a black eye, a split scalp, or a swollen nose. She was, after all, a competitive swimmer, someone who tried things.

Since John was too strong, and Paul was, too—well, if she failed, he might just kill her on the spot—she centered on Dianne. Mornings offered Barbara's greatest moments of freedom; she was on her feet, at least the lower part of one arm was free; the space in the bathroom was confined enough to make attack possible; and who else was there? Only proper and sometimes helpful Dianne. Moreover the thin girl was the most responsible member of the group; if she failed to go home, or went home badly banged up, inquiry was sure to follow. Yesterday, in the morning, Barbara had even done a little private rehearsal; she was sure she could *get* Dianne.

That certain delicateness that pervaded and marked Barbara's character, however, had so far prevented her from doing more than planning. Everyone was susceptible to love and charity, and the kids could be counted on to come through, couldn't they? She could see it to the end this way, couldn't she? Violence wasn't necessary, was it? So much for yesterday's generously liberal thoughts. Having been knife-scratched by a thir-

151

teen-year-old, raped by one not four full years' older, and threatened by the presence of an unknown prowler, however, she reversed herself. *Now,* lady.

In the morning next, then, she had dropped her washcloth and felt her whole system go on double time. Argument and argument came together: I must do it versus I can't do it. Then Dianne was bending beside her and then her own hand—it hardly seemed hers—was swinging out.

Once she had sunk her fingers into that neat hair of Dianne's—Barbara had to content herself with the first grip whatever it was—she knew that she had at least enough determination never to let go. When it came to hurting Dianne *enough,* however, she held back as she had been afraid that she would. Mentally she gave the command and momentarily the advantage was hers. A real swimmer's smash of the hips banging Dianne's head and face against the wash basin would have been the end of the game: if not, the next smash would have been. Even as she moved, however, she held back; being Barbara, she somehow hoped a *little bit* would do it. She thumped Dianne a good one, of course, but it was delivered with a mercy not returned; Dianne was not made of so tender a stuff as Barbara thought; and then the moment of opportunity passed, and the struggle was in progress.

Barbara never truly saw John's first blow coming save as a blur in the corner of her eye, but even with the bright green and white flashes that followed the explosion at her temple, she somehow froze him in memory. He, too, was made of harder stuff and would not hesitate to kill her, and then he hit her again, and she was falling. She had underrated them all.

When she went down, it was in a daze. Releasing Dianne too late and throwing her free lower right arm out too late, she struck the tiled floor unprotected, and then coldness rushed up to meet her face and hurt it.

For some time, it remained that way. She vaguely heard crying and voices, dimly felt things being done to her, but she was somehow anesthetized. There was a dizzy fog between the essential inside Barbara and outside Barbara. She was gratefully numbed. She would have liked to remain so, but pain and consciousness relentlessly returned.

She opened her eyes and found herself still on the bathroom floor, both hands tied again and her feet no longer just hobbled, but bound tightly together ankle-and-ankle. Her mouth was again stuffed with lumpy, damp cloth, and her lips were heavily covered with tape. Little dazzling shock waves of hurt—injured wrist, thudding head—went across her consciousness. Above her, on the other side of this flickering return to waking, John and Bobby stared down at her. Even though they came and went from focus, she knew they were white-faced and breathing hard, too. She turned her face down against the cool ceramic floor and made a sound of heartbreak.

She hadn't had it in her.

The pain at the point where Dianne's head had struck the sink, lessened and left in its place only a headache and slight swelling. When this became apparent to her, she was reassured and calm again, almost supernaturally calm. Drying her eyes, she got up from the sofa, went into the kitchen, opened the freezer, took ice cubes from the automatic ice-maker, crushed them in the ice-crusher in Dr. Adams' bar, wrapped them in a towel, wet it, and put it to her forehead. Her movements were as assured and positive as those of the various machines she employed. The rest of Freedom Five followed and stood milling around, watching her anxiously.

Although Dianne had not been knocked unconscious, there had been a moment when all time to that instant had stopped and then resumed. There was a short, blank space in her life. On one side of this interruption matters had appeared one way, and now on the other side, they appeared quite different.

For one thing, the faces of the other kids were altered, they seemed younger and less certain than before. Paul was trembling, Bobby was deeply shook, Cindy was silent and submissive, and even John on whom she depended, was uncertain and silent. About the four of them hung a common aura; they were waiting for her to speak.

It suddenly occurred to Dianne that they were waiting for her to speak.

The first thing she said—she knew it—would be jumped upon, acted upon regardless of what it was. It would seem a command, and it would be carried out. Freedom Five, disturbed and directionless for the last few minutes, had become hers to direct entirely. She felt full authority—it took but the thousandth part of a second—pass into her hands.

Still standing, still silent, still not more than a breath later, Dianne felt a slow, exquisitely sweet sense of freedom engulf her. She took the iced cloth from her head, dumped it out in the sink, wrung it out, and hung it to dry over the swing faucet. She surveyed the kitchen and found it neat enough.

"What're we going to do, now?"

"Take her downstairs," Dianne said.

The present Adams house had been begun when Cindy was six—four years ago—and in those seemingly ancient times, they had all lived in the tenant house in the field. They had driven down from Baltimore on Friday nights, stopping to let the children eat at Howard Johnson's and arriving at the farm fairly late. Black night or not, the first thing Dr. Adams always did was walk up the ridge along the river and see what the contractors had done since he had last been there: the house was his artwork of the moment. Cindy remembered it all quite clearly.

First came the bulldozers ripping out a long deep trench just behind the rise overlooking the water. Then came the cement trucks and block-layers building a fort. Afterward the machines came back and graded the earth up to the top on the outside. On top of this sunken, dark place, the weathered siding house was

154

slowly built, and though it had come first, the basement had never been entirely finished. Dr. Adams had specified that the contractor leave him a toy of his own.

To reach the basement, you went down one flight of stairs set to the southwest end of the hall that ran the landward length of the building. Once down, you turned left to three choices. To the left was the utility and laundry room: ahead was the storage area: to the right was Dr. Adams' recreation room-to-be. By plan, this room was to serve for about five years as his shop, and so it had. A surgeon specializing in the problems of the wealthy, the doctor had as well a carpenter's flair about him. It was here that he cut, shaped, mortised and glued up the shelves and odds and ends of furniture intended for the upstairs. Here repairs were made; here Christmas presents were built; here Bobby tinkered on rainy days; here the guns and yard things were stored; here—in short—everything rough was done.

At the end of five years, the room was to be converted into a special sort of room Dr. Adams was still creating. So far, in his spare time, he had begun to convert exposed overhead joists into imagined ship's beams with knees and ringbolts and painted-in scarfs, had begun to experiment with barn siding for walls and decks. When finished, it would probably look like an expensive restaurant without tables, the sort of thing the *Washington Post* would someday run in its Style section on Sunday. For now, however, it was semicomfortable chaos, a place of tools and spades and camping and boating gear, piled-up lumber, and barbecue grills (there were *two*).

Cindy had never like the room. The smell of paint and wood and tar and cement did nothing for her at all. With feminine disdain she never went in unless it was to ask a favor or get a toy of her own fixed by Bobby or Daddy. There was too much dead there—unused furniture, rusty equipment, dust, and a kind of wet feeling—and it reminded her of the deep pit of the well when it was open and the men were fixing the motor or something. Nonetheless, when Dianne spoke,

155

Cindy immediately understood the appropriateness; it *was* a little bit like a torture chamber.

If Freedom Five had been cautious about handling Barbara at first, then more confident, now they were rough and vengeful. She had startled them, attacked them even—they almost understood what she had intended—and she had frightened them, the most unforgivable thing of all. They reacted like a person who has bumped into a piece of furniture and then turns and kicks the offending chair or table to teach it.

Half lifting, half dragging her, they got Barbara into the hallway and pulled her to her feet. Although she offered—could offer—no resistance, she held herself stiffly and, glancing over her shoulder, made clear enough sounds of pain. They were not inclined to listen, however, even Cindy. Ever since the other night when she had ungagged Barbara only to have her start screaming, she had distrusted her. The scuffle this morning, the fact that Barbara had hurt Dianne, only deepened this. When the others began to carry Barbara downstairs, she wished that she was big enough to help; she'd bump her into something and *show* her.

"Watch it now—You still got her?" John and Dianne carried her by the upper arms, one to each side.

"Yeah. *Watch* it, Paul! Yeah, we're OK." Breathing hard and moving awkwardly, Bobby and Paul backed down the stairs, their hands locked beneath her knees.

"Not so fast—"

"I can't hold on—"

"Just don't let go *here*."

"There's not enough room for me to turn."

"Get *out* of the way, Cindy!"

Bumping and staggering, they slowly descended the stairs to the basement where they put Barbara down on the last step while Bobby opened the door of the recreation room and turned on the bare bulb over the work bench. Barbara leaned over and tried to rest her head against John's leg, but he pushed her away.

"OK, let's go." Moving more easily with level

footing, they carried her into the shop and put her down—hard—on the concrete floor. There was time-out for a puff.

"What're we going to do now?" Although he was outwardly quiet, Paul appeared nearly spastic with restrained excitement. His eyes darted back and forth with guilty, squirming pleasure.

They considered.

It was stuffy in the basement: the air conditioning did not reach here. John pulled the tail of his T-shirt up and wiped his eyes. Bobby looked uncomfortable. They all watched Dianne.

Tilting her head back and looking at the exposed pipes and joists and the heavy "ship's" ringbolts in the finished beams, Dianne said, "Let's hang her up."

"Yeah, that's tough!" Paul did what is known as a jump for joy (rarely seen). "By her thumbs!"

"Ah, you can't do that," John said.

"Why?"

"That's only like you read—"

"You'd pull her thumbs out of the sockets," Bobby said learnedly.

Barbara struggled to sit up, making noises through her nose.

"Just by the arms," Dianne said. "That hurts enough."

"Boy!"

The complicated maneuver meant another fight, however. They had to move her again—under the heavy, iron rings—and knowing what was coming, Barbara kicked out and sent the two smaller boys falling. Eventually it took even Cindy to help move her the eight or ten feet required.

"She's too tall," John said.

"What do you mean?"

"By the time you get her reaching all the way over her head, she could touch the pipe. Anyway it might not take her weight."

They hadn't thought about this, but it was clearly so.

"I know!"—Paul's moment had come (it was clear). "Leave her hands behind her like they are and pull *them* up!"

"It'll work," Dianne said slowly.

This was something that Freedom Five had not tried upon itself. It would be interesting.

Barbara's wrists and elbows (still tied together) were released from her body and rebound behind her. John ran a rope from her wrists up over the pipe and down again. He pulled and wrenched her arms up backward and her body down forward. Convinced that she must stand or have her shoulders twisted around and out of their sockets, Barbara allowed herself to be brought to her feet, and John pulled some more. It was no effort at all. To avoid pain, her heels cleared the cement, and she went up on tiptoe: the tendons behind her knees were sharply shadowed, and the muscles in her calves stood out. Her breasts hung, and her head (now) hidden by tousled hair pitched forward. John tied the rope off to a supporting column, and Freedom Five took a second breather.

In the some minutes of wrestling, Barbara's nakedness had lost all its novelty for Bobby and Cindy and much of its excitement for the others. Up to this instant, the morning had proved the prisoner to be a burden, a danger, an opponent, a spur to guilt and anxiety, but never the object of erotic attention. Now, however, forced, twisted, bound, and motionless except for a slight shifting of weight to somehow ease the agony, she became to them—still again—altogether astonishing.

"We did it." Paul could not believe it. "We really did."

Cindy looked at him and understood what he meant. Indeed, she felt that everybody did. It was the game for real. The game played so many times in imagination and so, innocence, had come true. What Paul had said went for them all, and there was a sense of deep complicity and commitment in the basement. They all knew that in "the game," there were other

158

things that could be done. It was suddenly a little scary—at least, Cindy thought so—and she didn't reply or say any other word.

"Well, what did you expect? That we couldn't, or something?" John bluffed a casualness that Cindy saw as false. He was nervous and not nervous, looking and not looking at Barbara's white, smooth, rounded behind.

Dianne alone acted. Standing in front of the captive, she reached out beneath the bent body and took the older girl's breast in her fingers and with deliberate coolness squeezed and twisted it as hard and as far as she could.

It is possible to feel someone else being hurt, and Cindy experienced it now. Barbara's flesh was soft and grotesquely distorted, and the hand was hard and thin and white-knuckled. Moreover Cindy heard it; the prisoner exploded in futile writhing and noises and was allowed to continue so for some seconds. Eventually Dianne released the breast, took Barbara's head up by the hair, and slapped her across the face just one hard time. Then the obscene moment was over.

Dianne did not dignify her actions by a single word.

Barbara's knees bent, and for a moment she seemed in danger of tearing out her own shoulder sockets with her own weight. She made the same old sounds of being hurt and all that. Then the greater pain took charge, and she stood on toe, legs stiffened once again.

It unnerved Cindy, the whole thing did. It imposed complicated thoughts and emotions and responsibilities she had no wish to have. She felt her face becoming hot as it did when she was about to go into a total-despair crying time. It was all bad. And Barbara was bad to have caused it all, and Dianne was right. With something akin to sudden, hot abandon, Cindy drew back a puny fist and hit Barbara, and then Dianne caught her arm and stopped her.

"No!"

Cindy understood. She had stepped into something personal.

"She didn't do anything to you," Dianne said, "and don't you hurt her—yet." She relented and patted Cindy. "But you were good. You helped."

Cindy looked up, still faltering angry, and saw that Dianne's face was not its cool, always right shape. Still, she did what she would not have done for her parents or Bobby or anyone else alive. She nodded and left the room with hands clenched. But she knew what was going to happen anyway.

"Listen!"

Because they had been in the basement for some time, the children hadn't heard the truck until it was nearly at the house. Within seconds after they identified the sound of the engine, it was there, an emergency brake ratcheted, a horn tooted—after the days of silence it was oddly cheerful—and a truck door slammed. There would be no footsteps immediately because the path around the house was of deep, loose, sun-baked sand and dust. Freedom Five stopped breathing all at once, and all for the same second's time. One by one, they looked up as if trying to see through the solid floor and walls above them. Cindy clapped her hand over her mouth.

Barbara's head—to the extent that she could move it—inclined with the children's. She tried to twist around, making startlingly loud (to them) noises through her nose. The unspoken words were plain to the hearers—*help me*. Instinctively John jumped forward and curved his hand under her taped mouth and close up under her nose. The sound all but ceased as Barbara began to suffocate. She reared hopelessly in tether.

"Will you shut *up?*"

"She'd better!" Dianne's whisper was as sharp as a .22 shot. "Go up and get into your bathing suits and come out into the kitchen." She was looking at Bobby and Paul.

"Bathing suits?"

160

"Hurry *up!*"

Now, at last, there was a thudding outside on the kitchen stairs and a knocking—nearly a pounding—at the river (kitchen) door. A grown-up was here.

"Come on!" Less rattled and more commanding each second, Dianne grabbed Cindy and went up the stairs first, two at a time. "Just a minute!" she yelled from the top. Then, stopping at the bathroom, she pulled Cindy inside and turned on the shower.

More knocking.

"Coming!"

Dianne was exasperated, trembling, but still in command. "You stay in here and *leave* the shower running. You understand? Leave it *be*. And if I say anything through the door, just yell back yes or no and try and act like Barbara. You got it?" She shut the door apparently not reassured by the child's look of bewilderment.

"Coming!" Almost trotting down the hall now, she saw from the first window that it was Tillman's delivery truck. Half a minute later, she was into and across the kitchen and opening the door for Mr. Tillman, who stood on the outside steps holding one brown bag and balancing another on his knee while he banged at the screen.

"I'm sorry. Come in."

"Thanks, Dee-Dee." He came awkwardly past her, a pungent mass of sweaty male skin, and put the bags down on the counter with a thud. Pulling a damp handkerchief from his pocket, he sponged off the back of his neck beneath the collar, his forehead, and face. Refolding the cloth to find a dry spot, he finished by mopping under his chin. "Man, it's really *right* out there today, I'll tell you." He pronounced right as "ruoigut" in the Eastern Shore manner. "What're you doing here today? Visiting? Where's the girl who ordered the groceries?" He hesitated over whether to call Barbara girl or woman.

"Bar-*bra!*" Dianne turned and shouted through the house. "Did you order any groceries from Mr. Tillman?" After a moment's silence, she turned. "She's in the bathroom." Here Dianne was a trifle private. "I guess she can't hear me."

"Oh, she ordered them all right. All she has to do now is sign."

"OK, I'll get her. Wait a minute. . . ."

"Better not wait too long. Them frozen things half melted already. Mind if I have a glass of water?"

"Sure!" From the door Dianne whirled around and came back. "Here's a glass"—she handed him one from the cupboard—"and ice water." She opened the refrigerator and put a tall green bottle on the counter. "Help yourself."

"Lord, honey, I don't need anything that fancy," he laughed.

"Might as well. That's what *they* do." She left, calling ahead of her, "Bar-*bra!*"

"Hunhh?" In spite of the running shower, the voice from inside the bathroom sounded frighteningly like Cindy's.

"Mr. Tillman's here with some gróceries. . . ."

"Sign for 'em, like Mommy does!"

Oh! Dianne could have killed her. No baby-sitter would have said that, but it was out now, and maybe Mr. Tillman hadn't heard. Making sure her own voice was loud enough to carry, Dianne yelled, "OK," and went back to the kitchen. "She said sign for it, and is everything there?"

Tillman had drained his glass and was standing in front of the air conditioner. Now he turned back, took a moist slip out of the bag nearest and frowned. "Well, we were out of some of the frozen dinners she wanted, but knowing the kids, I stuck a couple of fried chickens in for the turkey platters. Course now, she don't have to take 'em, only thing is, I don't know when the man's coming back with the turkeys because his truck's broke down to Bryce, and I figured I'd bring enough to eat anyhow." He showed her the delivery slip.

Dianne studied it.

"I guess so. I don't know—wait a sec." Dianne

took the slip and made another round trip to the bathroom. This time she returned with a signature and Cindy in tow. "She said it's OK, and thank you."

"We're going swimming!" Cindy, queen of the county so far as Mr. Tillman was concerned, ran up and gave him a hug around the waist. It was a natural, accidental, and inspired move. Mr. Tillman was fully, cheerfully distracted.

"Oh, you are, are you?"

"Soon as Barbara takes us." She looked up and gave him a crystal-bright smile.

Dianne sighed and forgave. Then Paul and Bobby came through the kitchen in bathing suits, their faces absolutely blank. They might have been going to the dentist's.

"No swimming until Barbara gets there," Dianne said.

"What?" Unprepared glances back and forth.

"That's what she said, and use the towels off the back line so she doesn't have to wash every day."

"OK." They stumbled out and down the back stairs. Once clear of the house, they broke into what Dianne could tell was a terrified run, but she supposed it could be taken as one of joy. Maybe.

Tillman looked after them. "Nothing better to do'n swim." He was silent long enough to have possibly remembered his own earlier days on that same river. "Nice place Dr. Adams built here. Cool."

Dianne nodded.

"Safe and peaceful, too. Great place to raise kids."

"Well, what *about* tonight?" John flopped over on his stomach in the fine gray sand. At his feet riplets no higher than half an inch fell fountain-soft on the minia-ture river beach.

Around him in various positions of after-swim re-pose, Freedom Five—except for Paul, who was on guard—lounged in the shade. Their nervous fits of giggling, their recollections of how scared they had been at various points of the day finally over, they con-

163

sidered what might come next. Though—it was just four o'clock—the sun was high and darkness distant, still the shadows which had shrunk all morning were now reversed and getting longer again. It was possible that a day of alarms could become a night of alarms.

"Well—" Bobby drew idly with his finger in the sand. "I mean about the Picker."

"What about him?"

"Well, like last night when I saw the fire, everything up here was quiet. Like everybody was asleep. So what if he's really hungry or something tonight, and he comes up here looking for something to steal? What if he comes to the door or looks in the window? It's just the two of us. We're alone."

Cindy—the other part of "we"—was not yet visibly alarmed, but she was clearly thinking about it all. With feminine daintiness she had picked what they called a sandspur and was cautiously testing its pointedness against the soft ball of her finger.

Silence.

"I mean, I can't shoot him. I can't really even shoot *at* him." Bobby ceased doodling and looked up. "Shoot a gun around here at night, and everybody in the neighborhood would come running."

"No, they wouldn't."

"They'd ask questions." Dianne agreed with Bobby. Sitting a little apart on her towel, she was—with equal feminine daintiness—plucking petals from a black-eyed Susan: *He loves me, he loves me not.* It was impossible to imagine Dianne using that particular nursery rhyme as accompaniment. Whatever alternative thought she had as she pulled remained her own.

"Keep everything locked up tight."

"Big deal," Bobby said.

"I wish we could shoot him"—John ignored the sarcasm—"even lay a couple of shots over his head in the dark. That'd get him."

They all giggled. The imagined sound of the bullet whine—something TV had made them all feel expert in—the sprinkling of severed twigs from overhead, the

164

sudden scurrying of night animals around the camp-site—amused them. It would be enough surely to make any ill-at-ease, itinerant Picker leave his temporary home and take off through the night, yelling for mercy. The pictured flight was funny. They endlessly invented new plights—falling in the marsh, getting stuck in the briars, stepping on a snake, etc.—that would accompany his flight.

"And then get run over by a car!" Cindy's laugh had a silvery, bright mirth to it.

"Yeah, but that's not what's going to happen." Only Bobby was morose.

"No," Dianne said. "Well, keep all the lights on that you can. No one will notice them out here."

"All night?"

"I wish it was *you* that had to stay here," Bobby said. He took in the whole group. "Alone with her."

"Me?" Cindy was offended.

"No. *Her.*"

"Oh." Agreement.

Talk dropped. It seemed so peaceful by the river that their entire present situation vis-à-vis the world seemed all but imaginary. Tonight they would all eat well and (except for Bobby and Cindy) bask in parental affection and approval. It was difficult—it was nearly impossible—to realize that *this* was what was real and their home lives were now completely irrelevant. They had willed it so.

At length John said, "The creek runs up by where he has his fire. . . ."

"So what?"

"I don't know, I guess—" John cupped his chin in his hand reflectively. "Maybe if I pushed up there in my rowboat, I could keep an eye on him. For a while anyhow."

"What good would that do?" Bobby said.

"Maybe scare him!" Cindy was still on the blood scent.

"Hey, yeah." Bobby looked at his little sister in

165

surprise. "If you could chunk a few big rocks in from behind, he might have something else to think about."

Now it was John's turn to consider the dangers to him*self*. He frowned. He knew well enough the darkness and the bugs and the water sounds and the rattling bushes and the crackling of years of leaves and twigs that could betray anyone in the woods. "Yeah, maybe."

"It might make him mad," Dianne said thoughtfully.

"Or chase him toward the house," Bobby agreed.

"Naw-w-w."

"I wish—"

"What?"

"I wish there was a way to blame it all on him," Dianne said. (*He loves me not.*).

"Blame what all?"

"Oh—her. Everything," Dianne seemed distant.

"Barbara?"

"Umnn."

"You couldn't do that."

"I just said I wished," Dianne tossed the denuded flower aside and snapped off another. "That's all."

"This isn't doing us any good." Bobby—his own problem still came first—sighed.

"Maybe nothing'll happen."

"Yeah. Maybe."

"I got it," John rolled over and sat up brushing the sand fron his chest.

"What?"

"What if we got the guns and all went up there now?"

"Why?"

"Well," John was disappointed at the lack of uptake, "if he was back there, we might scare him off a little. If he wasn't, we could kick the place up a little bit and make it plain somebody'd been up there and found out about him."

"Now?"

"Well, the rest of us've got to go home pretty soon. . . ."

166

Bobby tightened his lips thoughtfully. It was clear he didn't have much enthusiasm for the project.

"Anyhow, if he isn't there, it'd make you feel a little bit better, wouldn't it?"

"Yeah. If he *isn't.*"

"And even if he is."

Bobby picked up a handful of sand and threw it down again. "Aw-w-w, he wouldn't be scared of a bunch of kids like us. You know we wouldn't really shoot him. Even if we wanted to."

"He doesn't know it."

"Sure he does. What'd most likely happen is that he'd take our guns away, and then where'd we be?"

"There's *no way* he can take my gun away." John stood up suddenly.

"It's not yours."

"The one I use then."

"You ought to take Paul, too, if you go," Dianne said mildly.

"Paul?"

"He can shoot. He goes with our father. He *likes* to shoot."

"Yeah. Rabbits." Nonetheless Bobby got up with John, and then the girls. They started slowly up the path to the house, yelling for him.

Early in the afternoon they had lowered Barbara from the joist from which—by then—she was nearly hanging, semiconscious, head and hair pointed at the floor, knees nearly failing, heels flat even though that caused her more pain. She came down as if dead, knees touching the cement first, as in an attitude of prayer, then temple, shoulder, and hips. Her hands were quite bloodless and discolored. Except for averting her face from the concrete, she made little movement and certainly gave them no trouble. At John's insistence, they bound her—faceup—to a dusty picnic bench, and here, still later, Paul found her when it was his turn to guard.

If—this morning excepted—he had waited nearly a full day for his turn with Barbara, Paul was disappointed. The day had taken too much out of her, and she did not revive; actually she lay as if asleep or in a coma. She did little in response to his probings and torments—some of them were quite exotic for a small boy—and what reaction she did give was little more than a short toss of her head and a frown. It was as if he did not exist, and it infuriated him. Wildly he thought of all the things that *might* be done to snap her back in his power. His eyes roved hungrily over the assortment of tools and instruments in the basement, until his legs became weak and he perspired behind the knees. He was still half blindly in this world of imagination when they came downstairs and relieved him. Blinking, twitching, trembling, he followed John and Bobby back upstairs, felt the .22 being put into his hands and felt the cold handful of shells dropped in his pocket.

Outside it had begun to get darker in the west, not from any imminence of evening, but from the sky's daily effort to make rain. The sun, still high enough, began to dim behind a brown-copper haze of airborne dust and moisture, and silhouetted by the lesser light, huge thunderheads slowly boiled up for thousands of feet. As the boys went up the private road through the woods, it began to grow noticeably cooler.

More quickly, now that they knew the way, Freedom Five approached the campsite. This time, however, they marched in loudly and full of bluff, hoping any Picker would take flight before them rather than confront their (useless) guns. Whether or not they were successful, the campsite and pine-needle bed were as deserted as before. This was satisfactory, and it was not satisfactory.

"Well . . . I guess that's it."

"Yeah," Bobby said.

"Well, we've got to go home."

"I know." Troubled, Bobby turned and led the way back toward the road.

Only Paul did not contribute. Bringing up the rear of the file, he walked blindly as if still in his basement trance.

168

7

Again, there was lightning and thunder, and again rain didn't fall. It wanted to, John knew. In the darkness the air was heavy with waiting moisture and heat, but it just could not rise. Instead the thunder remained muffled and confused—everywhere at once—and the lightning was soft and diffused, not sharp and snapping as it should be.

Standing barefoot in his rowboat some distance up Oak Creek from his house, John held onto overhanging branches and tugged himself forward only in the rumbles. The lightning, such as it was, he used to search the water ahead.

A fish jumped, and he froze.

Behind him—he silently gave the signal by hand—the men in the other sampan stopped, too. It was eerie out in the Delta alone. A splash like that *could* be a fish, a rock thrown to draw fire and make him give away their position, or a swimming VC. For a long moment, he remained motionless: his job was to find, make hard contact with and then hold Charlie down. In the morning he would call in air, and afterward there would be a sweep of the area. He savored the thought; maybe they'd use napalm. He looked back during the next dull flare of lightning, and thought he saw the rest of his patrol, faceless, scared nonentities in uniform (he definitely saw war from the management position). He felt contempt for them; they wanted to live, not kill. Well, if they wanted to do the one, they'd

169

have to do the other. He motioned them to follow him. Lightning—pause—move on.

He reached up, trapped a mosquito against his sweaty neck, and smeared it.

Somewhere up in the woods in the darkness was a sentry. If John could get by him, he could get to the house. They had the girl there, torturing her. He had to get close enough to get her out or make sure the information died with her (another great plot). Part of the job. Well, on with it; not far now.

And indeed, this last was somewhat so.

By John's reckoning, he was nearly to the place where the creek was closest to the Picker's little camp. His musings and daydreams, idle if interesting, had brought him this far but faded as he drew nearer. The rest, if there was to be a rest, would have to be done by John Randall, aged sixteen, in person. Even if not done, he was proud of himself so far. Who else would come up here alone at night and do the spying he was doing? He thought about what a good story it would make tomorrow, and pulled on.

As it rose to its nebulous source—a spring-fed marsh half a county away—Oak Creek grew narrower and more choked and snagged with weeds and obstructions. At one point John had to lie flat in the boat and pull himself under a huge fallen tree—appropriately an oak—that spanned the banks. It was a spidery, scary feat.

He eased himself down, feet aft under the stern seat, back flat against the midship's seat. Hands up, he grasped the wet, black, rotting bark and slowly tugged himself and the boat forward. His fingers, expecting grubs or snakes or worse, moved gingerly. Wetness fell in his face. Once, the boat dragged between mud underneath and tree overhead, and he was stuck. Instead of giving way to panic, he rested—alive and well or at least as well as he had been an hour before at home— and thought. Reversing himself, he backed downstream, started again, and slowly wiggled the boat beneath the tree trunk until he saw light again. Compared to the blackness he had been through, the clouded night sky was luminous—surprising. Then the boat was free and upstream in the pool above the tree. He rested. There was slow thunder, lightning, and then thunder again. He stood up.

By daylight John knew the place. You could catch small sunnies here, dig in the mud, and find crayfish living halfway between salt and fresh water: you could build stick bridges out into the water if you were younger and there was nothing else to do with the afternoon. At night you could spook yourself a little bit for the fun of it, and look around.

Holding the bow upstream with his oar, John reoriented. There was a sharp bend ahead with the sand across the middle, the dumping place where the county trucks came down, and the path that went up to the road that ran back to his property. His house was behind his left shoulder; ahead of his right shoulder were "the pines," the clay bank on the Adams side, and—there was the Picker.

John's eyes must have passed back and forth over the same darkened area twice before his glance and a yellow flicker of cloud lightning showed him the figure of a naked man standing about knee-deep in muddy water not thirty yards away on the nearest—it would be the Adams'—shore. The man was bathing—how could John know that?—or he had been bathing. He was, at any rate, looking at John.

The tactical situation was immediately clear and to John's disfavor, not to say humiliation. He had been making noises as he wrestled under the tree. There was no retreat. The Picker was warned; he was five small jumps away; he was on bottom, and John was in a shaky boat with—he could not help but look down—a small pile of rocks he had intended to pitch into the woods and frighten his adversary. How silly. He and the Picker surveyed one another. It was light, and then it was dark; it was noisy, and then it was quiet.

As the silence grew longer and the situation grew more obvious, another fact made itself clear to John.

He accepted it with surprising equanimity: it was almost a given of the problem.

They were enemies. Any two people coming together in such circumstances must fear and hate one another. John considered it normal.

In books and comic strips silences are taken to be intolerable. People blurt out words. This silence, however, turned out to be not only tolerable, but quickly preferable.

Wordlessly the Picker bent down and scooped up a double handful of water and dumped it over his head. Wordlessly John moved his boat out toward midstream, pulling himself along the uncertain branches of the tree and then pushing away. When he was clear, he broke out the oars, and slipping them into the rowlocks, pulled away into the middle of the pool. There, insulated, safe for the moment, he rested and panted with simple emotion.

"Fish?" The Picker spoke softly, no louder than would be required to carry his voice across a room, and yet in the sound of "fish," the *sh* sound seemed to extend itself indefinitely. He had the Pickers' accent.

"Yeah."

The Picker turned and, wading slowly, moved up the bank, and gathered his dark, shapeless clothes around him. Instead of dressing and slinking off into the woods, however, he turned back and squatted comfortably on his heels, hands locked in front of his knees. After a bit there was the flare of a match and afterward the glow of a cigarette. John dipped his oars in the water and held position against the weak current.

John felt disgusted with himself, relieved and frightened all at once. For all his horsing around coming up here, he was now the one at disadvantage. A dozen better alternative plans—fruit of hindsight—came to mind, but then who would have expected the bastard to be wading around naked in the creek in the middle of the night anyhow?

"You ... up the house?" The Picker's calm, deep

172

voice came again. The *se* sound hung in the air menacingly near.

"Yeah—no," John said nervously. "The *other* house."

Silence.

"A lot nice house around here," the Picker said at last. To John the words sounded contemplative, those of the fox regarding the surprising number of chicken coops nearby.

"Nice," the Picker said judiciously. Everything hung; this time it was the *ce* sound. He might have had a black moustache and beard; he seemed to pull his chin thoughtfully. "Quiet."

"Yeah," John said again. This time he began rowing slowly upstream but without show of alarm. At the sand bar above the pool, the boat grounded and John had to step out and pull it upstream into fair water again. He didn't dare look around or appear hurried. Here was where the Picker could simply wade out in three decent steps and get him. (Why? They were enemies—that was enough.) John tugged. Sweat ran down into his eyes. He struggled with panic, and then the boat came across and floated again. Looking up, however, John could not see the Picker, he just simply wasn't there any more. Feeling terribly stupid, John called back into the emptiness, "See ya," and got back in the boat.

Nothing answered. It was scary.

Another fifty or sixty yards up the narrowing stream, he came to a sort of unofficial dumping ground—his own family put their cans and bottles there in a low place—and pulled into the bank. Making fast to a tree limb, he splashed ashore and quickly clambered over to the private road and driveway that ran back down his side of the creek to the Randall house. Once out on the dusty, two-track lane, he turned left and broke into a solid trot swinging his head left and right as he went.

John might feel big and strong around Freedom Five and even around an older girl if she was completely tied up, but in the Picker, he had seen what men are and boys only hope to be. The broad, powerful shape tried against fields and orchards, white where random lightning illuminated it, otherwise only a black voice from the woods, frightened him. The darkness sweated danger simply because he was there, and John wondered if he should tell his father about it. The nearer he got to home, however, the less he thought of the idea.

John was in; John was safe, and he had distracted the Picker a little. He just hoped Bobby wouldn't have to face that man alone.

Like the Adams, the McVeighs were not natives of the Eastern Shore. They had transplanted down from Philadelphia and after almost ten years still looked upon their move from the city as something on the order of Darwin's voyage in the *Beagle,* and life in the country a sophisticate's comic novel. Owning more land than their neighbors, they had acquired a few animals which they carefully named and endowed with imagined personalities; they had a local neighbor who cropped their field along with his own and who, all unknowing, became the folk hero of witty letters back to friends and family. Edna McVeigh still spoke of shopping in Bryce as "going into the village to do a few errands," and she always wore little checked, shirtwaist dresses that struck (to her) just the right note between chic and condescension. Mr. McVeigh often spoke of going to his office (he had been admitted to the local bar) as "going down to the feed store."

As one of their rituals, they drove out after dinner and up to the crossing of the U.S. highway and state road that ran nearby. Getting ice cream there fit the pattern of summer: it relieved monotony and gave them a droll, bucolic sense of adventure.

Dianne, when she went along (it was often beneath her) was allowed to drive the car as far as the state road and, from there, home again on the return trip. After two years of this, the novelty and privilege had worn off. She was a good driver, had learned quickly, and ordinarily had good judgment even when looking at headlights at night.

Tonight, however, she wasn't concentrating on her innocent little drive. Seeing her at the wheel, you would notice her overerect, overstiff. She swerved suddenly at things that weren't even near the road, moved the wheel when it didn't have to be moved, and braked nervous yards before the stop sign. Even later, under the buggy, stinging blue-and-white neon of the malt-stand-drive-in, she only absently ordered ice cream and only absently licked it with a dainty tongue. Instead she looked across the highway and appeared to be studying the slow, lazy heat lightning that silhouetted the trees beyond.

Whether or not leadership of Freedom Five had actually passed to Dianne McVeigh in the morning, she no longer knew. John, after all, was still the larger and stronger. What had passed to her, however, was the heavier thing—responsibility. She had seen *that* in their eyes, all right. No matter what they decided to do, she would have to be the one who said what the orders would be and what they would accomplish. No one else would. No one else could, that is, if there was to be any outcome of the Barbara thing other than letting her go and getting punished.

Dianne welcomed and resented this, welcomed it for the sense of freedom she felt and resented it for what it allowed her to understand of the children. The little ones had always known that they were going to give up and cry or something when it got hard; their appearance of reliability and courage had only been a loan to be called in as soon as the grown-ups' return was near. They hadn't said it, but Dianne saw that this was the way it was going to be and soon, if she didn't think of some other way out. Barbara might be free this time tomorrow night; they might be setting her free right this minute. And John, even John. Now that he was messing around with the girl (Dianne was too re-pelled to watch, but she wondered what it was like between a man and a woman), he too was undependable. He might even be the one to turn chicken first. Sitting ivory-cool and neat in the car with her family, Dianne thought about it.

It was getting trickier. The chances of interference, discovery, Barbara's escape, and their own loss of nerve, went straight up. They had had a fair run of luck for a fair time now. Dianne didn't look at it so analytically, of course, but her sense of wonder at their success and her clear foreboding that they were due for a change, was the constant weather of her mind. The dread end of the game—the dread of each one of them—was hers to carry. And she had the added problem of Paul.

Even regularly, he was erratic, predictable only in his strangeness, explosive, temperamental, and unstable. A clever little built-in baby-sitter for her brother for years, Dianne had learned a few ways to control him. Mother took tranquilizers and sleeping pills as a part of her normal life. By switching capsules for capsules and pills for pills, Dianne had been dosing little brother Paul for a long time now. The older she got, the bolder she got, and Paul withstood it all without effect. Fragile-looking and spastic, he could apparently burn off drugs in half normal time, and with the Barbara episode, he had become worse. He moaned in his sleep, shouted out, and waked up crying until she was sure he would blurt the whole story out. Caught between her responsibility to Freedom Five, her mother's finite supply of sedatives, and Paul's superenergy, she strung him along with hints of what would happen and promises and—when everything else failed—stole another pill and slugged him with it. (Even Bobby ransacked Dr. Adams' things for pills that might work, but there was little to find of any use.) Paul was holding on now only to a faint expectation Dianne had given him, a way out of the game that would be a lot of fun, *his* kind of fun.

It was all enough to make a seventeen-year-old girl just give up, free the prisoner and go forward to judgment, and of course, the alternative had occurred to her. Her punishment would probably be the lightest. She had entered only after they had captured Barbara; she had run the house, kept everyone fed and safe, and so on, and so on. She could make a good case of it. But ... and but. It wasn't what she wanted to do.

The game was right. They had done nothing wrong, not really. To this she clung. Grown-ups and children were on opposite sides; anyone who knew anything knew at least that. One was fair game for the other, and always had been. If there was fairness or loyalty between them, it was the grudging, exasperated affection between opposites ever opposite. Dianne could not—in pride—imagine crying at injustice, nor given the rare circumstance, imagine adults doing less. So out of proper beginnings, fortuitous circumstances, and good managing had come a logical (to her entirely so) situation that must have—sometime, some place—an ending in harmony with the opening. This was an article of faith with her, so much so that she began—she tossed away the dry, uneaten part of her ice-cream cone with the thought—to imagine in detail how they might conclude their little game.

At the state road her father got out and walked around to the passenger's side while Dianne slid over to the wheel. A fair amount was on her mind. The driving of the car was automatic, but at the touch of the wheel again, the movement of the gearshift into "drive," an outside, unbidden thought occurred to her as if someone had spoken it in her ear: "The Adams have a car." There was nothing more, not a clue, not a hint, not a suggestion of utility, just the miracle of the voice. The Adams had a car. She felt struck blind with some kind of wisdom. Barbara could be moved.

Suddenly Dianne wished that the going home, the watching television, and the going to bed were over and done with. She wanted very much to be alone where she could imagine things, *make* things. All at once, she had a "story" in mind.

Perhaps he had heard his name being called even as he slept. It came closer quickly in short, distress whoops. Then there was a white splash of light in his eyes and he was being shaken, pushed, and pummeled by Cindy, her face nearly against his own.

"Bobby, Bobby—there's someone looking in the window! Get up! It's a *man* out there looking in our windows. Bobby, wake up, I *mean* it!" The noise went on and on like a radio at top volume.

Somehow, between sleep and waking and still numb, Bobby knew that what he heard was true. It had been coming since he had seen the light in the marsh last night; it had moved from being one of the possibilities to that of being an absolute future event in his mind. Now Cindy's panic was the proof. They were discovered. And still she shook and pushed him and pulled at the sheet, whether to get him out or make hiding room for herself being unclear. "Bobby, *hurry!* He's here! He's coming," she was crying with fright.

The Picker.

He sat up so suddenly that his forehead hit hers, but neither noticed. "What?" he said though he knew what. "Where? Which window?" He looked—frightened—at his own, which was empty.

"The basement, Barbara, the rec room." All of Cindy's words poured out as one. "You know"—she was in agony—". . . *There!*"

"What kind of man?" Bobby made no move to get out of bed. In spite of the room's heat, he suddenly felt cold and sick.

"A man, that's all."

"Did he see her?"

"How do I know what he saw?"

"Are the doors locked?"

"You find out," Cindy hissed.

"Did you *open* any of them tonight?"

"I dunno—no—yes, I did. One. The kitchen."

"Did you lock it again?"

"No!" Cindy began to really cry now. "No, no. Just get *up!*"

He knew he had to do it, and yet everything inside told him that this was the end. Someone had seen their secret, had looked in the window of the basement, and seen it all—Barbara, the way they had left her, Cindy, the emptiness of the house, the whole works. Now there would be a pounding on the kitchen door, heavy shouts, big footfalls in the living room, pushes and shoves and hits, Barbara free and telling the whole story. "Be quiet," he said, and waited for the end.

"What're you going to do?"

"Just be quiet." He finally threw down the sheet, swung his feet out over the edge of the bed, and sat up. Cindy looked at him, her eyes wet enough but momentarily not crying, her springy hair curled up into spirals around her face, her lips pursed. They waited.

In fact, nothing happened, and it was very puzzling to Bobby. What was to happen was not occurring. There was only the sound of the cicadas outside, moths at the window of his room, and the very distant, almost soothing sound of summer thunder. He reached up and turned out the light. He did it slowly, fearfully, almost religiously.

"Don't do that."

"We have to."

"I'm scared—I want to *see*."

"Go hide then. I don't want him to see *us*."

"Hide where?"

"Anywhere."

"I want to stay with you-u-u-u. . . ."

"OK, then, but shut up, will you?" Bobby slowly stood up, testing the quietness of the house with his ears—they felt as if they were sticking out a mile beyond his head. "Get away from me, now. Stop getting in my way." He went to his window and squinted out. Nothing. Then he went out into the hall and looked out the windows there. Nothing.

"What do you see?"

"Shut *up*."

He went into the living room and stood in front of the .410 he had left there. It was far from a warlike

179

move. He felt now that if he took a gun in his hand and an adult really did come in—a *good* adult—it would somehow make their whole crime worse. It had all been well and good to go parading around with shotguns up to this point, but he knew, he just simply *knew,* that he didn't have it in himself to shoot anyone tonight. Particularly somebody who oughtn't be shot. If a grown-up came in and just found Barbara tied up and the two children being good (otherwise, of course), it would be better. There was no reasoning to this; it was just the truth. "Stay here," he told Cindy.

"What're you going to do?"

"Just stay *here.*"

Barefooted, he went out into the kitchen to the river door and looked out the unlatched screen (Cindy). In two lightning flares, everything continued quiet, and he opened the door and looked out, up and down the length of the house. Although he again saw nothing, every bush and tree beyond the immediate yard seemed a threat. He shut the screen, latched it firmly, and shut the inner door behind it. "Turn on all the lights."

"All of them?" Cindy said from the doorway.

"Everything. The television, too."

He turned on the kitchen overhead light, the counter light, and the stove lights. Cindy went from lamp to lamp in the living room, turned on the blank TV, and the little-used front-porch light. Together, they went down the hall from bedroom to bedroom until at last, they met in a bath of illumination.

"Are we safe now?"

"I guess so." In fact, Bobby felt the same as he had last night: the Picker could see in and Bobby could not see out. The difference was that in twenty-four hours he had lost his nerve. No going out there in the vegetable garden tonight—no way. He was on the scared defensive now.

"Well—" Cindy said.

"Don't worry." It was the first time in Bobby's life that he had ever done that thing that adults do so often, hidden his fear from others, but he did it out of

180

compassion. And maybe the lights might work. They sure made daylight out of everything.

"Where're you going?"

"Downstairs, stupid."

"I don't want to go down there anymore." Cindy crossed her hands over her chest. "It's scary."

"Then don't," Bobby turned and began his way down. He had no more enthusiasm for it than Cindy, but he had Barbara—even at the verge of surrender, he was responsible—as his next duty.

"Bobbye-e-e-e." Cindy began to cry again, but quietly.

That was all he needed. He wanted to cry himself. "All right, get in the closet or under the bed. I don't care. I've got to go down."

Torn, Cindy followed him halfway, her eyes looking back up at the fearful house and then down at the horrible basement. Still, step by step, she followed.

The door to the rec room was open as Cindy had left it, and looking at the window, Bobby was reassured to see no one there—no one who could *be* seen, that is. Moreover a glance told him that whoever had peeked in—he didn't doubt Cindy for an instant— would have had to look very carefully to see anything unusual.

Barbara was seated at the end of the picnic bench that had been pulled up against one of the steel poles that held up the first floor. Her wrists and elbows were tied behind the column, and rope was wound around her body, holding it upright against it. Her legs were entirely free and more or less gracefully tucked under the bench, and, of course, her mouth was taped. In this position, she was considerably to the left of the window and luckily turned away from it. Finally, the light which came from a naked bulb over the work bench, was a poor one that put her back and bound hands in shadow.

Hesitantly Bobby walked into the shop and more hesitantly over to the wall beneath the window, which

181

was up at nearly ground level. Cindy wouldn't come in but stood at the door looking cautiously at him.

He turned and imagined himself creeping up to the glass there behind his shoulder. There would be no noise, hence no immediate danger. There would be a quick look inside and just in front—nothing. Then, more carefully, there would be a look left and right. Finally, there would be the sight of someone sitting up on the work counter swinging dirty legs back and forth. The person—the child—would look up for some reason, see the peeker and scream. Afterward all the lights in the house would come on, and it would be time to take off.

Step-by-step deductions of this kind are attributed to people much older than Bobby without being true in any way. It was the same with him. He didn't think this; he *felt* it, felt suddenly safer. Moreover, it *was* the Picker, and he *had* run off; otherwise one of the good neighbors would have come knocking on the door long before. Even so, he reached up and turned out the one light.

"Bobby, that's scary. I don't want to come in. . . ."

"Come in or go somewhere else," he said. "I'm going to shut the door and guard. If you don't want to, OK."

"I'm tired."

"Go to bed then."

She didn't say again that she was too frightened; instead she came in and obediently shut the door behind her. It was black, but after a moment or two when their eyes got accustomed to the dark, there *was* a little light coming down from the window from all the rooms they had illuminated above. It wasn't half-bad once you got used to it, and after a while, they settled down nearly as uncomfortable as their prisoner. Now it was a matter of *listening*.

At the beginning of the fourth night after the fourth day, Barbara had been broken by the children,

182

although—since she was gagged—she could not tell them nor beg to them. The moment had been reached when, after the failed rebellion of the morning, she had been hung up backward by her wrists. If they had just released her then and given her a single moment's comfort, she would have—this was without deceit or trickery—done anything they asked and willingly. She would have waited on them; she would have let them beat her; she would have taken an oath of secrecy to protect them; just please end it all. And it was true, it was true; she thought it, and she believed it. The children, however, had gone through the day without suspecting or caring about it.

Indeed they had left her for the night in a position that Dianne had invented—tied back against the pole, hands and arms behind, standing on one foot with the other bound up behind to her wrists. It was not endurable and could not have lasted except for the ropes which, winding around the supporting column, her leg and body—ropes entirely supervised by Dianne—firmly held her in place. Even fainting, Barbara would have done no more than slump down an inch or two still standing up.

It's too much, it's *too* much, Barbara said. By tomorrow morning she would be in some unimaginable state nearly vegetable. The melodramatic pity with which she repeated this to herself—she could think of nothing else—was not so much due to present discomfort as to the fact that this, too, was added on.

The point of the game as the children had played it among themselves, was to inflict, observe, and experiment with the feelings of helplessness, humiliation, and—occasionally—pain. It was a tentative exploration in at least one of the relationships people have with other people. No one, however, had ever gone four hours let alone four days and nights as it. *Time* was the ingredient they did not understand, or—not understanding—wished to play with now. The *reality* of time.

Dianne understood it.

"Leave her alone now," she had said. Dianne had been angry all day, but now she was cooling: Barbara could almost see her slipping into the calm obedient role she would play when she got home half an hour later. "Leave her just like that. No letting her go or anything just because she makes a little noise. . . ."

"Chicken," John added.

"OK, OK, I won't." Bobby sighed.

"You better not." Paul, whose game with the knife had seemed to very nearly put him over the edge, was writhing beside Bobby.

"I said OK."

"All right then, let's go. We're late." And Barbara had watched them leave. She was broken, and they didn't care. She was broken, and that wasn't the point at all.

Tiredness verging on exhaustion prevented her from speculating specifically on what the true end of the game would be (since even she realized it *must* end). In place of particular ideas, her mind raised up only a general aura of dread. The morning's aborted struggle had polarized her own and the children's position. Yes, they were—to anyone outside of their own circle—a cold and unfeeling little group, and they had progressed almost smoothly, almost naturally, from the idea of capturing Barbara to the execution of the idea and steadily to the abuse of her. Until today, however, the process had been gradual, one in which tormentors and victim alike knew that forbidden things were being done. A wordless but agreed-upon limitation as to what could be done to her lay upon the house.

From the morning's battle on, however, a brutal streak—something beyond idle torment—had emerged in them. She had not believed that they, or anyone else outside of fiction, could actually tie a person's arms up behind her and then enjoy the consequent agony, but yet they had done it to her. She had not believed that just kids—John and Paul—were capable of real ferocity, the one by rape and the other by torture, and yet they had so spent their summer's afternoon with her.

184

She could not have believed that another girl, like Dianne, could condemn her to a night in this position, and yet, of course, Dianne had done so and shown every satisfaction in the act.

They were capable.

Barbara's mind only reluctantly supplied the end of the thought, They were capable of anything now. They might not even know it themselves—in fact, Barbara guessed they did not—but they were capable of doing anything, including killing her. They might not know they could, and she did not know if they would. To that extent, they were all adventuring together.

And still the minutes and the half hours ticked on. Barbara could no longer entertain herself with imagination or even fuzzy speculation—what various people would say or do if they knew of her plight, for example. The faces most easily summoned up—Terry, her mother, Ted, Daddy—all hung mistily unrealized and just beyond her vision, and with the failure of this picture-making, imagining function, she was wholly and finally isolated. Her world shrank until it included only her own, central, anguished, and most selfish self, and the bright, pretty, fleeting ring of children around her.

At dark, before Bobby went to bed, he came down and did a surprising thing: he took pity on her. He came into the cellar room as if fresh from a struggle with his conscience; he appeared guilty. Nonetheless, he untied her left ankle so that she could lower it to the floor and support her weight on both feet. After consideration (and walking around her a couple of times) he untied all the ropes except the ones that held wrists and elbows together behind the pole; then he pulled over the picnic bench to which she had been tied in the afternoon, and allowed her to sit down on it.

Though he retied her body to the pole afterward, he did not do it as tightly and as thoroughly as before. It hurt, of course—everything they did, hurt—but relatively she had more comfort than at any time since she had been taken. She stretched her legs and thought. Though he had been the one to put the chloroform rag

185

over her mouth and so sentence her to this week of misery, it was strangely enough Bobby—uniquely Bobby—who had never intentionally hurt her or shown any indication of doing so. (Even Cindy had hit her a harmless but vindictive little blow this morning.) Moreover, unlike the other two boys, his reaction to her nakedness was one of shyness and aversion; he was always reluctant to touch her even when he had to. If there had been no other difference, this would have made him the most normal of the five to Barbara's way of thinking.

As she watched him, moreover, it also struck her that he was the most tired and afraid in the group. He no longer seemed to like any of this. He didn't seem to like keeping her or hurting her, and he probably didn't like the idea of his parents coming home just three and a half days from now (to her it seemed forever, but to him it would likely seem like tomorrow). Most of all, he obviously did not like the darkness settling around the house outside. For a small boy, he was under considerable strain, and he showed it. When he had finished knotting the ropes and had stood back to check it all, Barbara saw that he was somewhat pale in spite of the constant sun each day, and when he gave the guard to Cindy and left, he looked really weary. Barbara watched him go.

Maybe he had come down here to free her and then could not make himself do it. Maybe she had an ally left in Freedom Five after all. Certainly he was behaving quite differently tonight.

But Bobby. If she couldn't talk to him (he would never ungag her again—her own fault) or use her sex on him as she had tried to do with John, how could she persuade him to let her free? Play sick? Moan and groan a lot?

She had nearly fallen asleep thinking about it— chin down on chest, things beginning to blur—when suddenly, Cindy began screaming almost beside her ear. The child was pointing her arm and screaming at Barbara as if *she* should be the one to do something

186

about something bad, and Barbara—startled—*tried*. She wrenched at her ropes and tried to get up before her waking senses returned and the true situation reimposed itself. Then, obediently, she turned her head as far to the right as she could and looked down Cindy's pointing finger at—did she mean the window? If so, there was nothing to be seen but a square of darkness.

Barbara was both frightened and puzzled. Then the child had taken off in a scuffle of sandals on concrete, her yells ringing up the cellar steps ahead of her.

8

It was late when Freedom Five assembled the next morning; it was also hot, the hottest day of the drought of late summer. When John and Dianne and Paul came out of the tree line along Oak Creek, their faces were shiny with sweat. The dust—it lay on every leaf and pine needle—stuck to their skin. Breaking clear beneath the broiling forenoon sky, they crossed the field, came past the vegetable garden and up to the Adams' kitchen steps in silence. Bobby and Cindy, nearly sleepless and certainly sandy-eyed, were waiting for them.

"Sorry we're late," John said.

"John had to leave his boat up the creek last night."

"He *saw* the Picker."

"He *talked* to him. . . ."

"We had to go up the creek this morning and get the boat," Dianne said.

Bobby and Cindy looked at each other. "He was here last night, *too*," Cindy said defensively.

"Who, the Picker?"

"I *saw* him."

"Cindy says she saw someone looking in the basement window last night," Bobby said. "She woke me up, and I looked around, but I couldn't *see* anything."

"You were scared enough!"

"I was not."

188

"Were too." Cindy stood firm. "You were as scared as I was."

"What window was he looking in?" Dianne said.

"I dunno," Bobby said. "Maybe he looked in all of them, *if* he was here. Cindy thought she saw something when she was guarding."

"Did he see *her?*"

"Barbara? Who knows?"

"Where is she now?"

"Still tied to the pole. She fainted. I had to let her sit down."

"What else?"

"Nothing. We turned the lights on upstairs and off downstairs, but nothing happened. Nobody did anything. At least not yet."

Freedom Five stood silent a moment. They were solemn beyond their ages. John rolled his hand—thumb, forefinger, and palm—over his forehead to remove the sweat. "I guess we better have a meeting."

There was a certain ceremoniousness about the Freedom Five meeting. Perhaps it was caused by little things like the hot weather, their own selfish, sweet-tooth wishes, habit, or the example of adults unconsciously observed, but there was ritual there. Dianne opened the refrigerator and got out the ice—it popped from the automatic ice-maker that was forever full—John and the other kids got out the soft drinks and glasses and put them on the kitchen counter. Then, like the grown-ups they disdained, they poured their own drinks—one, a Cola; one, an orange; and another, a ginger ale. Afterward they went into the living room and sat down formally for a change.

Only Cindy remained herself. She sat down at the piano and began her torturous attack on "The Happy Farmer"—dum, *dum, boom, boom,* dum, *dum,* (mistake), *boom, boom* (begin again)—with complete if temporary concentration.

"OK. Shut up," John said.

"You haven't begun yet." Cindy was offended in *her* house.

"Yes, we have. Now, stop it."

Cindy banged her hands on the keys with a discord effect, but she stopped.

Each member of the five looked at some other member in silence.

"Uh," John said, "I guess we gotta decide some things."

"What?" Bobby said.

"Well, everything." He looked around and received no help. "Well," he began again, "your folks are coming home three days from now. That's one thing. And the Picker—us getting caught—that's two. I saw him last night, I talked to him sort of, and he's big. If he gets the idea to come in here, we can't stop him unless we kill him. And, of course, we've got *her*."

"You mean, let her go," Bobby said. If nothing else he was logical; the mounting up of obstacles meant just one conclusion (which, naturally, would be his release from the responsibilities of jailer).

"Not yet."

"What then?" Cindy was impatient. She continued to sit on the piano bench, hands around one knee, swinging her foot. "I mean, if you're just going to sit around and talk, *say* something."

There was a pause. Outside, the cicadas began another cycle of their endless chant to summer.

"Kill her." Paul squirmed.

The words were blurted out in his usual way, and though he sat normally enough in his chair, he seemed to be crawling around in his own skin like something in a bottle. And they all looked at him. There was enough force in his voice to compel attention.

Beyond the walls of the house, beyond the automatic air conditioners, beyond the fields and the county road and the highway, lay the routine world. There—in the town of Bryce—adults did their own, incomprehensibly dumb things about stores and money and cars and all, and their kids just bumped along behind them, crying or complaining or carrying packages or just suffering it all in silence. The weight of this oppressive world was not in any way forgotten. Kidlike, however, Freedom Five held it a trifle away from them. After all, it wasn't bugging them at this very minute, was it? They were privileged in their own world, weren't they? They could at least think about things, couldn't they?

"Kill her," Paul said again, and this time more pleadingly, "We could kill her."

"And blame it on the Picker," John said.

"You're kidding," Bobby said. If he had been in school where everyone tried to keep up with swinging language, he would have said, "Man, you're putting me on," but in the actuality of emotion, he reverted to more antique slang. "You're kidding."

"No, I'm not. Dianne thought it up last night." John looked at her.

"Would you like to?" It was issued as a rather formal invitation.

"*Kill* her?" Cindy stopped swinging her foot in midair.

"Why not?"

"You know what'll happen to us if she tells. . . ."

"You know what'll happen to us if we kill her," Bobby said.

"I told you. We can blame it on the Picker. We can do it and go free."

This gave Freedom Five genuine pause.

Things were arranged in an extremely simple fashion for their benefit. The Voice said, Do this, or I will beat you. That, in essence, was the sound of their upbringing as they had heard it. Even John and Dianne at their present age still heard the melody: threat as reprisal for disobedience. The actuality of judgment and punishment—and for the oddest reasons—was clear in their minds. What would happen after *this* experience was beyond comprehension. They would not be killed, but then, that was probably the only thing they would be spared.

(In fairness, they had also been tampered with

191

along this line: "Do this because it's so much more fun." They regarded it cynically and had never been conned. Threats worked best; they were simply understood.)

The children also considered the proposition from the disadvantage of guilt. From the beginning, "the game" had been directed toward WHAT WAS NOT ALLOWED. Born in a welter of—nearly smothered by—TV, magazines, comics, and newspapers, they were aware enough that adults continuously killed other adults. It was only *around here*, in this neighborhood, that it was strangely out of fashion, but they were not misled. They played with the idea and liked it.

Everybody liked it—everywhere.

But that kind of play developed in them a stealth and guilt and—now, at the moment of discovery versus execution—excruciating indecision. They fell grave. Because of the sweetness and youthfulness of their faces, a difference and advantage they clubbed their elders with, the gravity had an almost comic effect. Cindy, in fact, giggled.

"We *can't* kill her," Bobby said. Here his tone separated himself and Cindy from the other three.

"Why?" Tears started in Paul's eyes. He was keen on it.

"Well—" Bobby paused. "She's—well, she's a—she's just a kid like us."

"Yeah," Cindy agreed.

And still again, Freedom Five stopped to think. They understood the argument Bobby had made without being able to put it into an articulate statement. Barbara might still be on their side of the war. Grownups killed each other and got beat up in accidents, so OK it was hard to care about a grown-up outside of your own family (and sometimes difficult then). But another one of *them*. . . . It had a strange force; they could identify with themselves or their equals, and not one of them had ever died or been killed that they knew of. It was something new, indeed.

"Aw-w-w, she's old enough to be Cindy's mother."

"Is not!" Cindy was insulted. "She's only twenty."

"*A* mother, then." (Mothers—for purposes of this discussion—had a fairly low cartel.)

"So's Dianne," Bobby said, "and John's old enough to be a father. They'll both be in college like her in a couple of years." He looked around and saw that his point was won. He had made it "serious."

Freedom Five appreciated quietly.

After a minute Dianne said (and she had thought about Bobby's point as if it were something new), "What difference does it make?"

"I dunno. It just does."

"We'd be in the same fix, and we'd have the same trouble if she was Cindy's age. Twice as much trouble. You're not supposed to kill *little* children."

"I'm not that little!"

"Oh, shut up, Cindy."

She did. Her expression showed that it was getting a little scary around here.

The other four were equally wordless, and yet somehow the tension had lifted one degree. *Ethically* speaking, they would never victimize a small child nor—if their play was rehearsal for life—would they think twice about an older person. Barbara was indeterminate. The matter could not be solved on the basis of age. The jury was still out.

"Anyhow," Bobby, ever practical, said, "how would you do it?"

"Any way."

"Ask Paul."

Paul said very little, but he went ashen with the effort of getting it out. More was passing through his mind than could be encapsulated in a single phrase, and he was in a near faint. He said, "Like we always do."

"Oh."

Bobby, who knew Paul, sat back in his chair and let this sink in as far as it would go.

"Oh." Cindy was awed.

John set his jaw.

Dianne never let much emotion show; if you knew her, you would say she had no surface feelings at all (and the deep ones you would grant only out of politeness). She listened to Paul and sat quite still as always, but she was rigid, and underneath the rigidity was a trembling.

"Well, that's what we always played we wanted to do, isn't it?" Paul laid it on them.

Freedom Five heard and sighed. In imagining such a thing, they were not going as far as childhood would allow them to go and remain children any longer, but they were going as far as being *adult* would ever allow them. Simply by considering the thing, they were going as far as dreams and dreams again would take them—certain dreams.

Dreams of. . . .

The philosophical ins-and-outs of one person's taking another person's life—a nicety that seems rarely considered in actual events—was beyond them. The point needs clarification: they could not have *discussed* it. The literature on the subject, the annotated codes of law prescribing the provocations and instances of retribution, the history of the matter—all of history with all its precedents pro and con—were unavailable, unreadable, and incomprehensible to them. They faced the subject anew.

Each person, after all, in his or her ability to create or destroy life is a god of some sort. If a person is born, two other persons (presumably; who knows anymore?) created him; if that person is deliberately killed, at least one other, equally human person did away with him. Being god on a local scale is possible; any child who has ever squashed a mushy caterpillar knows that.

"And we can get away with it," John said. In spite of the air conditioning, he appeared sweaty.

"No way," Bobby said.

"Dianne has it all figured out."

"You're going to get . . . well," Dianne said quickly, "Someone's going to break into the house tomorrow night."

"The Picker," John said.

"How's he going to do that?" Cindy said.

"Shut up."

"And he's going to force Barbara to lock you"—Dianne looked at Bobby and Cindy—"in the closet, so you can't get out. Then he's going to take Barbara out to the tenant house and kill her. Then he's going to run away, and we're going to come over here in the morning and let you out, and you're going to tell us what you remember." She stopped.

"The Picker?" Bobby said.

"That's the way it's going to *look*." John was selling.

"I have to spend the night in a closet?" Cindy was dismayed.

"It's only like playing." Paul twitched.

"I don't want to."

"You want to get a beating instead?"

Cindy said nothing.

"I want another Coke." Bobby got up and walked out into the kitchen, and the others gradually rose and followed him. It *was* hot in the house. When they had all come back and settled down, Bobby looked at Dianne and said, "What you mean is we're going to make up a story about it."

"Right."

"It won't work."

"Listen to it," John said.

"Well"—Dianne seemed to rehearse for a moment—"Well, we use the station wagon to take her down to the tenant house. Then we . . . well, we do whatever we do."

"Kill her."

"Right," Paul said.

"Anyhow that's the easy part," Dianne said. "After we clean up, and it's all over, we come back here and lock you and Cindy in the closet. Sunday morning,

195

when you're not at church, we raise a ruckus, and you get found and tell everybody what I just said."

"Up to getting in the closet," John said. "After that, you don't know *nothing*." (He was deliberately ungrammatical here.)

"That's right, nothing else," Dianne said. "Then somebody goes over in the field and finds the body and calls the police and—" She shrugged.

"It still won't work." Bobby's tone, however, held some reluctant giving way before the idea.

"*You* couldn't have done it; you were locked in the closet." Dianne was reassuring.

"What about you?"

"We were home before it happened."

"Fingerprints."

"Wipe them off. We never used the car."

"Footprints," Bobby said a little desperately.

"Rub them out with weeds."

"Time of death," he said. It was a sophisticated question for a thirteen-year-old-boy; it arose from TV watching and being a doctor's son.

"Yeah," John said.

"It'll be close," Dianne said. "That's where we're just going to have to depend that grown-ups won't suspect us. If we just go home on time and act *completely* natural"—here she looked at Paul—"the folks will never know. They don't know half of anything anyhow."

Bobby sighed an absolutely monumental sigh. He said very simply, "The Picker'll say he didn't do it because he didn't. He'll be somewhere else at the time. Then it'll have to be us."

"Not if we have him up around here doing some work and getting his fingerprints on everything." Dianne had waited for Bobby's top card with her ace. She smiled triumph.

Bobby was overwhelmed. Dianne was really mean. She had a twisted mind. Weakly, feeling the tide against him, he said, "He'll still say he didn't do it."

"They'll pick him up and beat him or whatever

they do." (Dianne had a rather nasty idea about police work.) "And no matter what he says, they won't believe him."

"Why?"

"Who cares what a Picker says?"

"Adults don't believe each other anyway."

"Fingerprints"—Dianne came back at Bobby with his own questions—"time of death. . . ." She let it linger.

"I dunno. . . ."

"You mean you *will?*" Paul said.

"No."

"But you would, if you could get away with it."

"We can't."

"Why?"

"Us." Without prior notice, tears appeared and began quickly running down Bobby's face. "We're just *kids.* Some one'll blow up and start blabbing the first time a grown-up get his hands on him."

"Chicken?" Paul said.

"If they can't make the Picker admit he did it, we won't admit it either," John said. "They'll have to choose between us and him."

"I think we can count on our folks to help," Dianne said judiciously. "If we say we didn't and cry a lot, they'll believe us."

"Paul'll tell."

"Who'd believe him?" John said.

Dianne sat silent.

On this point, there was a curious agreement among the children: Paul was different, quite different. They couldn't be rid of him in any way; they simply made a place for him, cripple though he seemed to be. But he *was* batty.

"No one," Cindy said, and it was true.

Paul jumped up in fury. Whatever else was odd about him, he wasn't stupid. He shouted in refute, "I . . . I . . . I. . . ."

Paul wished to say something that could not be put into words, that much was clear. Had he looked

197

around, he would even have found sympathy; they were all in various stages of self-concern. But he didn't look, and he couldn't speak. Instead, words failing, he lowered his head like a little bull and ran with full self-destruction straight at the living-room wall. He hit with enough force to make a sound that could be heard and fell to the floor, but he did not knock himself out. With that fragile-seeming and yet incredible energy, he appeared slightly "still there."

Freedom Five (or three of them anyhow) were stopped. They had heard of Paul's suicidal head charges, but no one except Dianne had ever seen one. They stared at him absolutely astonished.

Frustrated, hurt, still incapable of telling them what he wished to say, he lay sobbing on the floor. It was a heart-breaking sound, not simply that of a hurt child, but a sound of abandonment, of having been abandoned by whatever supported him.

Dianne jumped up and ran over to him. Dianne usually moved with glacial calm, but this time she flew with a child's movements, abrupt, clumsy, frightened. She rolled Paul over and cradled his head in her lap; she hurt *for* him, it was easy to see. And Paul, when he was not spastic or twitchy, was a normal enough boy. He had pale brown hair that was thin and curly: his eyes were brown and warm. Against the cotton of Dianne's short dress, he looked adorable. And pleading, somehow.

Dianne stroked his head for the bump. "Are you hurt?"

"I . . . I . . . ," he began again and again.

"Paul! Paul, listen to me. Hush now."

"I . . . what?"

"Paul, *you* can do it."

"What?"

"Kill her."

"Me?"

"Kill her," Dianne said. "Just like we said."

Paul was somewhat pacified. He slowed his crying.

198

"You can tell us what to do, and do it first. You understand me?"

"I can?" A clarifying light thinned the color of his eyes to amber—amber like that of a cat's.

Dianne looked up at the other three. She had asked for very little in her life and didn't know how. "He *can* be first, can't he?" she said. "It isn't fair, but he'd like it—"

"I . . . I . . . ."

"Be first at *what?*" Cindy said.

"Be first—kill her." Paul was still somewhat incoherent. He rolled over on his side and pressed his face against his thin sister's stomach as if he wanted to crawl into her womb. His legs curled up in the foetal position, he looked like something waiting to be born.

"He *can,* can't he?"

"Wait a minute," Bobby said. "We were having a meeting about it. We never voted. We never decided anything—"

John had to acknowledge this true, though it seemed to annoy him. "OK then, we'll vote. For killing her, who?"

"Me." Paul (well who else?).

"Me." Dianne.

"Me," John got in.

"Oh—I guess so." Cindy.

"No." Bobby. He had stopped crying, but he was still dismayed.

"Well, you wanted the vote."

"It isn't fair!"

"What isn't?"

"*I'm* the only one who doesn't want to—"

"That's what voting is for."

"—and I have to do something stupid just because you don't have the sense to see it. We're going to get caught. I'm telling you, they'll find out."

"The vote!"

"Wait a minute," Dianne said coolly. "We can go through the first part—get ready—and then if it doesn't look OK, we can stop. We can always let her go, even at the last minute."

"No hurting her until then?"

"Of course not."

"We're not crazy, you know."

Bobby was not satisfied with the meeting at all, but they had voted fair and square, and they meant to do what they said, if they could. That sort of brought it down to the inside thing, the last question.

"Well," he said. "OK." He needed time to think.

The rest of the morning was somber even by Freedom Five standards. Paul was persuaded to lie down and rest for a while, to give up his first swim of the day. No more than any other kid did he willingly take naps while the sun was still shining, but this time he relented.

"If you go home hurt or cranky, Mother's going to wonder why," Dianne said.

"You could mess up everything," John said.

"For yourself, too. . . ."

Even Cindy, the slightest unselfish trace coming out in her, put a soft little hand on his head. "We can play and swim after lunch," she said. "I'll go with you. If you want to. We can build bridges and stuff."

Bobby nodded, and Paul reluctantly shut his eyes. He was obviously in some lingering state of upset— pale, trembly, perspiry—but he tried to obey, and they left him.

Even at the beach, however, the mood did not lighten. It was terrifically hot: the water felt like luke-warm mud, and the sand flies with avenging appetite drove them down from place to place.

"It's really going to do it this afternoon," John said.

"Rain?" Bobby said.

"Squall."

"Yeah," Cindy said.

"What do you know about it?"

"I *know* . . . !"

"Yeah, it is."

"Are we really going to do it?" Bobby said after a bit.

"What?"

"You *know*. Kill her."

John sighed. They were sitting on the half-mud, half-sand bottom, about shoulder-deep in the water to keep away the flies. He picked up a cupped handful of water and let it dribble through his fingers. "I guess so," he said. "Dianne's got it figured out pretty well."

"Why?"

"I dunno." The fact that John said he did not know the reason in no way seemed to undermine his determination to go ahead and do it.

"Do we have to? I mean, what if we went up there now and told her she had to promise not to tell or she was going to get killed?"

"She'd promise."

"She'd fib!" Cindy said.

"Shut up."

"I don't have to. It's *my* house as much as yours."

"You ought to stop picking on her," John said gently. "She's got smarts, too. She's right. Barbara'd tell, anyhow."

"Yeah," Bobby conceded. "So we get a whipping, and it's all over. It's not going to kill us. We had our fun."

"That's not the point," John said.

"What is then? I mean, we proved we could tie her up and do anything we wanted to her. We've already proved we can kill her. All you have to do is go up there and get my .22 and—blowie!—she's dead. What's the sense of going to jail the rest of your life for it? What good is she, dead?"

John was in no way a Catholic, but he said, "If you don't feel it yourself, I can't tell you."

The antique argument was fairly effective with Bobby; it was also unassailable, but he tried. "So, tell me."

"You remember how we used to play when we were younger?"

It had been kind of neat then, Bobby remembered, but now that they were talking about real life, it was too gruesome to repeat. "Yeah, I remember," he said quickly.

"Like when we cut off the guy's fingers so he couldn't climb out of the well?"

"I *said* I remembered."

"Well?"

"Well, nothing. That was only playing."

"So's going out for football after school; only Namath made 400-grand for signing with the Jets. So's grinding out the grades; only some guys get sent around the world with scholarships for it. Free."

"I . . . ," Bobby struggled. "I guess that was fun, and this isn't. I didn't really mean it about killing people."

"I didn't either," John said. "It's funny."

"What?"

"Well I mean, I mean it *now.*"

"Will you just say *why?*"

"Killing—is—what—one—person—does—to—another—person—who—can't—help—himself." For John, this commonplace verged on profundity. His face grew stern with the effort of it.

"It isn't," Bobby said.

"Well"—John gave an annoyed shrug—"Maybe only when you're not going to be caught at it."

"Even still, it isn't that way."

"Then why does it happen all the time? Every time somebody gets the chance?"

"It doesn't. Not *all* the time." Nonetheless Bobby was swayed, bent by obvious fact, left without an answer that he could easily express. What was in the corner of his mind was the general argument, "We all ought to try and not do it," or something of the sort, but it was a dumb chicken thing to say because nobody but him wanted to try anyhow. In the—to him—avalanche of Freedom Five opinion, he could only say, "Anyway, I don't want to kill her."

"You don't have to. Paul will. Or Dianne. Or me, if I have to."

"Or me!" Cindy said brightly. She was becoming more savage as time went on.

"You better not!"

"I'll do what I like."

"Leave her alone. . . ."

"And I don't even want to watch."

"You don't have to. Go up and put your head under the pillows all day if you want to."

"Then what *do* I have to do."

"Stand your guard. Shut up. Or it'll be you instead of her. You can't get away from *us*."

Well, that was true enough. Bobby could not get away from John. They were sitting not two feet apart in the water. In such a tone does society speak.

Bobby sighed. A tear came down one cheek, and he clumsily washed it away with river water.

"Oh, cut it out for godsakes," John said. "It's going to come out all right."

"Yeah. Don't be a cry baby," Cindy said.

At that point Dianne appeared above them at the top of the bank. "Let's eat." She was as neat as ever but rather prettier and more animated than usual. "We have to clean up the house and get ready, and then we have to take her to the bathroom."

"What for?" Cindy said. "She hasn't eaten since Wednesday."

"To make sure she's purged," Dianne said.

When the kids were late, and when, after they arrived, they did not come down, and when she heard the muffled sounds of voices coming through the floor at the other end of the house, Barbara assumed that it was a meeting. The occasional formality of the kids when dealing as Freedom Five had not escaped her. But about what? A very strange tingling—was it so prosaic a thing as hope?—began inside.

203

Was it about the person, the man who, they thought, had looked in the window last night, the one who had been prowling around the woods the last couple of days? (His existence in her mind was absolute enough.) Was it about the Adams coming home? Something new? Was it about *letting her go?*

Freedom?

(Oh—my—god!)

The freedom. Freedom, so abruptly taken away from her, so persistently denied, returned like a chord of grand music (Ravel? Tchaikovsky? Wagner?) sounding through her head, a chord struck by a thousand-piece orchestra accompanied by choirs, cannon, and rockets. She was engulfed in the great A-major majesty of it. It was just plain silly in her situation to feel so momentarily free, and yet the sound echoed on. For a moment the strength in her returned until she felt she could simply fling her hands upward, snapping rope like thread. *Freedom!*

Characteristically Barbara's thought of freedom—its nearness momentarily believed in—did not come trailing any feelings of revenge. What she would do to and about the kids, seemed lost in an unimportant and somewhat irrelevant part of her brain. Instead—wholly instead—the flash of imagining herself free made her feel charitable, outgoing, philanthropic. It made her feel quite close to guilty. She had never been understanding enough, sympathetic enough, free enough with her warmth. What she would do when she was free again!

Let me go, Barbara said, just let me go and I'll. . . . The thought evaporated off into a rather splendid bath of emotion. Let her go, and she would do some deed—or deeds—so fine and unselfish that. . . . *Oh, damn it,* Barbara said, *if I could just remember this afterward.* But she knew she wouldn't—not entirely.

It was already fading.

Gently, irresistibly, the whole feeling dwindled until it was only a background glow against the influx of a new, quite cool caution, a caution of particulars. Caution, after all, was what Barbara needed now; caution was temporarily better. Grand deeds another day.

When they let her go—if they let her go—but if and before they let her go, they did some bargaining with her, made her promise certain things to do and not do, she *would*. That was caution; that was sense. Oh, yes, she would; she would, indeed. The power and authority over children that were hers in the outside world, might be passing back into her hands—in sixty hours, it would be hers, no matter what—but then, those remaining sixty hours or so were *real* time, Freedom Five time. This, she had no wish of experiencing; to anything they set forth, she would agree.

Yes, I will, Barbara said, and listened but only heard the distant, indistinguishable mingle of voices. There were no words. It was maddening: it was like listening to water. Not yet. Release was not yet, but it might be coming. Thus, by silent turns, her emotion went from illusion to reality to caution to a mild fear.

Normally Barbara was no more superstitious than she was open to overwhelming emotional floods. Her world ran level and loving. Nonetheless the gates were now open. As she had been saintly and exalted a moment or so ago, now she became tribal, deep, mystic. It seemed that if she anticipated too much, wanted too much, ached too much—particularly, right here toward the end—then somehow, it would not happen. Do not show Fate the face of your longing; you will be disappointed.

Be good. Be undaring and cheerful. But above all, be good.

When the children finally did come down then, when they undid and redid her, when they hobbled her and stood her on her own two legs, she went willingly. Willingly up the stairs with no trouble, willingly to the bathroom, willingly to the toilet, and willingly thereafter to the wash basin. The day before they had broken her, and today they could measure, if they wished, the results of their work.

From the bathroom, however, they led her back down the stairs. Where she had felt herself at the edge of reprieve, she was instead resentenced to the basement room. They led her to the workbench and put down a lunch—her first food in thirty-six hours—and left. All except Cindy.

There was a white chicken sandwich again—one—and a paper cup of some Cola. With her one hand free from the waist, Barbara ate; indeed, she gobbled. She lifted up the plate and awkwardly licked the crumbs and smearings, and then she drank.

"Can I have any more?" She was entirely used to begging for things from the children now. Her stomach hurt worse than her pride. "Can I have another sandwich?"

"You only got *that* because Bobby wanted you to," Cindy said. In spite of the fact that Dianne oversaw her and tried to keep her neat, Cindy had let her hair go. In the humidity of the weather and the brackishness of the creek and river, it had reverted to its wonted state; it curled, and the curls took curls, and the very ends went into spirals. She was frizzy and bright and unable to keep secrets.

"Bobby?" Barbara said.

"It's all low residue."

"Low residue?"

"Bobby says you have to have something on your stomach when. . . ."

"Something on my stomach, when, what?"

"Well," Cindy said importantly, "if you have a lot in your stomach and you're hurt or scared, you mess yourself. You go poo-peee." Cindy giggled. "But if you have just enough at the right time, you don't, and nobody knows the difference."

"Who's nobody?"

"The coroners." A bright smile.

"Coroners!"

"That's what Bobby says."

"What do coroners have to do with it?"

"They're doctors who. . . ."

"I *know!*"

"Well"—this delicious piece of knowledge, Cindy slipped out word by word—"they're going to kill you, and you have to look like everything was OK before."

"They," Barbara said very quietly.

"Well, us," Cindy said.

Barbara stiffened and looked at the empty, tongue-licked plate, the last offering. Then she opened her mouth and began screaming. Every ounce of her being was concentrated in every scream, and forth the screams came, sound after sound.

Freedom Five came down the stairs almost wearily. They knew their Cindy, and they were not surprised.

John took Barbara's hair and jerked her head back until she could not close her mouth. Dianne put the rag down in the hole from which the sound was coming, and Paul and Bobby taped the lips and jaws. Afterward there was only a moaning sound. They did not look at each other very much, and they could not seem to look at Barbara. Instead they put Paul on watch and took Cindy with them back up into the house.

As they had done earlier in the day, Freedom Five looked at the sky and frowned. Above them it was silky blue with summer puff clouds here and there, but to the west—out toward the county road—it was brass colored and, still beyond that, there was a dim shadow just over the tree line. The sun had lost its blinding light—you could look almost right at it through the gathering haze—and its blistering edges had become indistinct and pale; they leaked off into the haze. There was no discernible wind, and the heat was unbearable. The world was a box of discomfort.

Of the four kids sitting in the scant shade beside the river—only Paul, on guard, was absent—Bobby frowned the most. Always the least likely of the conspirators, he was nonetheless the most conscientious. Their joint problems weighed upon him.

While he really didn't think it had been necessary to capture Barbara, strip her (he wished they hadn't), or toy with her, he had gone along because everyone else wanted to. What was to come, however, was disaster. He could smell it. He could smell it coming a piece at a time.

Dianne's plan was neat enough. He acknowledged it. There was even the possibility that on TV or something, an idea like that would work out. But everything had to go perfectly, and already it wasn't.

"It's going to rain," he said finally. Every time he spoke now, he knew that he was arguing uphill against all of the rest of them.

"It's *really* going to rain," Cindy said innocently.

"So what?"

"Car tracks."

"What?" John said.

"Car tracks"—Bobby shrugged—"Like if it rains, everything will be muddy tomorrow. If you take her down to the tenant house, there'll be a set of car tracks to show it. It'll have to be us."

"The Picker drove."

"Fingerprints." (Again.)

"Anyhow, nobody ever *drives* down there." Surprisingly enough, Cindy understood the technicalities of the plot now.

They were quiet. In the trees between them and the house, the cicadas started up again.

Dianne narrowed her gray eyes and agreed. "We'd better take her down before we go home. If it rains, it'll wash out the tracks. If it doesn't, we can brush them away."

"It will," John said.

"And guard her there all night?" Bobby said. "Uhnn-uh."

They knew what he meant. It was a frame house, old, cheap from the start, open-chinked and almost windowless, spooky enough in the daytime (which is why they valued it as a clubhouse) and unapproachable

208

at night. On top of it all, if it rained with lightning and thunder. . . .

"Why do we have to kill her *there?*" Cindy said with inspiration.

Bobby looked at his little sister with thanks but said nothing.

"Because we do."

"Yeah. It ought to be there," John said.

There was nodded agreement. The tenant house was a non-place, a building where you could do what you would not do in Dr. and Mrs. Adams' nice house. It was a point on the fitness of certain things at certain times and places.

"Well, *I'm* not staying down there to guard her," Cindy said.

"You won't have to."

"And I'm not staying alone in my house either."

"You have to do one or the other."

"I want Bobby with me, and I want to stay in *my* room."

"We could take Barbara down there and tie her up so good that she couldn't possibly get away," John said.

"And leave her alone all night?"

"Why not?"

"No way," Bobby said.

"I don't see why not."

"What if someone tries to get in out of the rain and goes there?" Bobby said.

"Who's—?" John began and stopped. They all looked around at one another.

"Now do *you* want to stay down there and do the guarding?" Bobby said.

"The Picker."

"Yeah."

They looked at Dianne. She was mind-made-up. "Well, we have to anyhow," she said.

"You heard what I said," Cindy was flat-foot adamant.

"You can come home with us and spend the night," Dianne said.

"Why?"

"You just said you didn't want to stay here."

Cindy lost her bearings. Her point was that she was scared and did not want to be alone or guard in the tenant house. She was so intent on it that any other thought got through to her only slowly.

"You can come home to dinner and spend the night with us," Dianne said. "We . . . can bake a cake to surprise Barbara and your parents with on Monday."

"But Barbara. . . ."

"That's what we're going to *say*," Dianne said.

Cindy took slight hope. "Oh."

"It's a good idea," John said.

"But what about Bobby?"

Bobby looked at John.

If you ran down the roster of participants, there was no one left. Put Dianne, Paul, and Cindy in the McVeigh house and Bobby guarding the prisoner alone, and there was only one spare—John. Bobby looked at him.

"Maybe I could help," John said.

"How?"

"I don't know. My folks wouldn't want me going out in the rain at night except to check the boat or something, but they go to bed early."

Some things don't need to be spoken, but Bobby's need was large. "Could you sneak out?" he said.

"I dunno. I guess so," John said. "Well—sure."

"When?" Bobby said. "How soon? How long?"

"Umnn." John frowned.

"How soon can you get away from your *parents?* How long can you guard?"

John tried to be honest. There was no room for horsing around. "I don't know. It all depends on when they go to sleep. I guess I could get here around eleven or twelve, and I'd have to go home about four. Something like that. Maybe a little bit later." John looked around for sympathy. "Well, I just can't go banging around there any old time I want, you know."

"And I can't sit up for two days straight," Bobby said.

"Yeah."

"So are you coming over tonight or *aren't* you?"

"I'll be here."

"When?"

"I said I'll *be* here."

"It's the last night, you know," Dianne said.

They looked at her.

"I mean, this time tomorrow night, it'll all be over."

"Yeah, over," Bobby said.

9

The tenant house stood across the access road which came in from the mailbox to the Adams' property and formed a turnaround. It was south on the away-side of the river and perhaps seventy-five or more yards down into a field of well-picked-over and drought-burned corn that now rustled and clattered in the lightest breeze. The height and the smothering closeness of the dying crop—the field had been cultivated right up to the walls of the house—hid the building up to the middle of the first-floor window frames, so that it seemed to float like a gray, wooden island in a brown tide.

What was left to see was typical of the region. It was a weathered board-and-batten, two-story, all square house whose pine sides had warped and curled and pulled out their rusty nail fastenings, until the wasps could build nests in the walls, the squirrels run freely through the attic, and the mice live rather comfortably under the floors. For the rest, everything was in keeping: rusted-through, brick-red tin roof; rotted sills and window frames; broken panes; a door that wouldn't close, and a path leading out from that door to the turn-around.

Although the house had been the Adams' summer and weekend place until the new house was finished, it had gone back downhill afterward. It was allowed to stand now because it did no one any harm and be-cause—in Dr. Adams' mind—it was a rich source of oak "barn wood" that was becoming unavailable anywhere else. Also, it had always been there.

Taken purely as a scenic object, it could be viewed two ways. Because of its age, abandonment, weathered condition, and isolation in the field, it could appear—particularly under a gathering squall—rather mournful, sad, and even ominous. Approached in another way, it could—under similar conditions—be peaceful in the peculiar way that cemeteries are peaceful, a reminder of the rural and distant past, of the simple virtues, of the quiet life and the acquiescing, accepting of death.

These things were not lost on Freedom Five. Though they could not express themselves on the subject—to them it was merely spooky and sometimes "neat"—they felt the presence of time there. It was an *old* place; it lent authority to their discussions. This, too, was one of the influences that contributed to its becoming the obvious and "fitting" place to conclude the whole thing with Barbara. It was right.

But Barbara did not go willingly.

Though they wrapped her in enough rope and clothesline to hold several hostages, the children were nonetheless forced to leave her the writhing, twisting movements of a snake. A number of purely practical things—her weight, going around corners, clearances—prevented them from carrying her on some sort of litter. And Barbara, desperate, was still strong.

The struggle began in the workshop-rec room and proceeded out the door, up the stairs, into the carport, back over the cement to the rear of the gaping station wagon, and then up into the rear of the car itself. John and Dianne began by carrying the weight of her body by the shoulders: the three smaller youngsters carried her legs. Her convolutions and twistings overpowered them all, however, so that Dianne had to trade places with Paul and Cindy and let everything begin again. Several times they dropped her, and after a while she was obviously skinned up and bruised.

"It's OK," Dianne said on the second occasion.

213

"When the rapist dragged her out of the house, the same thing happened."

"What do you mean?" The change in verb tense and levels of reality was confusing.

Bobby was clearly panting. "She means," he said, "that from now on, any marks on her body would have happened anyhow. I mean . . ."

"It fits the story." John was pale. Both the exertion and the obvious erotic influence of the journey made his voice shake.

"The coroner's report," Bobby said.

"Oh." They did not understand—Paul and Cindy—but they weren't going to admit it.

"OK, let's go."

Beneath the pile-on of the kids, Barbara made sounds one does not hear in everyday life, or at least not often. The various tones could be taken as sobbing, embarrassingly so. Freedom Five, however, was becoming used to such things. Dianne found it rewarding; John found it arousing (as, indeed, everything about Barbara was arousing); Bobby found it unbearable; and Paul and Cindy found it irritating, they wanted to smack her one, anything to shut her up.

"Come on."

Once again the kids untangled and tackled their squirming burden. Now they moved back along the country-dusted sides of the wagon, bumping and sliding along its metal panels.

"Don't let her touch it. . . ."

"*We* can't help it."

"Keep going. . . ."

"We'll have to wash the car."

"Leave it out in the rain."

"*If* it rains."

"It'll rain, all right."

They looked up.

"Hurry!"

"Get her around the corner now."

At the lowered rear gate of the station wagon, the major battle occurred. Barbara would *not* be put in.

214

She kicked and squirmed; she tried to roll under the car; she butted with her head. She could not be grabbed nor held, and the fight continued until at last, John, losing his temper, hit her with all his might. He intended to wind her, but instead he hit up near the joining of the rib cage, and Barbara went limp.

"What happened?"

"John hit her."

"Oh, no." Bobby had seen it. He looked sick.

"Oh, no, what? What could we do?"

"You don't *ever* hit anybody there."

"Why?"

Bobby went quickly over the unconscious girl. "Because," he said, "because you can rupture their heart."

"Aw-w-w...."

"Is she dead?"

"Let me see." Dianne knelt beside Bobby. John went red. "Can you feel her pulse?"

"With her *hands* tied up that way?"

"Her heart then."

Dianne inclined her ear and touched Barbara's naked chest. "Be quiet."

They all strained to hear what only she could hear.

"It's beating," she said. "Listen."

Bobby, who did not like to touch Barbara at all, found nowhere to avert his eyes and not see her at the moment of touching. Instead he shut his eyes and put his ear to her body.

More silence.

After a moment or two he said, "Yeah."

"Boy"—John was relieved.

"Why?" Cindy said. "You're going to kill her anyway."

"Not like this," Dianne said. "That'd ruin everything." She straightened up. "OK, let's get her in. Everything's all right."

They got her legs up on the tailgate, and then,

215

with them to support part of her body, they all got together and packed her up and in any old way.

"She's all dirty now," Cindy said as if in criticism of their work.

"Not really."

"Yes, she is." Cindy had her standards. "And her hair is all messed up."

Dianne looked at Cindy woman-to-woman, a first-time event, and agreed. "We'll have to wash her."

"And brush her hair. That's what you make *me* do."

Bobby had paid neither one of them any attention. "I'm going to take off her gag," he said.

"And let her start screaming all over the place here?"

"We got to. She's not breathing very well."

"No!"

"She won't scream," Bobby said.

"OK, then you do it. It'll be your fault."

"You want her to die here? *Now?*" He needed help, and he got it. They straightened her out in the back of the wagon, rolled her up on her side, and held her while Bobby removed tape and cloth.

"Here, I'll take it." Dianne reached over. "Cindy, go get some more tape, the whole roll."

"Why?"

"Fingerprints. I'll have to throw this away with the stuff that gets burned. And anyhow we have to regag her."

Momentarily Bobby seemed to cut in on Dianne's thinking. "That's right. Tape is the best fingerprint thing in the world. Do what she says." He returned his attention to his patient. His face again turned to a miniature version of his surgeon father—grave, concerned. "She's not breathing good enough yet." He was really worried.

"Why?"

"How should *I* know?"

"What do we do?"

Bobby thought. He supposed that in a similar situ-

216

ation a real doctor would do something quick and smart—oxygen, a stimulating injection, but *something*. Unfortunately, he was only a doctor's son, not a doctor. There were none of those things around. Then he remembered "Mouth-to-mouth resuscitation."

"Yeah."

"Who?"

"John hit her. . . ."

"John?"

"OK," John said. (Actually they all could have done it to some extent. They had gotten instruction in it at the Bryce pool from their water-oriented parents, and the older ones had it still again in school.)

"Roll her to me." John climbed up into the wagon, and the rest of Freedom Five moved Barbara. "We don't have an airway," he looked around as if apologizing for failure in advance.

"Just do it."

"We have to open her mouth."

"Here—" With some awkwardness Bobby managed to open Barbara's jaws. "Now."

As if reciting the lessons learned, John took a deep even breath, bent down, married his lips to hers, and breathed steadily in. He recovered his wind and did it again. There was resistance.

"Hey, great! Keep it up."

"It's working," Dianne said.

John inflated his athlete's lungs again and breathed into the girl again. Because it was Barbara, he did it tenderly and perfectly (even though he was committed to help kill her tomorrow).

Now she actually complained. "Don't. . . ."

He did it one more time.

"I don't need that." She tried to roll her face away, and since she was a swimmer, too, John stopped. She would know when she was OK.

Cindy came back into the carport. "What's going on?"

"Nothing," Dianne said reassuringly, reassured herself. "Everything's OK. Get in."

Four rode in the back of the station wagon with Barbara. Dianne drove.

She got self-consciously into the driver's seat, put the key in the ignition, pumped the accelerator the way she did on their own Chevrolet, turned the key, and started the motor. The station wagon came to expensive life: lights came on and went off, the air conditioner started sighing, and they were ready.

"She OK?"

"Hurry up," John said. "The rain. . . ."

With the rigid expression of someone taking a driver's license test, Dianne dropped into R, let off the hand brake, touched the accelerator, and found herself moving. The car backed out into the drive, jockeyed roughly once or twice, and then went around to the path that led to the tenant house. Here Dianne stopped. "I can't back up to the house like I thought. The path's too narrow. It'd show."

"Carry her."

"Drag her."

"Whatever we're going to do, for Christ's sake, let's go." John again looked overhead.

"What if someone sees us?"

"Who's here to see?"

"Too late for that now." They all piled out.

Barbara seemed more than halfway back to reality. She heard. She seemed to understand. Her eyes conveyed that she *knew* what she was here for. "Please. . . ." The sound was exhausted, drawn-out, pleading.

"Gag her again," Dianne came around to the back. "Hurry."

They gagged her. It wasn't difficult; she was unresisting. New cloth replaced the old; new tape sealed itself over her lips.

"Can we make her walk?"

"No."

A sigh. With an all-together-now effort, they pulled her out onto the tailgate and sat her up. Then, all five at the upper arms and shoulders, they dragged
218

her down the path toward the tenant house. Her bare heels left two parallel tracks behind them.

At the door to the building, they bumped her up over the splintered and rotted sill into the tiny, gray-colored hall and let her drop. Although it was still mid-afternoon, the clouds from the west were moving in, and the sun was prematurely fading into a dark blue haze. Inside the house, it was oddly dark for that time of day and, as oddly, cool.

"Where?"

"Upstairs," Bobby said firmly.

"Oh god, no."

"You can see in all the windows down here. Listen, John, you can *climb* in any one of them you want to. You know that."

John was silent.

"If I have to guard her, I want it up there. That way there's only the stairs to watch."

"You don't have to do it all night alone."

"If *you* want to guard her then. . . ."

John slouched, but the nature of his resistance changed. From obstinacy he went to grudging doubt and then agreement.

"Bobby's right," Dianne said. She was as tired as the rest.

"Yeah. OK."

Without further talk, they again took Barbara by the arms and began the steep creaking ascent up the wooden stairs to the second floor. Barbara still resisted but more feebly. Even so, along the way they had to set her down and take a breather. At the top they were virtually in a state of collapse.

"Which room?"

"Either one, I guess," John said.

"No," Bobby said. "That one."

They looked at him.

"The storm's coming from *that* way," he sighed. "This room'll be the driest."

It was now growing quite dark for that time of the afternoon. A copper-colored light pervaded the upper rooms. Little animals—rats, squirrels?—scratched across the attic over their heads.

"OK."

Now that they were near the end of the job, Freedom Five lifted and pulled with new strength (and now that she had lost, Barbara seemed to go limp). They took her to the most protected part of the southeast room and put her down almost gently for a change. It was done. They all straightened up in relief.

"We've got to get the car back to the house and wipe it off."

"Inside too...."

"And get some weeds and sweep off the tracks," Dianne said.

"And the path!"

"We can let that go until tomorrow. We'll be coming back," Bobby said.

"What about *her?*"

"She can't get away," Cindy giggled.

That seemed obvious enough. Barbara lay, shoulders and breasts mostly down against the cracking, once-linoleumed floor, her hips up, her legs bent in an S shape. She was rather ridiculously swathed in rope, but they weren't sure. Her escape was the one chance they could not possibly take now that she knew.

"Well, maybe—" Bobby frowned.

In the end, they finished by rolling her completely face and stomach down and pulling her ankles over behind her and tying them down to her wrists. No further movement or sound was possible.

"That ought to do it until Bobby gets back."

Freedom Five began to cover its movements as quickly as possible. Dianne got in behind the wheel of the wagon and whirled it back around to the main house. There she and Cindy and Paul wiped it clean inch by inch. There was no sign that it had ever been used nor that Barbara had ever been in it. Behind them John and Bobby swept back along the turnaround with branches, removing the car tracks.

It was now premature night, however much too early, but nightlike all the same. The classic signs of squall were in the distant but visible sky.

The west was an impenetrable blue and black; the sun had vanished; and there was just the beginning of a faraway "beard"—little, dirty, soapsudsy clouds—making up before the storm. The children were indecisive. There was a lot on Dianne's schedule yet to be done, but. . . .

"We better split," John said. "It's going to blow hard."

"Yeah." With Barbara in the tenant house alone, Bobby didn't want to see them go. What was going to happen, however, just had to happen.

"I'll be back tonight," John said, "but it may be late."

"What about Cindy?"

"I'll take care of it." Dianne, cool and polite as could be—what a wonderful daughter—called home and got permission for Cindy to spend the night. With minimum time for niceties, she scrubbed the little girl's face, brushed her hair—six licks to a side—threw some things in one of Dr. Adams' flight bags, and was ready to go. Outside, John, Paul, and Bobby waited, scuffling around in the dust and looking anxiously at the sky.

"Ready?"

"Ready." Dianne and Cindy came out of the kitchen and down the steps.

"Let's cut and run then," John said.

Freedom Five—down to four—took off at a fast trot down along the garden, across the field, and into the trees along Oak Creek. By himself Bobby watched them go, sighed, squared his thin shoulders, and went inside.

Without the kids and the magnetic presence of Barbara in the house, the rooms seemed quite abnormally silent and empty. The electric motors whirred—refrigerator, kitchen clock, window air conditioner—but that was all. Outside, even the cicadas were silent.

221

And, of course, there was the distant rumble of thunder.

He was lonely, self-pitying, and sad.

The loneliness was self-apparent and would continue until at least midnight. Bobby was not optimistic; midnight would be the first he'd see of John, if *then*.

The self-pity was equally obvious. He had done the biggest share of the work and taking risks all along, and *they* had had the fun. Now he was stuck with the worst job so far. For hours it would be just him and *her* and a Picker out there—maybe—and the weather and the rest.

The sadness was more difficult; he could not have explained it in any one way because it was a thing of so many sharp-cornered parts. When he put his mind on it—and he did—things became a blur too indistinct for him to unsort.

Where, for instance, Bobby should have welcomed relief of any kind, in fact, he regretted—dreaded—the adventure's coming to an end, particularly the end planned. Like each other one of Freedom Five, he had formed an individual relationship—if known only to himself—with Barbara, and it was a dear one. After the initial capture, after the fears of her escaping had passed, he had fallen to paying more and more attention to her for herself. Although he did not feel any true body lust for her that could be consummated—indeed, his shyness of her remained almost overpowering—still he was not so young that he could not observe and admire. Barbara was beautiful.

Her shape—since she was his first experience, she both set and met all standards—was pretty. Like Paul, Bobby was not without some idea of the female form—in a doctor's family, surely not—and he found the girl's youthfulness and suppleness and slight immaturity all to the good despite the many bruises that marred her now. Her grace even in the difficult things they had made her do, her differentness from him and from them all, was compelling. Her voice, her words, though she had been allowed to say little enough, were quite enchanting. If he had a wish, it was that he could

222

keep her here for a long, long time—like a wild fawn or vixen, and train her and tame her—until she could be let run free without a leash and come back at his call.

From here, Bobby's thoughts reached over toward an emotion a little too adult for him, but, in fact, it was tenderness, protectiveness, what grown men feel for grown women. He struggled with the feeling of wanting to cradle and shield her and found it just too complex. Other things intruded.

Her struggles the morning she had waked up a prisoner, the ones that almost tore the bed apart, her kickings and thrashings about, her attack on Dianne, her fight this afternoon, told him well enough that the Barbara of his entirely private dreams was not there at all. Inside of her was another person, indeed, and a possibly dangerous one.

Still beyond was his duty to Freedom Five, a duty that involved the penalty of *not* performing the duty. Here again was a world he could not have been expected to understand, that honor and responsibility became tangled up with loyalties which became tangled up with requisites which—finally—involved personal pain and loss.

They could not keep her because his parents were coming home. For the same reason they could not let her go free and be themselves caught. It all confused him and made him sad, but as usual, he was in charge and there were things to be done. For the second time since coming in the door to the kitchen, he squared up and set to work.

He closed all the windows against the advancing squall (his mother would be mad if the wallpaper was streaked when she got home) and locked them all except one. That was Bobby. He might want to get in unobserved some time later on. Then he went down to the rec room and gathered up his rolled sleeping bag, his old windbreaker, and a good flashlight. These he took upstairs and assembled neatly on the kitchen counter together with his small shotgun (which he still favored for its short-range pattern spread) and extra shells. Finally he ate. He didn't feel like it, but his father said that the body was like a fireplace: if you put fuel into the thing, it would run; otherwise not. Further he made himself a second sandwich, carefully wrapped it in plastic wrap, got a quart of soft drink from the refrigerator, and rolled everything into a camper's pack.

Lights on or off? Bobby wondered.

After some thought, he decided to leave them off. If the Picker—his chief caution now—was drawn to shelter from the rain, he might be inclined to go for the darkened house rather than the tenant house where Bobby definitely intended that there be at least some light. All this decided, all this accomplished, he took the back-door key from its hook, shouldered his roll, locked his way out of the house, and went off around by way of the vegetable garden.

It was cool and growing quite dark now—cooler than it had been in weeks—and fitful little breezes stirred over dust that was strangely fragrant. The squall was both near and far away. It was clearly 45 degrees up in the sky, but Bobby had seen them like that, squalls that only grumbled around and went straight up into the air like last night. Again, they could cover the remaining miles in ten minutes or less. He hurried a little.

Inside the tenant house, he paused only a moment to listen—there was nothing—and then he resumed. He closed the door which would not latch and pushed Freedom Five's old meeting table up against it more against the wind than against possible intrusion. It wouldn't hold out Cindy. Then he went upstairs and put his things down by what would be the driest wall when the storm hit. Barbara, of course, had not moved except to somehow fling herself over on her side. She raised her head and looked at him when he came in, and then dropped back again, eyes once more closed. That was all. His sadness returned.

Leaving her nonetheless, Bobby went back down the dimming stairs and rummaged around in some "junk" he kept in one of the closets his father had built he summer they lived here. The object finally found, urned out to be a gasoline lantern with a burnt and opsided chimney, but a lantern that still worked. In keeping with his nature, Dr. Adams had thrown it out the minute it became defective, and true to his own, Bobby had salvaged and fixed it. He had also provided himself with matches in a jar. With a sense of the woodsman's pride then, or as much as he could lay claim to, he got the lamp going, the mantle adjusted, and the closet neatly closed. There remained the problem of where to put it.

Upstairs it would be comforting, but if anyone— specifically, if the Picker—broke in, it would be Bobby in the light unable to see and the Picker in the covering scary darkness. Still, Bobby did not part with his lamp easily. Further thought. Finally he set it in the middle of the second lowest step, so that it lit the front and only usable door and room while giving off at least a little reflection upstairs. With this he could manage, and he climbed back upstairs to Barbara.

Again, of course, she had not moved, and this time she didn't even lift her head. She seemed as if already dead from the torturous position in which they had tied her, from fear, or from exhaustion, and she seemed unnaturally white in the lightning flashes that successively lit the room. In some alarm Bobby knelt and touched her. She was cold—poor circulation, he guessed—but she moved at once and opened her eyes intelligently. Had she been dozing and dreaming, and did she suddenly think that this was the morning? *The* morning, he reminded himself. Running his fingers down her upper arm and feeling the ropes merely as ridges on her skin because they had cut so deeply into her flesh, he felt that complicated emotion of tenderness. He was sorry for Barbara, but he still had time to decide about all that.

Getting up, he went to the wall and unrolled his meager possessions. The soft drink he carefully placed by the wall itself; the sandwich he put by its side; the flashlight he turned on; and the shotgun he loaded and

225

stood in the corner. Then he took the sleeping bag over and unrolled it beside Barbara, pushing it as far under her side as he could. After unzipping it and unfolding it, he took her ankles and rolled her gently over from one side to the other so that she was off the floor entirely and on the softness of the down. Finally he got busy loosening some of the ropes, removing others, releasing her legs so that she could stretch out, and chafing the indents on her arms and legs. When he had made her as comfortable as he dared, he covered her with the top part of the sleeping bag and put his folded windbreaker under her head for a pillow.

Being Bobby, he did not expect any flashing looks of gratitude. He would really have liked to talk, to have *her* ease *his* loneliness by the sheer sound of *her* voice. Later he would give in and do it, but he was still busy.

The front of the squall reached the Adams property perhaps an hour later. The little fitful winds evaporated, and it became theatrically silent as if they were both beneath a proscenium arch, as indeed they were. The low, dragging beard before the rain—Bobby saw it only in flashes of lightning—seemed barely above the trees when it passed over. The temperature dropped again, possibly ten or more degrees this time, and then the first, few pelting raindrops hit the tin roof overhead. The attic-dwelling animals stirred, too, and then the wind came.

It sighed through the distant trees, across the fields, and against the house as if testing, simply testing. It paused a moment. Then it came like a sustained rising chord of noise, beginning half the county away and rattling over the land like drumroll. When the first gust hit, the tenant house physically gave before it. Half a thousand and more pieces of board tugged at enlarged nailholes, plank grinding on plank in a many-voiced complaint.

Traveling inside the wind came the true rain; a sea of raindrops, shattered into tiny bits, drove into the wood like shot. The sheets of tin that were the roof bumped up and down and tried to fly and could not.

226

Gusts rumbled over them creating a sound equal to the thunder—thunder inside and thunder above. Now that they were within the squall, moreover, what had seemed sullen flares of lightning were revealed as branches, trees, rivers of energy discharging for miles in every direction but always down toward where they were (or seemed to be). The old building twisted in their light; rain drove in mist through the windows and across the room even though they were on the lee side of the house. Bobby kept lighting his flashlight and looking around.

He understood these things. His father—always the researcher, the explainer—had told him about this kind of squall. Somewhere up above him, stretching possibly several miles into the sky was a "hole" leading up from the hot earth into the cold upper levels of the atmosphere. There—by cold—hot air was separated into downpouring rain and freed. Uprushing air pulled more in behind it. The electric charge of the uprising air—was it plus or minus? Bobby could not remember—collected and redischarged back groundward. That was the lightning. All very interesting to the boy's mind, and even possibly true. He remembered standing out in the rain with Dr. Adams and listening to such explanations and thinking that there just might be something to them after all. Nonetheless he had never been exposed to one of these freakish squalls under such dramatic—if self-imposed—circumstances. Children are children, and the fury of nature is ever the fury of nature.

There was a gust and the building moved; there was a gust and the building moved; there was a gust and the building moved again. The repetition of it forced recognition of insuperable forces. The boards beneath Bobby's feet slid in and out under the cracked linoleum; the windows shrilled where the glass was broken; and the ceiling ran water like a sieve. Nor was the sound confined to the room in which they waited.

In the other room of the upper floor—more open to the wind—the rain drove like bucketsful of water against the old oyster plaster. A closet door banged, and junk—who could remember what had been lying around up here?—clattered over the floor. Downstairs the noise—as easily heard where Bobby stood against the wall—was equal. There was a tinkle of glass—wet cornstalks forcing an already cracked pane—things banging and flapping. At one instant, there was a sudden, rumbling sound as if the house had been mortally wounded, but it was the old, abandoned field gate being blown down from its leaning place against the building wall. In the cold, Bobby perspired.

The sky sounds were of several subtle intensities. There was the rain-dulled thunder that was far off. There was the unexpected, hand-smack sound of very nearby lightning, a pause, and then the sound of a direct hit that never quite was. The entire house tried to squat down beneath the explosion of winds above. Thereafter there might be a lull, almost a toying, playful lull before the next bolt of lightning and thunder. Near or close? Now or never? Bobby listened, felt, and waited.

His eyes particularly watched the field between the tenant house and the pine woods along Oak Creek. Weather like this would have to drive any tin-can camping Picker for shelter somewhere—assuming he had returned tonight—and the Adams place was closest. Would he bypass the tenant house? Would he come here? Would he come in a straight line, blundering through the growth toward protection, or would he skirt along the turnaround and then make a dive for the building?

In one medium flash of lightning, there seemed to be nothing but dead corn beaten flat and writhing under the rain like a vast muscle on the back of the earth. In another, more brilliant flash, Bobby would think he saw a hunched, shadow-highlighted figure in the field. He would hold his breath. He saw him; then he didn't, until with every eruption of light, he saw men coming at the windows from every direction.

Bobby held on to Bobby, however; in this he was a remarkable boy. He jumped with childish fright at one explosion of lightning and then waited: when he had confirmed that there was nothing there after all, he refastened his grip on things. It was all imagination. Nonetheless a tickle in the corner of his eye would tell him that the Picker was really over *there*. To look again was irresistible; he picked up his gun. Another flash—nothing. Perhaps the Picker was just now coming out of the woods; perhaps he had been there all along on the other side of the tenant house.

Forcing himself away from what he thought was the best lookout window there was, Bobby made a trembling tour of the other three sides of the building in turn. The worst window, the one directly open to the squall, he left for last. Edging up to it in splashes of light and voids of blackness, holding his gun shielded behind him, he looked out straight into the storm. There was nothing except those twitches in the bottom of his eyes.

The window was located over what had once been a back porch and later merely a sheltered lean-to for farm equipment and things not in use (junk). He looked down, his sight slanting in under the broken edges of the tin roof, and saw in the next flash of lightning the figure of a man. The eye's snapshot was indelible. Man . . . black, dark, shiny wet shoes . . . dirt-colored trousers rolled up . . . light shirt sticking to dark skin . . . leaning against post . . . hand with handkerchief, wiping face . . . head turned up toward his own. Then there was blackness again.

Lightning.

Confirmation.

He was there.

In the instant or two between flashes, Bobby flung himself away from the window and against the dry wall of the four. With fingers as wobbly as soda straws, he felt the shotgun. It would be easy enough to fire out the window over the roof and not be heard *now,* and it might frighten the Picker away. Then he remembered Dianne's plan for the man. He didn't know what to do. And *Barbara* was in *there*. In dilemma he behaved like a real soldier; he peed red-hot urine into his already soaking jeans.

"God . . . ," he said. Then he remembered what his father had told him, and what he told himself every week at Sunday School.

He didn't believe in a pray-to god.

"Turn off the lights before you come up."

"And don't watch television all night."

"OK." John rose and kissed his mother on the forehead. He was already much taller than she, and an obedient son. "If it quits raining before I go to bed, I'm going down and bail out the boat."

"Don't go out while it's storming."

"I won't, don't worry. Anyhow, it's almost all over now."

John watched his parents go upstairs and then went and got himself another Coke from the fridge. He did so with a distant sense of guilt: he thought that Cokes gave him a stitch in the side when he ran, and football practice began in another week. It was important to him to make the real team this year.

Afterward he returned and took his father's chair in front of the TV and forced himself to wait through two more segments of the movie. When he sensed that things upstairs had settled for the night, he turned off the set and went and got his oilskin jacket with the hood. Like Bobby he had made some preparations (in stealth and underneath his parents' noses). He had a knife, a flashlight, and a whistle in his pockets, and he, too, had a sandwich. He also had his own gun—a .22— in its gun case waiting for him under the house. He was as ready as any scared boy can be.

He slipped out the front door quietly, pulled the gun out, and went down to the rowboat. The grass was tall and full of water, so that as he walked, he kicked up moisture as high as his shins. By the time he got out on the dock, his moccasins were soaked.

The boat was a third full of water. He guessed that they must have had several inches of rain in the brief two hours of the squall. Still, the job was there to be done. He laid the gun on the dock, kicked off his shoes, and stepped down on the wet, wooden thwart barefooted. He could feel every paint flake and plank edge separately; the boat rolled beneath him soddenly, and anyone less experienced would have capsized it right there. His balance, however, was perfect. He sat down gently in the very corner and began to bail quietly, one coffee can after another. It was exasperatingly slow work, and he gained by the half inch.

When the boat was mostly dry, he gathered his things off the one-plank pier, slipped the painter, and paddled—he did not risk the noise of rowing—himself across the creek to the Adams' side. There he secured to the black, wet tree stump that was his normal mooring and stepped down into the muck of the creek shoreline. Back at his own house, all was black and silent and thus—good. With the cased gun in one hand and his shoes in the other, he climbed the bank and slipped into the woods.

There was still some wind sighing through the distant tops of the trees, and with every gust the pines unloaded a fresh shower of water that splattered down through the needles onto the path he walked. About twenty yards in, he halted, put on his shoes, shifted his gun to the other hand, and got out his flashlight. It was dark, scary, and bug-stinging down in the middle of nowhere. It was also now quite exciting. Not an hour before he had been watching TV with his parents (at his age, almost the very word itself was repellent), and now he was very much in the middle of something infinitely more exciting and real. Less than half a mile away, the beautiful girl lay in captivity awaiting his coming. And it was true. He wondered what his friends would think if they knew what he was doing right at this minute.

At the edge of the field that virtually surrounded the Adams' place, he stopped. The main house, lying squat and low beyond the vegetable garden, was entirely dark. The car—a lump—sat out in the turnaround illuminated only by the receding flares of lightning. The tenant house was nearly invisible from where he stood. Only the dark, peaked roof stood out over the beaten corn in diminishing flares of lightning. There was no one around—at least, not near—and he felt oddly courageous. It was one of those transient feelings.

Picking his way gingerly around the puddles, he came to the turnaround, crossed over the grassy center of it to avoid leaving tracks in the mud, stopped to pull the sandspurs out of his ankles, and crossed again to the path leading to the tenant house. There he stopped. As he had more or less expected, there was a faintly wavering light from the broken front windows—Bobby's gasoline lantern, he guessed—but to imagination's eye, it seemed forbidding. At once, the finality of their adventure, rather than the erotic aspect of it, seized him. Everything around here was terribly and specifically quiet. He could hear the trees sighing in the dying wind, of course, the sodden clash of stiff cornstalks and the workings inside his own body, but from the house—nothing. Well, what did he expect? The Rolling Stones?

What John had expected was to march up the path, like the good F.F. leader that he was, and relieve the watch. Now instead, he faltered and entertained a number of fantasies and possibilities in his mind. The Picker had come and overpowered Bobby and was waiting inside for him . . . the Picker was somewhere close, watching the house as he was . . . Bobby was sitting behind that door with a gun ready to blow John's head off by mistake. . . . John was not at home in bed, and that was being discovered this very moment. These and other thoughts—perhaps there was no Picker here at all tonight—jostled back and forth. Except for the fact that Barbara was probably still in there, he would have gone straight home to bed.

Instead John took out his whistle and blew a measured sound—shrill where he was but not calculated to carry home across Oak Creek—and he pulled out his flashlight again. Getting off the path, he moved wetly through the corn to a place where he could sight

232

one of the front windows and yet hopefully be out of any normal line of fire Bobby might choose. Now, he whistled twice and waited again. After a few seconds, he thought he heard an answering whistle from inside, but there was enough instant thunder and weed noise to make him unsure. Aiming the flashlight at the window, he sent the signal "F–F". Overhead, the clouds were beginning to shred into streamers behind the squall. He looked up and thought he saw a star.

At the tenant house, the door swung open a lighted inch. "John?" The voice sounded smaller than Bobby's.

"Yeah." John bent forward and moved through the weeds and old corn as quickly as he could. His gun case was wet, and he set it with the contents of his pockets on the table. The two boys looked at each other in the light of the gasoline lantern.

"He's here."

"Who?" John knew well enough.

"He's *outside*. Like we said. Getting in out of the rain. Under the shed," Bobby said. "I saw him, and he saw me."

"Where were you?"

"Upstairs."

"How's she?"

Bobby shrugged.

"Does he know about it?"

"How could he unless he saw something last night?"

"Where's he now?"

"Like I told you,"—Bobby pointed through the unused room at the boarded windows in the back— "under the shed roof, I guess."

"Did he try and get in?"

"No. I was waiting." Bobby had, in fact, been holding his shotgun since he let John in the house, something that seemed so normal to John that he hadn't seriously noticed. Now, however, he unzipped the case on his own .22 and got it out.

"What're we going to do?"

John looked down at his own hands, clean, wet, boy hands, taking out the rifle, checking it, loading it, and he shook his head. "I don't know. . . ."

On cue, thunder rumbled—still more distantly— and the house echoed slightly. John shoved the bolt home and locked.

"Kill him? Shoot over his head?" Bobby said. "Stay in here? I'm sleepy." One idea was as hopeless as the next, and Bobby's tone of voice betrayed it.

"I dunno. Maybe talk to him. He sure can't hurt us."

Talk, reason, persuasion, the endless mouth-running of city people—chatter, understanding, polemics, postponements—John felt his taste go sour even as he said it. Nonetheless, he and Bobby were too young to handle a killing by themselves, and besides, Dianne wasn't here to say what to do. Maybe she wouldn't even like it. But it would be fun. It would be like real life, and it would solve the problem, too.

"Just talk to him." John recovered from reverie. "Find out what's up. Talk to Dianne tomorrow."

"You mean just go around the house and start talking?"

"I've talked to him before. It isn't so bad." John cautiously opened the door. Outside, of course, there was no one. He put his foot out and into the weeds.

"Are we going to leave her here alone?"

"Have to."

"Uh-h-h . . . now?" Bobby said.

"The longer we wait, the worse it gets. Coming?"

"Yeah." Enormous lack of enthusiasm.

They went around the corner of the house, John leading, and stumbled on the gate, which had been blown down. After that, there was no hope of surprise, and John turned on the flashlight the rest of the way. The Picker—the *man*—was there as Bobby had said, waiting for them to come. He was sitting up on a dirty, old, enameled table, which had once been used in the kitchen, and in the flashlight's beam, he was watching them with rather lidded eyes.

234

"Who're you?" For the boys, the mystery of the Picker was over, the fright half gone. Now that they saw him, now that they had guns in their hands, the game was over.

"Cruz," he said carefully. "My name is Cruz."

"What're you doing here?" John's voice was a little high-pitched.

"De rain," he said and shrugged. He made no move to go. He was not alarmed.

John and Bobby stood where they were, out in the open, out of their fortress, in the mud and a little uncertain. The Picker continued to sit where he sat, feet up out of the wet, back solidly against the boards of the tenant house, arms folded across his large stomach. Of the two parties, he was the more comfortable and sheltered; the distribution of his weight and his bulk advertised ease. Between him and the boys lay a no-man's-land.

The boys were silent, and John, at least, was angry. They couldn't order the Picker out and make it stick; they couldn't just walk up and beat the hell out of him; they couldn't shoot him; and they couldn't let him stay where he was. Barbara weighed on them too heavily. What would Dianne do?

John lowered his gun and cradled it casually in the bend of his arm. "Are you hungry?"

"Hungry?" There was amused disbelief in the Picker's voice, but there was a hint of interest, too.

"Food." Bobby lowered his shotgun and patterned himself after John.

"Where?" the Picker said.

"Up at the house."

"What?" Everything the Picker said seemed to drag itself out, like the *t-t-t-t* of "what."

"I dunno. Different stuff. We're going to get something to eat. We're hungry." This was nearly always true; it had the ring of sincerity to it.

"C'mon," Bobby added.

"To'd house?" There was the drawn-out sound *se* again.

235

"There's nobody there for a while."

"They're out."

"We're just down here camping for the night."

"Oh, camping." There was irony in the Picker's voice.

"Well, it's better than standing out here." In his bravest move of the evening, John turned his back on the enemy and started back for the front of the tenant house. Taken in by the show of confidence, Bobby did the same. "Let's go."

After the longest time, there was a sound behind them and the heavy bending of weeds and corn into the mud. The Picker was following.

"It just might work," Bobby whispered ahead.

"Shut up."

In the morning the grass and weeds were doubly heavy from the rain and dew, and Dianne stood on John's small dock feeling soiled and not-perfect. Her long, stiltlike legs were wet, her white socks sagging, and there was mud on her sandals. Summer-end weeds and chaff stuck damply to almost every part of her body, and even the fine white hair on her arms held downy bits of field fluff loosened by the night's storm. Behind her, silent and trembling, Paul stood—he was in a state that might be called anticipatory shock—and he was equally rumpled and disorganized. His neat blue shorts, immaculate fifteen minutes ago, were now black-streaked and wrinkled where he had pushed through the path to the Randall house ahead of her. Behind him—the dock being narrow—Cindy sat on the lone wet board swinging her feet overside and staring indefinitely off into space. For the morning of the day *it* was going to happen, everything seemed unfair and conspiring, but Dianne held her disappointment and waited in her stiff, self-held way.

John's bailing can scraped rustily along the paint-flaked chine of the boat. "He spent the night there," he said.

"Where?" Everyone was speaking in stage whispers.

"In the rec room. On the floor. On a sleeping bag." John emptied the can and continued bailing without looking up. "Bobby stayed in his room with the gun, and I stayed down at the tenant house with her."

Dianne looked at him, and when he said nothing more, assumed that their precious prisoner remained just that way—captive, helpless and waiting. Nonetheless she felt bitter and angry.

Through the night she had coped with strains far above the heads of most seventeen-year-olds. There had been the business of helping Cindy make a cake for the Adams' homecoming—(a project Cindy despised)—of smuggling Paul a sleeping pill and making him take it, and of keeping herself cool and in command. Above all, however, there had been that problem of herself, almost of the person-within-the-person normally called Dianne.

In a sense, it was a new phenomenon. Like everyone else, Dianne had always confided in Dianne, self to self, intimately and privately, but the conversations or interminglings of idea had always been controlled by the outward Dianne whom everyone thought to see. The one Dianne proposed, and the other supplied: Dianne set forth the subject, the fantasy, the daydream of the moment, and from within came the details, the variations, the entire rich contents of cooperative, if inventive, imagination. This commonplace, Dianne thought unique to herself—again she was seventeen— and guarded it behind her pale gray eyes as if it were some source of magic or wealth. As indeed it was. She rubbed the lamp of *what if*, and the genie appeared.

During the Barbara adventure, however, from the moment she saw Barbara tied to the bed and knew what Freedom Five controlled, Dianne's genie had not been so entirely docile. The improbable having been done—she had first mentioned it to Paul, and he had blurted it out to the rest of Freedom Five—the still more improbable suggested itself to her.

237

There was an inner spoken phrase connected with this. It had come to her almost as a physical sensation, one of boundless joy and power, and it began with the words, "We could. . . ." (Sometimes it occurred as "*I* could. . . ." The jinn of imagination spoke, and she was momentarily blinded, blurred by the potential implicit in the beginning of the sentence; her interest quickened, the tips of her fingers burned.

Later in the week—when she had been helping clean the Adams house or watching naked Barbara or dreaming on the river beach—an amplification of this sentence came to her: *"We could do it so beautifully that. . . ."* And Dianne was startled. By those words sounding in her mind, apparently independent of her will, she was informed: to the limitless if urgent realm of possibility was added the factor of beauty and symmetrical completeness. Mythology. Like in her book. It was as if the wandering, innocent hand, having begun to draw a segment of arc, discovered—the line surely commanded and not the person—the inevitability of the circle. To each fair beginning, solution and finality are promised.

"We could kill her so beautifully that. . . ." Dianne had stood up—electric, rapt, visionary—and nearly wept. "We could kill her so beautifully that. . . ." Her plans for the execution had begun immediately. "We could kill her so beautifully that. . . ." She had told Paul that.

Of course.

Of—course!

The vision waned, the mystic transport of mind evaporated, and Dianne frowned. To give her credit, she had thought a moment or two about the fact that if they were successful, they would be killing a person like themselves. To the sort of credit she would prefer, however, she dismissed the motion in favor of the grand design upon which they had—was it unknowingly?—embarked. It was not a coldness.

Given the crisis, Dianne would have been one of those cool-headed persons who throw themselves on the bed and forcibly breathe life into a newborn baby still trailing—if knotted—the severed umbilical cord. Given an adult life or the power over that life, she was equally disposed to extinguish it.

Still standing, still frowning, Dianne had decided for Freedom Five (assent assumed) to kill Barbara. The decision was not made on any basis of moral right or wrong, of human sympathy or brotherhood, or even of cause and effect, crime and punishment. It was simply that the great wheel dipped close, silently, unstoppably spinning, its bright, inner workings momentarily visible and available to the touch. Put your finger here, and you create life; put it there and you alter it; put it yet there and you erase it. Unguided, untutored, unhindered, she reached out her hand—or was it drawn into the wheel?—and touched. So much for Barbara, whoever she was. Dianne breathed deeply and guiltlessly.

"What're we going to do?"

"What?" Dianne was startled.

"What're we going to do about the Picker?" Cindy asked.

Dianne turned around in a sudden flush of emotion, of longing and desire and frustration and anger all mixed together. They were so close to doing something marvelous now, something out of sight, something *real,* that they couldn't let it be stopped. The design so inadvertently discovered *had* to be completed, and so—in mind—she put out her hand and touched the shiny spinning wheel again. "We'll kill him, too," she said.

"What?"

"It's part of the story. . . ."

"Cool it!" John whispered in a shout, or shouted in a whisper. "Mother might hear us down here."

"Kill him"—Dianne immediately dropped to a whisper, too, but the words kept coming out—"Like I said. If we go and let *them* out Sunday, and they tell us what happened to her, and we go up in the field and find him with the body, we *have* to shoot him." She turned to John. "Can you? You're the only one who can."

"Stop making so much noise," John said. "Let's wait until we're over in the woods to talk about it. On the other side."

"Yeah." Even Paul understood the tactics of secrecy.

"Yeah, let's," Cindy whispered.

"But *can* you?" Dianne said.

"Get in."

10

After the children left her in the tenant house alone, Barbara had struggled in a sorry way with the ropes that held her, rocking and squirming around on the cracked linoleum, trying to see if there was anything that might be useful for escape. Being left unattended in a new place for an hour or two gave her hope. In all of this, however, she accidentally rolled over, landing with a hurt on her side, and that ended possibilities of doing more. As Freedom Five had foreseen, getting away was out of the question. Barbara let her head fall, cheek against shoulder, closed her eyes, and wished, not that she were free now, but that she was. . . .

The word was *dead*.

With any kind of true presence, of course, she might have dismissed the emotion. After all, not so much had been done to her. She had been captured and confined; she had been embarrassed; she had been forced to grant sexual intercourse—it was far short of fatal—and she had been underfed and overguarded. The children had even hit her a few times and yet, to a strong, athletic girl, the grand sum total of punishment could have been endurable if spaced out. The body is a remarkable machine, her coaches had told her; and it was true. In training and in swim meets she had hurt for periods of time, ten seconds, thirty seconds, possibly a minute and then she had been able to give up and spring back again.

Now there was no springing back, and the period

241

of that time reached beyond her imagination which reached only beyond the next zillionth of a second. Time was a terrible curve in which the first second was two seconds long; the second, five; the third, fifteen; the fourth, thirty; and so on. People in pain live by a different clock, she thought; it *never moves.*

Her back, shoulders, arms, and legs were gathered together behind her in a web of rope and unreachable knots. Heel ground on heel, ankle on ankle (and the flesh over them was deeply bruised). Wrist ground on wrist, elbow on elbow, and her shoulders arched in a bow-strung tenseness that could not be released. The weight of her head bent the neck and forced her nose and forehead down on the dirty linoleum, and her breasts, ribs, and belly ground against the rough floor.

It was the doling out, the unremitting constancy of pain—as a migraine is constant—that had worn her down to a state near to hysteria. The very thoughts and emotions that made Barbara, Barbara, were scarcely present any more: they were drowned out by the single phrase, "I wish I were dead (rather than this)."

No! She raised her head suddenly and stared out across the dirty floor through the window at the storm sky—never so free and violent and beautiful-seeming—her eyes wide at the horror of self-betrayal. No!

"Dead," in fact, was what was promised. They were going to *do things to her*—in pain she could not conceive of more pain except in a blackness of mind that she pushed away from herself—they were going to kill her or said they were. Such things happen.

The children had the power, opportunity, imagination, and more than an inclination, but did they have. . . ? Barbara lowered her head and intensified a new ache somewhere in her body. Were they that *inhuman?* Life just wouldn't be possible if a person had to go around in the knowledge that the next person she met would—given any kind of chance—kill her. But *didn't* they? *Don't* they, Barbara said. All the time? Every day?

242

I don't understand, Barbara said. I can't believe it. They're only innocent *kids*.

However, if not-knowingness and humbleness are the beginnings of religiosity, Barbara was now more religious than she had been at any moment of her former, childlike faith. And if wordless need and trust are prayer, she prayed.

No one is used to being operated. That is, no one is used to having their life lived for them, to breathing only when someone allows them to breathe, moving only when the other person allows them to move, gaining comfort—relative—only when another human being grants it to them. Nonetheless, so broken to this system had Barbara become, that she was absurdly thankful when Bobby spread down his own sleeping bag, rolled her over onto it, slackened her bonds, and pillowed her head on his windbreaker. Suddenly he was there in the house again, and she was not alone. Suddenly there was at least softness against her body. Suddenly there was privacy and a shred of human dignity beneath the sleeping bag top. Suddenly kindness hurt her.

Barbara's legs, allowed to extend, did so with electric-seeming shocks, and pain long blocked by numbness flashed through to her. She tried to stretch, to move her toes and fingers, and could feel nothing but prickles and hotness. She throbbed both in relief and in pain and thankfulness. They *were* good children, or at least this one was. Thank you, Bobby, Barbara said.

He had removed the unnecessary ropes from around her upper arms and body; he had eased her ankles away from her wrists, so that she could straighten herself; and he had made his support for her head. At the sound of her sob, moreover, he looked at her with alarm and sadness and offered the ultimate gift—he removed her gag.

From the beginning, gagging Barbara had been one of Freedom Five's problems. If they hurt her too much, and she began crying and her nose filled up (how well they knew it as coughy kids), she would not

243

be able to breathe and would suffocate behind that adhesive tape and rag. That—this being the situation—she would die of imposed anguish, self-pity, and so on, was irony lost on Freedom Five. They simply knew that she could die if they did not take care. In their watches they had listened to her breathing, and in their torments of her they had listened with even greater care.

So it was that Bobby now ungagged her quickly and nimbly. The tape came off with an audible, tearing sound, and the rag came out to lie at her side. Barbara sniffed and licked her dry lips with a dry tongue. Outside, it had grown quite dark and still. Older girl, younger boy, they were astonishingly—each felt it—alone, and he had let her talk, and she couldn't say a word.

Can words and eyes and tone of voice alone persuade? Can anyone convince anyone else of anything at all? Is it ever possible to change the direction of things that are about to happen?

What Barbara wanted to say was the everything of everything, the *me of me*, the absolute necessity of necessity. Words, sentences, paragraphs, speeches, books, entire libraries of appeal, should have filled her mind, but they would have boiled down to the one thing. *I must live.* And would he understand even that? She looked at Bobby and knew that she could not make him know. Not now. Not really. One day he might create life, and—tomorrow—he might help end it, but he couldn't understand what it meant to lose it. He was too young, too rich in life-yet-to-come. It wasn't that valuable, yet. What she actually said was, "Can I have a drink or something, please? I don't need much. Just something?"

What he said was, "All I've got is a soft drink." Still, he got it for her, opened it, lifted her grown head in the bend of his arm, and let her drink. When it dribbled down the side of her cheek, he wiped it with his hand and then wiped his hand on the sleeping bag. She coughed.

"I'm sorry," he said. "Is everything OK?"

244

The absolute monstrousness of the question, she ignored. They were going to kill her—Bobby, too—and he was being nice. Unbelievable. Nonetheless that was the situation that they were in. Reality has its force; God helps those who help themselves.

"Bobby," she said, "are they really going to kill me? Are *you* going to kill me?"

Bobby pulled the sleeping bag top around her shoulders and sat back on his heels. She looked up, and he seemed very far above her: he was a boy-god. "I dunno," he said seriously. "I really don't know. I guess so." He seemed thoughtful enough, even unsure.

Barbara stared at him with an intensity that she had never put forth in her life. There was goodness in Bobby. It seemed strange under the circumstances to recognize it, but she had been right. He could be appealed to. He had breeding, nobility, courage to work hard, and give up things, and he was sweet. Among his peers he would shine out—*had* shone out—among children he was the one a prospective parent might pick for her own. Some day he would be a credit to the human race, and yet he was ready to kill. That was the one thing he could not be made to know. When she died, everything *stopped:* it didn't, of course, but to *her,* it did. She considered infinity while he balanced units and percentile figures.

"Why?" she said. *"Why,* Bobby?"

He shrugged. He encompassed the entire history of oratory in his shrug. "I dunno," he said again. "I really don't know. Honest."

"Bobby . . ." Her ropes held her, her nakedness held her, her helplessness held her. "Bobby, *think* a minute."

"Yeah. OK."

The thunder came closer and the first advance drops of rain hit the tin roof. This is insane. I'm dying, Barbara said. "Bobby, think about it carefully."

"I said OK."

All of the time that he sat there—back on heels, fair, young face alight, consideration at the forefront—

245

he still seemed remote. Bobby's compassion and humanity were under a strange control. It seemed charity against getting caught, kindness against duty. She was only relative on his scale of things, and she had never realized that such a thing was possible between people. He was on the other side, a side she had never considered to exist at all—another race of human beings entirely separate from herself—and yet the separation was blade clean.

The hopeless, alien strangeness of another complete, isolated human being, another person—*the* other person—engulfed her. She did not think it in words, but the feeling chilled her nonetheless: we are not alike. The way I think is not the way he thinks. What works for me doesn't work for him at all. He's other. *I'm* other to him.

At the thought Barbara's friendly and trusting life did finally come to an end. The rather sweet, milky, vague possibilities of general love diminished and vanished. The cruelties of captivity endured were real, not play. They were planned and intended. The fact that they were administered by children did not count at all. Long ignored, a certain coldness and uncaringness, running through all life, appeared to her. She understood; she wished to tell Terry.

We're alone, Terry, she said. There's nobody here but people, and the closer we get, the more we're alone.

Terry was silent.

"Bobby," Barbara said, "you're hurting me. I can't move. It hurts so much I can't even think straight." She let her head sink onto his windbreaker and closed her eyes. "Bobby—one last try—why did you do this to begin with? Really? In the beginning?"

"I dunno," he said for the third time. He shifted himself around and sat down cross-legged. "Because we *could*, I guess. It seemed like fun."

She opened her eyes and looked up. He seemed so innocent and pretty that Barbara almost understood what he meant. "It's not true."

"What?"

"Fun."

Bobby said nothing.

"Is it? Is it *now?*"

"Well . . . not so much, I guess."

But he wasn't going to untie her, not yet. He wasn't ready to let her live. Barbara said nothing.

Thunder came again. A nervous puff of wind shook the tenant house. Bobby looked over his shoulder and out the window and then composed himself a while longer. He seemed as lonely as she ". . . not so much," he echoed himself. "It's funny."

"What's funny?"

"Like the way it didn't come out that way," he said. "Like when we were all figuring out if we could do it, it seemed like something we *had* to do. You know? Like if you think you can do something, you *have* to."

"You don't *have* to do anything. You don't *have* to hurt people."

"I know what you're going to say, but—" Bobby suddenly clamped down in stubbornness.

"I'm sorry." Barbara was stretched out and comforted, and she was allowed to talk. I can't let him stop now, Barbara said.

"It's OK," he said.

She nearly died with relief.

He didn't notice. "I dunno, it was like something that *ought* to be done. Like we couldn't help it." He stopped and looked at her moodily. "And it was OK at the beginning. Then it was a drag. Now . . ." this was a long speech for Bobby, and he suddenly seemed to realize it. "The reason I took off your gag is that I'm sorry."

"About what?"

"That it's you."

"But it *is* me." Something in Barbara let go, and with all her strength she pulled at the cords and knots that held her. "I'm me." She collapsed again. "I'm— me. You like me. You don't have anything against me. Just let—me—go. Please!"

247

"*I* would," he said, but I can't." He seemed finished with the talk; he had known what she was going to say anyhow. He put his hands on the floor to get up.

"Bobby, don't go."

"I'm not going anywhere. I mean, not away from here. Just around"—he actually seemed solicitous—"Don't be scared."

Monstrous, again.

"I *am* scared," she said. And she was. In pulling against her ropes, she had hurt herself again, and the hurt would not stop. In pulling against Bobby's orderly but other-oriented mind, she had seen the possible future, and that hurt would not stop, either. Desolation. She raised her head and shouted his name, and that didn't help either. She let her head fall and cried.

In all the time and through all the things the children had done to her, Barbara had never really cried. Adult dignity had held out that far. But now she cried, and it was ugly. Her diaphragm heaved; her nose ran; her face streamed water; she made unmaidenly sounds: she cried.

Bobby watched her—she saw him watching her and not doing anything for her—and he appeared distressed. When the crying did not stop—she could not stop it—he got up with his small shotgun and went someplace else. It was beginning to rain now. The boards and nails, the floors of the tenant house, everything moved beneath her. There was no solidity anywhere in the world. They were going to kill her if they could; all of this world would cease all too soon. Her mind could hardly encompass the thought.

Yet so tough is the human creature, that the crying eventually stopped. The body—unbidden—ignored its pain and despair and repaired: it fought for itself. She subsided alone and lay sniffling alone, and after a bit, Bobby came back and bent over her. He took a damp, crumpled paper napkin—it smelled "sandwich"—out of his shorts pocket and let her blow her nose on it, and afterward he wiped her eyes with the same piece of paper. She looked up at him.

"Bobby—" How much can be put into a word? How can you convey the end of the end? "Bobby, just tell me. Why won't you let me go? *Now?* What's stopping you? I don't want to die."

He looked—aside from his concern with the squall and everything else—Bobby looked contrite. He said, "They wouldn't like it."

"They," Barbara said. The rain swept over the building and a livid streak of lightning seemed to hit quite nearby. "They is *nobody*, Bobby. You're the one who's doing it. You're doing this to me. You started it. *You're responsible." Oh, god, tell it to a wall.*

"We voted," he said, "and I lost." Duty, democratic principle, morality, desire, confusion. He seemed genuinely tragic enough, a young boy caught up in a large web of philosophy and religion and man and forever and all of that. "I tried all along. I was on your side," he said, "but I can't help it now."

"You *can!*"

"Well . . . I could, I guess."

"You can! *Do* it."

"Not yet, anyhow," he said. Bobby was getting more and more nervous as the storm grew. He kept darting his eyes around. He was ready to leave again.

She desperately tried to hold that attention on herself. *"Bobby, what's more important, me or those other kids?"*

"Well, I said I'd do my part. . . ."

"Me or them?"

"Them."

Afterward before he left her, he put the gag back in her mouth. First he reached for the chloroform, but she protested, and so they agreed. He stuffed the rag back in her mouth, down the tongue where it nearly made her retch, and then he retaped her.

Help me!

What help?

The squall brought the night. There would be no swift passage and then the reprieve of sunset that so often followed these summer storms. Rain gusted through the broken windows of the upper rooms of the tenant house and made thin mud of the linoleum floors. It grew cold and quite black. Bobby patrolled and then repatrolled the windows on the second floor, his shotgun in arm. Barbara watched him until there was barely enough glow from the stairway lantern to see anymore, and then she listened to him come and go.

Listening, she strained. Little terrors went up and down.

Thunder and lightning and gusts of wind were bad; they increased her desolation. Footsteps were good; he was back again. The sealike sound of wind and rain curling over the tin roof was the worst. She listened for more, anything more, and there was more but only by intervals.

She heard Bobby make a sound in the other room. She sensed his fright. She heard the silence after the squall that was so thinly stretched that a cricket sound would have sounded like an explosion. She heard John's whistle when he came; she heard the whispered conversation between boys downstairs. She could hear them talking to the Picker and then, a long while later, she heard John coming back into the tenant house, up the stairs to guard her. He brought the gasoline lantern with him, its mantle still turned low. He put it on the floor by the wall that was dry, and it underlit him, sending long shadows the wrong way up his body and face.

Where Bobby had seemed sad, however, even consoling, John seemed a number of—and conflicting—other things. Barbara looked up from the zippery pillow for her head that Bobby had made and thought that John looked frightened, and of course this heightened the fear in her. He did not seem to be afraid of anything concrete, such as the man he and Bobby had found outside (now that it was over, at any rate), as he was—perhaps—by this entire situation which would be followed by tomorrow's entire situation. Again, the word was *death* as approached by the young and unready.

John's whole posture—his baby eyes shone in the

lantern light—indicated that something *big* was going to happen that would change the world, the entire world as he experienced it. He dreaded it, and yet he awaited it. He told Barbara that, yes, she would die, and did so by doing no more than standing still and looking down at her, his cut-off shorts and blue chambray shirt black from the rain, his blond hair slightly down over his eyes.

John also told her something else—how much is exchanged by an instant glance—he told her that he valued her for the purse between her legs and that he wanted her tonight. Though he might become one of her killers, though he was terrified at the prospect and the imaginings of what might happen afterward, though he had the *world* to think about in a very fundamental way, it was all overridden by a kind of doggy, randy, panting look around the eyes. She saw it and knew men.

John toured the house perfunctorily; he looked out the windows; he checked his unfired gun. Then after whatever time it took him to work up his resolution, he came to her and uncovered her. He handled every part of her body, and then he moved her.

In the last few days John had learned his trade of jailer well. He tied each of her calves to its thigh, released her feet so that her legs could be parted, and rolled her over on her back. She was presented to him belly up, hips supported by bound hands, knees ajar, open and prepared for the act of rape. So he had intended, so he would perform. He began to take off his few rain-wet clothes, and she watched—what he had done, what he intended to do, she now understood well enough—and she waited for him.

A number of things went through her mind. Nothing superseded the central fact that the children had voted to kill her, and yet a number of other things went through her mind unbidden. They were simultaneous and not clearly separated, one from the other.

He's going to hurt me, Barbara said. It was strange to think of so little a thing as a vaginal hurt when death

251

was the next step in the process, and yet such was the self-protective concern of the body, that in fact, she did think, he's going to hurt me. And he isn't going to care.

None of them will, Barbara said. None of them ever will. It was an odd thought.

Because of John, Barbara was no longer virgin: because of him, her only experience had been painful. Yet because of John, the world of beyond virginity had at least been disclosed. From this point, a wider view was possible. The lovers—so she categorized the yet faceless, somehow powerful and (hopefully) compelling men who might inhabit her life if she was to have one— the other lovers stood invisibly behind John. And they wouldn't care either.

Even now—when she couldn't know who (or even *if*) they would be—she knew that. They were simply waiting their turn at her.

Barbara did not say, I am outraged. It's unlikely that anyone ever does. She saw John and understood what she thought to understand, and simply *was*, thereby, outraged. I am for using. Moreover, she consented. John, the parking-lot sniggerers, the blank-faced lovers all in a line, were too much. The weight was too much. They would have her; they would unstoppably pour into her. Whether I want or not, she said.

He's handsome enough, Barbara said, and this was an even more impossible thought. John was prone to fat after a lazy summer, and the hard, muscular, tendon-sharp corners of his future shape were still encapsulated in softness and roundness and unformedness. Man-child, child-man, he was frosted in baby-fine body hair. And yet he was tall, as tall as she: and yet he was strong even now, stronger perhaps than she. And he was here, and he was going to do it to her. (Her never-anything-but-polite mind could not translate the exact term describing sexual intercourse into any other word but *it*.)

He's the only one, she thought, the one and only, first and maybe—it now became terribly possible— maybe the last person who would ever enter my body.

The waste, the waste. How much I have to give and never knew it. I can give, I can do, I can *be*. I *could* be.

He's going to kill me, Barbara said, her thought cycling back to the one central issue between them. He might be the one who, in the end, did the *real* 'it' to her, somehow and by means of his own choice. The rape-to-be was only a premature killing. We are enemies.

Men and women are enemies, Barbara thought.

If she lived, if through some careless charity of unknowing children, she was allowed to live, that part would still be the same. A man would change her life, lift her out of being into motherhood, and being something else and having done so, would not himself be changed. Men altered women; it was the female sentence. In the now-case, she might be altered to "dead."

I have power over him, Barbara said. By just being me. Right now he couldn't live without my living. It was clear.

John, looking down on the helpless her, was himself made helpless enough. He was compelled. His nose flared; he breathed in short breaths as he got out of his shorts and stood naked. His rubbery *thing* rose (Barbara's nicety again). It led him; he must do it. He seemed confused and blank-eyed. He was not in control of himself, and it was because of *her*. Whatever happened hours from now, she directed him for the moment, and in that moment and in that direction, might somehow escape.

This all occurred to her, not as sequential thought, but as a flash of recognition and hope when she looked up into his eyes. All at once. She realized that she did not know how to act nor had any time to learn.

She did not know whether she pleased him more as resisting slave or as cooperative lover. She had as little idea of how to please him as he had of her. And yet she *had* to please—it was the key word—to become valuable, too valuable to kill. I wish I knew how whores do it, Barbara thought desperately.

It was all going too fast.

Barbara—the body of Barbara—writhed in girlish fear and directly for his benefit. It was sincere enough at root. Never in her life had the feeling of being truly afraid had any semblance of reality at all, but it was real enough now. It was also accentuated: Sexy Barbara (who was, after all, barely amateur) helped. Her not-so-exciting breasts heaved; her more-than-enough hips strained upward; her less-than-killing eyes flickered. Is that it? Barbara wondered. Is it *enough?* She flung her head sideways and closed her eyes in a not entirely acted anguish, and she waited.

John knelt in a state of adolescent reverence, the boy for the girl. He parted her doubled legs and lay down on top of her and kissed her and was lost. That was it. I *have* him, Barbara thought. It was not that she would not have been forced anyhow; it was that she had elicited a measure of affection aside from and above simple lust.

They nuzzled, everything at his instigation. That is, he rubbed his face into her, and to what extent seemed likely to her—after all, there was no precedent to follow—she accommodated him. A neck against a face, a taped mouth against a chest, a breast for a mouth. They rolled. When it was time at last, he used spit—how necessary and instinctive such acts are—and it was done by a young-people, short and friction-torn intrusion.

It *did* hurt for a bit, but it was done—had been going to be that way anyhow—and within her, he rested securely. The interrupting penis was like a thing of her own deep up within her, its tip against the unexplored inner tip of her body. She fisted her bound hands beneath her and waited—pretty child, silly boy, killer-man—and lowered her eyes.

John rested that way, long and disciplined for someone with only one experience and then he began to pump her. Barbara thought of the old description, the town pumphouse. John was pumping her with that distant look in his eyes—asking—and by such direct

254

means, he would probably *get*. There was no way now to reach him, no, plead with him later.

Her flesh grudgingly slipped outward, and her flesh grudging slipped inward. It was pulled as it was pulled. Someone else was within her as deep as she could imagine that deep could go. Beyond the thrust of his penis was only the her of her, and it did not hurt as much as before. In view of the fact that her lover was her rapist and possibly her killer, her body's complaisance shocked her.

I will not, Barbara said. I will not; I will not; I will not.

Oh god, I might, Barbara discovered. Sometimes it is possible to be made to enjoy.

Please, *not*.

John gave a sound and completely expended himself in her—she sensed it more than felt it—and then fell on her. There was a pressure that thrust as high up as her navel.

I can't, Barbara said. Not if he's going to kill me.

Hold on, Barbara said, just another second. . . .

As slowly as Christmas coming, John removed the tape and rag from her mouth and kissed her as he should have done days ago. They lay together, and he kissed her, and every possible part of his body was touching and sticking to every possible part of hers.

Now, now, Barbara thought. No, dammit, not now. Not ever with him.

They were loving enemies, and he extended a trusting tongue into her mouth and along her teeth, and again she absorbed him. She did not bite. She reached inside of him and explored all the hardness of his mouth.

Oh, no, not love now, Barbara thought. I don't want it. Don't give me any part of it.

Yes, *now,* Barbara admitted.

It is not possible to describe an orgasm, certainly not possible to describe the first, possibly only and last orgasm of a beginning lifetime. It is a death as has been agreed upon; it is a death which may—with

255

luck—be repeated. It is a death to be extended death-
lessly, a death to be sought, a death one willingly dies.

Stop it, Barbara thought, and could not stop it.

John was talking something to her and kissing her,
and she was kissing him back and could not have cared
less in any situation. Oh, John, stop it and let it be.

"Oh . . . ," this was the principal, intelligible
sound that came from his mouth. She understood.

"Oh . . ." was similarly the only decent reply, and
still he rested within her and on her and seemingly all
around her. "Oh . . . ," and then they collapsed.

Each one collapsed, and they lay still and one together, and looked out across the wetted room and the
mud of dust on linoleum and the cracked plaster ceiling
and the streaked plaster walls. And since there had
been a squall—how far away it seemed now—there was
in addition the thunder of distant thunder to be heard.

"John"—she kissed his cheek—"Johnny?"

"What?" He spoke from beneath her ear, in her
hair.

"John, why are you going to kill me?"

He was silent. He thought or seemed to be thinking. In the hesitation alone was danger. It was not a
matter of whether but—to arrive at the exact point—
one of answering her question of Why.

"John. . . ."

"I know."

"John"—she kissed his ear—"why when you can
be like this instead?"

"I don't know"—he kept his face buried in the
turn of her neck.

"John, don't do that now."

He said nothing.

"Just tell me, if you're going to do it to me."

"I said I don't know."

"Yes, you do."

"Not really."

"Do."

Some women move their inner organs to please a
man; others to defend. Barbara didn't know that this

could be done, but she did it with ancient instinct and expelled him.

"W - h - y?"

For a moment, he seemed extinguished. He lay on her as a dead weight and hurt her bound hands that held them both. Then—how quickly the young revive—she felt the movement of his arms. He gathered himself and raised up on elbow to look at her. "Because it's the next thing that happens."

"I won't tell. I've promised that. . . ."

"I don't mean about telling."

"I mean, I won't tell *anybody*."

"Oh. . . ." He raised his head, looked beyond her and sighed. "That doesn't matter so much anymore."

"Then what *does?*" Barbara said. "John, I'm me. I'm a person. I have a right to go on being me. *That's* what counts."

"I guess so."

"What do you mean, you guess so?"

"I guess it's pretty hard. I'm sorry." He seemed so. He hugged her with seemingly genuine enough affection. His strong baby-arms went around her shoulders, and he kissed her on the forehead, but all of that was over now.

Barbara could not even act for him. She said over his shoulder, "Then why does it have to be the next thing that happens?"

"I dunno. I . . . guess it just went too far." He released her and very slowly sat up and back on his heels.

She was cold where he had covered her. "The game."

"Yeah." He reached over for his shorts, got up, and started putting them on.

"How, for God's sake?"

"Well . . . like when you came, the first thing was could we do it, and that's all anybody thought about it. And then when that happened and it was boring, the next thing was. . . ." He shrugged. By the movement he

257

indicated her nakedness, her just-past rape, her fear. ". . . this."

For every step, there had been another step. Bobby had been right: it began because it could. The sheer possibility was irresistibly compulsive, addictive. Was that all anybody needed to become torturer, rapist, killer, just the possibility and then the power and then a way out-free? Barbara saw back over the past days as a single, horrible revelation. "Oh."

John picked up his damp shirt and put it on. He said nothing.

"But why didn't you stop? You could see what was happening, you can see what's happening *now*. It's still going on."

"Because we didn't know, I guess."

"But you do now!"

"Yeah, I guess so." He finished buttoning up and stepped into his moccasins.

"Then stop it now."

"I can't."

"Yes-you-*can!*" Barbara shouted. "Let me go. Now. Right this minute. It won't even take a minute. And then it'll all be over, and you'll be safe. It's your life, too, you know. They'll catch you no matter what you've thought up and you'll spend the rest of your life in prison. You know that."

John's expression showed that he had, indeed, considered the matter, still had to consider it, of course. It also showed that *the risk had been accepted.*

"You won't. *Oh, god!* You can, and you won't." Barbara began to cry again. "He won't," she said aloud to the world around, "he won't, he won't, he won't. . . ."

"It's too late." The regret was fading from John's voice. She had lost him for the last time.

Barbara looked up, and though John's face was water-blurry to her, she saw where his thoughts had begun to wander. It was so horrible that she wet the sleeping bag and herself. He was thinking about—about a world she would never know, a time (could it be as little as twelve hours from now?) that was beyond any time she would ever experience. He was thinking *beyond her lifetime.*

It was impossible. He was thinking of something as ordinary as Saturday afternoon or Sunday, perhaps, and it was all beyond her lifetime. And where would she be? In the heaven she'd been told about? Cold and stiff in death and half hidden by the weeds of a country ditch? Sunk in the river? Buried?

She could not even become hysterical. The look on his face, though not really intended for her, was too numbing for there to be anything save the reactive spurt of urine all over her legs. She even stopped crying. It was like being in shock. She went dead-cold; she trembled uncontrollably; her breathing was irregular; she felt that she had forgotten how to blink her eyes. They felt dry and wide open and unfocussed. She barely felt what was being done to her.

John almost idly bound her ankles together again and them to her wrists again. He rolled her on her side and closed the sleeping bag over her up to the neck, and then he passed clothesline around the sleeping bag until she was cocooned. Then he gathered up his things, looked around carefully for mistakes, gagged her, and left. She could hear him going down the stairs and then gone.

Barbara understood.

She wasn't going to escape; she wouldn't die; and the prowler, whoever he had been, had gone. There was no longer any need to guard her.

Nobody was coming.

Late in the morning Dianne came. Dianne came up the stairs of the tenant house and knelt beside Barbara.

The dawn had come kindly over an unkind world for Barbara. The rain of the night had washed out the dust and the haze and the mosquitoes from the air—and through the window—the sky had been as green and clear and blameless as the sea, as green and cold-blue

259

as autumn, or the promise of autumn (which it was). There were corners and edges of unbelievably soft, white-gray clouds which she could see through the window. Bound, naked, shivering even within the sleeping bag, she had seen and felt the chillness of the dawn and of the promised fall.

The day—to her limited field of vision—had grown in the same way, grown into a great, white towering day of the change of seasons, summer and yet not any more summer, not winter and yet winter to come. The day had grown into something of indescribable beauty to her, something inscrutable, ironic, cruel, and yet still beautiful.

Is this the last and only one? Barbara said.

She had the hungry desire to be outside and in it, free and naked and bowed on her knees, her forehead to the earth: she had the ravenous want to open her mouth and bite the wholesome dirt, to feel the cool, damp grit and sand in her mouth and between her teeth. It was a more ancient form of prayer than she had known before. I want the dirt in my mouth, and then it will be all right, she thought. I want the dirt on my whole face, dirt in my hair, dirt against my whole body and then I'll be safe. On the earth, with the grass and weeds lay anonymity, oneness, inviolability.

Is this the last and only day? *Dirt, I pray to you.*

And a little while later, Dianne came up the stairs. She came slowly and coolly and quietly, and she carried impossible things. She carried a pitcher of water—country style—a washrag, a fresh, bristly nylon hairbrush, and—as Barbara saw—cologne.

Before anything else, Dianne set these things down and took off her shorts and blouse. This was done primly, obviously more out of a want to stay neat than from any near attempt at disclosure. (It was difficult to imagine Dianne ever being naked entirely. Perhaps she never was.) Afterward, Dianne knelt down and mostly untied Barbara. She undid the ropes around the sleeping bag, opened it and undid the rope that John had put on hours earlier until only three were left—ankles, wrists, upper arms. Everything else lay on

260

the floor around them. Blood pushed through bruised arteries and again burned in Barbara's body. Dianne was good. It was a simple thank you: Dianne might be going to help kill her, but Dianne was kind. Barbara straightened out stiffly. Then Dianne began to bathe her.

She did it with knowingness and gentleness and womanliness. So completely knowing was Dianne's touch that Barbara had the feeling it was her own hands touching herself. She bathed Barbara's streaked face and her neck and upper body and rinsed them softly. She reached between Barbara's legs where John had forced her to orgasm and where she had peed on herself, and washed her gently *there*. She washed her legs and feet and dried them, and afterward she patted on the cologne she had brought. Finally she took Barbara's head in her lap and brushed her hair.

There was sensuousness in it. The soap was mild and scented, and the wash cloth was from an expensive monogrammed set. The cologne was summery, and the stroke of the brush was gentle and lulling. Feeling all of it and knowing that she could be killed soon now, Barbara took these little pleasures in bitterness.

If nothing happens, she said—what a big "if," what a steadily vanishing "if," what a never-was-there "if," what a totally, impossible "if"—if nothing happens to stop what is happening, I'm going to die. And O god, the sun's already up *that* high, the morning's going, help is far-off, and I can die at that. I really can. Barbara, feeling the sensuous strokes of the hairbrush said, maybe there's no way out after all.

But I didn't *live* long enough, Barbara said. I never lived at all. Not until now, and why now? Why at the *last minute?*

No.

I will *not* be dead, Barbara said. No matter what they say and no matter what they do, I'll live. I *have* to live. I've been fooled. The horror of what they call horrible just isn't all that bad. No matter what they do, I'll endure it and live. I've been fooled. It doesn't even have to be my way: I'll give them that, too. I lost and I need.

I - will - do - anything - to - live.

And the brush stroked her hair, and it continued. Dianne went on stroking her hair with the brush—right and left, back and front; Barbara could not resist—until the short, springy hair became as fine and airy as the webs of spiders that spin silver webs. It lifted. Barbara rested her side-of-face against Dianne's thin, tanned thighs and let it happen because she could do nothing else. I'm dead beautiful, she said.

I'm *not* dead, and I won't ever be.

Forever is long, and I'll live forever, and I'm afraid.

The closeness of death, the sensuousness of death, the utter sensuousness of now-it's-coming-and-I-will-be-gone death, the soft, pulling stroke of the hairbrush against her hair and the closeness of her face to Dianne's body, created a bond between them.

Barbara felt that her part-killer loved her. So much, loving kindness.

Barbara felt that Dianne loved her and envied her, envied her in her dying. I can't understand it, Barbara said. I can't understand and I'll never understand how you could want to kill anyone and at the same time envy them and yet I do understand. It's the big experience, the biggest one you can think of, and I'm going to do it—die—and Dianne cannot. Each eye filled with one big smeary tear.

"Don't" Dianne said soothingly, "not now." She dabbed at Barbara's eyes, put down the cloth, and removed the gag. Then she dabbed around Barbara's mouth. "It won't help." She might be speaking to Paul or Cindy who had just skinned a knee.

For once, Barbara wasn't thirsty. She might never be thirsty again. Held right and left, hand and foot, she lifted her eyes and said, "Why?" She sighed. "Just why, Dianne? Is it because you think you'll *like* killing me? You'll see something new, feel something new, become something new?"

"No-o-o. . . ."

"Then"—Barbara wrenched in (to her) unexpected frenzy and still could not move—"then (O god) why, Dianne?"

Dianne was not afraid, and she did not throw words. She looked down at Barbara—they were upside down to one another—but she looked down and with elementary slowness said, "Because somebody has to win, and somebody has to lose."

"Win what?" Now Barbara no longer spoke loudly to anyone, not to Bobby or Paul or Cindy or John or even to herself. Nonetheless the urgent need to know was in her voice. Oh, the pretty day. "Win what?"

"The game," Dianne said.

Dianne was as cool as when they had met.

Barbara said it very slowly: *"W-h-a-t g-a-m-e?"*

Dianne touched Barbara's cheek with her fingers. "The one that everyone plays," she said. "The game of who wins the game." She seemed content with her circular and unapproachable logic. "People kill people," she said. "Losers lose."

"But you made up the game," Barbara said. "You made up *this* game."

"No, we didn't"—Dianne put down the brush—"I told you that. Everybody's always been doing it, and we're doing it, I guess. It's nothing all that new."

"But you're children . . . !"

"What difference does that make? Anyhow we're not as dumb as you think."

Barbara was nearly defeated. She said, "Dianne, why do you hate me?"

"We don't hate you," Dianne stroked Barbara's hair. "Paul doesn't hate you, or John or Cindy or Bobby or me. It's funny."

"What's funny?"

"We like you. John's sort of in love with you. Well"—she looked a little sad—"I guess you know. But we all like you."

"Like me?"

"Umnn," Dianne nodded. "I never thought it would be like that with somebody. . . ."

Barbara finished the sentence for her, ". . . that you were going to kill."

Dianne nodded again. "That's why it's got to be pretty, as pretty as I can make it."

"Why *pretty?*"

"Oh. . . . Because you're pretty and it's a nice day and we have the *time.*"

"Time for what?"

"You know."

"Dianne," Barbara ignored this because of her fear, "Dianne, listen. Why don't you have a meeting? With *me* there? Just one more meeting? There's time; you said it. . . ."

"Why?" Dianne was astonished.

"If I could talk to you all at one time instead of just one by one, if we could all be together just once, if you'd all listen to me for just a few minutes. . . ."

"Well, *we won't!*"

Without warning, Dianne dropped her loving mood. She emerged out of her seemingly mental cage with fury. "Well, we won't. How do you like *that?*"

"Dianne. . . ."

"You think you're so pretty and so smart and have all the answers," Dianne said. "You come down here and"—here she mimicked Barbara's voice in the old schoolyard way, the Miss Sassy-Frassy way—"you come down here with, 'Why don't we all get together after church?' and 'Why don't we all go swimming?' and 'It'd be more fun if we all did it this way or that way.'" Dianne dropped Barbara's head on the windbreaker and stood up.

"Well, we 'won't all just' do anything, not this or that or anything else. Not anything at all for anybody. Never. Why should we? Do you know who you're talking to?"

"No."

"Us. We're us, and we have a right to be us. We're going to go right on being us, and you know why we're going to kill you?"

"No."

"Well, we may like you OK, but we *hate* you.
264

You make everything bad with your love, love, lovey-dove talk. That's not the way it is. It's not the way we are, and we're going to show you. We're going to prove it. You'll see. You're going to get it." And she gathered her things all neatly together by the door and began putting on her shorts and blouse.

"I do see." O day, Barbara thought. She looked out the inescapable window at the day. "It isn't right, you know." She felt herself losing fight. To one extent, Dianne was correct; here, at least, love was in poor cartel. "It really isn't."

"You're a teacher, all right." Dianne had her back turned to Barbara. She appeared to be buttoning her blouse. "You'd make a good one like all the rest and tell us lies about what isn't so."

"Then what is so?" Barbara could not stand to look at the day she could not live, and she shut her eyes. "What is so, Dianne?"

"Well. . . ." Dianne neatly tucked her blouse below the waistband of her shorts and zipped up the side and buttoned the flap. "It's like on a beach when people go walking along and pass each other and hate each other. You know? Paul and I were on the beach hunting for shells last summer, and these kids came walking up from the other way, and when we passed—without anybody ever saying anything—we were all looking around for something to throw or a stick or a board or something. And I'd never seen them. Neither had Paul. I mean, we just hated each other because it was right, and it was fun, and I was scared, and some of the other kids were a little scared of Paul and me. That's the way I mean."

"Do you like it that way, Dianne?" Barbara rested and did not open her eyes.

"I don't like to use modern words."

"Modern words?" Barbara did look up at her now.

"Groovy. That's just a word little kids use. It isn't real. But it was groovy."

"Dianne. . . ." By inflection and tone of voice, Barbara somewhat changed the subject. "If this was all

265

the other way around and you were me and I was you, would you want me to kill *you?*"

"I wouldn't *want* you to. . . ."

"Would you think I ought to?"

"You'd be winners. It'd be up to you." Dianne was fully dressed again and cooler again. "But I wouldn't be worried." She faced around.

"Why?"

"Because I don't mope and groan and cry around like you do, and anyhow, you wouldn't do it. You're not good enough."

"Good enough!"

"*Brave* enough," Dianne said. "In the end, you'd let me go, and then I'd win anyhow. Sooner or later. All that stuff you believe in that isn't true—I'd win sooner or later even if you were on top."

There was truth there. She's right, Barbara said. I'd do it. I'd let her go. And why? At the enormity of the question Barbara became very nearly sorry that she had ever been Barbara at all. In no way did she agree with Dianne, and yet in no way could she disagree with the girl. There were more Diannes in the world than Barbaras, and the child was right; the Diannes won every time. It was a matter of when and where and *how*. It had always been going to happen, and now it was a matter of negotiating the way out, and Barbara said, "Kill me."

Dianne, having touched her hair, looked down with clarity and alertness. She said nothing.

"Dianne, kill me. Now. Here. Please."

"What?"

"Listen."

Dianne was still.

"Kill me."

Bound, Barbara looked up in helpless appeal. "Kill me," Barbara said. "Kill me right here and now. There's the bottle of stuff over there and a rag in it, and if I breathe enough of it, you'll kill me. You win. You can do it yourself and win. And I *ask* you to do it. Please. If ever anybody ever asked anybody for anything, I ask you, Dianne. Just do it for me now."

Dianne's pale smooth forehead wrinkled.

"Please," Barbara said. "Be kind."

"I can't," Dianne said. "That won't be for an hour yet."

Words, words, words. Somebody said that, Barbara thought. They said, "Words, words, words . . . ." It comes out of a poem or play. Maybe Shakespeare, Barbara thought. Probably Shakespeare. Words, words, words.

Words.

If you think about the word that means "word," it all falls apart. It's an ugly sound that doesn't *do* anything, and if it doesn't, then I can't tell her. Ever.

I'm going crazy, Barbara thought. I'm going insane because I'm so frightened and I'm going to be killed and what is the word that means "help" so that she can understand it. Or the word that means me not being any more. She looked up at Dianne standing above her and knew there was none. I'll never understand her, Barbara thought, and she'll never understand me. It wasn't right, and she didn't understand it, but it was so, and that left only the matter of mercy.

Barbara lay her head back down on the pillow Bobby had provided; it was the only kindness around her. What was the word for mercy? How could she die gracefully? How could she hasten toward the vague, wavery god she both believed in and no longer believed in?

"Dianne, kill me. Really," Barbara said again. "You've got to."

Dianne's face was cool and white and curious.

"No, you're wrong," Barbara said. "You think I'm pretty, but I'm not. You think I'm grown-up and all with all the answers, but I'm not. You think I go around being nice and kind because I want to do something to you—change your mind or something—but I don't. You think it's right to kill me, but it's not. You're wrong, wrong, wrong. I can't tell you how wrong you are, but you're going to do it anyway," Barbara said. "Anyway.

"So kill me now," Barbara said. "Do it the nice

way between us. You can, and I won't feel anything except what anyone feels." She breathed deeply.

What more can I say? Barbara thought.

"I don't want them to cut me or burn me or whip me and laugh at it," she said. "You're a woman, Dianne. You know that . . ." And the day outside was in the act of becoming a golden noon that filled the whole universe and shined in on the muddy floor of the tenant house. *"Do you understand?"*

"Yes," Dianne said. She did. "I really do, but I 'just won't' do it. You won't get out of it just by sniffing a funny bottle. That's *that.*"

"I don't know." Barbara rolled her head and shoulders back so that she could look up and see Dianne clearly, really clearly. Now that all the rest was over—had it bored Dianne?—now that it was almost time, there was a rather subtle animation about Dianne's thin face. She had begun to look forward to it, Barbara could see it in her whole attitude. So there *was* a way to like hurting and killing people: there really *was* another kind of person in the world after all. And how many other kinds after that? "I just don't know." She closed her eyes. "How are you going to do it?"

"That would be telling." The child's phrase was not Dianne's. It was used with sarcasm.

"You know," Barbara said into the darkness behind her eyelids, "if anything happened so that I'd live, I'd hate you the rest of my life. I'd hate it all. I'd hate and I'd hate and I'd hate."

"That's right!" Dianne's voice sounded both surprised and pleased, that of a teacher with a slow pupil who has managed to grasp something at last. "That's what I've been telling you. That's the way it is."

Somehow in the end—or very nearly in the end—Barbara had made the girl happy.

It was later than noon. Because of the washed air and quiet breeze, it was a blinding, blue-white afternoon and strangely cool, and now it was time for the children to come and get her, and they came up the stairs and got ready. They had already regagged her,
268

but in a different way. They had wrapped rope around and around her mouth until the pressure of it forced her lips and teeth apart, and the rope slid into her mouth and held her tongue down tightly.

"It's going to hurt," Dianne had said, "and you're going to cry a lot. You have to be able to breathe through your mouth. I'm sorry."

Then, they had picked her up to go, and they had learned even since yesterday. Bobby had invented the means and instructed them. They simply picked up the sleeping bag on which she was lying—five pairs of hands—and she left the room of the tenant house as if on a litter.

When there was still even a little time left—she didn't know how much, one hour, two—Barbara desperately hoped. Her thoughts centered on the last three possibilities. The first was that the prowler, the man she had never seen, was still around and would somehow interrupt.

This was destroyed when she *heard* him. Below, outside, the children came chatting down the path to the house and she heard the man's deep voice.

"Here?" He sounded odd. The *re* sound seemed to trail out to some length. There had been a metal clanking sound.

"Yeah, that's OK."

"Thanks."

"And come back tomorrow morning and help us clean up," this had been Dianne. "There'll probably be a few more things to do."

"Sí, I will." The *ll* was again a drawn-out, soft sound, and, then—how could Barbara know?—he was gone. The children had him in tow as completely as they had her.

The second possibility, the one that had always been there and always been disappointed, was the chance of outside visitors. She had listened for a car. Never in her life had she ever so much wanted to hear the sound of a car, the sound of a horn, but none

269

came. There were only the sounds of the country nearly asleep on a Saturday afternoon.

Then, with revulsion, she had heard brief flames and had smelled smoke, and this had crossed out the last chance. There would be no last-second change of plans by Freedom Five, not even any quick thing like shooting her. It too had all been thought out: it was going to be like they always played.

The children had done well not to feed Barbara. Her bowels heaved but were empty. She retched in terror, but it was only a dry convulsion. Then they came and got her.

Freedom Five took Barbara down the stairs somewhat twisted around on the sleeping bag. It bumped; she bumped; but they finally got her down into the space beside the tenant house and got her to the big field gate that had blown down during the night. They bound her to it, all four limbs spread—it took a while and a fight—and bound her to it tightly.

There was a surburban—pressed and painted—metal type of barbeque grill set beside the gate, and it was smoking, and on top of the coals was the living-room poker from the Adams house. Everything had the Picker's fingerprints on it, because he had been paid five dollars from Barbara's meager change purse to clean the inside of the house (leave fingerprints there) and bring the grill down. To preserve all this, Freedom Five had several pairs of gardening and work gloves there.

The lazy white smoke rose and dissipated for a time, and they looked down into the grill. Finally they were ready.

They squatted; they hunkered. They looked at Barbara and at her unmarked skin like students on a field trip. Innocent curiosity. Something new. And then Paul picked up the poker and found it nearly red-hot.

Cindy, in her ten-year-old judgment had been quite correct. Paul had a fetish: he lived convinced that a woman's psyche was to be found in the bottoms of her bare feet. This being the case and Paul having the first "touch"—unanimously Freedom Five had granted it to the weakest—he put the poker to the pale sole of the girl they had known as Barbara. The result was startling, even to them.

The heated metal went in and in. It might have no end to its course. It went through the skin, through the subcutaneous layer, through the nerve endings and blood vessels to the swimmer's tendons and nearly into them. And when it came away, it came pulling black flesh. Afterward the wound bled, but not as much as Freedom Five had expected. It was nearly cauterized, and most of the blood came slowly and thickly.

Paul was rewarded in all of this.

The victim, whoever she was, spasmed in an unimaginable way and made a sound utterly wonderful to him. He had never heard it before and would probably never hear it again, but it was gratifying and altogether satisfying. He would have done it again, but he had to pass the "touch" to John, who returned the iron to the fire for a minute or two.

The other kids, excited faces alight with learning, squatted and leaned closer. Then finally John was ready. He swallowed.

O day, O day, Barbara said. When she had finished fighting, and the children had her fast to the gate, she said, O day, O day. It's not only the last one, but it's the last minute of the last and only one.

Oh, she said. I want to fall up off the earth into the sky and just disappear. It might hurt, but then it would all be over, and I wouldn't have to be human anymore. No one can bear to know humans and bear being human.

But it won't happen. It never happens when you need it.

So it began.

Barbara raised her head and saw most of what was going to occur.

Paul took the metal from the fire and looked at her with the clearest, the most curious and terrifying eyes she had ever seen. Innocence is the most frightening sight of all.

271

He quite truly seemed to want to know what he didn't know, and he truly felt unsure about the result. He turned and bent, and the iron disappeared behind her own foot, which she moved—it could move a frantic inch or two—as best she could. If he did *that*, then he and the others would do what she could not even imagine. And behind Paul all the rest of them stood invisibly: the parking-lot sniggerers, Terry, Ted, the rest —the practical ones—not as torturers but as notaries. However they might later hear of it—really—she saw them impassively gather to certify what happened to people like her.

End, she thought.

End, end, end.

But nobody ever comes to the real end, do they? We talk about it, but it never really happens to really us, does it?

Then it all went swiftly.

She felt the poker touching, going through her, into her and then back out again, and she felt all that happened in the process. But, it occurred as a sudden, nearly fatal blackness of the mind after which nothing could ever be the same again.

This is the end; this is what the end looks like and feels like and oh, god, he's still got it in me. And after Paul regretfully removed the iron, she still felt it in her. She would forever as long as forever could last.

The wound was born inside of her like another personality whose power overcame all of her own, virtually wiped out all of her own. She shuddered as if in electric shock. Nothing could allow life to go on being as it was at that instant. She raised her head looking for something—anything—to stop it, and saw John bending over her.

He put the horrible metal to her breast; then Dianne laid a vivid stripe across her belly. Even Bobby and Cindy took their turn dabbing at her and were thereby edified.

Afterward, the last inhibitions gone, they did all the things to her—under the circumstances—that they had ever imagined doing to all the invisible, meaningless

272

people of their imagination, and while it was far different from what they had imagined, they persisted. It all took a while.

Approximately halfway through the program, Barbara cheated them. She ceased to leap and make appropriate sounds, and lay still and did not react to their torture. After a while, Freedom Five's game became boring—as usual—and so they killed her and got done with it.

They twisted a rope around her neck and put a piece of wood in it and twisted until the rope cut into her throat and no breath was possible. This had been thought out before, and the hands that did it were gloved, and there was only the traceless rope constricting what was left of life.

At the end, at the very end, when it would least have been expected, Barbara surprised them one more time. Her long-closed eyes popped open, wide and staring but suddenly extremely intelligent and clear, and she stared at them. She didn't stare at any one of them in particular—her eyes seemed to include them all without moving—but she stared at them as a human to humans, and her eyes formed the shape of the letter O. And their mouths and eyes opened in silent answer and formed the same, silent letter O.

Then that part of it was complete.

Freedom Five wept.

Oddly, with love.

Epilogue

One event inevitably fathers another and other events. Some of them are worth note in this case.

The people who get most of their adventurous life from the news led very interesting lives for several days after Barbara's death. It is barely possible to turn away from such headlines. (It is conjectural to wonder about those who read: elderly ladies in homes, train-commuting husbands going to town, secretaries on coffee break, housewives yawning before the real day begins, the kids who throw out the evening papers? The thread continues forever.) Some of them read:

BOYS AVENGE BABY-SITTER'S
TORTURE SLAYING IN MD.

LOCAL GIRL DIES IN BIZARRE CASE
SUSPECTED KILLER SHOT BY BOYS

As a follow-up:

SLAIN CO-ED TOOK HOURS TO DIE

And so on, and so forth.

Cruz, of course, was killed. It was as planned. John visited the Adams' house Sunday after church and let the kids out of the closet (Cindy was a wreck). He and Bobby waited for Cruz and told him to go down and bring back the barbecue, and they followed him with guns.

The tragic look on Cruz's face was less for his own death—he never anticipated that—it was for what he had seen just before he turned around to look at the boys, his mouth in the shape of a soundless O. He had never known, and when he finally knew, could not believe. They very nearly cut him in half at close range.

He got a very small notice in the papers.

After they had strangled Barbara, Freedom Five still had to clean up. The sleeping bag had to go back; the gloves be returned; and the house and path swept down, so that only Cruz's footprints would be clear the next day. They went about it robotlike, pale, silent, talking in whispers. Dianne was the last one out of the tenant house, and she swept her way downstairs with a handful of weeds and with tears running out of her eyes. (They had to give Paul a shot of Scotch to get him moving home, but he came around when he had to.)

Freedom Five—all of them, of course—were questioned.

Dianne, her eyes carefully cooled back down to pale gray, could tell them very little. She and her brother, Paul, and John Randall went over to the Adams' every day and used their beach to go swimming. The middle of last week, Bobby Adams had mentioned that there was someone camping down just beyond the pines, but she had never seen whoever it was, and besides, none of them thought much about it. Not even Barbara. After all, where was the harm? (And she did mention Cindy coming over and their baking a cake for Dr. and Mrs. Adams' return and all the rest of it.) Throughout, she remained very thoughtful and tried to remember everything she could, but she was still just a teen-ager, and there was only so much to remember.

The questioning of Paul was given up as not only

useless but possibly harmful to the boy. The detective was the only one of the Bryce Police Department so designated and was, of course, a part of the community. He knew the McVeigh family and the doctor who attended them, and in the end he knew Paul quite well. The boy was very delicately balanced—on the verge of insanity to the detective's mind—and so the questioning took the form of a friendly casual chat, which was terminated when Paul literally went into spasm. Barbara's death was hard enough for adults to stomach, much less a nervous young boy. The detective thought in pity that the thing might have marked Paul for life.

The questioning of John took place as that of one athlete talking to another. The detective had—not all that long ago—played football for the same high school that John now attended. He followed the teams of his alma mater with year-around fervor. In the summer he followed the fortunes of the Baltimore Orioles, who at the time were richly rewarding his interest with another pennant. The detective didn't think John was great, but then John was young. He could stand watching for good things.

John told him as little as the rest of the kids. There was this guy camping down in the woods, and no one thought much about it. Then the Adams kids didn't show up for Sunday school, so afterward he went home and changed clothes and rowed over to see what was with them.

They were locked in a closet, and so forth. He and Bobby had each taken a gun from Dr. Adams' rec room because they were afraid, and they'd gone out to see what there was to be seen. Eventually they found Barbara, and there was a man with her. That is, there was a crazy-looking man in the tenant house near her.

The point was gone over closely. Had John seen the body? Yes. What did he think? He wanted to throw up. Was he emotionally disturbed at the time? Certainly. He had raised and fired his gun at the man that Bobby said was the man.

Good for you, the detective thought. That took guts for a sixteen-year-old kid.

The detective had seen Barbara's blackened, fly-covered body. He had seen a number of deceased in his day, and this particular deceased was no glory. Nonetheless the detective had marked out the blonde hair, the freckles (which had faded in death), the daintiness of the girl in general, and there had been a pressure at the inside corners of the eyes that meant unmanliness. He could see an adolescent boy doing what he did.

The questioning of Bobby and Cindy was close but short. Dr. Adams was there to see that they were not overtaxed.

Bobby, who was the more reliable observer, detailed the man who came in with a knife (Cruz had one; the children had found it) and forced Barbara to lock them in the closet. That was it until John came and let them out. In every other way his story corresponded with the other kids' stories.

The detective looked over at Dr. Adams and decided to question no further. People like that shouldn't be put through criminal proceedings.

Cindy went last, and she seemed the most untouched. By this time the detective had heard how she had sobbed and cried in the closet all night because she was afraid. It certainly didn't show in questioning.

Now she was out, and the detective noted how swiftly things pass with the young. Her mischievous little eyes sparkled: she almost seemed to enjoy the attention of being questioned. She seemed already a woman with secrets. She was coy and cute. Even if Dianne were included, the little girl seemed to be the least scared of any of the children who had been with the deceased. What was odder yet—this was the detective's opinion only—if Cindy could have her dearest wish, she would want to look like and be like her dead baby-sitter.

The Pickers in the county were also questioned, and they answered evasively and nervously. Yes, some of them knew Cruz. No, he wasn't a troublemaker exactly, but he was funny. He refused the wage sometimes, and he refused to live in the quarters provided. He went off by himself sometimes, they never knew where. Yes, they had seen him just before the white girl was killed; he hadn't been working, but he had money to spend at Tillman's store. *Go him with god*.

The detective talked with the county coroner. The girl had been sexually assaulted, tortured, and killed by strangulation at or within a time that corresponded with the five kids' stories. There was no way of telling if the man, Cruz, had done it; the coroner had to examine him in virtually two halves. The detective could go for the rest of his evidence to the fingerprint material supplied by the state police. (The place stunk of fingerprints: only someone stupid would have left them in so many places, they said.) That closed the case; the detective's work was done.

The girl's body lay in the morgue, waiting for her parents. Not far away lay the body of her killer.

Stupid waste, the detective thought.

The Adams came home, of course, but they knew about Barbara's death before they got there. Dr. Adams had called from New York with the happy news of their arrival, and he had gotten the unhappy news from a neighbor who was substituting for the dead baby-sitter that Barbara was dead. And the children were all right so far, but get home fast.

So the long-awaited—awaited by so many people for so many reasons—took place. The Adams came into Baltimore on the shuttle down from New York and were met by another neighbor, Mr. Tillman, and driven to a desolate home and crying children.

Within the year they moved.

The house was drenched in sorrow. The trees hung that winter; the sky hung overhead; and it rained all spring. Pretty, springy, athletic Barbara in the blue cotton dress with the floral print, the girl who got off the bus in Bryce, had been killed there, and the whole land was sick. Dr. Adams moved, and afterward the

278

house stood vacant nearly half a year—weeds grew up through the kitchen steps by the river; the rooms (Barbara's, of course) and the hall and bathroom and intended rec room, fell to dustiness—and eventually it was sold to a new group from Wilmington with noisy dogs and drinking friends who loved the place, but they were never very happy there. A fundamental sorrow infected the very ground. (This was true, although they razed the tenant house, and planted over it the second season following.)

The children, of course, had future lives that began immediately. What would happen as their future histories unrolled is open to wonder.

Did Paul crack? That would be a question. And if he began to show signs of it, did Dianne have to take steps to stop it?

A more mundane thought. Did John make the varsity, and if so, what did he think about during that season? And if he did and found a girl who liked football players, whom did he think of when he kissed her, and what did his eyes look like to her then?

Bobby and Cindy—Cindy with her love of telling things sooner or later—what became of them? When Bobby's sense of duty—excellently executed—was balanced against his later judgment on what he might have done, what became of him? When—possibly years later—he had the intellectual tools to think about god and man and philosophy and what-ought-to-be-done, what did he do then? How did it affect him?

Cindy, when she became the housewife and silken pussy cat on a cushion she was always going to be, did she drink too much? Did the failing of telling secrets come to the fore?

Did Freedom Five ever meet again *per se?* What did they talk about? Did they ever play the game again? Even years later when they were grown-ups themselves with more adequate means? Or did life complicate and close them off forever?

Touch the petal of a flower and shake a star.

Little things intrude.

What of Barbara's role afterward?

Barbara, who thinks of you?

Barbara's mother and father were, of course, equally killed. It is not possible to lose a child; it runs against the current of things. Barbara's parents went on living, but only because they had to; they kept pictures of her around their ever silent house.

Barbara's nominal boyfriend, Ted, read about her death in the newspapers and had a very unpleasant thought. He was shocked, unbelieving, sad, deprived of something in his life, and he was genuinely sorry for Barbara. Since he had never had her, however (in fact, he had only had one girl so far and paid for that), she exited from his life as the forever unattainable girl. Her worth was heightened, and he wondered what it would have been like to do *that* to *her*. Simply by having the thought, he changed his own life. He knew himself, and that is a sort of death in itself.

He would have made a good but rather a strange husband for her.

Terry—this would certainly have astonished Barbara—was the most nearly destroyed of them all. She heard about it when she got back from her summer at the Cape. She went down to the newspaper and dug up the stories of Barbara's death and then went home to fling herself on the bed and cry in a way that people rarely cry.

Barbara, you were the prettiest thing in the world (it's strange how people thought of Barbara-in-death as beautiful when they never thought to do so during her life), but you were the nicest, dumbest thing in the world, and now that world is gone. Terry could barely think of her.

It stirred up memories of Barbara washing her hair in the bathroom when Terry wanted to get in there. It stirred up memories of swimming meets that Terry had attended and so seen Barbara when Barbara felt most alone—thin and tanned and white-lipped, and about to throw up before her event. It stirred up all the things not thought about someone until that person is dead.

It stirred up everything, and Terry was nearly destroyed. One thing held her.

Barbara, Terry said, you dumb-ass. You're the thing I wanted to be and never knew it until I met you. You're the one thing in the world that was worth being, and now you're dead.

Terry felt that Barbara had cheated her.

Barbara, there are so many things I wanted to talk to you about this year. I think I was getting it, but now I can't. You got away from me: you got yourself killed.

I don't know why I'm not more surprised, Terry said. I'll miss you the rest of my life, but I don't know why I'm not more surprised.

Barbara—and here, Terry echoed the unknown Dianne's thought—Barbara, I hated you for being so easy and simple and happy. You deserved it (and here she again echoed the unknown Dianne who continued to feel the same), I hated you, too.

What will I do without you?

I hate you.

Goodness, go out of the world.

I knew goodness, Terry said. I knew it and lived with it and never knew it until it was gone. Goodness, go out of the world. Barbara, go home to wherever home is. Get yourself out of my life, Terry said, for god sake *get off my back* (by now, she had nearly cried herself out). We have enough to do without you, too.

I'm me, and we're us, and we're all us, and we can't be anything else. Get off our backs, Beauty, and go home and be done. We don't *want* you.

You ruin everything and make everyone think it's possible to be what's impossible. We shouldn't be tempted, and you're responsible.

Beauty, go away, go away home and be finished. I knew you, and I never want to see you again. It's just not right.

Goodness, go out of the world so that we can live in it.

Barbara, go to hell.

If any chilly, marginally reasonable stance is taken, it is impossible to imagine Barbara in apotheosis. After all, Barbara is done; that is clear.

Still . . . and still.

It is possible—the mind will be tempted—to picture her as yet present, looking down and back on her brief experience as a human being. Everyone once was.

She looks at the people who were once her fellow people, all of them (to her this is possible). Now, of course, her face floats free of the normal boundaries of imagination and sits high and omnipresent in the mind. It is *there*.

Her mouth is taped, and she is silent. Though she cannot be seen below the shoulders, it is presumed that she is bound as she last was, unable to intrude further on anyone's life. It is in this state that she looks out on her former, related human beings.

There is a look of recognition in her eyes.

I know you now.

The look—the meaning of it can only be guessed at by inspection of the eyes—is rather uncomfortable to bear: I know you, now; I didn't, but I do now.

No words come, of course. They are not possible. Nonetheless, it is imaginable to hear her saying, "You are . . . you are. . . ."

Even if she were allowed, she could not say it.

We are through.

Beauty, go home.

I am gone. I go willingly.

I never meant to harm you.

Now she *is* gone. What follows, quite naturally, is emptiness.

This is not the end, either. Despite human protest, the end of the end goes on forever.

ABOUT THE AUTHOR

MENDAL W. JOHNSON has written for a variety of newspapers and magazines. He and his family live in Annapolis, Maryland, where he is able to indulge in his favorite hobby of sailing. This is his first novel.